# CERTAINTY

# CERTAINTY

— A NOVEL —

## VICTOR BEVINE

LAKE UNION
PUBLISHING

Published by Lake Union, Seattle

www.apub.com

Amazon, the Amazon logo, and Lake Union are trademarks of Amazon.com, Inc., or its affiliates.

ISBN-13: 9781477825457
ISBN-10: 1477825452

Cover design by Eileen Carey

Library of Congress Control Number: 2014938950

Printed in the United States of America

*For Sofia, my mother.*
*And for James Gatz.*

*Children of the future age,*
*Reading this indignant page,*
*Know that in a former time,*
*Love, sweet love, was thought a crime.*

William Blake

•—•—•

*This story is based upon actual events.*
*Some names have been changed to protect the innocent.*
*And the guilty.*

• • •

## PROLOGUE

*Newport, Rhode Island, June 1919*

William Bartlett had visited the Newport City Jail only once before, on his ninth birthday, when he'd been treated to a tour of the facility by the police commissioner himself, a longtime acquaintance of his father. The elder Mr. Bartlett, an attorney, had worked on numerous criminal cases, some quite prominent—he'd represented an interested party in the infamous Lizzie Borden murder trial in Fall River back in '92—and so had considerable experience with the comings and goings of a jailhouse and the inhabitants thereof. To his young son William, however, it was an illuminating and sobering experience. The commissioner's office, the squad room filled with policemen in uniform, the booking room where prisoners waited to be processed, all these were interesting, but the jail cells themselves, most filled with drunks or vagrants on that particular day, held an unexpected fascination for the boy.

Here, it suddenly seemed to the nine-year-old William, was the logical extension of the penalties that had been meted out to him by his father at various times for one infraction or another—confinement to his room, being made to go without supper, or being restricted from using his bicycle. It was now evident that once a man reached adulthood, if the required lessons had not been learned, if the individual continued to do as he pleased willy-nilly in disregard of the rules, the father's gentle hand would be replaced by the iron grip of the state.

William could not recall whether any of this had been verbally suggested to him at the time, either by his father or the commissioner, or whether he'd merely heard it in his head, but he did remember being mesmerized by the confinement of these men in so exposed a fashion, by the ability of one person to completely deprive another of his freedom and dignity, and he came away convinced that the sooner one learned the well-defined ways of the world, the better.

So it was with some discomfort that William, age thirty-five, returned to the jail to collect the Reverend Kent, whom he found imprisoned with several wholly inappropriate men in a holding cell in the basement of the building. Kent was a trifle disheveled, having been roused from bed the night before by the arresting officers, but other than that, the man seemed himself; he was seated, strong and tall with his characteristically calm, contemplative demeanor, almost as if he were sitting on a park bench for a moment of reflection. One of Kent's four cellmates, a crusty soldier, was ranting, obviously drunk, while a peeved Navy man was threatening that if the first didn't shut up, there would be trouble. The third, an ordinary-looking fellow in a seersucker suit, appeared to be feigning sleep, while the fourth, a rumpled derelict, stared off miserably into the shadows. Kent regarded the men with interest and compassion, each in turn, as if marveling at the unlikely circumstances that had brought them all together.

"Reverend Kent?" William uttered.

Kent looked up and flashed the warmest smile William had ever seen. There was not a hint of relief, nor hope of salvation to be found in it, just joy at the sight of an old friend.

"William!" Kent stood up and moved toward him, the bars interfering with their reunion.

"Officer!" William shouted. "Open this cell immediately!" Then to Kent, "Are you all right, Reverend?"

A moment later a middle-aged policeman, who could easily have passed for Kent's double, burst through the booking room door. He was sweating as he pulled out a set of keys.

Kent nodded. "Yes, William, I'm just fine. It was an experience I never expected to have, and that much more interesting for it." He laughed. "Though I can't say I'm not pleased that it's over. Thank you for coming."

The policeman opened the cell door. He spoke nervously. "Sorry for the delay, Mr. Bartlett, Reverend. Bunch of sailors were just brought in. Drunk and disorderly. Always causing trouble of one sort or another." The man glanced at Kent and flushed, suddenly embarrassed. "Pardon me, I wasn't referring . . . that is, I'm sorry about all this," said the officer. "I'm sure it will be . . ." He trailed off.

William gave the officer a terse nod, then gently took Kent by the elbow. "Come, let's get out of here." He spoke in Kent's ear, "Don't say another word until we're alone."

Kent looked at him, puzzled. "Very well, William, as you wish," he replied.

William led Kent up through the crowded squad room and out into the merciless sun. It was uncommonly hot and close for June, and though his black sedan sat parked no more than twenty feet away, it seemed to William that they would never reach the dark safety of the automobile. William glanced around. There were people on the street, but no one appeared to be looking at them. Even if they had been, William told himself, they would hardly have guessed the reason for Kent's presence here. He might have come to minister to an accused or convicted man, helping the poor soul make peace with the justice, or injustice, of his incarceration.

"Reverend Kent!"

William and the priest turned at once toward the young male voice. An energetic fellow in his mid-twenties, dressed in a cheap coat and tie, approached them with a smile. Kent stopped.

"What is it, Reverend?" asked William.

"I don't know, I . . . do I know him?" Kent looked at William.

"*Providence Daily Journal!*" the young man announced eagerly as he pulled a pad and pencil from his pocket.

Kent simply stared at the fellow with a bemused look on his face.

"Come along, Reverend," William urged.

"Can I get a statement?" the reporter asked.

"Permit me," William said as he grabbed Kent by the arm and pulled him to the car. "Get in, please."

William yanked open the passenger door. You could have baked a pie in the car's moist, wooly heat, but Kent slid in without a word of protest.

The young man persisted. "Don't you even want to deny the charges?" he shouted pleasantly in a clear, bright tenor.

William slammed the car door with a force that might have loosened its hinges. "We won't dignify them with a denial," William snapped as he made his way to the driver's side, got in, and started the motorcar's engine.

"Who was that boy?" asked Kent.

"Newspaper reporter," William replied.

Kent laughed. "Why on earth would he want to talk with me?"

William looked at Kent a moment.

The reporter tapped on the closed passenger window, his face no more than a few inches from Kent's. "You gonna let that man speak for you, Reverend?" he shouted through the glass. "Wouldn't you like to defend yourself?"

Kent looked at him, confused, his mouth open a bit as if he were about to speak.

William gunned the engine. "Move away from the door!" he barked at the reporter.

The fellow took a step back, raising his hands in surrender. "Whatever you say, mister." He shrugged with a slick smile. "But we're gonna have to print something!"

William put the motor in gear and sped off down the street.

"What did he mean?" Kent asked. "'Print something?'"

"The papers, they . . ." He stopped himself. "Don't think about that now, sir."

Kent fell silent a moment. "How strange this all is," he observed.

"Yes, it is, very strange," William agreed. He could never have imagined he would confront something like this. "But let's try to deal with just one thing at a time, shall we?"

"Very well," said Kent. "May I open my window?"

"What? Oh, yes, of course," said William, at a loss. "I suppose that's as good a place as any to start."

## ONE

*Seven months earlier, November 1918*

William walked briskly along Thames Street, Newport's main thoroughfare, the collar of his greatcoat turned high against the wind whipping off Narragansett Bay. Winter was closing in now, so the colors that filled Newport in the summer season—white sails dotting the sea, the azure tint of the sky, bright flower boxes and striped store awnings—would have been faded in any case. But they would not have been replaced so thoroughly, in normal times, by khaki and navy blue.

Twenty-five thousand U.S. Navy recruits had descended upon the city since the start of the war eighteen months before. Add to that the several thousand soldiers stationed at Fort Adams, and there were more military than civilians in Newport. The Island, as the local Naval Training Station was called, was equipped to handle only a fraction of that number under any kind of proper conditions, and the tent cities that had been thrown up to accommodate the excess had turned into the worst breeding grounds for the Spanish flu. Brawling was routine, as were improper suggestions to wives and daughters of all stations. Complaints were regularly lodged with the Island's commanding officer, but everyone knew the situation to be beyond his or anyone else's realistic control. And there was no greater symbol of this new disorder than the Army and Navy YMCA that dominated Washington Square, the historic heart of William's beloved city.

The square itself, where dozens of sailors could be found loitering on more balmy nights, had been mostly cleared this evening by the bitter cold, with all but the hardiest seeking shelter somewhere indoors. But as William crossed the park, past the central statue of Commodore Oliver Hazard Perry, hero of the War of 1812, he did spot two sailors bundled in peacoats, warmed by the bottle they were sharing, no doubt, and a third, quite young, who sat alone on a bench. William could not be sure if it was just the shadows cast by the streetlamp above, but the fellow seemed to wear an especially forlorn expression.

The building was not unlovely, William would concede, and might be worthy of praise in another setting, say, Boston or Providence. Here, however, it was a Renaissance monstrosity, occupying an entire city block, five stories tall and completely out of proportion to the colonial structures that surrounded it. Even the old courthouse, the redbrick Georgian building that anchored the square at one end, was restrained in its grandeur. William recalled the cottages that had made way for the YMCA just seven years before, modest, shingled dwellings rich with history. They too had become symbols for him, of the vanished, graceful world that he had so taken for granted.

Crossing Washington Street, William pulled on the heavy wooden door and entered the lobby, uncomfortably warm after the outside, and thick with the smell of humanity, cigarette smoke, and steam heat. As his eyes adjusted, he made out a landscape of shadowy men, two hundred or more, those missing from the square and more, packing the chairs and floor, mumbling and coughing and hooting at a motion picture flickering at the far end of the enormous room.

"Mr. Bartlett!" an older male voice whispered fiercely. William turned to see a tall silhouette waving at him from behind a counter, pointing him toward a door to his left. William stepped into the white glare of the projector's beam, causing an immediate uproar as his shadow blotted out the black-and-white drama. He stood frozen for a moment, disoriented, and the crowd began to shout.

"Mr. Bartlett!" the voice called out again. "Step out of the light! This way!" William moved closer, able now to distinguish an impressive figure in a clerical collar, six feet tall at least and sturdy. William extended his hand, composing himself.

"Reverend Kent?" he inquired. "William Bartlett."

"Welcome, Mr. Bartlett, a great pleasure to meet you," said Kent, with a genuine smile as the two men shook hands.

"My God," exclaimed William, referring to the crowd, "there's so many of them! Is it safe, do you think, their congregating like this? With the epidemic, I mean."

"Nothing to be done, I'm afraid. Since they closed the saloons, the poor boys have nowhere else to go." Kent shrugged. "And there's no avoiding close quarters, regardless of where they are." He placed a hand on William's shoulder. "Come. There's a small office in back. I just changed reels. Things should run smoothly without me for the time being."

William followed Kent through another door into a tiny office with a small desk, two chairs, and a pair of overstuffed filing cabinets.

"And how is Mr. Hart doing?" Kent asked, gesturing to one of the chairs. "Sit, please," he urged in a reassuring voice. "I won't tell you to make yourself comfortable, as that is clearly impossible under the circumstances."

William did as instructed while Kent took the other chair, the knees of the two tall men nearly touching. "He may not make it, I'm afraid," William replied soberly.

"Oh, no," Kent responded, his wide, handsome face suddenly

filled with sadness. William would have estimated the priest's age at around fifty, yet there was a youthful eagerness about the man's kind brown eyes that belied his years.

"John was a boyhood chum of mine," William explained. "This Seaman's Institute project of yours is very important to him, so when his office called, it seemed the least I could do. Damned flu. I appear to be the only attorney in Newport still on his feet."

"Well," Kent said comfortingly, "God must be saving you for a reason."

"I doubt that," William said dryly. "My wife's the do-gooder in our family. I just shuffle papers and do as I'm told," he added with a chuckle.

Kent smiled, gazing upon William as he might a favorite son. It seemed almost as if he'd forgotten the purpose of William's visit.

"Uh, speaking of papers, Reverend," William said. "Might you have them handy? I'm, well, rather anxious to be on my way."

"Oh, of course!" Kent glanced about his cluttered desk for the documents in question. "I had them not long ago. Wait!" he said and reached into a drawer at his right. After a moment of digging, he pulled out a sheaf of papers and held them high, a smile on his face.

"Here we are! Unforgivable of me really, waiting this long," Kent said as he leafed through the pages.

"I need to drop them at the city council office before midnight," William added, "or the resolution will expire. Here, let me help you." William took the papers gently, turned to the signature page, and returned them to Kent. "Sign here."

Kent paused as he looked down at the document, not yet moving to sign his name.

"Is something wrong?" William asked, concerned.

"No, no. Pardon me, it's just that, well, I can't believe it's really happening," Kent said, shaking his head in disbelief. "You see, Mr. Bartlett, the moral guidance of young men has become more or less my ministry over the years. That's why I was brought to Newport from Lehigh University when the war began. Emmanuel Episcopal, where I serve as pastor, provides a small allowance to take the occasional man on an outing, to shows and such, but it's not nearly enough. And what with my work here and at the hospital, I haven't a spare moment to do much else for them. But this . . ." He trailed off, gesturing to the papers. "This Seaman's Institute has been my dream since I arrived here. Now that it's happening, it's almost too much. I suppose that's why I've been dragging my feet."

William thought the man overly modest. "It wouldn't be happening at all if not for you, sir. The city fathers refuse to break ground until you sign off on the project." William paused. "My wife, Sarah, speaks of you often, in such glowing terms in fact that, well, it sometimes makes me rather jealous."

Kent's face lit up. "Sarah Bartlett? Ah, of course. I might have known. Extraordinary woman."

"Indeed, she is," William agreed, and smiled wryly. "Never met a cause she didn't like." He felt himself blush at his sudden openness, then added earnestly, "As I said, I'm no do-gooder, but it's clear this project is long overdue, for the good of the city. All these men, from Lord knows where, simply loitering about, it's . . . troubling, to say the least."

The reverend looked away. "I suppose it's just such fears that prompted the city to act as quickly as they did."

"It's not typical, I assure you," William agreed.

Kent chuckled. "Well, I'm never one to look a gift horse in the mouth, but"—he lowered his voice and leaned an inch toward William—"may I tell you a secret?"

William didn't like secrets, especially when divulged by complete strangers, but there was something about the man that urged him to lean in at least as far as Kent had.

The man whispered, "Newport survived blockade and starvation during the Revolution, and it will survive this, with or without the new Seaman's Institute." He paused a moment and sat back. "No, it's the boys themselves that concern me. Torn from their families, with who knows what ahead of them. They deserve more than this during what may be the final chapter of their lives."

"Of course, Reverend." William did not consider himself an expert in human emotion, but Kent's compassion appeared genuine enough. Perhaps his wife had been right about this fellow.

The priest shifted his attention down to the document on his desk. "Sign here, you say?" asked Kent.

"Yes, sir." William watched with interest as Kent signed the paper. "Oh, you're left-handed. I am as well. Nuisance, isn't it? My father tried to make me use my right when I was a child, but it was no use." William reached for the pen. "I'll need to witness it now, Reverend."

"Odd, I suppose," Kent replied as William countersigned, "but I've always rather enjoyed being left-handed in a right-handed world. Builds ingenuity. Or perhaps I'm just naturally obstinate."

"I doubt that, Reverend." William laughed. One couldn't help but like this man, William thought as he blotted the signatures. In fact, in that moment, he felt certain that he liked Kent more than anyone he'd met in a very long time.

"That's it, then?" Kent asked.

"That's all there is to it." The two of them rose and William extended his hand to shake with Kent once more, struggling to find some appropriate words of farewell. "May I . . . may I say, sir, what an honor it's been meeting you."

"The honor is mine, Mr. Bartlett," Kent stated simply.

And he meant it, William knew. There was no evading it; this was an extraordinary man before him. Likely, he could have done any number of things with his life. And yet, Kent had dedicated himself to helping others, most of whom, from what William had seen of these recruits over the last months, were neither grateful nor worthy of such devotion.

"Mr. Bartlett?" Kent asked. "Something on your mind?"

William blushed. "I . . . well," then he shook his head.

"Speak freely," Kent assured him. "Please."

William looked at the other man a moment, then took a deep breath. "Very well. It's a subject over which Sarah and I often disagree. Do you truly believe, against all odds, that you're making a difference by what you're doing?"

Kent took a thoughtful pause. "My pride would like to answer, 'yes.'" He sighed. "But the simple truth is that I haven't the faintest idea." Kent looked at William and smiled. "Does that shock you?"

"No," said William. "I appreciate your honesty."

"Good." Kent nodded, genuinely pleased. "The whole issue of whether I'm making a difference, I've come to the conclusion that it's none of my business, really, in the end. What I *do* know, however, beyond a shadow of a doubt, is that I am performing the job I was placed here to do."

"By the church, you mean?"

Kent looked at him oddly. "No, Mr. Bartlett, by God. Everything else, everything, is just human vanity, the dash on the headstone between the day we're born and the day we die."

William looked at him, puzzled, but said nothing.

"Yes?" asked Kent, with a hint of a smile.

"Well, *how* do you know? That you're doing God's will?" William asked earnestly. "If not by your accomplishments, then by what evidence?"

Kent again took a moment to search for a response. He seemed never to have one close at hand, no catalogue of easy answers suitable for every occasion, as did most of the men William knew. Finally, the reverend shrugged. "I just know."

Had William ever been that sure of anything in his life? Until that moment, he would have said "yes," but in the face of Kent's simple willingness, William felt himself fall short.

## TWO

Hospital Apprentice Second Class Harold Trubshaw, eighteen years old, a mask over his nose and mouth, tried his best to tidy up the bed of the nearly lifeless body before him. He had gotten used to the color the worst of them turned, first blue, then black, as they were slowly suffocated by the disease. It was the cups of blood they coughed up that made him queasy. Trubshaw couldn't figure out why *he* hadn't come down with it, considering all the exposure he'd had in the last month. He'd caught a pretty bad flu the previous spring—a lot of the men had—but it had been nothing like this, and none of those previously infected were coming down with this more virulent strain. Whatever the reason for his continuing good health, Trubshaw figured he must be doing something right. Besides, someone had to help these men die with a little bit of dignity at least, and it might as well be him. He'd always had his heart set on being a nurse once he'd left the Navy, and this was giving him valuable experience. Not a manly profession, he'd been told more than once by folks back in Alabama, but then, no one had ever called Trubshaw manly.

13

He'd heard many names for what he was since arriving in Newport—fairy, queer, pogue. In one way, it had helped him make sense of feelings he'd had for as long as he could remember. The strong boys who wanted things from him, who knew instinctively that he would do what they asked, made his heart leap and the first few times, in the midst of the act, it had felt so right. Then, inevitably, would come the laughter and the name-calling by other men he didn't even know. He'd been hurt by it, but then the flu had arrived, and he'd buried his shame along with other trivialities in the hapless battle of life and death.

He picked up the soiled linen, wrapped it in another sheet, and carried the foul bundle through a set of swinging doors into the laundry room. Ironic, he thought, how a couple of weeks before, these men, many of whom he remembered from their induction physicals, had been preparing to cross an ocean and go into battle, filled with excitement or fear or a mixture of both, all sturdy and many beautiful, ready to lay down their lives for their country. And now they were lying here instead, in their own blood and shit and piss, without ever having so much as seen the enemy. The Grim Reaper was capricious at best, Trubshaw decided, a malicious jokester at worst.

He turned his head, hearing footsteps in the ward, and . . . voices? It might have been Reverend Kent, arriving early for his nightly rounds of prayer and comfort, but the priest always came alone, and the footsteps sounded hurried, and made by more than just two feet. A door opened, then sharply clicked closed, and the silence returned. Very peculiar.

Proceeding cautiously, Trubshaw went back out to the ward to investigate, but saw no one. Just Death and his minions, the young man supposed, weary war-workers rushing to complete the day's list of impossible tasks by the same simple means as the rest of us. Moments later, through a second set of swinging doors, the Reverend

Kent arrived. Trubshaw watched from the shadows as Kent stopped to regard the suffering all around him. "Evening, sir," Trubshaw croaked.

Kent turned to him and smiled. "Good evening, Harry."

Trubshaw glanced around. "You alone, Reverend?"

Kent looked at him oddly. "Yes, of course. And so are you, it seems. Where has everyone gone to?"

"You mean the staff? Oh, they all went home," he said matter-of-factly. "Scared they're gonna catch it, I guess."

Kent placed a light hand on his shoulder. "You're a good man, Harry."

Trubshaw shrugged.

"Who needs me most, son?" Kent surveyed the room.

"One boy's just about gone." He led Kent to the bed of a semi-comatose fellow, slightly purple around the eyes and lips, but still recognizable as human. The fellow moaned periodically between labored breaths. An intermittent and bewildered panic flashed in his eyes, as he felt his young life rapidly drawing to its close. "Keeps calling for his mother."

Kent looked down at the sick boy. "Yes," he said sadly. "I'll sit with him for a while."

"You should be wearing a mask, Reverend." Kent was the only real mentor Trubshaw had ever known, always supportive of everything the boy hoped to do and be. It would be an overwhelming personal tragedy for Trubshaw if something should happen to the man. And not just for him. The tireless reverend meant a great deal to a great many. "We can't have you getting sick, sir."

But Kent dismissed the suggestion with a wave of his hand as he pulled up a chair beside the sickbed and sat. "Only the good die young, my boy." Kent smiled sadly. "Or is it that only the young die good?"

Trubshaw sighed, too tired to insist, and went back to resume his long list of duties, leaving Death to complete his own.

Kent removed a clean washcloth from the bedside table, dipped it into a pitcher of water, and laid it across the forehead of the delirious boy. He gazed at the young face and gently clasped the fellow's hand, ablaze with fever.

"Have no fear, my son," Kent murmured gently. "God is already holding you in His arms."

This had become to Kent, this end of his every day, the most critical and most dreadful aspect of his duties here in Newport. He had reveled in the work at Lehigh University, felt significant and full of purpose as he ministered to undergraduate men bound for unknown adventures—careers, wives, children, a future as open as their unmarked faces. They had often come to him, weighted down with cares, with secret guilts and inchoate fears, and though he sometimes struggled to find the right words, to distinguish their unique torments from his own, he was almost always able to send them off lighter than when they had arrived.

How could he ever have imagined that sunny road leading to this one, this endless procession of young lives dissolving in his hands? The horror that he might one night encounter a precious face from his Lehigh days had given way, in his own sleepless delirium, to seeing those faces in every dying boy he encountered here. Keeping vigil at their bedsides, two, sometimes three a night, Kent was tormented by visions of the life each had been happily assigned by everything bright and good in the world. How could he answer the stunned awareness in so many eyes that the dark and malignant had triumphed, had strangled the sweet urgency of their youth and turned the blush of their innocence to ash?

The only answer, the final answer, he knew, was prayer. But what could he pray for, night after night? Health, when they were blue with suffocation, puking blood? Deliverance from suffering, with choirs of cherubim to sing these boys to heaven? No, it was faith that he prayed for, passionately, fervently, a renewed faith that all of this made sense somehow, that some divine and inscrutable plan lay behind the horrendous suffering and loss. But each morning he came away with the same growing bitterness, the same conviction that what he truly required of God was an apology, abject, full of tearful regret and pleas for forgiveness that He, the Almighty, had allowed the obscenity of war and a prolific, putrid disease to sweep the world.

Not yet insane, Kent expected nothing of the sort from the Divine. Instead, he pressed his forehead to the hand of this boy, dying horribly before him, and settled in for a long night's watch, praying again for whatever God, in His infinite wisdom, would deign to provide.

—•—•—

It was the last place on earth Seaman First Class Charlie McKinney wanted to be at that moment, ambling down a dark, empty hospital corridor, surrounded by the stink of bleach and death.

Charlie had always figured he had more to live for than most, blessed as he had been by Nature herself with those endowments that made life worth living for a mug like him. Without breeding, money, or class, on his own since he was twelve, Charlie had thrived on the often brutal streets of New York, honing a cagey wit and a ready charm, and an unfailing talent for getting over with minimum effort. Now, at twenty-three, with uncommon good looks and an impressive physique, the black-haired, blue-eyed McKinney was rarely on the losing end of any negotiation. And at six feet even, it was still more rare that Charlie found himself the shortest man in any cohort. Now he walked between two giants, his six-foot four-inch, copper-haired pal Claude loping behind, and a few steps ahead, Ervin Arnold, the chief petty officer they'd only just met. An ugly man as tall as Claude, with a pockmarked face and a powerful build, Arnold had emerged like a nightmare from the darkness, lying in wait, it seemed, in an alley behind the Y where the boys had gone for a lewd assignation with a person of ill repute. Charlie was not an easy man to bully, but Arnold had succeeded, roping him and Claude into this crazy mission of his, the nature of which remained a total mystery.

The monstrous chief peered through a set of swinging doors to see if the coast was clear. Satisfied, Arnold gestured with an abrupt flick of his big head for the boys to follow him into the ward. A creak and a rush of rank air announced their entrance as the doors swooshed closed behind them. No one amidst the row upon row of horribly sick young men paid them any mind. Charlie turned toward Claude for confirmation of his worst fears and found a face fully flushed with wide-eyed panic.

"Damn, Charlie," Claude whispered in his Texas drawl. "Look at these guys!" Charlie was way ahead of his friend.

"Chief?" queried Charlie in hushed tones, so as not to disturb the good-as-dead. "Correct me if I'm wrong, but these poor sons of bitches, they got the Spanish flu, right?"

"That's right, sailor."

Charlie looked around again. He had beaten the odds on six U-boat–infested North Atlantic crossings and he had no interest in giving Fate the finger in quite so stupid a way as this. "Ain't that real contagious?" Charlie offered, fearing that the man they were following was indeed insane.

Arnold snorted. "Thought you were tough."

"Tough, sure," Charlie replied. Then to himself, "Not fucking crazy."

Reaching the far side of the ward, the men approached a solid oak door with a darkened window and the word "Utility" written across the top. Arnold looked around again, reminding Charlie of a detective in a dime novel, then unlocked the door and hustled the boys and himself inside, turning the deadbolt behind them.

"Ow! Shit!" yelped Charlie, bumping his shin against a footstool. "You think we could turn a light on in here?"

A face that looked to be carved out of solid granite materialized out of the darkness, nose to nose with Charlie, shadows hiding the deep-set eyes.

"That would not be a good idea," said the granite man in deep, crisp tones.

"Jesus Christ!" Charlie said as he jumped back. "What the hell's going on?" Then he flashed a wry grin. "Wait a minute. I get it. This is all a joke, right? You're just doing this to scare the crap out of us, some kind of an initiation. Come on, who put you up to it, huh?"

"Anything to report?" demanded Arnold, ignoring Charlie.

"No, sir," replied the phantom, whom Charlie could now identify as an unknown, dark-haired seaman first class of an age, height, and build similar to himself. Charlie still could not see the man's eyes, but he could feel their energy boring a hole in his skull. The SFC moved his head only slightly to direct his response to Arnold, keeping his hidden eyes always on Charlie. "Nothing but that orderly swishing back and forth," the man uttered with disgust.

"Good." Arnold nodded. "Bart Rudy, meet Charles McKinney and—"

"How the hell do you know my name?" Charlie asked sharply.

The chief smiled. "Your fame precedes you. And your friend?"

Without taking his eyes off the chief, Charlie answered, "Claude McQuillen." This was getting worse and worse.

"Welcome aboard," Rudy offered grudgingly.

"Aboard?" Charlie repeated, stupefied. "Aboard *what*?"

All heads turned as three soft, rapid taps erupted on the door's window, as dramatic as gunfire in the solemn silence. Arnold peered out, then unlocked the door and admitted a man in his mid-forties, about five foot ten, balding, wearing oval spectacles. His blue Navy uniform bore the stripes of a lieutenant and the insignia of a naval doctor. Arnold pulled him into the cramped closet and urgently shut the door behind him.

"Hey, Doc," Arnold said as the men shook hands briefly.

"He's coming," warned the doctor, with excitement.

Charlie and Claude watched, perplexed, as first the doctor, then Arnold and Rudy positioned themselves by the window and gazed out, confident that they could not be seen, like little kids with paper bags over their heads.

"Get up here, you two," Arnold barked over his shoulder. "I want you to see this."

Charlie and Claude glanced at each other for confirmation. Then Charlie shrugged in surrender and the two men moved up slowly, finding a place behind the others from which to view the scene apparently about to unfold.

Across the ward, a familiar-looking older man entered through the swinging doors.

"Hey," said Claude. "It's that preacher from the Y."

"Kent," said the doctor.

"Indeed it is," Arnold concurred with contempt.

Charlie felt a shiver. "Givin' last rites more 'n likely," he murmured.

"That's what he'd like you to believe, anyway," Arnold snarled.

"Who's that?" asked Claude.

Charlie craned his neck, able now to see a young orderly, his face masked, standing beside Kent.

"That's the assistant pervert," Rudy said.

The orderly led the priest to the bed of what must have been a very sick young man. Kent pulled up a chair to sit and the masked orderly went on his way. After a moment, Kent took hold of one of the young man's hands, clasping it between both of his own.

"Look at that!" said Rudy, horrified.

"What?" asked Claude. "What?" he repeated, unable to see and fearful that he was missing something historic.

Charlie watched carefully as Kent brought the boy's hand to his lips, then pressed it to his brow, lowering his head in what appeared to be prayer.

"Disgusting," muttered Arnold.

"Now," the doctor declared, "we wait."

Charlie felt a gentle tug on his shoulder. He turned to face Claude, the man's confused expression a silent plea for some sort of explanation. But Charlie merely shrugged. As someone who took great pride in knowing every game three moves out, he had every reason to feel as worried as Claude now looked. Life, however, had taught Charlie McKinney just how abruptly things could change, how situations that seemed to bode the worst for a man's future could sometimes turn on a dime to his advantage. So he would take the only sensible advice he'd received all night. He would wait, knowing that with the dawn might just come the opportunity of a lifetime.

— • — • —

Charlie sat uncomfortably, surrounded by Arnold, Hudson, and Rudy. It was now well past dawn and things were still not looking up, as far as he could tell. He had watched Kent depart sometime after the boy had expired many hours before and a new orderly had stripped the soiled linens from the bed.

He glanced over at Claude slumped on the floor of the utility closet, sleeping like a baby. Charlie doubted that he had ever slept like a baby, even when he was one.

He turned back the clock in his head, to the poker game early the previous evening when everything he desired had seemed within his grasp. Nearly forty bucks in his pocket, a fortune really, his eye set on a fine night with Dottie, his favorite girl, a bottle of something strong and sharp to share between them, and enough dough left over to spread some goodwill for a day or two. Then he'd let that barrel-chested Army sergeant convince him to stay for one more hand. "Sure," Charlie had said, and why not? He'd marked the cards himself. Naturally, he kept raising till all he and everyone else had was on the table, convinced he would walk away from this game a rich man.

So when Army proceeded to lay down aces over kings, no one was more surprised than Charlie. The smug faces on the guy's doughboy pals told him it was Army vs. Navy from the first. Where the hell had Claude been when he needed him? The Texan's sheer size made him count for two at least and together they might have stood a chance. Alone, however, Charlie had seen no choice but to walk away empty-handed.

"Chief Arnold was a private investigator before joining the Navy," said Lieutenant Erastus Hudson, the Navy doctor. "Hunting down sexual deviants was his specialty."

"I can tell a fairy just by the way he walks," Arnold announced proudly.

Charlie sighed. "Holding the kid's hand? I seen a lot of shit in France, Chief. That don't make the guy queer."

"Says you," insisted Arnold. "Couple months ago, I was laid up in here, touch of rheumatism in my hip. One night, some orderly, a real sissy, he's hovering around, fussing with the bedclothes. Finally, he leans over, lets me know in so many words that he'd be happy to play with my private parts if I'd be inclined to let him."

"Christ!" Rudy exclaimed. "Can you believe that?"

"I grabbed him by the throat," Arnold continued. "I asked him, 'Who told you it was all right to suggest things like that to another man?' He kept saying, 'Mother Kent! Mother Kent!' Didn't know who he meant, but I found out soon enough."

"Healthy young men have strong drives," the doctor explained. "We know that. We also know that there simply aren't enough willing women in Newport to accommodate them."

Arnold sneered. "Plenty of willing fairies, though, ain't there?"

"We don't blame the men, McKinney," Hudson continued. "We blame those who put this kind of temptation in their path."

"My suggestion, Doc?" Charlie offered. "Bring in more women."

"Don't be a wiseass," snapped Arnold.

"All right, fair enough, Chief." Charlie yawned. "I see your point, but what's any of this got to do with me?"

Arnold spat on the floor. "As if you didn't know."

Charlie's body tensed as he weighed Arnold's implication. Fairies were a part of life and always had been, as far as he could tell, and like everything in Charlie's world, they had their place in his vast array of stratagems. Some would pay as much as five bucks to go down on a guy, and when the poker game had gone awry, Charlie had needed money fast to save his evening with Dottie, who was *never* one to give it away for free. When Arnold had accosted them, the boys had been headed down an alley behind the Y, well known for such boy-on-boy action. Poor Claude had scant luck with women so Charlie had convinced his pal to come along, setting him up with a friend of a friend, not the first time he'd done such a thing and likely not the last, always making a buck or two for himself on the transaction. "Just close your eyes," he'd assured Claude, "and you'll have a helluva time."

"We're well aware of your familiarity with these people, Mr. McKinney," Hudson insisted.

Charlie looked from the doctor to Arnold and back again, beginning to get the picture.

"Oh, it's no use denying it, son," Hudson continued. "We know it's true, we know the extent of your behavior, and it's your good fortune that we've chosen not to look too deeply into what it says about you. The simple fact is that you hold a certain appeal for these types and for whatever reason they seem to trust you. We want you to help us get close to them."

So, that was their angle, Charlie mused.

"You're asking me to be bait?" he asked.

Arnold smiled. "Something like that."

"But not simply that," Hudson rushed to add. "We have big plans for this operation. Once we've successfully completed the pilot program here in Newport, we'll be expanding to other cities, New York primarily, to attack this problem root and branch where it festers and grows. We've seen how you are with rank-and-file sailors. You're a natural-born leader, McKinney, and we hope those qualities will help us to recruit other undercover operators, and, uh . . ." Hudson hesitated, ". . . train them, as it were. You would of course be relieved of all other duties, and you'll receive a three-dollar-a-day stipend—that's in addition to your regular pay—to defray any . . . expenses you may incur." The doctor offered a broad smile. "And if you're all we hope you to be, promotion and decoration is not unlikely."

Here it was, the opportunity he'd been waiting for. Three bucks a day. Easy money, and a future to boot, something he'd *never* figured on having. But when he opened his mouth to say, "Hell, yes," the words refused to come. The worst thing someone could be in Charlie's world was a snitch, and as low as queers were in the pecking order, it still didn't sit well with him.

"I been called a lot of things, Doc," he found himself saying, "but a rat ain't one of 'em. 'Fraid I'm not your boy."

What the hell was he thinking? Charlie asked himself. What did it matter in the end? It's not like he cared about protecting the fairies; they knew the risk they were taking bending over and getting on their knees for other guys. And even if his choice *had* been made out of sympathy for the poor dopes, it's not like this whole thing was just going to go away. Arnold and Hudson would simply find some other lucky bastard to fill Charlie's shoes if he refused. But when he looked at the shocked expression on Arnold's hateful face, all regret vanished from Charlie's heart, and he offered the two older men an innocent smile. "Can we go now?" He glanced at his sleeping comrade as he started to rise. "Claude, wake up!"

Charlie was violently thrust back into the chair. Arnold loomed over him, his breath reeking of onions and stale cigarettes.

"Now, you listen to me, you fucking pimp, 'cause you're only gonna hear it once. We're offering you a chance to save your skin. Either you help us do the right thing, or I will personally see you locked up for a very long time. Is that understood?"

Charlie glared at Arnold silently, fighting to contain his rage. He wasn't used to having his back up against a wall and he didn't like it one bit.

"IS THAT UNDERSTOOD?" Arnold bellowed.

Fueled by their mutual hatred, Charlie found himself wondering who would kill whom first in an all-out slugfest.

"There's one other thing," Hudson added buoyantly, perusing a file. "Do you know someone by the name of Dorothy McCann?"

Charlie turned to the doctor, forgetting Arnold for the moment. "Maybe." Charlie shrugged, feigning nonchalance.

Arnold backed away, relaxed now and smiling. "Your mick whore," he sniggered.

"Quite a resourceful little thing," said Hudson. "It seems she somehow managed to escape the Catholic Decency League's crusade to clear the town of prostitutes some months back. Lucky for her, too, since she'd likely be back in Ireland by now, eating rotten potatoes in some cold-water shanty."

Both men glared at Charlie. Charlie stared back at them. He was willing to take a chance with his own skin—he'd likely come out on top in any case—but Dottie was another story. She was no angel certainly, but somehow the thought of her being sent back to Ireland, of never seeing her again, tugged at his insides. He was definitely going soft, damn it, he cursed himself.

Arnold knew he'd won. "Welcome to the cause, McKinney."

⬩ ⬩ ⬩

It sounded like gunfire, thought Charlie, the rivets of driving rain pounding the brick walls of the infirmary. Then came a rising tide of shouts, men's voices booming in counterpoint to sirens and truck horns, to bells and fire whistles. Claude awoke and got to his feet as Charlie and the other men exchanged puzzled glances in the dim morning light.

"Maybe the Germans have landed," Charlie quipped.

Arnold shot him a glare, then opened the closet door, and the men piled out. At the other end of the ward, a young fellow in an ensign's uniform dashed in through the swinging doors. His blond hair soaked from the rain, wet face shining like a beacon, he shouted, "It's over! It's over! The kaiser surrendered! The war's over!" For just a moment, his breath seemed to stop as he took in the desperate state of his bedridden audience. Then he dashed out just as quickly and thoughtlessly as he'd entered, not seeing Charlie and his companions standing at the far end of the room, and not willing to squander his rapture on those with no purchase on the future.

# THREE

*Six weeks later*

The written orders were remarkably straightforward, even for such a poor reader as Charlie knew himself to be. The men were instructed "to obtain information and evidence pertaining to cocksuckers and rectum receivers and ringleaders of this gang, arranging from time to time meetings whereas to catch them in the act, getting their full names, rates, and where they live and where they are stationed. This evidence is to be corroborated leading to their conviction." There were two other short paragraphs stating that the men should also keep their eyes peeled for "women that are in the same business," as well as for "cocaine and booze joints," but the heart of the document and of the operation was catching fairies, to be sure. In case there *was* any doubt, and Charlie knew that some of the twenty-four boys he'd helped to recruit were not the brightest fellows, the following "advice" had been added: "Any man attached to and serving on this staff must keep his eyes wide open, observing everything, and keep ears open for all conversation, and make himself free with this class of men, being jolly and good-natured, making them believe that he is what is termed in the Navy a 'boy humper.' Be careful not to arouse suspicion."

But the section that Charlie found to be the most amusing stated that "any man attached to and serving on this staff who by any reason allows himself to give any information or to let his own family know what work is being carried on will be convicted of perjury." Now, Charlie himself had no family to speak of, an aunt he remembered only dimly, and a cousin or two that he wouldn't know if they spit on him, but he couldn't imagine bragging about this to anyone. And he certainly couldn't imagine that any of the raw recruits who he'd enticed, convinced, or browbeaten into "volunteering" might include in their next letter home, "Dear Mother: My current duties include having other men suck my dick," which, presumably, was the only foolproof way to "corroborate" secondhand evidence against any individual who, according to Arnold, "walked funny."

Their headquarters, secured through Doctor Hudson's acquaintances in the Newport medical community, were in the large basement room of the local chapter of the American Red Cross, a stately brick building on a corner in downtown Newport. It was here that the men would be expected to file their reports each morning, in triplicate, on their activities of the night before. And it was here, on this night, that all the squids were gathered to sign their orders, according to standard military procedure, in the presence of their "commanding officer." Though a few had been handpicked by Arnold and Hudson themselves, it had in truth been Charlie, with Claude's help, who had recruited most of these boys, culled from the more than one hundred that they had paraded before the doctor and the chief. Arnold and Hudson had personally screened each of the prospects for suitability before letting any of them in on the secret, presumably having them walk before Arnold, thereby making certain to the chief's satisfaction that they weren't fairies themselves. Most were rejected for any number of reasons, none of which were ever revealed to Charlie.

Charlie went from group to group, making sure that each of the young sailors had affixed their names, or marks, to a copy of the document. He had met a hell of a lot of Navy men since he'd joined up at the start of the war. Many had been pasty or pimply, with buckteeth, or no teeth at all. Some had been too tall and hunched over, and others so short you could have used them as a barstool. Some were rail thin, or fat as a house, with huge noses or no chins. But as he looked around the room at this carefully chosen cohort, Charlie realized that there wasn't a single man present that he could describe as anything other than good-looking.

"Ch-Charlie," someone stammered. Charlie turned to see a young recruit with downy cheeks hovering nearby, the folded document in his hand.

"Can I . . . could you . . . ?" the fellow continued haltingly.

"Did you sign it, Barker?" Charlie grabbed the document out of his hand and checked the last page.

"Yes, yeah," Barker said, nodding, aiming to please.

"Good boy," Charlie said, as he saw for himself the fellow's signature affixed where it belonged. He looked back up at the kid's enormous blue eyes, with their perpetually startled expression, like some Katzenjammer Kid in a comic book, and wondered once again what the hell he'd been thinking, allowing the Nebraska farm boy to sign on as an operator. The kid had insisted, complaining that he'd arrived too late, that the war was already over, and that he wanted to serve his country. Finally, if only to stop Barker's painful stammering, Charlie had relented. Why the hell not? he had reasoned. Charlie himself had done a lot worse by seventeen, and this fellow was downright pretty, just the type Arnold wanted as bait. Now, he thought better of it. As much as he claimed that he had nothing against fairies, Charlie had to admit that some were vicious, and would eat Barker alive. He'd just have to keep an eye on the youngster as best he could.

"I . . . I wanted to—"

"Sorry, kid," Charlie cut him off. "I'm busy. Later, all right?"

Barker nodded, flushed and embarrassed, as Charlie moved on, making sure there was no one he'd missed. It was then that he saw Claude seated by himself, his lips moving as he struggled to read the document. Charlie walked up and sat beside him.

"What's the problem, Claude?"

"I don't understand half of this, Charlie. And the half that I do, I wish I didn't. 'Cept maybe the part about the motorcycles. We gonna get to ride motorcycles?"

Charlie recalled the odd reference to motorcycles on page two of the orders, as if that had to do with anything. "Anytime we want, buddy." Charlie nodded with confidence.

Claude still seemed hesitant. "I don't know. I mean, I heard all the reasons they gave us and they're good ones, I guess. For what we're doing, I mean. But I just don't know."

"Listen up!" Arnold bellowed. Charlie and Claude turned to see the chief standing on a small platform at the front of the room, Hudson beside him. "Nobody goes out that door tonight until every last document is signed. You hear me?"

A chorus of "yes, sir" rose up on all sides.

Charlie put his arm around Claude's shoulder. "You heard the man, Claude. Now, sign it, would you, so we can get out of here? Dottie's waitin'."

Claude looked at his friend.

Charlie cooed, "Just keep thinkin' about the motorcycles, Claude," as he flipped to the last page and handed the pen to Claude, who dutifully signed.

• — • — •

The basement door was located at the back of the Red Cross building, allowing the men to stream out later that same frosty December night more or less unobserved. Not that it mattered, thought Charlie, since few upstanding citizens would be found on the street at this hour.

Christmas had passed. Fading decorations still hung in leafless trees and dangled from lampposts, as a new year, 1919, and after that a new decade loomed ahead, bursting with possibilities for feast or famine, adventure or desolation.

Charlie felt no shame about what he was doing. Once joined, any action became as natural to him as eating when he was hungry or hustling some rube when he was broke. He had no illusions. He knew that if it turned out that there indeed was a hell, a one-way ticket would surely be reserved in his name. But he doubted the existence of such a place, as he doubted the existence of leprechauns and guardian angels. If God *was* real, as real as other things, like high-speed torpedoes that could rip a hundred men apart in the blink of an eye, then He had set up this game, and it was of no consequence to Him what a man like Charlie did to survive another day.

At that moment, he remembered Barker, and the burning question that had left the boy flushed and nervous. Charlie scanned the crowd for the youngster.

By and large, the men had not dispersed, but lingered in the alley and vacant lot behind. Posses had begun to form around one natural leader or another, as each sought out those with whom he felt a kinship and to which, either by a shared sense of humor or of purpose, he could belong. Like Barker, most of them had missed the war by mere weeks, and the sense of destiny that had been blooming in their hearts had left each man with an odd and stubborn sense of his own importance. The swagger and giddiness that now rippled through the small crowd suggested to Charlie that tonight perhaps they had found an outlet for that urge to prove themselves, and they were anxious to be led somewhere other than back to their cramped quarters.

But there was no swagger or giddiness in Barker, who had perched hesitantly near a group of laughing, eager young men. As Charlie approached, stopping just behind Barker, he could see Bart Rudy standing at the center of that group. Charlie's initial dislike of Rudy had only grown since that first night in the hospital—the man had proved himself to be a braggart and a shameless toady of Arnold—and Charlie watched with distaste as Rudy regaled his new followers with a story of life on the sea.

"Last ship I was on, big destroyer," Rudy announced, his square jaw jutting out, "there was this one cocksucker, must have made his way through half the crew. One night, me and some of my pals, we threw the son of a bitch overboard."

"Barker," Charlie said softly. Barker turned with a start, his wide eyes landing on Charlie's. With a quick jerk of his head, Charlie led the fellow a few yards distant.

"So," said Charlie, "what was it you wanted?"

Barker flushed again, then shrugged, looking down.

"Just speak your mind, kid, will ya?"

Barker looked up, mustering all his courage. "Well, I need . . . could I ask you somethin'?"

"I'm all ears."

"Hey, Charlie!" Charlie looked toward the voice and saw Claude approaching the pair. "Been looking all over for you!"

Barker looked down again, his fortitude now gone. Charlie could feel the youngster ready to creep away, so he grabbed him by the arm.

"Claude, you remember Barker, right?" Charlie said sharply as the other man arrived.

Claude flashed a broad grin. "Course I do. How's it going, kid?" He offered the younger man a warm handshake.

Charlie laughed to himself. The good-natured Claude was exactly the kind of fellow Barker needed to spend time with if he was ever going to become a proper man. "Claude," Charlie said, "Barker and I were just having a little chat, so . . ."

"Oh?" Claude said, then, "Oh! Sure." He winked at Charlie. "No problem," he drawled. "I'll catch up with you boys later on, then," said Claude as he turned and walked off.

Charlie looked at Barker. "Walk with me," Charlie commanded softly as he turned, leading Barker toward the street and away from the others. "So, what's on your mind?"

"Well, I don't . . . I mean . . ." Barker struggled.

"Barker, if you don't just spit it out, I swear to God . . ."

"Well," Barker jumped in, then blurted out the rest in a rush, "Can you tell me, um . . . what's a fairy?"

Charlie stopped in his tracks, looking at Barker in disbelief. "You're pullin' my leg, kid, right?"

Barker shook his head, very earnest.

"Barker," Charlie uttered with a shake of his head. "What the hell are you doing here?"

"I . . . I wanted to serve my country," Barker said simply.

Charlie sighed. "A patriot."

"So," Barker continued, "can . . . you tell me?"

Charlie looked at the boy, considering how to start. "A fairy is, well, he's a guy who, uh, kinda thinks he's a woman."

Barker looked at him, a puzzled expression on his face. "How could he think that?"

"Well, he don't *really*," countered Charlie. "He just acts that way, sorta girly. And he likes to do things with other fellas. Sex stuff."

Barker got a faraway look in his eyes, as if he were remembering something.

"What?" asked Charlie. Barker looked at him hesitantly. "Come on," Charlie insisted.

"Once . . . I, well, at the Y one night, when . . . when I first got here, we was . . . we was watching a movie, and there was this fella, real friendly, who wanted to . . ." The boy went beet red.

"Right," said Charlie knowingly. "What'd you do?"

"I . . . I got up. Walked away, far as I could."

Charlie laughed. "Well, there you go. That's a fairy."

"Oh," said Barker, beginning to understand. Then another thought arose, and he looked confused again. "But ain't that what *we're* gonna do?"

"Huh?" asked Charlie.

"For the op . . . for the operation. Do . . . well, you know, do stuff with other men."

"No, no, no, not at all," Charlie insisted. "Well, sort of, but the difference is that they, the fairies, they *want* to, see? Have sex with men, I mean. Besides," Charlie added pointedly, "anytime we go out, we'll always be the man, you get me? Goes without saying." These were simple facts to Charlie that folks in his world took for granted, but the blank look on Barker's face told him that he was not getting through to the youngster. "All right, listen," Charlie continued, getting frustrated, "sometimes, well, there just ain't no women to be had, know what I mean? But a man's still got needs." He offered Barker a wink and a wry smile, but again received nothing back but the blank look. "Wait a minute," Charlie said to himself, a sudden awareness dawning. "Oh, Jesus. You ain't even . . ." Charlie muttered, recognizing the problem at last; Barker was a virgin. "Christ, McKinney," he cursed to himself. What had he gotten this boy into, and how was he going to wise him up fast?

Charlie couldn't recall anyone ever explaining this stuff to *him*, it was just the natural order of things; he had no ready words for it, so describing it to Barker would take some effort. But who better to do it than Charlie, he asked himself, to set the kid straight, so that no one, woman *or* man, could ever play Barker for a chump?

"All right," said Charlie with confidence. "Easy enough to fix. Old Charlie'll get you done up right, guaranteed. But take my word, kid"—he pulled his new protégé in close, offering a warning, man-to-man—"once you get a taste, of a woman, I mean, you won't be able to think about nothing else. There are *times*, though"—he thought about his old neighborhood on the Lower East Side of New York, about the immigrant guys with wives back in the old country, and how there was always a neighborhood fairy to take care of them. Nobody talked about it, but nobody bothered them neither—"when you're out at sea, for instance, months at a time, fella gets wicked horny. So, the fairies, don't ask me why, they're willing to . . . to be the woman for you, relieve you one way or another. Nature's way, I guess. Keeps a guy from doing something really crazy. 'It ain't queer unless you're tied to the pier.' Know what I'm saying? And nobody thinks any worse of you for it, long as you're a regular sort."

"So, then"—Barker now seemed to be following Charlie's trail of logic—"why are we trying to . . . ?"

"Because some people, like the Navy, they *do* think worse of the *other* guy, the fairy. I mean, for us, it's just a squirt. We don't feel nothin' like we'd feel for a woman. But fairies, see, they'd rather do it with a guy. They *like* takin' the woman's part. And they'll fall for you just like a dame would. That's why they get no respect."

Barker went silent for a moment. Charlie waited, giving his young student time to digest the subtleties of the master's argument. Finally, Barker looked up at Charlie and said, with conviction, "Don't seem fair."

Charlie looked at him, taken aback. Where had that come from? What bedtime story had Barker been told, what lesson at his father's knee had suggested to him that the world was fair? Charlie snorted, then with a bitter laugh he said, "The big fish eats the little fish, kid, and so on down the line, and the only guy who really wins is the one who makes the rules. Just be glad that, this time at least, you ain't the little fish."

Barker nodded, seeming to accept this wisdom; then he turned and walked away, disappearing around a corner into the winter darkness.

"That is one funny kid," Charlie muttered to himself as he watched him leave. He'd have to watch out for that one, Charlie told himself as he made his way toward Dottie's waiting arms.

# FOUR

*Seven months later, June 1919*

William's office faced Thames Street, which was the only thing that could be said for the cluttered space other than that it was inadequate. When his employers, the highly respected attorneys Rathbone Gardner and Abbot Phillips, decided they needed to hire a junior lawyer, they simply added a desk to the small room they had been using as a law library and printed William's name in gold on the window of its door. Most of the forbidding legal tomes still remained, collecting dust on the built-in mahogany shelves, so at least William never had far to go for a reference volume.

But in the seven years that he had been in the employ of Gardner & Phillips, first as a legal clerk during summers off from Harvard Law, then as an attorney, he could count on one hand the number of times his work had required any demonstration of legal precedent whatsoever, and those few had been decidedly prosaic, dealing with estate and property claims rather than the soaring heights to which the law might reach. Like Isaac Newton, William was keenly aware that he stood upon the shoulders of giants; greatness surrounded him, encrypted in these volumes, from Solon to Marshall to Holmes, whose uncluttered reason had spread the light of civilization over a dark and brutal world. But that vision now seemed a distant dream, hidden in so many forgotten tombs, as if greatness were a quality from another time and place, no longer required for the petty nastiness of his daily legal practice.

"The reading of the Strathmore will is to be delayed indefinitely," William announced, remembering the bright-eyed young clerk, Edgar, who stood before his desk, "pending the return of Mrs. Strathmore from Europe."

William watched Edgar scribble and saw himself, ten years earlier, trying to absorb all he could, still thinking that all of this mattered.

He glanced down at his neatly arranged desk. There were framed photographs of Sarah and their three children, a collection of sharpened pencils in a blown-glass holder, a lead crystal inkwell, and a finely wrought gold and enamel dipping pen from E. S. Johnson & Co., New York, which had been his mother's gift to him upon his graduation from Yale. Two folders lay open on his desk, with several documents in each. He stared at them blankly.

"Mr. Bartlett . . . ?" Edgar queried.

William looked up. "I'm sorry, Edgar. Where were we?"

"No, sir. Look." Edgar was staring out through the glass office door. William could hear raised male voices offering effusive greetings.

He joined Edgar by the door. They both watched with interest as William's employers fawned over a tall, distinguished man in his late forties, dressed in black clerical garb. The man returned their greetings, but with only the briefest of nods, as if he were a prince, and an unhappy prince at that, disturbed at having to deal with the common folk. With great deference, the two gray-haired lawyers led the man toward Rathbone Gardner's office.

There was something familiar about the visitor, thought William. Not that he had ever met the man, but rather that he recognized him as a personage of some specific importance.

"Who is it, sir?" asked Edgar.

"I'm not sure," said William as the three men disappeared into the elderly attorney's sanctum. "But I feel I've seen him before. Or perhaps his picture."

The intercom on William's desk buzzed loudly. He leaned over and flicked the switch.

"Yes, Mr. Gardner?"

"William?" Gardner's voice crackled. "Would you come into my office a moment?"

"Of course, sir, right away." He released the intercom and looked at Edgar, the two sharing a moment of intrigued curiosity.

"What do you think, Edgar?" William asked as he grabbed a pencil and writing tablet. "A little excitement, at last?"

Edgar smiled. "I hope so, sir."

"Me, too. But I wouldn't count on it."

—•—•—•—

"Close the blinds, William," said Abbot Phillips, the younger of the two general law partners. Phillips was nearing sixty, with mostly gray thinning hair, perpetually slicked back and strongly scented with pomade. Though not more than five foot nine, and despite the tight round belly that had grown by roughly an inch each year that William had known him, the man maintained an impressive stature when upright. In his usual state of repose, however, seated in a massive wingback leather armchair, the attorney had a languid quality, as if he'd seen far too much of the world to be interested in anything other than his own bank account and the state of his manicure.

Rathbone Gardner, on the other hand, the senior partner, was a kind and cultivated patrician in his late sixties. Six foot two inches and thin as a college freshman, Gardner had a mane of pure white hair and eyes as blue as a mountain lake. Until this moment, William had always looked upon Gardner as a trusted mentor to whom he might turn in moments of professional crisis. But the look of aggravated concern on the old man's face gave William a sudden indication that Gardner's native forbearance did have its limits.

Gardner cleared his throat pointedly.

Remembering himself, William turned back toward the chamber, dark and heavy now with heat and silence. Velvet drapes drawn across the street-side windows stilled the air. Slivers of sun streaked across the room, landing here and there like jagged bits of glass, illuminating pieces of things—the foot of an ottoman, a square of Persian carpet. As his eyes began to adjust, he noted the elderly Gardner, perched like a great gray eagle behind his huge mahogany desk, upright and alert, while opposite, Phillips and the mysterious cleric sank half-hidden into the pair of dark leather armchairs. With a flick of his head, which William could feel more than see, Abbot Phillips directed the younger man to a lonely seat on the broad leather divan that yawned beneath the draped exterior windows.

His feet heavy, William made the long trek across the room, feeling eyes on his back. A moustache of sweat dampened his upper lip as he turned and dropped into his designated place. The sofa was ancient and sank beneath him, leaving William at an undignified disadvantage, a head and a half at least below the other men.

"*William!*" Mr. Gardner pronounced ritually. "This is the right reverend Bishop James DeWolf Perry Jr. of the Episcopal Diocese of Rhode Island."

*Of course!* William thought to himself. No wonder the man looked familiar. Perry's portrait hung in the foyer of the church that William and his family attended each Sunday. A person of note, indeed! At the time of his elevation to the bishopric eight years earlier, Perry had been thirty-eight years of age, the youngest ever to be so honored. And William had also been right in thinking the man a prince. As a direct descendant of Commodore Perry, whose bronze statue dominated Newport's main public square, Bishop Perry was the scion of two great and wealthy New England families whose influence could not be underestimated in his rapid rise to power, though, to be fair, the man was known to be a capable if somewhat remote leader.

"Bishop," Gardner continued solemnly, "*this* is William Bartlett."

William looked at his mentor, alarmed by Gardner's tone, which seemed to carry the burden of accusation.

Perry leaned forward just enough to clear the wing of the leather chair. He examined William curiously, as if attempting to fathom how any man living could commit such a horrendous, though as yet unnamed crime. William stared back, flushed and baffled and frozen with guilt over he knew not what. It was only his deeply ingrained manners that pulled him out of the sofa to his feet, whereupon he offered a modest half bow.

"It's an honor to meet you, Bishop."

Discomfort ensued, during which the man appeared to be assessing the value of William's gesture. Finally, Perry nodded at William, accepting that perhaps he had the wrong man, after all.

"Please, proceed, Bishop," Phillips offered with a tight, forced smile.

Perry sighed with the weariness of a much older person. "What is at stake here, gentlemen, is nothing less than the future of Christian brotherhood. Can one man show loving kindness to another without being accused of . . . ?" He trailed off.

The others sat in silence. Finally, Abbot Phillips picked up the thread.

"Bishop Perry, this firm does not normally attend to the legal affairs of the Episcopal Diocese. Though we are extremely honored, I feel the need to ask you, why have you come to us?"

The bishop looked again at William. "The Reverend Kent specifically requested that Mr. Bartlett handle the case."

*Kent?* William asked himself. He reached back to the memory of that night six or eight months before, another world really, when disease and war were ravaging the country and turning his city upside down. The priest had been a bright spot in the midst of it all, wonderfully kind with a calm, gentle manner, fully committed as saints are to an impossible task. He had not seen or spoken to Kent since, though he had often thought of the man as a symbol of what the world was rapidly losing, the simple goodness of a more civilized past.

"William?" asked Gardner, that same unpleasant tone still ringing in his voice.

William felt like a boy of five as he looked up to find the three older men staring at him questioningly.

"I . . ." he stumbled. "Pardon me, but . . . what is this about?"

The bishop seemed to narrow his gaze.

"I understand you're acquainted with Reverend Kent's work amongst the men," said Perry.

"No, not really," William stammered. "I did some pro bono work for the Seaman's Institute, on behalf of the city council, nothing more than that, but it was months ago, just before the war ended." In his defense, he added nonsensically, "I hear the project has been abandoned."

Phillips grazed William with a look of bitter displeasure; then the silence fell again.

"What case?" William queried.

The older men looked at one another.

Gardner dropped his head an inch or two, preparing to parse his words. "There have been some unpleasant accusations," he offered with as much decorum as he could muster.

"Against Reverend Kent?" William asked, perplexed. "I find that hard to believe. What sort of accusations?"

The bishop's eyes closed as his jaw tightened, the muscles bulging with restrained fury and chagrin. William had no doubt that if the man could have discreetly covered his ears, he would have instantly done so.

"The unspeakable vice of the Greeks," Gardner continued reluctantly. "That is the crime to which we are referring."

William looked at Gardner, then at the other men. He recognized the phrase from his undergraduate days, something bandied about to explain certain expurgated portions of Plato. He even remembered several of his classmates joking about it afterward as they mocked their elderly classics professor, who had been something of a sissy. But it had never taken root as a real concept. "I'm sorry, gentlemen," said William genuinely. "I still don't understand."

"Oh, William!" Phillips sighed, exasperated. "Sodomy! Do you understand now? Three young sailors have accused Kent of making depraved advances upon them."

A cold, wet stone filled William's stomach. He laughed nervously. "That's preposterous."

The bishop smiled. This was apparently the answer that he wanted to hear. "Of course it is," he said. The man moved his head awkwardly, as if to free it from the strain of the tight clerical collar. For the first time, William noticed the purple trim. Perry rose abruptly. "Good," he pronounced. "It's settled, then."

"What's settled?" William demanded as he again struggled to rise from the low sofa. "What's settled?"

Gardner jumped up with surprising agility and escorted, or rather, rushed, the bishop to the door.

"You have our full support, Bishop Perry," Gardner cooed.

"That's a tremendous comfort," the man responded absently, his eyes on the exit. "Thank you. We'll speak soon?"

Gardner nodded gravely as he held the door for the nervous aristocrat, who quickly slithered out and never looked back. The gray-haired lawyer closed and locked the door, then returned to his desk and sat, seemingly ten years older than he had been a moment earlier.

William remained standing, looking after the vanished clergyman. *What had just occurred?* he asked himself. He looked at Gardner, then Phillips, but neither of his employers seemed ready to acknowledge William's relevance to the matter at hand. He felt invisible as Phillips began to speak.

"He'll obviously have to plead guilty."

William looked at Phillips, stunned.

"To a lesser charge, of course," Gardner was quick to add.

"And that would be?" Phillips asked, skeptical.

"How should I know? In all my years . . ." Gardner visibly shuddered at having to deal with such unpleasantness. "Indecent something or other."

"But, gentlemen . . ." William blurted, not believing his ears. "Sir, you can't . . . !"

The two old men looked at him.

"Yes, William? What can't we do?" Gardner inquired.

"Well . . ." William hesitated. "If . . . if we're going to take the case—"

"Little choice," Phillips grumbled. "Thanks to you. What do you mean, moonlighting like that? Don't you think you should have informed us of your little mission of mercy?"

William racked his brain for a satisfactory answer. The fact was he had been repeatedly told how important it was to foster good relations with the city fathers. Newport was a small town, controlled by a tight tapestry of founding families, and one hand always washed the other. William had made a snap decision at the time but had always thought, until this moment, that he'd made the right one.

"My friend, John Hart, it was his business. He was ill, and I thought to do a favor . . ." William said defensively.

"What difference does it make now, Abbot?" Gardner asked. "What's done is done. William, you don't refuse James DeWolf Perry, and you don't refuse the Episcopal Diocese of Rhode Island. The case is ours to . . . resolve," Gardner pronounced.

"All right, then," William continued, "but . . . well, the charges you mentioned, they're outrageous. This man Kent is . . ."

"What?" Phillips snapped. "He's what?"

"Well, he's . . ." William laughed. "It's impossible, really. If you knew the man . . ."

"I thought you said you only met him once," Abbot shot back. "Is that the truth or were you dissembling?"

"No," insisted William defensively. "I mean, yes, I only met him once. But there are some individuals, well, once is all it takes. The man is as near to a saint as anyone I've ever met. It makes no sense."

"I've never had the pleasure," Phillips drawled on a sigh, "so I will personally reserve judgment. But I suggest you ask yourself, William, what sort of fellow even gets accused of something like this?"

The two old lawyers shared an indecipherable look.

William took great pride in his self-control, considering it a mark of maturity and distinction. But there had been rare instances, three or four perhaps in his memory, when his blood had been brought to an instant boil.

Upon reflection, he could discern amongst these incidents a single common thread—a face-to-face encounter with shameless injustice. Whether the bully at school he'd witnessed beating a weaker child, or the policeman he'd seen mistreating a colored man at Yale, or a man striking his wife or children, any person exerting unwarranted authority over another could trigger in William an almost irresistible urge to shout down the abuser, or worse. He never expected to find himself in such a circumstance in his place of business, standing before his employers, upon whom the future of his career and the welfare of his family depended.

"William?" Gardner asked. "Are you all right?"

"I . . ." William fought to keep a civil tongue in his head. "Gentlemen," he said, invoking all the endowments of that word, the call of civilization to reasonable behavior and discourse. He took a breath. "Shouldn't we at least hear his side of the story, before we—"

"I'm sorry, William, but Abbot is right," Gardner insisted calmly. "A trial would be a disaster for everyone, not least of all your friend Reverend Kent."

"The Navy doesn't want to send a clergyman to prison." Phillips shrugged. "A slap on the wrist, they'll assign him to another parish, and we'll all be spared a lot of embarrassing publicity."

Gardner stood and walked to William, placing a hand on his shoulder. "Son, I can see you're struggling with this," he said sincerely. "I have no doubt that Kent is the man you say he is, but his guilt or innocence at this point is irrelevant. This accusation, once made public, would destroy his life irrevocably. The sooner we're all done with it, the better."

As difficult as it was to accept, William sensed that Gardner was right. But it rankled him nonetheless, railroading an innocent man into a guilty plea, and for such a crime as this. Those men he'd tried to help, little better than rabid dogs most of them, had turned on him for some unknown reason or another. Just one more example, William noted, of a world still at war with itself. And here he was, once again being called upon to play his small part in the unraveling.

"Believe me, my boy, as men of the world we must accept Abbot's suggestion as the only course of action available to us. What you are contemplating would cause more sorrow than you can possibly imagine, and it certainly would not be to the liking of the bishop, who is after all, footing the bill. No, your job in this, in deference to your relationship with the reverend, is to convince Kent exactly where his best interests lie. I have total confidence in you, William. I'm certain you'll have little trouble helping him see the light of reason."

*Reason?* William asked himself. How do you reasonably ask a man to accept a scarlet letter on his back? He had always suspected that somehow, someday he would have occasion to speak with Kent again, to delve deeper into the man's obvious wisdom, but never in his wildest dreams could he have envisioned that it would have been under circumstances such as these.

# FIVE

The wooden parish house had recently been painted, blue with white trim. Still, it seemed sad and stingy to William when compared to the impressive stone church beside which it sat. Two stories with a covered porch on one side, it could hardly be said to have a style. It was simply a house, with the first floor occupied by administrative offices, and the second, up a private staircase with creaky treads, the residence of whatever man happened to be pastor at any given time.

William stood in the center of the main room, surveying the austerity of Kent's modest quarters. He felt even more awkward here than he had at the jail, glancing at the few meager furnishings and Kent's fewer personal effects. A worn print sofa and slipcovered side chair faced a blackened fireplace. A plain oak table with two high-backed chairs sat near an open kitchen with a small stove, sink, and icebox. A door on the far side of the fireplace led, presumably, to a bedroom and bath. Folded against one wall was an extra bed with a metal frame and a thin single mattress. The hardwood floors were scratched and highly polished, covered in part by a faded oriental carpet and two newer hooked rugs defining the kitchen and dining areas. This was not a home but a way station. Many had stopped here for a period of time before moving on, and many more would do so in the future, a future unlikely to involve the Reverend Kent.

Kent himself sat in a large wingback chair beside the room's one generous feature, an enormous double-hung window that gave out on a spectacular copper beech in full bloom. The tree had a massive trunk and a copious crown of deep red leaves fifty feet across at least, and standing in the room one felt nearly a part of it. It was a perfect summer day, with a warm, familiar wind sweeping off the bay, and the beech was putting on an extraordinary show of light and rhythm, thousands of leaves dancing and rustling in great waves and sudden patterns.

Kent's physical presence seemed diminished, fading into the worn upholstery and the embrace of the great tree behind him. He lifted his head from the document he had just signed approving the firm's plea bargain strategy. He attempted a smile. "Seems as if you always have me signing something or other." He held it out to William.

William approached and took the sheaf of papers, handling them reluctantly, as if their touch was somehow poisonous. "Thank you, Reverend." He looked at the older man for a long moment but could think of nothing more to say. "Well," William resumed feebly, "I'll have to be getting back to the office."

"Of course," Kent said.

William nodded, then walked to the door in silence and discomfort.

"William," Kent said.

The lawyer stopped and turned. "Yes, sir?"

"What does it mean?"

William flushed red with panic at the thought that he had been negligent somehow. "I'm sorry. I'm so sorry. Did I fail to explain it to your satisfaction? It . . . well, it means that you give our firm permission to . . . to negotiate on your behalf. You will plead . . . guilty to a lesser charge, so that we can keep you out of court. It will all be done as quietly as possible, so as to—"

"I understand all that, William," Kent interrupted calmly. "You were very clear in your explanation. But what do you think it means in terms of . . . my life. Will it change dramatically?"

William looked Kent squarely in the eye. "I have no idea, sir. I've no experience with this sort of thing."

Kent laughed sadly. "Neither do I."

Another moment passed in silence as William tried to think of something reassuring to say. But he had told Kent the truth. To do less than that now, to retreat into false comfort, would not be worthy of the man.

"If there's nothing else, Reverend . . ." William said.

Kent shook his head no.

"Good-bye then, sir." William turned and walked toward the exit. As his hand fell on the knob, he caught sight of an old photograph hanging on the wall at eye level just beside the door. The subject of the photo was a woman, flanked by two young men in their teens, one a few years older than the other. The woman might be forty or sixty; hard work and worry had likely stolen her youth long before. The older male to her left seemed shy and hesitant, but the fellow on the right, the younger brother who strongly resembled his mother, was an eager and strapping lad with a broad jaw and an especially bright smile. This was a fellow out to set the world right, with the strength and intelligence to fight or outwit any foe.

William wondered where that woman and elder brother might be right now and, if still among the living, what they thought of their knight in shining armor, their Don Quixote. Was there an awareness even then, that sadness in the mother's eyes that William thought he could discern, that her son was destined to tip at nothing but windmills his whole life, that he would wind up as broken and dispirited as she? William's hand held the knob, but he was unable to proceed.

"Reverend," he spoke with difficulty, "I must ask this question—" He turned to look at the other man, who still sat in his chair, looking at William curiously. Again, William drew a blank, unsure of how to begin.

Kent smiled wearily. "I've done nothing wrong, William," he said, "if that's what you're wondering."

William felt suddenly ashamed. "Of course! Please don't think that I . . ." But what *else* was Kent to think under the circumstances, with William as proxy for all the interests urging him to plead guilty? "That wasn't what I was implying."

"Even if it was," Kent said evenly, "it would be all right. You're not inside my head. How can you be expected to know what's true or isn't true about me?"

William hesitated. What he was considering was insane, against every law of self-preservation, not to mention the best interests of the man before him, but Kent deserved more than to be railroaded into a guilty plea. He deserved a choice. William made what he knew would be a fateful decision, and a sudden sense of calm descended upon him.

"Sir, may I sit with you a moment longer?"

Kent nodded, perplexed. William grabbed one of the wooden dining chairs and pulled it up to sit opposite the priest. Now that William had made his decision, he felt electrified, his mind clear as a bell. He looked in Kent's eyes and began earnestly. "I want you to think, sir, is there anything, anything at all, that these three men could have misinterpreted? Some action on your part that might have been misread?"

Kent reflected for a long moment. Finally, he looked at William, shaking his head. "Nothing."

William pulled the indictment from his breast pocket, flipped the page, and read, "Henry Dostalick?"

"I took him to a Navy show one evening," Kent replied, as a simple matter of fact. "We had a pleasant ride one Sunday in my automobile along Bellevue Avenue."

William glanced down at the next name. "Bart Rudy?" he asked.

"I met Bart several times at the Y," Kent replied. "He's a devout Methodist. He said he was interested in pursuing a career in the ministry. I gave him my advice over a meal here in the rectory, here in this room. Mrs. Donnelly, the housekeeper, brought it up for us."

William nodded, then read the third and last name. "Charlie McKinney?"

Kent fell silent. He seemed troubled.

"What, Reverend?"

The priest sighed. "McKinney took sick during the flu epidemic. I sat with him in hospital. He recovered, one of the lucky few." Kent's eyes grew moist and he closed them to ward off the approaching tears. "Ridiculous," he insisted, wiping his eyes. "I'm sorry. A moment of self-pity, I'm afraid, but it's still difficult for me to think of those months." He smiled ironically. "As if I were alone in that." He took a deep breath, restoring himself. "We've all seen too much death."

"Yes," William replied, sympathetic. "Indeed we have."

"These boys, William"—Kent was searching for the words—"I fool myself into believing that I remember what it was like to be that young. You may, perhaps, but I don't. And what they've been through, torn from their families or wherever they've come from, with nothing but horror ahead of them. At this point, they're like stray dogs, many of them, beaten once too often. A kind word or look and they react with fear, suspicion. It's my duty, no, my *privilege* to look beyond that, to respond with love, regardless of their hostility."

Here was the man William remembered from their first meeting all those months before, and though he surely did not share the

Reverend Kent's compassion for the sailors who had accused him, he could not help but be impressed by the man's certainty. William knew more surely than he'd known anything in a very long time that he could not simply allow this man to swing in the wind, as his employers and the bishop would have preferred. "Reverend, as your attorney, I'm bound by law to keep anything you share with me in the strictest confidence. In what I am about to say, I must ask the same of you."

Kent smiled. "You're a lawyer, I'm a priest. Many of the same rules apply."

William laughed. What an unfailing talent Kent had for putting people at ease, even in the face of his own desperate circumstances! But William could not allow any sense of good fellowship to obscure for either of them the momentous nature of the step they were about to take.

"There's no point in lying to you, sir. It won't be pretty. The prosecuting attorney will no doubt make all sorts of horrible claims. But in the face of your testimony, of your life, I can't believe there's a jury in the world that would find you guilty of these charges."

Kent looked at William, confused. "What are you saying, William? I thought—"

"Yes, I know. But it's wrong, what I was trying to do. You must be given the chance to defend yourself against these monstrous accusations," William protested, as much to himself as to Kent. There was only one other way out at this point and William grabbed for it, despite all his fine sentiments. "If that's what you choose."

Kent thought for a moment. "And you would be willing to defend me? To speak in public of these things?"

"What?" William was confused. Then, horrified at the realization of what Kent was imagining, he blurted out, "Oh, no, sir, you misunderstand. I'm not the lawyer for—"

"But then who else—"

"No," William insisted. "Believe me, this is a serious matter. You need someone with real trial experience," he urged. The picture of him standing in the courtroom defending Kent flashed through his head. Twelve jurors and a silent crowd listening with rapt attention was an appealing fantasy. It was also a terrible suggestion that would ultimately lead to disaster. "There are a dozen attorneys I could recommend," he announced, "far more qualified than I."

"I see." Kent fell silent for a moment, crestfallen. "Then I'm afraid it's out of the question."

"What?" William said, alarmed. "But why?"

"I'm a poor man, William. In this matter, I am completely at the mercy of the bishop. He appears quite comfortable with the choice of your firm, and once his mind is made up . . ."

"Perhaps if I spoke with him?" William offered, desperate to save the day. But that question fell to the floor, each man allowing, in the quiet of his own conscience, that such a conversation could never take place. Were William to take such a liberty, he would undoubtedly lose his job. And Kent was a soldier of God, William knew, who did as he was told.

The lawyer stood. "I . . ." He trailed off. There was nothing more for either of them to say, but William found himself unable to move. So this was how it would end, he thought to himself. A good man, perhaps the best that William had ever known, would be ruined, and the world would continue as before, with one more black mark against it, gone unnoticed.

"Reverend?"

The priest looked at him expectantly.

"You're a man of God," William continued, looking everywhere but at Kent. "You can look into the hearts of men—"

Kent protested, "William, please, believe me, I have no such ability—"

"Nonsense," William insisted. "I know you've told me to have compassion for these men, but how could they turn on you like this? After all you've done for them, to ruin you in this vicious way? I don't . . . It's beyond even my expectations of them."

Kent sighed, then turned to gaze out the window. After a long moment, he said, "This tree has been my constant companion for over a year now. I sit for hours sometimes, gazing at it, and just when I think we're well acquainted, the seasons change."

Kent paused for another moment, then turned to look at William. "The only soul of which I can hope to claim knowledge is my own, William, and it's been an imperfect study at best. As for other men, I offer no judgment or tidy conclusions. I simply pray for them what I pray for myself—God's indulgence as I stumble through life."

What was William to say to that? What was he to do? He tried to imagine the world as it must look through the eyes of Samuel Kent, but it was no use. William's own soul was a mystery to him, rarely considered. But somewhere within, he recognized that in seeking to give Kent a proper choice in his destiny, he had stumbled upon a crossroads of his own. The righteous path lay clearly marked. So too did the prudent. If his life history had any bearing on his decision, William felt certain that he would choose the latter.

## SIX

*Two days later*

Ice cream socials were a much-loved tradition in New England, modest affairs where family and neighbors would gather to celebrate the arrival of sunshine and warmer weather. But never had there been such a one as this, William suspected. Ice cream was served, to be sure, and in great abundance to hundreds of people, but it seemed to him a devilish trick to link that most American of confections to a political agenda. And although the day brought some memories back to William of a simpler world, the motives behind the display, the uncontrolled extravagance, and the odd assortment of guests made it all feel like more a mockery of the past than a return to it.

Rumor had it that the hostess of this astonishing event, Alva Belmont (formerly Vanderbilt before her very profitable first divorce), had hired a private train to pick up various notables on its riotous way across the country to Marble House, Alva's palatial summer "cottage" before which, in an enormous blue and white striped tent, William was now encamped with those notables in support of women's suffrage. Though he would not even pretend to know who most of these people were, he did overhear bits of chatter as the famous or near famous drifted by, and a few caught his attention.

There was a dour-looking man with a pointy gray beard who, it was whispered, may or may not have been the notorious Austrian sex doctor Freud on his first trip to America. And it was indeed the Hollywood star Clara Bow who sat perched near the ice cream bar, dressed in a white frock cut scandalously low in back, and surrounded by a mostly male entourage. Teddy Roosevelt's second cousin Franklin was there, in his sparkling white uniform. The dashing naval under-secretary was busy flirting with all the pretty girls, while his poor, homely wife, Eleanor, the former president's niece, fervently discussed the issues of the day with anyone who would listen.

Of the Newport elite, most of the important families were repre-sented. The Whitneys and various Vanderbilts (those still on speaking terms with Alva) were there, along with the Berwinds and the Kings, and several of the Gallatins. The Wetmores managed a brief cameo, their late arrival made even more gossip-worthy by the absence of patriarch and former governor George Wetmore. Had it been gout that kept him home, or politics? And Tessie Oelrichs, silver heiress and Alva's sworn rival in all things social, made a dramatic entrance with her longtime friend, the famed Jewish magician Harry Houdini. The prestidigitator had done a few tricks upon arrival, several involving a floating cigarette that even William had found unsettling. But the performer had long since abandoned the confines of the tent in favor of the great lawn beyond, where five hundred working-class individu-als of various hues and ethnicities had been granted access to gawk, gobble ice cream, and pretend to care about women's voting rights.

William's wife was in the tent, off somewhere rubbing elbows with the leaders of the movement, who were difficult to distinguish since it seemed everyone was dressed in white linen or lace. He stood rooted near the thirty-foot-long ice cream table, where vats of the frozen confection in strawberry, chocolate, and vanilla sat packed in ice. Behind each vat, a handsome Negro stood, his dark skin set off by a white jacket, a silver ice cream scooper at the ready. Children ate their favorite flavors from Lenox bowls with silver spoons or piled high on waffled sugar cones. The adults drank sweet lemonade from lead crystal tumblers, or sipped jasmine tea, dispensed from four sterling samovars each the size of a fire hydrant.

Was it only he, William considered, who heard the deafening buzz bleeding under the tent, the hum of the great unwashed as they milled about the lawn awkwardly, modest vanilla cones dripping on their fingers in the unforgiving summer sun? A sudden punctuating scream of delight made his head turn, as he wondered with what new sleight of hand Houdini might be enthralling the crowd. But no trick, William reckoned, could have seemed more fantastic to this mob than that which had allowed them to enter here, where magic was standard and an entirely different set of values held sway, different from theirs, and certainly different from his own.

Nothing hammered that point home to William more than the teacup he held in his hand, and which he now examined for the first time. Those lovely blue squiggles on the bone china that from a distance had seemed a simple decoration resolved themselves, upon closer inspection, into something far more subversive. He turned to the mounds of cups, bowls, and saucers piled high on the long white table, and sure enough, across every piece, the words "Votes For Women" had been inscribed in periwinkle, baked right into the porcelain in cursive script. It was not the sentiment that offended him, but rather the willful extravagance that seemed to reduce the most important issue of the day to the level of frivolous vanity.

"Just like old times, eh?" a deep Australian baritone mused. William looked up to see a tall heavyset man with a red face, nearing sixty, William guessed, standing quite close.

"I'm sorry," William replied. "Were you speaking to me?"

"This party," the man explained. "Reminds one of the good old days before the war."

William glanced at the plates again. "Not so much."

"Ah, yes, well," said the man, understanding William's meaning. "Everyone needs a hobby, I suppose, now that we've 'saved the world for democracy.' Can't hate the Germans anymore." He chuckled as he picked up a saucer and examined it. "You've got to admire the thoroughness, though. Shows real commitment."

William shrugged. "A little heavy-handed if you ask me."

The big man smiled wryly, his interest piqued. "Opposed to women's suffrage, then, are we?" he asked.

"If I were," William responded defensively, "why would I be here?"

"William!" He turned to see his wife, Sarah, her blond hair worn stylishly up, waving at him from across the crowd. He smiled and waved back at her.

The big man chuckled. "A husband will do an awful lot to keep peace." The fellow then took a scooper from a startled Negro and helped himself to a generous second serving of strawberry ice cream. He put the bowl beneath his nose and breathed deep. "Ah! The smell of fresh strawberries!" He raised the spoon to his mouth and shrugged. "Frankly, it amazes me how many otherwise intelligent men make public fools of themselves over the issue. Why, just the other day . . ."

Sarah, in a long white cotton dress, ran up and took William by the hand, green eyes flashing with delight. The fellow was right, of course. Even after twelve years of marriage, he would still do nearly anything for her.

"Come, dear. I want to introduce you to—"

Nearly anything.

"I was, um . . ." William said, reluctant to move, "talking with this gentleman." He turned to the large stranger. "I didn't catch your name, sir."

Sarah looked at the Australian with a nod of recognition.

"Mr. Rathom," said Sarah, pleased. "It's good to see the press covering something uplifting for a change."

"All depends on your point of view," Rathom said, glancing at William with a smirk. Then, graciously, he continued, "But I'm afraid you have me at a disadvantage, ma'am."

"Sarah Bartlett." She extended her hand with a cordial smile, then presented her other half. "My husband, William. Dear, this is John Rathom, editor in chief of the *Providence Daily Journal*. He's from Australia, where they've had universal suffrage since 1901."

William gave a nod and the men shook hands stiffly. So, William thought, this was the man responsible for that young reporter's assault on poor Reverend Kent outside the city jail.

"A pleasure, Mr. Bartlett." The journalist turned back to Sarah. "I was just telling your husband how the other day, we reported on two U.S. senators who had the temerity to claim that giving women the vote would be against the will of God."

"That's absurd." Sarah laughed. "It was Saint Paul himself who wrote, 'In Christ there is no male nor female, for all are one in Jesus.'"

"You left out the rest, ma'am," Rathom corrected her gently. "'No Jew nor Gentile, no slave nor free . . .'"

"Of course." Sarah smiled graciously. "I did so for brevity's sake only, I assure you, Mr. Rathom."

"I have no doubt, Mrs. Bartlett. But we must be very careful about these things. They say that *patriotism* is the last refuge of scoundrels," remarked Rathom. "But I rather think it's the Bible." He turned to William, raising an eyebrow. "And you, Mr. Bartlett? What *is* your position?"

"Jews *can* vote, the last time I checked," William asserted, annoyed that this obnoxious fellow had presumed to correct his wife. "And we abolished slavery a very long time ago."

Rathom exchanged a glance with Sarah, who looked down.

"Quite," Rathom replied. "I was merely pointing out how often people tend to pick and choose from Holy Writ as it suits them, just as those senators did."

William blushed, aware that he was not keeping up with the conversation, so focused was he on his immediate and intense dislike of this fellow. What kind of man, he asked himself, sows discord between a husband and wife purely for his own amusement? Sarah took his arm supportively.

"My husband is a staunch supporter of the movement," she assured Rathom. "With some reservations."

William glanced at Sarah, annoyed.

"And *they* would be?" Rathom probed.

William took a breath. "What concerns me, what concerns *many* of us, are the uneducated classes. Obviously, a woman of my wife's station is capable of casting a responsible vote after reasoned discourse with her husband. But doubling the franchise amongst the poor and the immigrants seems ill-advised."

Rathom snorted. "Some women are more equal than others, is that it?"

"No," William said firmly, determined not to lose his temper. "But there are certain values upon which democracy and a civil society depend. Given time, those now living in a state of ignorance will be taught the wisdom of those values and act accordingly. I believe in progress. I do. But I also believe it's the duty of those of us who know better to make sure we don't lose what's fine and good along the way."

"And what about the women who don't *have* husbands?" Rathom asked.

William searched for a response but none came to mind.

"Awfully young to be a dinosaur, aren't you?" Rathom remarked, amused. "Probably in favor of prohibition as well."

William was about to protest that he was not in favor of any such thing, that it was in fact his wife who supported that absurd experiment, but Rathom never gave him the chance.

"You know," Rathom pronounced, "the Romans had a saying . . ."

"Seize the day?" offered Sarah hopefully.

"No, ma'am." Rathom looked down at William. "Let go or be dragged. The tide of history is a mighty force to struggle against, Mr. Bartlett. You sure you just don't want to let go and join the party?"

If this was the party, William thought, and Rathom was on the guest list, then he was quite sure he would rather send his regrets. But outnumbered as he was, and not willing to cede the field to his opponent, William chose to hold his ground as he stewed in what even he recognized as impotent silence.

—•—•—•—

Sarah Clarke had grown up less than a mile from her future husband, the love of her life, but although they were distantly related, both descendants of Dr. William Clarke, one of the founders of the Newport colony, and though they were of the same social class, their awareness of one another as children had been dim at best. It was not until she'd begun attending dancing school at age fourteen that Sarah noticed the awkward boy who had been chosen as her opening partner on the morning they first learned to waltz. His movements and manners were painfully stiff as he attempted to lead her around the floor, and his brief bow and rapid disappearance elicited little more from Sarah than a bemused shrug as she moved on to her next partner. Over the years, however, she often found herself glancing at William from a distance, wondering why this ever more handsome young man remained so shy and serious. He proved himself to be good at nearly everything—schoolwork, sports—as was she, and he seemed to have a close circle of chums, as did she, but he rarely looked as if he was having any fun.

Then, at high school graduation, she saw him with his parents. There was little to be said about his mother, a bland woman who appeared pleasant enough, but as he stood beside his father, William seemed to visibly shrink. The older man was tall, stern, and distant. He seemed to have chosen this day to bestow some small measure of approval upon his only son, which William, sweating in his over-large blue blazer, tried to absorb in a manly and decorous fashion. But it was clear to Sarah that the boy was in fact starving for it. So different from her own family, she thought. Sarah's own father had willingly bestowed his hopes of posterity on his eldest and her two younger sisters, and had encouraged them to be all that society would allow, reminding one and all of their direct blood connection to the fiercely independent founders of their fiercely independent city, which had after all been first led by a woman.

It was not until the summer following her second year at Smith College that she again encountered William, this time at the annual Fourth of July celebration on Washington Mall, Newport's historic main square. Cheering citizens crammed tight, spilling from the sidewalks, as a parade of sharp naval cadets from the War College and seasoned soldiers from Fort Adams marched to a military band. Belching tubas and bright coronets flashed gold in the relentless sunshine, while a dozen snare and bass drums echoed off the buildings' brick facades. Vendors sold small American flags and hot dogs and beer and lemonade and popcorn and ice cream to the noisy, overheated crowd, who seemed perfectly thrilled to be perspiring together into their holiday clothes.

And there, in the small park that anchored the center of the Mall, on the stone pedestal alongside the statue of Commodore Perry, stood William, his arm around the bronze hero's neck. He seemed changed somehow in his straw hat and white linen suit, jacket slung over his shoulder, sleeves rolled up. Perhaps he was drunk, she thought. But when he saw her and jumped down and came to her, she knew that, though he may have had a beer or two, the change she had perceived was more fundamental. He seemed more curious and a bit lost, more willing to engage in conversation, and certainly much quicker to smile than she had previously known him to be. He loved Yale, he told her, and though it had been a difficult year, with the sudden death of his father in February, his family was doing well, his mother and younger sister were holding up fine, and he was now the man of the family, or so he was told, and he was still trying to figure out what that meant. There was no question that he would finish school and then go on to study the law, as his father had done, but would she perhaps at least *consider* marrying him when it was all over or maybe even before that? She looked at him a moment, stunned, then burst out laughing, and he joined her seconds later, but as the laughter faded and their eyes met, an awareness of shared destiny passed between them, and William stole the briefest of kisses.

Two years later, almost to the day, they were married, and so began their life together.

---

As they pulled up to their home, William turned off the motor's engine but did not move to go. He watched Sarah collect her souvenirs nestled on the floor at her feet—a flowered centerpiece from one of the party tables, a printed event program, and a commemorative silver spoon, which she had laid carefully on her purse.

A chorus of crickets filled the silence as William considered the day's events. So many women, his own wife among them, determined to change the world, and there he had stood, unable to utter a single coherent position against that newspaperman.

"I envy you," he said simply.

"What?" she asked, turning to him.

"You have principles," he replied absently.

"As do you, dear," Sarah said with a wry laugh. "I can certainly attest to that."

So he had always thought. "But how willing am I to sacrifice for them?" he mused aloud.

Sarah laid her hand on his. "What is it, dear?"

He avoided his wife's gaze as he tried to imagine a circumstance in which he might tell her of Kent's predicament.

"Something has come up at work," he offered. "Something not very nice. I had hoped to, well, exert a positive influence, but I appear to have little say in the matter."

He sighed.

"What's happening to the world, Sarah?" he asked sincerely. "People have lost all sense of decency, it seems."

She smiled at him. "You haven't."

He looked at her. She had meant it as a compliment, he knew, but it felt like an indictment.

She leaned over and kissed him tenderly on the cheek, then said, "We are only bound to do that which is in our power to do. The rest, we leave to God."

She sounded like Kent, William thought. "As simple as that," he said, equal parts statement and question.

"No," she replied. "Not simple. Sometimes it requires a great deal of thought to recognize the difference."

William sighed. He had already spent more time on this than anything in recent memory, but he had no doubt that much more thinking lay ahead.

# SEVEN

It took about an hour for William to drive his Dodge Brothers sedan from Newport to Providence early the next morning. He did not know what demon had possessed him to embark on the thirty-five-mile journey to the *Providence Daily Journal*, but possessed him it had. By rights, he should have gone directly to the offices of Gardner & Phillips to report on his successful interview with Reverend Kent. But in light of his own cowardice, the least William felt he owed Kent was an attempt to exact a promise from his new acquaintance Rathom that there would be no undue publicity. If William's ultimate goal was to salvage as much of the reverend's reputation as possible, then it seemed there could be no better place to start than here.

As he approached the four-story French Revival building that took up an entire city block, William suddenly felt himself very much the small-town lawyer. Why must it be, he wondered, that every edifice built in the last forty years had to resemble a king's palace? This was a monolith he was facing, a hungry beast with a mind all its own, and William seriously doubted if Rathom would even grant an audience, much less agree to his demands. Still, he had come this far, and he was not about to turn back, no matter how poor his odds might look at the moment.

He approached the main entrance, a revolving monstrosity flanked by two sets of glass doors trimmed in brass, which were never still for more than a moment as people hurried in and out. Above the doors, bronze letters proclaimed proudly, "The Providence Daily Journal, founded 1829, Oldest Daily Newspaper in America." The lobby was large and cool, with black marble walls and floors. An inlaid inscription in shiny brass, polished even now by the tread of busy feet, pronounced, "I have sworn upon the altar of God, eternal hostility against every form of tyranny over the mind of man—Thomas Jefferson."

"Can I help you, sir?" an overly eager young man asked. William turned to him. The boy might have been but was not the cub reporter who had cornered William and the reverend outside the jailhouse. "I . . ." William hesitated, then found his voice. "Where might one find the office of the editor in chief?"

The boy's eyes brightened. "Mr. Rathom?" He laughed. "Glad it's you and not me looking for him! Room 401," he announced, pointing to the elevators as he headed out the exit.

William boarded an elevator with a group of people, mostly men, all of whom seemed to know each other as they laughed and conversed. The elevator man, a well-groomed, middle-aged Negro in liveried attire, announced with a heavy Southern accent, "Goin' up!" as he closed the doors. "What floor, sir?" the fellow asked William respectfully.

"Uh, fourth, please," William replied as the elevator jerked to a stop.

"Second floor!" the operator yelled.

A man with a small trolley shouted, "Getting out! Getting out, please!" then jostled William from behind. A second man got off as well, while two women, secretaries by the look of them and deep in conversation, joined the crush. The doors closed and the car bounced up again, leaving William's stomach behind.

"Third floor!"

Another abrupt stop, and the doors slid open. The roar of high-speed presses spitting out the news in great sheets filled the elevator, making further conversation impossible. It did nothing to deter the secretaries, however, who simply raised their voices over the din as they advanced into the huge open space, which was dark with machinery and heavy with oil, ink, and industry. Workmen in overalls manned the presses much as they do machines in all factories, William supposed, accustomed to their routines, except that here, the product was information.

"Goin' up!" The doors closed. The mechanical din quickly faded as the elevator rose once more.

"Fourth floor! Editorial!" the man proclaimed as he opened the doors again. William peered out at the vast array of desks before him. There was another sort of din here, of typewriters clacking, and a strong smell of coffee and cigarettes.

"Mistuh?" the Negro queried.

William looked at him.

"This is your floor, sir."

"Ah, yes," William replied. "Of course it is." He reached into his pocket and pulled out a quarter, which he offered to the elevator operator. "Thank you," William added.

"That's not necessary, sir," the man demurred proudly and did not take the coin.

"Oh," said William, embarrassed. "Uh, very well."

He put the quarter back in his pocket and exited the car as others pushed aboard. The operator shouted, "Goin' down!" and the doors closed behind him.

William stood a moment to observe the people working at their desks, dashing from place to place, or pushing trolleys with files or mail or newspapers, each filled with purpose and energy. Light poured in from huge windows. Great iron columns in the Doric style held up the high ceiling, while twenty or more pneumatic tubes, strategically located, snaked from ceiling to floor and beyond to ensure that messages were delivered faster than humanly possible. News, after all, was only news right now, and that urgency seemed to generate not merely a physical but a mental vigor as well. William suddenly understood the appeal of the newspaper business.

Along the far right side of the vast space was a line of private offices. William had expected so important a man as Rathom to have a small army of underlings marshaled against uninvited visitors, but everyone was far too busy to pay him any mind whatsoever. At the very far end of the room, William found office number 401, the gold lettering on the door inscribed "John Rathom, Editor in Chief."

There was an outer office, with a male secretary at a desk. The man, balding slightly with rimless spectacles and likely in his early forties, was on the phone.

William approached him. "Um . . . excuse me, sir, but . . ."

"Just a minute, Mike." He covered the mouthpiece of the phone he held to his ear and looked up at William, annoyed. "You're late. He's waiting for you." He returned to his phone call. "Yeah, Mike . . ."

"I'm afraid you're . . ." William protested. But the secretary simply waved William toward the inner office and continued his conversation.

The referenced door was closed and William could see no noticeable movement through the frosted glass. In contrast to the melee without, the stillness seemed downright odd. Perhaps the man was not in, or sleeping, or dead. William straightened his jacket and knocked, firmly but politely.

"Come!" the man within exclaimed, the Australian accent discernable even on that single word.

William turned the knob and entered and there the big man sat behind an enormous desk. He was wearing reading glasses, engrossed in some typewritten text or other.

"Take a seat!" Rathom half offered, half commanded. "I'm nearly finished with this, today's 'letter from the editor.' It's amazing to me how well my staff can ape my writing style as well as my opinions at this point. They may be better at being John Rathom than I am." He laughed heartily, looked up, and held out his hand for a proper greeting.

Still standing, William extended his own hand, though the memory of the many reasons he'd found to dislike this fellow was quickly returning to him.

"Why are you still standing?" Rathom asked, perturbed. Then he pulled off his reading glasses to take a closer look at William. "You're not the water commissioner."

"You're quite right, Mr. Rathom, I'm not," William quipped. "I'm glad someone finally noticed."

"Well then, who the blazes are you?" He called to the outer office, "Jasper!"

Jasper stuck his head in the door. "Yes, Mr. Rathom?"

"This is not the water commissioner," Rathom complained.

Jasper looked at William, confused. "He's not the water commissioner?"

"What did I just say?" Rathom insisted.

"Well then, who is he?" asked Jasper.

"That's what I'd like to know," Rathom demanded as he scrutinized William. "And what is he doing in my office?"

"Who are you?" Jasper echoed his boss angrily. "And what are you doing in Mr. Rathom's office?"

Rathom rose. "Wait a moment, Jasper." He looked at William anew. "You're clearly not the man I was expecting, but I do know you, don't I?"

"Yes," said William calmly. "After a fashion."

"Don't tell me," Rathom barked, thinking. "The memory seems to have both pleasant and unpleasant aspects to it."

"Picture me in white linen," William suggested.

"What?" Rathom asked. "Why would I do . . . ah, yes!" he said with a smile. "Now I remember, the young prig from that fiasco at Alva Belmont's house. You have a charming wife. Congratulations again on that."

"Thank you," William said coldly.

"You'll excuse me if I've been less than gracious. You've caught me a little off guard. I was expecting someone else—"

"The water commissioner, yes," William offered.

"Quite right," said Rathom, amused. "But more to the point, there's no one I'd less expect to see standing on that carpet than you, sir. Mr. Bartlett, wasn't it?"

"That's correct," William replied formally. "I apologize for the unannounced visit, but there is a matter of some urgency that I need to discuss with you."

"Fascinating," said Rathom.

"Would you perhaps have a few moments to spare?"

"Yes," said Rathom, brimming with curiosity. "Absolutely. Please," he insisted, taking a seat and again offering the one opposite the desk to William. "I'm all ears!"

William glanced at Jasper.

"Oh," said Rathom. "Yes, of course. It's all right, Jasper. Mr. Bartlett is a gentleman of Newport. I'm in no danger whatsoever. Leave us, please."

Jasper gave a nod and left the room, but not before throwing a last suspicious glance at William.

"I must confess, Mr. Bartlett, it's not often that people surprise me. You've just succeeded in doing so, which earns you more than a few credits."

"In that case, I'd like to redeem those credits immediately," said William evenly.

"Very well. What can I do for you? It must be something big. If

71

I remember correctly, you have nothing but contempt for me. Does your law firm need a little plug in the press? Do you need an introduction to some powerful politician? No, you're probably related to all of them. So, pray tell me, what is it?"

The man was even more insufferable than William had remembered. But Rathom was right, his motivation was indeed a powerful one—William would never have come here otherwise—and he would not take no for an answer.

"Well? Speak up, man!" Rathom encouraged. "Ask and ye shall receive, ha-ha!"

"Three days ago," William began, "a reporter of yours accosted a client of mine outside the Newport police station."

"Three days ago?" Rathom asked.

"Yes, sir. A young fellow, very aggressive."

"That describes most everyone on my staff, I'm happy to say. But it had to be Hank Judson. Accosted, you say?"

"Yes. My client was released on bail and I was simply escorting him from the jailhouse to his residence and this Judson fellow would not leave us alone. He followed us to my car and tried to intimidate my client into giving him a statement for publication. When my client refused, the young fellow let it be known that the *Journal* would be printing something about the case, regardless of whether we issued a statement or not."

"I apologize for his rudeness," Rathom offered in a patronizing tone, "if indeed he was rude. But that's a reporter's job, you see, to get people to talk even when they don't want to. If the reporter smells a story, that is. Would you mind telling me your client's name?"

William hesitated, then said, "I have come here in good faith, Mr. Rathom. Can I trust you as a gentleman to treat this interview as confidential?"

Rathom raised an eyebrow. "Would you really trust my word as a gentleman? Perhaps we should use one of your credits."

"As you wish," William agreed.

"Very well. This conversation is officially off the record."

"My client is the Reverend Samuel Neal Kent."

Rathom was silent a moment. "Kent? I see," he said, subdued. "Hmm, a very unfortunate situation. And you've come for my assurance that I will keep his name out of the papers?"

"Exactly that, Mr. Rathom," William said with sincerity. "In exchange for any remaining credits that I may have, or that I may have in the future, or that my wife may deserve of you. Whatever has been said between us in the past, I would swear to you my undying appreciation for this consideration."

Rathom looked at William for a long time before speaking. "You're willing to give a great deal for very little."

"Little?" William replied, irritated. "Are you implying that the destruction of a good man's life is a little thing?"

"Calm yourself, Mr. Bartlett. I am implying no such thing. I'll offer my response in the form of a question: When was the last time you saw the word 'sodomy' in print? Even if there were cause for suspicion of guilt in the matter—and I tend to agree with you about Kent, that he is a genuinely good man—my hands would be tied. Judson is inexperienced. His instincts are right and he'll make a great reporter someday, but he was given a dressing-down that very afternoon and was told that the story would go no further. To his great disappointment, I'm afraid."

William was shocked. Was it to be that easy, then? "So, you're telling me you have no intention of printing anything about these ridiculous allegations?"

Rathom sighed. "Have you read the papers lately? Race riots, civil war in Russia, the damned Prohibition. There's no lack of genuine news. So unless Kent got one of the sailors pregnant, which would be a story that I could not ignore, you won't see a word about him."

William decided to let that last remark pass without comment.

"Well," he said amiably, "I'm very pleased. And I know the reverend will be too."

"That's refreshing," said Rathom. "I rarely have that effect on people. And I release you from your pledge of . . . what was it? Undying appreciation?"

"You have it nonetheless, sir. Well, I won't take any more of your time. Thank you." William rose to leave.

"Mr. Bartlett." Rathom stopped him. "May I ask why you failed to mention anything about this when we met on Saturday?"

William flushed. "It was hardly the time or the place, sir."

"Hmmm. Uncomfortable with the subject, are you?" Rathom asked rhetorically. "Can't say I blame you. But you do realize that it's not as simple as just keeping it out of the papers. Word will get out. Ironic, since no one will even name the thing, but people will know. I doubt he'll be a priest much longer. Unless of course he's completely exonerated, which would mean a court trial." Rathom smirked. "Not likely, I suppose."

William froze as Rathom looked him in the eye. The man was so smug, so unbearably sure of himself, that the words left William's mouth before he had time to think. "That is exactly what we intend, Mr. Rathom. Reverend Kent is an innocent man, and we will prove that beyond a shadow of a doubt before a jury of his peers."

"Really?" Rathom eyed William skeptically. "And does that mean that *you* will be representing him?"

William paused for a moment, hearing it from someone else's lips for the first time, then uttered, "Yes. That's correct."

"Humph," Rathom grunted, then offered a brief nod of respect. "You're a man of *many* surprises, it seems, Mr. Bartlett."

Rathom raised his great bulk to standing. "I look forward to watching this as it unfolds," he said, adding for reassurance, "as a private citizen, of course." He extended his beefy paw in apparent good fellowship.

William looked at Rathom for a moment, then, with sincerity this time, shook the big man's hand. The snide comments had rankled William, but what unsettled him even more was the odd joy he felt at having won the editor's grudging respect. He had made his declaration primarily to prove Rathom wrong about the fundamental nature of his character. Now that it had been said, William knew that there was no way he could go back on it.

—•—

The two men stood over William, red-faced, making no attempt to contain their fury. William had seen Abbot Phillips spout off many times, but never had he witnessed Mr. Gardner in such a fit of rage. The man looked as if he might have a stroke.

"Did you impress upon Kent the risks inherent in this foolhardy course of action?" Gardner railed.

William's first stop after leaving Rathom's office had been the church rectory, where he had informed a very grateful Kent of his decision before either he or Kent had the chance to change his mind. Now, William tried to hold his chest high as the furious assault continued. "Yes, Mr. Gardner, I did."

"And is he aware"—Phillips picked up the attack—"that if he's found guilty he faces up to twenty years in state prison?"

The image of Kent in a prison cell, worse than the one from which William had liberated the man, suddenly flashed through his mind. Kent would likely never see the outside world again. He would die in prison.

Phillips sneered, "You left out that little fact, I suppose."

William had never felt real hatred, but at that moment he was aching to punch Phillips repeatedly, this mean and narrow cynic, determined to sow the seeds of doubt in William's mind. The truth was, Kent would only go to prison if he were convicted, a virtual impossibility as far as William was concerned. Once these spurious allegations were held up against the facts and history of the reverend's life, Kent would be cleared, of that he was certain.

For William had not been idle during his days of torment over Kent, but rather had finally made use of those weighty volumes in his office. Even back to colonial times, it seemed, when the penalty in Rhode Island for such acts had been death by hanging, the crime of sodomy had rarely been prosecuted. Either Rhode Island had been an especially virtuous place, or prosecutors through the centuries had realized what a difficult and unpleasant thing it was to prove.

No, the problem here was not Reverend Kent's innocence; the problem was the discomfort that others experienced around the subject. He himself was not immune to these feelings, but what William had come to realize was how far afield the demands of decorum were wont to carry the cause of justice. Kent was being called upon to sacrifice himself solely so that other, more important men might avoid embarrassment. And this was unacceptable.

"The reverend is well aware of the risks, Abbot," William responded with equanimity, "and he has chosen them over pleading guilty to crimes he did not commit."

"You smug little bastard!" Phillips raged. "Privileged upstart! You're so cocksure, aren't you? You have no idea the kinds of men that are in this world, the things that are—"

"Abbot!" Gardner cut Phillips off before he could say any more. William could read the anxiety in the older man's face; they were about to plunge into the abyss, leaving all dignity behind, and that was something Gardner would not allow. "After all," the old lawyer continued in sudden resignation, "we can't force Kent to plead guilty." He stared down at William, his gaze narrowing. "And you're prepared to try this case? These are unspeakable acts that are being alleged."

"Alleged, yes, sir," William replied. "I . . . I won't pretend that it will be easy, but if there is any shame in this whole business, it seems to me that it's the sailors, and the Navy perhaps, that must bear the burden of that, sir."

"What a load of tripe!" Phillips shouted, and stormed out of the office, slamming the door behind him.

Gardner watched his partner go. The old man looked defeated, as if he'd just heard that his family had been lost at sea.

"Mr. Gardner, sir? Are you all right?"

Gardner looked at William curiously. "Oh, I wouldn't worry about me, son. I'm an old man, at the end of my career, and my life, give or take a few years. But I hope you realize what the consequences will be for you, if things fail to turn out as you envision. We would be forced to let you go, of course, and I doubt if any other established firm would touch you. Then there are the social implications for your family. It's quite the gamble. You're not a trial lawyer, William. Your father was, and I believe you have the makings of one, but this is not the sort of thing I would have chosen as my first outing. Juries are tricky animals. And justice does not always triumph."

William swallowed. He was not a fool. He had accepted that, win or lose, he would likely be separated from Gardner & Phillips for insubordination.

But the "social implications"—what would those be? he wondered. Should justice fail to triumph, or triumph only partially, how would William's standing in the Newport community, or that of his family, be affected? Defeat, and his association with so shameful an episode, would no doubt follow him as surely as it would follow the reverend. William looked at Gardner, hoping that his former mentor's speech would end with an encouraging flourish. But William found only hardness in the old man's eyes, a clear message that William was fully on his own in this matter, and that should he fail, he would indeed be left to swing in the wind.

# EIGHT

The backyard of the Bartlett home was large and sprawling, with a broad well-manicured lawn and trees that gave shade, flowers, or fruit as spring and summer waxed and waned. There were red maples and oaks, ornamental cherry trees and dogwoods, gnarled apple trees of various sorts, and a large cling peach tree, a species not meant to thrive in the New England climate. On a summer day in 1886, against the expert advice of a host of afternoon party guests, William's grandmother Sophie planted the pit of an especially luscious peach she'd just eaten and, to her great satisfaction, survived to see the thing bear fruit enough for several seasons' worth of pies and preserves.

The home itself, subdued in overall design but magnificent within, had been built in the early eighties by Sophie's husband, John Bartlett, owner of a successful chain of hardware stores. After the railroads went bust in the Panic of '93, John Bartlett had been forced to abandon all but his original store on Thames Street, which he'd inherited from his father. By that time, however, enough wealth had been amassed to assure the family a comfortable lifestyle throughout the rest of the century and beyond. When their next-door neighbor, a banker ruined in the Panic, burned his house to the ground and went to prison the following year, John managed to buy that parcel at a discount, cleared the wreckage, and added the land to his domain.

John and Sophie had four children: William's father, Henry, who from the first had been a stern, joyless little fellow; two daughters, Adelaide and Emma; and a fourth child, John Jr., who died of scarlet fever at the tender age of three. The two girls married and moved away, one to Falmouth, the other to New Bedford, but after law school, Henry returned to Newport, married his sweetheart, Edith Coggeshall, a descendant of one of Newport's eight founding families, and moved in with his parents to start life and raise a family, turning what had until then been merely a stately residence into the ancestral family home.

Henry and Edith's first child, William, was born on April 23, 1886, the year of the infamous peach pit, followed two years and some months later by a daughter, Lucille, a quiet, intelligent girl, who later married a prominent Wellfleet physician. Old John Bartlett, plagued by gout in later years, died in his sleep in 1904 at age seventy-three. He had been an outgoing man, well liked and a pillar of the Newport community, and the list of names in his funeral guest book read like a genealogical treatise of the city. Sophie followed her beloved husband one year later, but it was the sudden death in 1906 of their eldest child, Henry, forty-seven years old and at the height of a brilliant legal career, that shocked the city, making his boy William, then in his third year at Yale College, the nominal head of the family.

Edith continued to manage the house and the hardware business as she finished raising her children. She watched William graduate from Yale, then Harvard Law, and she was overjoyed when he chose the lovely Sarah Clarke, a distant relative on her mother's side, as his bride. But when Lucille married the doctor and moved to Wellfleet, Edith followed, deciding that after three hundred years, the Coggeshalls (or her branch of them at least) had had enough of Newport. She sold the family business and retired to a modest cottage in the dunes of Cape Cod, just far enough away from her daughter, leaving the grand Victorian on Harrison Avenue, its duties and its legacies, to her upstanding firstborn and his extremely capable wife.

—  •  •  •  —

As William turned into the driveway on that summer afternoon in June 1919, his own children, nine-year-old twins Annette and Bernice and five-year-old William Jr., were happily at play in the yard, unburdened by the history of which they were the heirs apparent. The girls, with blue eyes and straw-colored hair like their mother's, had tied one end of a long jump rope to a hook on the side of the former carriage house, now the family garage. Annette, the more proficient jumper, practiced her double-under while Bernice twirled the loose end for her sister, the two chanting their favorite new rhyme.

William drove past his daughters and into the garage. He turned off the motor but remained at the wheel, trying to devise an acceptable way to explain to his wife how and why he'd put their future in jeopardy. He tried to retrace the steps that had led him into this peculiar situation, but it was as if he were searching some other person's memories, some stranger who had taken control and made each fateful decision. The confidence he'd felt at Rathom's office had deserted him.

He withdrew from the car at last, stepping into the rose-colored sunshine of summer's early evening and into this garden, a place where innocence still ran pure and sweet, and the high, clear voices of his girls chanted their rhyme as they jumped.

"I once had a bird and her name was Enza! I opened the window, and in-flew-Enza!"

William looked at them, stunned as he put the word together. "What on earth are you singing?" he asked abruptly.

"Hello, Father," Annette called, out of breath.

"It's a rhyme, Father," Bernice added, answering his question. "Annette's friend Dorothy taught it to us."

"Well, it's horrid," he barked. "Sing something else."

"But why, Father? We like it," Annette insisted, still jumping.

"Yes, Father," Bernice chimed in. "It's funny!"

"It's *not* funny, it's horrible," he snapped, raising his voice louder than he'd intended. "I told you to sing something else! Now stop it!" William did not often shout at his children, so when he did, the effect was profound. The two girls stopped singing and jumping altogether and seemed on the verge of tears. William shook his head, realizing what he'd done.

"No," he said regretfully. "I shouldn't have shouted at you. Father's just upset about other things. Please," he implored. "Go on playing."

But the two girls merely looked at him, thoroughly confused by their father's odd behavior.

He put his hand to his head, sighing. "Where's your mother?"

They both shrugged.

William took a deep breath and set off across thirty yards of lawn toward the back of the house. Nearer the residence, half a dozen ten-foot clotheslines stood guard, arrayed in dry white sheets whipping brilliantly toward the blue-orange sky. Fanny, the housekeeper, a woman of some girth in her middle fifties, struggled to harvest the clean sheets, while the wind, mistaking them for sails, aimed to carry them off. But it was not only the wind that worked against Fanny's efforts. Another force, something unseen, attacked the sheets from below, and the woman shouted at her feet. Though the breeze muffled Fanny's words, her aggravation was evident.

As he drew closer, William caught sight of the pint-sized phantom amidst the billowing white, his five-year-old son who staggered like a blind man, laughing hysterically as the sheets blew in his face.

"Master William!" Fanny shouted in her thick Dublin brogue. "You'll be goin' without supper tonight if you don't start behavin' like a gentleman!"

"Willie!" Sarah shouted from the back porch. "Stop that this instant, young man! Let Fanny do her work!" But the boy romped on, either indifferent or oblivious.

William's instinct was to call out, echoing his wife's reprimand of their son. But though he had lived his entire life in this house, though he himself had spent countless hours as a child at play in this very yard, he felt oddly like an intruder today, and an insubstantial one at that, a ghost dropping in on his own funeral. "Will!" he finally shouted, expecting no response.

The little boy instantly poked his head up, cried "Father!" and ran into William's arms. Any need to reprimand his son quickly vanished as William scooped the boy up.

"I was flying, Father!" the boy announced, exultant. "Did you see?"

"What I saw," William announced as he feigned a look of disapproval, "was a naughty little boy making extra work for our Fanny." He turned to the housekeeper. "I'm sorry, Fanny, should I punish the little rascal?"

"It's all right, Mr. Bartlett, sir," said the woman, out of breath. "Boys are devils, that's God's truth, but what would we do if they weren't?"

"William." Sarah appeared at his side. "I hadn't heard from you. I didn't know what time to plan dinner."

"I, uh . . . I was out of the office for much of the day," he replied. "Something unusual has come up."

Sarah looked at him, curious.

William deposited his son on the ground. "Go play with your sisters." He turned the boy around and gave him a pat on the behind. "And behave yourself!" he added as little Will scampered off.

"What's wrong, dear?" Sarah inquired, concerned. "You look terrible. Are you ill?"

He avoided her gaze. "No, it's . . . Can we go inside?"

"Of course." She looped her arm through his and led him toward the house. "Fanny," she said over her shoulder, "would you mind starting dinner?"

"Certainly, Mrs. Bartlett."

"Now," she said to her husband, insistent, "what's happened?"

Halfway to the house, William judged them to be safely out of earshot.

"It's not pretty, I warn you," he said.

"All right," Sarah acknowledged evenly.

"I thought of telling you the other day in the car, but . . ." William muttered. "It's Reverend Kent."

Sarah gasped. "What? Has something happened to him?"

William sighed as they mounted the porch steps. "Not in the way you mean, Sarah, but yes, something has happened to him."

They passed through a set of open double doors into the conservatory. Brutally hot at midday, it was the coolest room in the house in late afternoon, with two great whirring ceiling fans and plants and flowers of all varieties. Large windows on three sides, thrown open to the evening, made for a lovely breeze. William sat with his wife on a white wicker settee.

"William?" she pressed.

He took a moment, then, looking away, plunged ahead. "Several sailors, men he worked with, I suppose, have accused the reverend of making lewd advances upon them."

"Advances?" Sarah asked, perplexed. "What sort of advances?"

William shook his head. "Sarah, please don't force me to go into detail. Suffice it to say that the claims are scandalous. And completely outrageous."

"I . . . all right," she said simply. "But there's more to this. What is it?"

"Kent has asked me to act as his defense attorney. And I've agreed," he blurted out.

Sarah said nothing.

William looked at her, interpreting her silence as disbelief, or worse, apprehension. He could feel his heart beat faster, his breath grow short. He stood and began to pace.

"I don't know *why* he chose me, Sarah," he hurried on defensively. "Perhaps I'm the only lawyer he knows. Gardner and Phillips both thought it best we keep it all out of court. Come up with some sort of wretched plea bargain. And none other than Bishop James DeWolf Perry seems to agree. He considered it important enough to make the trip from Providence last week to inform us himself."

"He came to the office?" Sarah asked, surprised.

William nodded.

"Goodness," Sarah said. "I didn't think he ever left his airy perch." She took a breath. "And what does the reverend want?"

"He wants to fight it, Sarah! Of course!" He shook his head hopelessly. "And I encouraged him. What on earth was I thinking? I could have gotten him to go along. He was *ready* to go along. But then I looked at his face. All he's worked for, Sarah, destroyed in an instant. It's so unfair! I felt he deserved a choice, at least. I tried to get him to consider another attorney, one with real trial experience, but he wouldn't hear of it, the old fool!"

William collapsed back onto the settee, defeated. "Well, there you have it." He sighed, prepared to hear a catalogue of reasons for reversing course. "I've made a horrible mistake, haven't I? Why didn't I just keep my mouth shut?"

Sarah took his hands in hers and smiled. "I'm very proud of you."

William looked at her. She had entirely missed the point. "Don't say that, Sarah. Please. This isn't about me. A man's future, a very fine man, is in my hands."

Sarah brought his hands to her lips and kissed them gently. "Such capable hands."

It was fruitless, he thought. How could he have ever dreamed of a more practical response from Sarah Clarke? She was Florence Nightingale, after all, working on behalf of all hopeless causes. For the first time in his life he wondered if perhaps he should have married a more conventional woman. Fear, chastisement, a demand that he change course immediately before any more damage was done, any of those would have at least put him back on solid ground, but this? He rose and walked away.

"I had hoped you would talk me out of it," he said.

"You have misgivings," Sarah said reasonably. "That's only natural. But you'll do splendidly. I know you will."

"Nice of you to say, dear," he uttered more harshly than he'd intended, "but I'm not so sure."

"Forgive me," she said, looking down, "for having so much faith in my husband."

He should have been grateful that she would support him even in this, and he was. He sat beside her again and put his hand to her cheek.

"What man ever had such a wife?" he said. "Of course, there's a part of me that believes you're right or I never would have considered it." He sighed. "But I fear I may be out of my depth."

"In what way?" she asked gently. "Tell me."

"My lack of trial experience, for one." He fell silent a moment. "My father could have done this."

"Perhaps. But he wouldn't have," she added sharply.

"Yes," he agreed. "Too much good sense. Next, the accusations themselves—how do I find the words, even to deny them, without thoroughly offending the jury? These are literally 'unspeakable' acts, Sarah."

"The prosecution will face those same challenges," she countered.

"That's true," he said with a smile. "You should have been a lawyer." He turned away. "And these men," he continued bitterly, "his so-called accusers, where do I begin? I simply cannot conceive of the malice it takes to concoct a lie of this magnitude. They're just common sailors, of course, from God knows where, but what motivation could they possibly have? Why would they target Kent? Can you tell me?"

Sarah smiled demurely. "Sailors are hardly my area of expertise, darling."

"Of course!" He went red with embarrassment. "Good Lord! Here I am just going on about this. I can't believe I'm even . . . ! But it's the crux of my case, and I don't know who else to . . ."

Sarah put her arm around him. "Well, dear, what I *do* know, what every woman knows, is that boys, regardless of their backgrounds, are capable of just about anything, given half the chance." She paused a moment. "May I ask an indelicate question?"

He looked at her warily. "Of course."

She took a breath. "You're quite certain they're lying?"

"What?" he asked, doubting his hearing. "What on earth are you saying?"

"Well," she replied delicately, "at the risk of . . . this *is* the twentieth century, dear. You must consider the possibility—"

"You're joking," William interrupted. He laughed in spite of himself. "You *must* be joking."

"William, I didn't mean to offend you, or the reverend," she maintained, then continued, searching for the words. "But, obviously, he's . . . well, a very kind, selfless soul. For these men, with their upbringing, that might seem . . . odd, foreign. Perhaps some action of his was . . . well, misinterpreted."

She was backpedaling now, but he knew what she meant, and it was unforgivable. "Misinterpreted? Would you care to read what they've claimed?" He reached in his breast pocket and pulled out the affidavits as if to offer them for her perusal.

"No, William," she insisted, "I most certainly would not."

"In that case, take my word for it, 'upbringing' is hardly a word one would associate with any of those degenerates!"

"Why must you always be so harsh, William?" Sarah asked with growing annoyance. "They're very young, you know, and they've just come through a war. You might take that into consideration."

"You're defending them! I can't believe my ears," he snapped. "Do they seem downtrodden to you in some way? And as for the war, these men are a disgrace to their uniforms and to the country they serve!"

"I see," Sarah replied, her tone measured. "And have you so much as met even one of them?"

William shouted back, "No! But I *have* met Samuel Kent! You yourself said he was one of the finest men you'd ever known. And I didn't have the luxury of choice, Sarah. I was required to read these affidavits! There's no room for 'misinterpretation'!"

"William, please." Her gaze had drifted to the open doorway. "Calm yourself," she urged.

"No, Sarah!" He was angry, he knew, overly so and it was directed at the wrong person, but he could not stop himself. "You're a compassionate woman and that's to be commended, but you *are* a woman and sometimes too forgiving. If there is such a thing as evil, and I believe that there is, then this is an evil act these boys have committed. And believe me, if it is in my power, I'll see they live to regret it!" He was breathing as if he'd run a race. "What on earth are you looking at?"

His fury spent, William turned to follow her gaze and found his three children standing together less than ten feet beyond the open

French doors. They had stopped their play and stood transfixed, watching the argument with concern.

A moment later, Fanny arrived to gather the little ones.

"Come, children," she said with a forced lilt in her voice. "Come into the kitchen. I have some freshly baked cookies for you, all soft and warm." The three were happy for the distraction and allowed Fanny to huddle them off. "That's right, children. They're likely to spoil your supper," Fanny sighed as she threw a last withering glance at William, "but I don't think your father will mind."

William watched the group depart, then turned to his wife, who had not moved from her place on the settee. "Sarah, I . . ."

Sarah put up a hand to stop him. She shook her head, then stood and left the room abruptly, leaving William just as alone as he had felt himself to be.

# NINE

Preston Barker was born on the Great Plains, or as he described the place, an immense, beautiful, and frightening expanse of nothing between two nowheres. The sky was enormous and so blue in summer it hurt your eyes, and the land beneath it, stretching flat endlessly as only the sea could do in the East, was either loopy with corn, swaying like a vast yellow and green ocean, or white and horrifying, dead like every one of us would someday be.

Once upon a time, rivers of buffalo had thundered across these lands like a dozen surging Mississippis. Indians had whooped and swooped in on horseback, felling the roaring beasts and scalping settlers, leaving their Christian bodies to putrefy amidst rows of rotting grain.

He'd seen all this depicted in books in the one-room schoolhouse where he and his siblings and their father before them had learned to read and reckon numbers, but truth be told, Preston found it hard to believe that anything so exciting had ever happened in Nebraska.

He was the fifth of eight children. His two older brothers had died when he was only a boy, one of whooping cough and the other falling off a thresher, so he was left the eldest son, with two older and two younger sisters, and a younger brother. His father at first had high hopes for Preston, as he was smart and had a natural way with animals, but he was a dreamer who would likely follow his older brothers to an early grave, or so his father said. Thus the family's hopes were transferred to the youngest boy, who was built thick and seemed more suited to farmwork.

His father had wanted to be a preacher but had instead been enlisted to take over the family homestead after his own brother and father had passed on within months of each other when he was just nineteen. Preston had no idea what he wanted to do with his own life, maybe move to town and work as a postman, or maybe be a cowboy, but when the war came and it looked as though he might be drafted, he took the advice of the proprietor of the local dry goods store and joined the Navy. He was young, just seventeen, and had to procure his parents' written permission. He had never seen the ocean and thought he would like to once in his life.

At the hour of Preston's departure, the family assembled in the parlor, quiet and somber, and at their mother's nod, each of the girls stepped forward to give Preston a peck on the cheek. It was in fact the first time such a thing had occurred and it was awkward. His younger but already larger brother sidled up a moment later and shook his hand manfully, blurting out, "Good luck!" Then he backed away, looking down as if to hide the emotion that Preston could feel welling up in them both. Finally, Preston faced his mother, who looked drawn and older than he remembered her looking yesterday, and she leaned in, giving him half a hug as he kissed her on the cheek.

"Be careful, son," she said.

He nodded and made his way to the screen door, which everyone tried to hold for him. His father was waiting in their horse-drawn wagon, reins already in hand.

It was windy but unseasonably warm for October as the two rode in silence to the train depot, a trip of a little less than an hour. Preston hopped down, and his father, a sturdy man of fifty with a weathered face that had once been handsome, came around and insisted on carrying his son's bag. The two walked the twenty yards to the platform, then stood facing one another.

The father laid a heavy hand on his son's shoulder and said, "Don't disgrace yourself, boy." Then the man blinked hard and Preston watched as a tear escaped his right eye. The young man had never seen such a thing, not even when his brother, the joy of his father's life, had died in the thresher accident. Perhaps he had cried in private, but never before in public view. *He must be that convinced,* Preston thought to himself, *that I'm going to die in this war.*

The older man's mouth pulled into a tight grimace. He yanked a handkerchief from his back pocket and wiped his eyes gruffly, then turned and left and with long strides made his way back up onto the wagon. With a double click and a snap of the reins, he whirled the beast around and after a final wave, he headed back from whence he'd come. Preston watched his father shrink into the prairie, until the approaching train whistle drew his attention back where it belonged, on his immediate future.

——•——

Their duties over the last six months had been light and mostly nocturnal, Charlie noted gratefully, and they had been slow to start. He and a couple of the other fellows who were already on friendly terms with the fairies had introduced the operators into the queer circle a few at a time so as not to arouse undue suspicion. Fairies were not, in general, a stupid bunch. They should have wondered why their luck had suddenly turned, why so many good-looking boys had found their way into the secret society all at once; but they didn't, preferring instead to believe, as all men are prone to believe, that the world had simply come around to their way of thinking, and that they were in fact as irresistible as they had long imagined.

Ironically, this self-deception seemed to be greatest when they were faced with fellows like Bart Rudy, a twisted pig of a man in Charlie's estimation, who, judging by his statements in private, seemed to hate queers more than he'd ever hated Germans. The slightest encouragement on Rudy's part and three or four boys would fall at his feet, stepping over each other for the chance to be his date for the evening. This man, who could barely hide his scorn for the fairies even while acting his part, was by his mere presence proving them right, that it was in their power to be accepted by even the manliest of men, and for that he was given the keys to their kingdom.

But amongst the operators, Rudy and his slack-jawed sidekick, Henry Dostalick, who aped Rudy in all things, proved to be the exception rather than the rule in their extreme hatred of queers. Most of the men had shifted more or less in Charlie's direction, their outright hostility waning the more time they spent with the fairies.

The simple fact was that the queer parties were fun. There was always good hooch, which was getting harder and harder to come by with the onset of full prohibition, and the latest records were always playing on the Victrola. The queers themselves went from the outrageous, dressed up in glamorous evening wear in imitation of their favorite female screen stars, to young guys who didn't seem much different from the average pimply sailor. Apart from the operators, there were other straight fellows there who were genuinely captivated by the "girls'" charms, one of whom was a short, squat chief petty officer of fifty or more with a face that even a mother would have a hard time loving. Even he got attention from the drag queens, if only because he was a man paying attention to them.

To Charlie, it was a job like any other and an easy one at that, light paperwork mostly, and the occasional necessity of being on the right end of a blow job. He'd had to look out for Claude a good deal in the beginning, appeasing his friend's remarkably persistent conscience, which had, thankfully, surrendered the field with time.

Truth was, Claude had never seen so much action, and though there was no doubt that the big Texan preferred ladies, he had learned to enjoy the attention he got from the fairies, and their impressive oral skills. It worried Charlie only a little that Claude had started to speak with affection about a hospital apprentice second class named Trubshaw, who would soon be on a list of defendants. But Charlie knew it to be merely Claude's nature to treat with kindness anyone who had done the same by him, and when the young man had remembered Claude's birthday a few weeks before with a gift of Claude's favorite chewing tobacco, the big fellow had been touched profoundly.

Barker was more of a problem. So flustered was he by the attentions lavished upon him by the fairies that he could be counted on to slip away from the parties at the first opportunity, when Charlie and Claude were otherwise engaged, retreating into the night back to the safety of his bunk. Early on, the operators had naturally divided into "squads" of two or three, based on personality and preference. Charlie was clearly the leader of his squad, so he was able to more or less cover for Barker's dereliction of duty, though he could not protect the boy from the jokes that circulated at his expense, mostly that Barker couldn't keep it up 'cause he was afraid one of the queers would bite it off.

More serious for Barker were the weekly visits to Cliff Walk that he and all the men were required to make. A ribbon of asphalt that ran atop the jagged cliffs overlooking the Atlantic, Cliff Walk was a popular tourist attraction by day. Families, young couples, sailors, and the elderly would stroll along its winding path, several hundred feet above the crashing waves, while on a rise just above the walkway, some of the grandest of the summer "cottages" stood on display. Elaborate mansions with names like Rose Cliff, Clarendon Court, and The Breakers proved to any who were in doubt that life was plainly not fair, but folks came anyway, feeling a little richer just by brushing up against so much extravagance.

By night, however, Cliff Walk took a decidedly different turn. The darkened twists and sharp curves of the walk and the brush-covered ledges that sloped down below afforded all the privacy one might need for an illicit tryst. It was here every night that a dozen or so men could be found seeking an encounter with another fellow, either because there was no party, they had not been invited, or, more likely, they could not afford so public a stage for their desires. It amazed even Charlie at times the mix of men he would see here from week to week, sailors, of course, but also men of business side by side with servants from the houses above. One night, he even spotted the colored janitor from the YMCA, who seemed unashamed when he noticed Charlie, flashing him a smile and a casual wave.

It was here that the operators felt most accurately the seriousness of what they were about. Queer parties were like parties everywhere, more or less, with music and alcohol and wild times that could justify many an unlikely "lapse" of memory. But here, out on the cliffs in the dead of night in all kinds of weather, with just asphalt or the hard ground to lie or kneel upon, it was clear that any man here had come for one thing only.

Every Monday morning at the meeting in the Red Cross basement, the squad leaders would pick their duty assignments from a hat so that the boys might find themselves assigned to Cliff Walk on any one of that week's seven nights. Chief Arnold wisely avoided the parties for fear of giving away the operation, leaving the men more or less on their own in those settings. But Arnold did visit Cliff Walk unannounced to observe the men and the work they were doing, so it was far more difficult for Charlie to shield Barker from the regular performance of his duty under those conditions. Instead, Charlie was forced to turn the kid loose and hope for the best, sending Barker off alone into the darkness with a look on his face like that of a man on the way to his own execution.

Charlie had come to a conclusion. He had resisted it at first, had watched and waited, biding his time, certain that eventually his instincts would uncover the actor behind the mask. But after six months, having failed to witness a single misstep or false moment, Charlie had concluded that young Barker was indeed the first genuinely good person he'd ever had the occasion to meet.

To start with, Barker never failed to put others first, which in the military could cause a man to starve. Next, he never had an unkind word for anyone. Even in the midst of a crowd of raucous sailors, Barker would clam up as soon the group started in on one individual or another. If the onslaught continued and he could not slip away, Barker, stammer notwithstanding, would defend the man, be he friend or foe, officer or enlisted man, pointing out some overlooked quality that the fellow possessed. Even if it meant risking the fury of a guy twice his size, Barker would never shy away from speaking up when he was moved to do so. And there was nothing opinionated or aggressive in his statements, no desire to prove anyone else wrong; he simply voiced his thoughts pertaining to the situation, as if he didn't know how to do otherwise.

But Charlie knew better. At the root of it all, he was sure, lay the simple fact that Barker only spoke his mind wherever and whenever he found something that needed saying. He was trusting and guileless and assumed the same of those around him. The idea that one person would lie to another, or worse, lie to himself in order to gain some advantage, was completely foreign to the boy.

But as much as Charlie and others stood in awe of Barker's forthrightness, he also knew that the fellow would face a miserable road ahead armed with nothing but his honesty. The notion of this kid going through life a helpless mark for hucksters like himself was not to be borne, so Charlie was determined to wise him up *and* find him a woman before they parted company, which more than likely would be soon. The war had been over for more than six months now, demobilization was seriously overdue and could be expected at any moment, and there was no way Arnold could keep this cockamamie scheme of his afloat a whole lot longer. Indictments were being drawn up, seventeen or eighteen in all, which seemed like a small number to Charlie considering how much sucking and fucking had gone on, and once the arrests were made and their cover was blown, Newport would shut down tighter than a drum and the party would be over.

Truth be told, these last six months had in many ways been the sweetest in Charlie's short life. For the first time, he'd been able to reach into his pocket on a regular basis and find a few extra bucks, with whole days free to enjoy his newfound wealth. For the first time, he'd been spared the choice of hunting down the next hustle or going hungry and sleeping on the street.

And for the first time, he'd found a woman who could keep up with him, in bed, yes, but out of bed as well. Dottie was a shapely woman, five foot five, with hair the color and texture of pale silk, breasts creamy white and full but not so big that they outclassed the rest of her. And when she spoke, her Irish brogue played at the faint edges of his memory, of time spent as a babe in someone's arms.

But Dottie was no fool and she didn't accept as gospel whatever crap Charlie dished out like every other woman had done in the past. Three, four, sometimes five times a night they would make it, trading off the dominant role as each surrendered to the other in some new way. It had gotten so that he could not envision parting from this woman without a touch of anguish, so he chose not to think about the end of things, staying in the moment as much as possible.

There had been just three aspects of the operation that from the start had rubbed Charlie the wrong way. First was Arnold, who made him want to spit every time he had to look at the guy. Charlie prided himself on his understanding of human nature, but Arnold was a mystery to him, for beyond being an ugly son of a bitch, which seemed too easy an answer, Charlie could not figure out how one person could be filled with so much anger and hatred, and so much crazy suspicion of everyone around him. In the end, he decided the guy wasn't worth the effort. This would be no more than a brief episode in his life, Charlie reminded himself, and he would soon be rid of the monster, so he simply chalked it up to the unique insanity of the career military man and avoided Arnold as much as he could.

The second problem, and one that was harder to justify, was tricking the queers. It had never been difficult for Charlie to make any woman or fairy burn with desire for him, and it was no secret that Charlie had often used that power for his own ends. But other than tears and heartbreak, the transaction had never caused any real harm. This was different. Charlie had no idea what lay in store for the fellows who were to be turned in, but he knew it couldn't be good. He had done his best to protect certain of the queers who'd been friendly or helpful to him in the past, gave him money or spotted him a meal on occasion. But as for the rest, some of whom could be nastier than the meanest bitch of a woman, Charlie tried to tell himself that they had it coming.

The fact was, and society would agree, that by doing what they did with other men, these boys had already forfeited any natural-born rights they'd ever had as males. They were clearly on the wrong side of every law ever written, and though Charlie had nothing against even the worst of them personally—"each to his own" as they say—they could not be called men. Therefore the rules of fairness that should apply within that original brotherhood did not pertain to this case.

Besides, looking back, how many times had Charlie been made to suffer unfairly for reasons not of his own making, because he was hungry and stole some bread as a kid, or just because some cop hadn't liked his looks and beat him with a nightstick for being on the wrong street corner at the wrong time of day? No, he would never be able to make the world a fair place, so he may as well take his turn on the plus side for a change and put the fairies and their future out of his mind.

The third and last thing that bothered him, maybe worst of all, was Dottie's persistent curiosity about his work. Keeping secrets was second nature to Charlie, in part because he rarely hung around people long enough for it to matter. But after all the intimacy they had shared, Dottie was growing tired of the mystery, and he was quickly running out of convincing dodges. One recent morning, with Charlie still lazing abed as content as any man could be, the horny beast within him fully sated, his woman before him sliding into a new pair of silk stockings he had bought her, she started in again.

"If you've found a way to outwit the ruling class," she theorized, "good on you. I'd just like to know your methods is all."

Charlie sat up and turned away, his feet hitting the floor. The room, his room, theirs now, was small, and badly in need of paint. There was a gas hot plate for making coffee, and a twisted ceiling fan that whined, doing its measly best to stir the fetid air. The walls were thin and it was noisy most hours of the day and night as sailors and other transients did their business. But Charlie was wise enough, most of the time, not to look beyond the double bed, wise enough not to ask too many questions of her, content to believe that he was the only one, more or less, that she wasn't turning a few tricks here and there for extra coin, which he knew she was. Why couldn't she show the same wisdom? Why couldn't she simply accept that he was doing what needed to be done in the best way he knew how?

He reached for a pack of cigarettes from the bedside table, pulled one out, and lit up.

"Sleepin' all day," she continued, laying the brogue on thick and syrupy. "Dough in your pocket, living in the lap of luxury—"

Charlie laughed bitterly. "Some luxury. And it's just 'cause there's still no room on the base."

"Yeah, but you don't *do* nothing."

Charlie inhaled deeply and blew out a long plume of smoke. "Says you," he added as punctuation. He could see out of the corner of his eye that she had stopped dressing and was now looking at him, her arms crossed.

"All right, then," she demanded ever so reasonably. "Tell me. What do you do?"

He kept his voice low and under control. "I write reports."

She sighed, exasperated. "About *what*?"

He put out the cigarette and glared at her. "Ever heard of top secret?"

She laughed, then covered her mouth. "I'm sorry. Maybe they didn't tell you, Charlie, but the war's *over*."

"So what? You think we ain't got no more enemies? What do you know, you dumb mick?" He turned away dismissively. "You ain't even a citizen!"

"Oh, is that so?" she replied angrily. "Well, if there's one thing I do know, boy-o," she smirked, "it's sailors! I know when somethin' ain't right, and *this* don't smell right."

She was not going to let up, Charlie knew. Eventually, one way or another, she would force him to spill the beans. If he still didn't comply, she'd go cold on him, then simply stop showing up in his bed every night. He didn't think she was ready to do that yet; the attraction between them was still too strong, but it was always a negotiation with them, so maybe . . .

She came up behind him, pressed her breasts into his back, and wrapped her arms around his middle. "Come on, Charlie. You know I don't care what it is you're doing. Is it some sort of graft that you're taking? Is somebody paying you to keep silent about something? Are you fucking an officer's wife? Ha-ha, that would be a laugh, wouldn't it?"

He chuckled grimly. "Yeah, you don't care. You just want to know."

What had they done it, three, four times last night? And he was ready to go all over again. He'd have to give her *something* in exchange, some tidbit of information, but what? The blood in his body was rushing to an organ other than his brain, and damn if the truth wasn't all he could come up with. But he'd signed an oath, under dire threat not to reveal the nature of the operation to anyone. He owed that much at least to the guys he was working with. And there was something else that prevented him, something that surprised and displeased him, a fear that she *would* disapprove, that she would feel a special kinship with the fairies and tear into him for what he was doing. He would never have cared about that in the past—let her go fuck herself should be his attitude—but today, this morning at least, on many levels, coming clean to her was not worth the risk.

"Sorry, Dot, I can't tell you," he said simply. "And that's my last word on the subject," he added with finality.

Hard as he was, he did not turn to her as he felt the words sink in. He did not turn as her touch and body left him, nor when she stomped back to the spot where her clothes lay.

"Where you going?" he asked, still facing away.

"Well, now, if I was your wife, and not a whore," Dottie quipped, "I might have to answer that."

She finished dressing, strode out in her high heels, and slammed the door behind her.

# TEN

The "Church of the People" was how it had come to be known, spiritual home to the servants and mill workers of Newport's fifth ward. And though it had grown over the decades, from a simple wooden meetinghouse at its founding in 1852 to an impressive Gothic Revival stone structure with a four-story tower and two massive bells, the Emmanuel Free Church still held to its proud tradition of "equality before God." Here, during the summer months at least, the prayers of Newport's richest and poorest would mingle in a single silent chorus; the poor would find comfort after another week of grinding labor, the wealthy an hour's respite from their dazzling social whirl. Servant and master, they sat side by side, like actors backstage in some great performance. This comity, seasonal though it may have been, stood as a living testament to the original spirit of the Newport colony, a spirit of tolerance and brotherhood that spoke to the best of what men and women hoped to be, regardless of the roles fate had temporarily assigned the players.

And all agreed that none was better to bear the standard of this noble tradition than the Reverend Samuel Kent, a man who had experienced much of the world before finding his way to the cloth, and who, in a city where wealth had become more and more the measure of worth, seemed to see no difference between the highborn and the low. Few knew his history in any detail. Few thought to ask, as if the cassock and collar had placed him in a realm beyond the personal. But as his mother, long deceased, used to say, "Knock on any door, and you'll hear a story." In the years since, Kent had taken that adage a step further; look into any face, he would have assured her, and you'll see the same.

Samuel Neal Kent was born and raised in the factory town of Lowell, Massachusetts, birthplace of America's industrial revolution. The younger of two sons of a hardworking mother and runaway father, Sam quickly proved himself to be the answer to every jilted mother's prayers. He was unusually bright, with a sunny disposition and a sympathetic ear, and his powers of persuasion were proven at age ten when he convinced their landlord to halve the family's back rent, then two months in arrears. The famously heartless old man simply laughed and, with a ruffle of the boy's hair, assured Mrs. Kent that her youngster's future was bright.

It was not until Sam reached the frontiers of manhood that trouble began to brew. Like his brother before him, indeed like most of the local young men of his station, Kent's first job was in one of Lowell's many mills, where for nearly a year Sam affixed heels to several hundred pairs of shoes each day. His brother, Levi, had had no problem with the tedium; he was grateful for the job. But Sam could not be contained in such a dismal routine and it was not long before the other men on the line complained about him. When he wasn't simply daydreaming, they reported, he could be counted on to distract the others with jokes or stories that put them all at risk of injury. Finally, while on break one day he was caught kissing a female worker, who in order to save her own job claimed that his attentions had been unwanted, and Samuel found himself suddenly unemployed. His foreman insisted that though he had nothing against Sam personally, the young man was clearly not suited for factory work. He left Kent with a last piece of advice: "Perhaps you should be an actor." And though the foreman's face had looked sincere enough, Sam was quite sure he'd been insulted.

Word spread quickly in Lowell. The fact that Kent had been fired did little to improve his prospects for future employment. At night, as Sam lay in bed wondering what would become of himself, the foreman's parting words returned to him in a new light, spinning inside his head into the gaudiest of fantasies. Perhaps he *should* be an actor, he told himself. His father had taken him to see the James O'Neill play *The Count of Monte Cristo* when he was a child and the memory of it still thrilled him, as though all the magic and mystery of the universe had been drawn together within those walls for a brief span of time, only to vanish in the thunderous applause at the final curtain. He had never thought of himself as having a life in the theatre, never realized it was something someone could choose to do, but now he could think of nothing else. When finally he announced his intention to his mother, that he would leave for New York to pursue his dream, there were tears and hand-wringing, shaking of heads, and shouts of reproach from his brother. The thought that he was abandoning his mother and, like his father, betraying her hopes for him tore at his heart, but it seemed as though another force now guided his life and his course was set.

On the day of his departure, while his brother refused to speak to him, his mother gave her favorite son forty-three dollars, money she'd saved from seamstress work, kissed him, and wished Sam either great luck or a quick return to his senses.

He saw many things those first days. The Bowery remained the center of New York nightlife and theatre at that time, filled with all manner of entertainment, high and low. He saw streetwalkers of both sexes, women in scanty outfits and men—or rather creatures that could only be described as half-man, half-woman—shamelessly plying their trade. Drunks and aristocrats mingled in nightclubs and restaurants, street vendors sold aromatic chestnuts hot off the roaster and sausages in thick bread, and, in the midst of it, to the sound of drums and brass, the Salvation Army girls fought a losing battle against the devil. A lesser man might have lost himself to any number of wanton pursuits of a night. But wantonness was of no interest to Sam, and so he remained safely an outsider, his sole focus the dream he carried in his heart.

Even in the big city, Sam's abundant charm continued to serve him well, for it was not long before he'd landed a job in the office of a minor theatrical producer—as a runner and coffee boy, true, but still, Sam felt sure he was at last knocking on the door of the life he'd envisioned.

A year went by, then two. He developed a circle of young friends, all in similar straits, and all involved in one creative endeavor or another. It was with two of these, a fellow actor and a writer, who he shared lodgings, a single room in a residential hotel on Second Avenue near St. Marks. The actor was studious, like Sam, and the writer drank too much, loudly pining over a mysterious ballerina with whom he was hopelessly in love. Sam had a couple of minor flirtations himself during that time, one with an actress and another with a salesgirl from Woolworth's, but nothing came of either of them.

Sam wrote to his mother twice weekly, claiming that he was lonely and that he missed his home and family, though he knew it was a lie. The young man had never felt so alive, and although he certainly experienced moments of despair, when all his efforts seemed fruitless, there were other times, more numerous, when he was sure he was on the brink of success.

It was on a morning when neither fame nor failure seemed imminent, as Sam busily filed casting sheets, that Mr. Birnbaum, the producer for whom he worked, called the boy into his office. On the previous day, with a slew of actors waiting to audition for Birnbaum's new play, the regular "reader" had called in sick, and Sam, the only other male within shouting distance, had been pressed into service as a desperate last resort, reading all sorts of scenes with all sorts of actors. He'd made a terrible hash of it, or so he thought, stumbling over words, his voice seemingly beyond his own control. He'd hoped to put it behind him, never think of it again, but now, in a sudden panic he thought perhaps that he was about to be fired for his ghastly "performance," and what on earth would he do then?

"What's wrong with you, boy? Sit," commanded Mr. Birnbaum, a large man with extremely hairy hands.

Terrified, Sam pulled up a chair and sat. "If this is about yesterday, Mr. Birnbaum," he stammered, "I swear—"

"Indeeeeeed!" Birnbaum interrupted, extending the word in the way he often did. The man, who must have come from Europe by the way he spoke, looked skeptically at Sam, adding, "Such a bundle of nerves, I've never seen."

"I apologize, Mr. Birnbaum," Sam blurted desperately. "I can only say, in my defense—"

"Do you think you could do that again?" Birnbaum queried.

"Excuse me, sir?" Sam squeaked.

"How'd you like to play that small part at the end, the boy who reads the telegram to the leading lady?"

Sam was speechless.

"As a dramatic moment, it's awkward," Birnbaum continued. "But somehow, your nervousness made it work in a way we haven't seen before. It's only one scene, but it's a decent speech. The actress is no Bernhardt, but she'll do. Couple nice laughs in it if you can repeat what you did yesterday. And it's in the third act, so the critics will remember you. Interested?"

In utter shock, Sam nodded, formally auditioned later that afternoon to make certain that he could in fact repeat the previous day's performance, and after twenty-four sleepless hours, received word that he'd won the part.

Now, under any normal circumstances, one might expect that day to have gone on record as the fateful one, the turning point that set Sam on his path toward a successful theatrical career, the answer to his prayers, the fulfillment of his dreams. And though at the time, Sam himself would have sworn by all he held dear that it had indeed been the most important day of his life, another moment, not far in his future, lay in wait, a moment more profound and obscure and against which all others, before and after, would glow with only the palest of lights.

The show opened to adequate reviews. Samuel got his hoped-for laughs, and people did indeed remember him afterward. One critic even mentioned Sam by name as "a presence both boyish and profound who delivered the all-important news with just the right air of knowing naïveté." His mother and brother made the trip down from Lowell for opening night and left the next day, beaming. Three months now into the run, and Samuel Kent had acquired the confidence and persona of a working actor. He had an agent, auditions, and was the envy of his friends.

Then on a night like any other, after a light meal at Luchow's with a new acquaintance, followed by two hours of card playing backstage with various cast members, Samuel made his entrance. Looking back, if he had to point to anything unusual, Sam might have said that he'd felt more relaxed that night than ever before in his young life, that he could not have imagined himself anyplace but there doing that very thing. He got out his first laugh line, and it was a big success, so much so that he had to fight a satisfied grin from appearing on his own face.

And then it began.

Over the next ten years, he would try to describe the experience he had that night to himself and others, but since it had not occurred at the level of human understanding, his attempts were always unsuccessful. It came closest to say that, in that moment, the line that separated Samuel Kent from the infinite utterly gave way. The human Sam, the actor, continued to say his lines, to play his part, but the boundaries of past, present, and future, the desires and frustrations that up to that point had made Sam unique, simply melted away and suddenly he was vast beyond measure, his consciousness filling every corner of existence, like floodwaters surging through a valley once a dam has burst. And as he surrendered to a sort of ecstasy he had never imagined possible, the universe in turn yielded up its deepest secrets, the knowledge of all things, of love eternal, and he wondered how they had ever seemed to be secrets at all.

It was a single truth, he knew with sudden certainty, out of which all the rest grew like limbs on a tree, and the truth was this, that separation of any kind, of one place or person from another, of desire from its fulfillment, of secret held from secret revealed, was simply a matter . . . of Time, which if it flowed at all, did so in both directions at once. Destiny and free will, those mortal enemies, had never been at odds, it now appeared, since all outcomes were both accidental and predetermined. And bathed as it all was in this sea of bliss, Sam could not help but see all choices and hence all human lives, however great or humble, as equally perfect and splendid.

He had never been particularly religious, and in no way had he asked for this epiphany, yet somehow in those moments, it seemed to Sam as familiar a body of knowledge as the play script he had memorized months before. For some reason, a door had been left ajar, and Sam had wandered into the mind of God and life would never be the same again.

Then, as abruptly as it had appeared, his vast consciousness began to ebb and with a sadness so profound he thought his heart would break, Sam found himself hurtling back into his humanity, where the former Sam had not missed a beat in his performance. The laughter resumed, louder than ever, and the applause at the final curtain seemed oddly astonishing to him.

Removing his stage makeup, Sam gazed so hard at himself in the dressing room mirror that another actor, an older man who played the father of the leading lady, asked if he was all right. Sam smiled and assured the gentleman that all was well. But later, as the group set out boisterously for drinks and a midnight supper, Sam slipped away unnoticed, heading home to his apartment, where he lay on his bed in the dark, staring at the ceiling, unable to sleep. What had it been? What had it meant? The ocean of wisdom in which he'd been immersed had by now fully receded, leaving behind the bare remnants of his revelation on time and destiny, a notion he could still grasp but no longer fully comprehend. Most of all, there was the lingering sadness at the sudden loss of such unmatchable, unimagined bliss.

But if it happened once, he told himself, it could happen again. Whatever it took, he would find his way back. Next time, he would be better prepared. Next time, he would comprehend fully, absorb all of it, and never again would he or anyone he touched need to feel fear or want or anything but the pure, clear rapturous light of the divine.

And so, he watched, and he sought. And he waited.

— • — • —

William stood at the wooden doors of the stone Gothic church. He had walked the long three miles from his home, stopping at his office on Thames Street to review the sailors' depositions in solitude, and to search through endless law journals for precedents on which to base his defense of Reverend Kent. The summer heat had been oppressive during most of his journey—he'd removed his tie and jacket, and his shirt was soaked with sweat—but with the rising of the moon, a cool breeze had risen off the ocean as well, sending a delicious chill across his wet back and chest.

The stained glass windows of the church glowed red and yellow with a welcoming light. Beside the peaked arch that framed the entryway, a white wooden sign informed William that evening services should be nearing their end. He tried the heavy door, half hoping it would be locked, but it gave, so he pulled it open and slipped inside. At the far side of the church, on a raised platform in front of the altar, Samuel Kent, in full vestments, made his closing remarks to the handful of women scattered in the pews facing him.

It seemed odd to William suddenly that after a lifetime spent in Newport, he had never found occasion to visit this church. The Bartlett family, when they worshipped at all, had by tradition always gone to Trinity, the much larger institution on historic Queen Anne Square. Since at least one of William's ancestors had helped lay the cornerstone of the great, white Episcopal edifice, the practice seemed entirely justified. Still, Emmanuel Free Church, where he now stood, was clearly a gem. Its great stone columns and exquisite stained glass windows invoked sufficient majesty, yet it was small enough to remain warm and welcoming. In front of the pulpit, in the midst of a carved mahogany sanctuary, a magnificent bronze angel rose to the height of a man. Behind the figure, on its outstretched wings, a Bible rested.

"The mass is ended," Kent pronounced in soothing tones. "Go in peace."

"Thanks be to God," the women murmured in response. Then one by one, as if reluctant, they each collected their things and rose to leave. As Kent stepped down into the aisle, some of them welcomed his action as a cue to pause and exchange pleasantries with the reverend or to thank him for his sermon.

The man seemed so much more at home here than he had at his residence, thought William, as though he were bidding farewell to honored guests come to share an evening meal at his home. It was clear why the women lingered. They were older, most of them, and likely widowed or as good as, and Kent, with the lightest touch, showed authentic concern for their welfare as he gathered them within his circle of intimacy. He had done the same to William on the night they'd first met. It was a great gift Kent had, greater still because it felt genuine.

Standing here, his recent incarceration must have seemed as much a dream to the reverend as it did to William, as if it had never happened at all. But William knew that it had, knew the seriousness of the charges Kent faced and how precariously all aspects of the man's life hung in the balance. Midweek evening service on a hot summer night would never bring the faithful out in throngs. Still, William couldn't help but wonder whether this especially poor showing, with not more than seven solitary women present, wasn't indicative of some more sinister meaning. In a small city like Newport, rumors had a way of spreading quickly.

"William!" Kent called out, striding briskly down the aisle as the last of the widows made for the door. "How long have you been here?"

"Just a few moments," William said apologetically as they shook hands. "I'm afraid I missed your sermon."

"Good thing, too!" Kent laughed. "Not my most inspired." The man flashed a broad smile as if he hadn't a care in the world.

Then, as if a light had been switched off, Kent's face went gray. He shook his head and laughed ruefully. "Do you know, I'd actually forgotten my . . . troubles for a moment." He paused, then continued in a wistful tone. "Do you think the day will ever come when you and I can simply gather as friends?"

"I have no doubt of it, sir," William offered gently.

279858 Costco 13
10000 MickleBerry Rd
Silverdale WA

Member# 111859336410
Invoice # 55599
Date            10/11/16
Time               15:08
Auth #           044950

VI Acct #
XXXXXXXXXXXX2027

Pump  Gallons  Price
09    9.482  $ 2.399

Product
Unleaded        $ 22.75
Amount

Total Sale      $ 22.75

SALE - Card Swiped
APPROVED
TranID#105170

Kirkland Signature
gasoline meets and
exceeds TopTier(tm)
performance
standards.
Learn more at
Costco.com
Search 'fuel,'

"Yes. Life is long." Kent managed a chuckle. "Well, I appreciate your optimism anyway." He forced another smile. "So, what brings you here at this hour? Something more for me to sign? Have I been accused of still more ghastly crimes?"

"Goodness, no, sir," William protested. "Nothing of the kind!" He looked down, hesitating. "To be honest, well, I . . ."

"Yes? What is it, William?"

"I am, uh . . ." William looked away, flustered. It was a question that had burned within him all of his adult life, lurking always somewhere in his awareness. At most times he could simply push it away, but in moments of greatest doubt, it had loomed large, like a finger punching at his chest. Pity that the first person he had ever thought to share it with, a man who could perhaps shed some light on his quandary, was now his client.

At best, William's decision to come here tonight was inappropriate. Kent's vocation notwithstanding, it was William who must now be the rock for Kent to lean upon, not the other way around. Instead, here he was, exposing his own insecurities to a man whose future was now in his hands. "I'm sorry, sir. It's nothing, really. Let's simply forget I came here tonight." He moved to go until Kent gripped his arm.

"No," said Kent. "Under no account shall I allow you to leave until you tell me what's troubling you."

William looked at Kent. "Very well. I came seeking personal advice. In light of our new professional relationship, it was a poor decision, which I regret. Please, allow me to take my leave before any more damage is done."

Kent looked at him and smiled fondly. "My goodness, but you are a serious young man." He sighed. "I appreciate your reluctance to add to my concerns, William, but it's misplaced. Helping others is what gives my life meaning. Besides . . ." Kent paused for a moment. "You've stood up for me when no one else would. Convinced me to stand up for myself. We've barely begun, but even if we were never to see one another again, I would already owe you more than I can repay. So, please, if I can help in some small way, allow me to do you that service."

William took a deep breath and surrendered. "As you wish," he said, feeling a little light-headed.

"Come," Kent said as he led William up the center aisle toward the altar. When they reached the communion railing, William hesitated a brief moment before proceeding.

"It's only a railing," Kent advised, as if reading William's mind. "There for convenience only, I assure you. This way," Kent encouraged him. "Just here."

At the end of a dark, narrow hallway, Kent opened a door and flicked on a light, illuminating the church's modest sacristy. There was a handsome oak desk with a chair beneath a single window. Two leather armchairs sat opposite. Against one wall, a large armoire stood beside a smaller cabinet, presumably for the holy vessels.

"Make yourself comfortable, please," Kent urged as he removed his heavy clerical robes, revealing ordinary trousers and a short-sleeved shirt beneath. "Too hot for these!" Kent opened the armoire and hung the vestments on a wooden hanger.

William looked around the room, recalling a dim memory. "Believe it or not, I once considered entering the ministry."

Kent turned to William, surprised. "Really? Let's sit here." Kent led them to the side-by-side leather armchairs.

"Strange," William mused. "I haven't thought of it in years."

"Tell me," Kent encouraged him.

William took a moment to recall.

"I couldn't have been more than ten," he began. "I remember sitting at Sunday service with my parents, watching and listening intently. It came into my head that the only one who knew anything at all about God was the priest. The rest of us just seemed to me like a bunch of imposters, sitting there, acting as if we could see or hear something. I concluded that I must either join the clergy, or stop going altogether."

"And you chose the latter?" Kent smiled.

William nodded, looking down. "All too common, I suppose."

"Not your self-reflection. That's quite rare, I think, especially in one so young. And do you still believe we know something you don't?"

William shrugged. "One would hope," he said, then fell silent.

"So, what is it that brought you here tonight?"

William looked at Kent, searching for the proper words to begin. "I, well, this evening . . . I had an argument with my wife, you see. I'm afraid I lost my temper."

Kent took a moment before responding. "That just proves you're human."

"My children witnessed it. So did our maid. It was quite unseemly. I felt ridiculous."

"Fair enough," Kent continued. "What did you argue about?"

William knew that the reverend himself had been the subject of the argument and he glanced away before Kent could repeat his mind-reading trick. "It's not important," William demurred. "My wife is an extraordinary woman, with very strong opinions."

"And you find that difficult?" Kent asked, eager to get to the bottom of William's upset.

"No," William blurted, then thought better of it. "Yes, sometimes. But that's not . . ." He trailed off. Kent waited.

"It's my father, you see," William continued finally. "He was a towering figure. Successful, imposing, respected by all. I remember people coming to the house, how they would defer to him. My mother was cowed by his intellect. Even his own father would follow his son's opinions in most things." William laughed ruefully. "And, believe me, he had an opinion about everything, and he was never shy about sharing." William paused. "There was one maxim of his in particular; if he said it once, he said it a thousand times—his life's motto, I suppose—that the true measure of a man lay in his ability to distinguish right from wrong. When I was a child, no further explanation seemed necessary. My father had said it; therefore it must be so. But as I got older, at critical moments, his words would often play over in my head, and I would wonder how I measured up . . ."

William sighed. "He died suddenly while I was still at Yale, and my greatest regret is that I never found the courage to ask him if he believed this quality of discernment to be inborn, or something one acquired along the way." There. It had been said. William looked at Kent, who looked back, unflinching.

"And you want to know what I think?" asked Kent.

William nodded gravely. "Yes."

Kent sighed. "Very well." The priest took another moment. "I suppose it's no surprise that I'm old enough to truly remember the world before electric lights. It was an extraordinary moment, when cities suddenly became illuminated. There was so much more to see. So many hidden things that were suddenly revealed." Kent paused. "For your generation, the war, I think, was that kind of moment. It changed everything. No one, not anyone on earth, could ever have imagined that such suffering, such inhumanity was possible. And all in the name of virtues we had always held as irrefutable."

Kent paused to look at William, and the younger man prepared himself.

"Your father was . . ." Kent stopped himself. "Well, let's say he was a very lucky man, William, to have lived when he did, in the way that he did. I'm afraid life is just not that simple anymore. And it never will be again."

William said nothing. Everything was nuanced with Kent, and though he appreciated the man's wisdom, he had hoped at least for a way forward.

"I'm sorry if that's not the answer you were hoping for, William." The man smiled sadly, seeming to read William's mind. "Unfortunately, it's the only one I have."

"I'm not sure what I expected," William uttered. "Of course, I suppose you're right. You're much more a man of the world than I am, but may I make a confession?"

"Please."

"It's not very modern of me—I could never admit this to my wife, of course—but I prefer things as they were. In my father's day, that is. And I think I always shall."

A silly thing, William thought to himself, but it felt as though that were the most private opinion he might have shared. As he searched Kent's inquisitive face, in one respect at least William felt gratified. He knew now that he would never be judged harshly by Kent for any honest statement. For that alone, whatever Kent's imagined debt to him, William considered the balance to have been amply repaid.

# ELEVEN

An edition of *Newport Illustrated* magazine, dated June 1919, the month Kent's trial began, ran a photo essay on Washington Mall, Newport's main square. The colorful photographs showed the square as it might have been on some particularly glorious July Fourth in the years before the war, packed with happy people, festooned brilliantly with flags and an excess of red, white, and blue bunting. The text went on to describe the square as "a small triangular park around which are centered the many interesting buildings and events in Newport's history, including the Old Court House. Built in 1739, it is of red brick, with window caps and other projections of freestone. The roof is surmounted by a cupola, in which there is a bell and there is a fine clock over the front. The building for many years served as the seat of the Rhode Island Legislature, and it was from its lofty flight of steps that lead up to the main entrance that Major John Handy first read the Declaration of Independence to the citizens of Newport on July 20th, 1776."

A noble history indeed, William noted when he saw the piece. But a three-dimensional square, or triangle, as this square happened to be, has many more sides than those that first meet the eye. And it was with these unseen aspects that William had of late become acquainted, the dark world of restless sailors and streetwalkers, and the expansive one of Samuel Kent, whose life it seemed stood as a portal between the darkness and the light. Though most, William firmly believed, made their home in one or the other, he himself had stumbled improbably in the less agreeable direction and he feared that he would be changed irrevocably. Thirty years of memories insisted that he reckon his brush with the darkness a loss, but as he climbed those "lofty" stairs in search of justice, with Reverend Kent keeping pace at his side, William felt somehow richer just for having known the man.

He had done his preparation as diligently as Rhode Island's poor system of record keeping allowed. But though the state had one of the most consistently severe penalties for sodomy, William had confirmed his initial findings that crimes of this sort, or at least their prosecution, were extremely rare. During jury selection, he had remembered his wife's sage advice that people's natural discomfort with the subject would cut both ways, and that those men most repulsed by the thought of it would also be those most likely to be swayed by Kent's otherwise blameless reputation, compared to that of his three accusers.

The building had no proper lobby. Passing through the main doors, William and Kent entered one vast open room, with high coved ceilings and polished wood floors. Designed, William presumed, to accommodate large crowds of unruly colonists eager for direct democracy, the room had long since been given over to lawyers and bureaucrats, who, accustomed to a more discreet use of space, hurried uncomfortably toward their destination. William considered it a hopeful sign that he and Kent drew scant attention as they crossed the floor to the wide staircase, an indication that the proceedings might somehow remain dignified and routine.

But upon reaching the second floor, the crowd of a hundred or more gathered in the large foyer outside the courtroom told a different story. The first person William identified was Captain Campbell, commanding officer of the Naval Training Station. A short, solid man in his middle fifties, he stood near the courtroom doors, a stern look on his face as he conversed with two other naval officers. A crew of soldiers and sailors milled about near them, while a sizable assortment of Newport's male citizenry awaited the opening of the courtroom doors, presumably eager to grab the best seat. Most curious of all, however, was a small group of older women who stood to one side, huddled together, looking confused. The women saw the reverend and gazed hopefully in his direction, as if for guidance. Kent nodded at them and managed a tight smile.

"Who are they?" William asked.

"From my church," said Kent. "Come to lend their support, I'm afraid."

"It would have been useful to have supporters in the gallery," William sighed. "But the judge has barred women from the proceedings. Naturally."

Kent looked down and nodded. "Naturally," he said. "They're kind hearts, all of them. But I doubt they even know the nature of the charges against me. Nor would they understand even if . . ."

The reverend stopped abruptly and gave a hard glance to his right. Three young sailors, led by a court officer, were settling themselves on a bench to the right of the courtroom doors. They were smartly uniformed in dress whites, looking far more wholesome than William could have imagined possible, and it took him a moment to connect the names he'd despised for months with the faces he'd first seen at their depositions two weeks ago.

Their statements had been lengthy, the interviews hours long, and like all good lawyers, William had used the opportunity to take the measure of each man's character as best he could.

Closest to the courtroom doors sat Dostalick, first name Henry, blond, slack jawed, and to put it plainly, as dumb as a stump. His blue eyes were watery, dull and empty, and as pale as his skin. The young man's mind, it seemed to William, was a blank, upon which anything could be written given the proper influence. He was a born follower, and William considered it fortunate that he had been chosen to testify first, before his brighter cohorts could define a clear path for him and the jury.

Next in line was Bart Rudy, twenty-three, tall and well put together, with dark hair and a square jaw. Rudy was smart, no question about it. He'd taken his time when answering questions, especially those that involved dates and times, as well as other queries that might convey multiple meanings. He had also appeared to be tightly wound, a trait William hoped to use to his advantage.

Finally, seated a discreet distance from Rudy was Charles McKinney, the flu survivor for whom Kent had held vigil in the Navy hospital. McKinney was the most intriguing of the three, William had noted, handsome enough like the others, but with a native intellect and self-possession that his cronies lacked. He seemed unpredictable, which the lawyer in William did not appreciate.

For their depositions, all three sailors had behaved in a manner both humble and compliant, model citizens doing their patriotic and now civic duty. But there was something ugly about these men that William could sense but not yet identify. Perhaps it was the uniform, or the knowledge that they'd lived through a war, but they seemed to harbor a grossly outsized sense of their own importance for which William could discern no logical justification. If he could somehow encourage this arrogance to reveal itself under cross-examination, it might turn the jury of twelve men against them and in favor of the truly humble Reverend Kent.

McKinney must have felt William's gaze, because he looked up and nodded. Then the sailor shifted his look to Kent, to whom he offered a restrained smile. The reverend, by instinct it seemed, nodded politely in turn.

Suddenly, the doors to the courtroom swung open. William took Kent by the arm.

"Come, sir."

The room was not the conventional rectangle one expects, with a judge's bench and a well, and rows of gallery seats stretching back behind the defense and prosecution tables. Befitting its former life as a statehouse, it was more of an amphitheater, with a curved gallery wrapped around on three sides, to encourage, William supposed, the deliberative process. The jury box was little more than an after-thought, tucked up into a corner to the right of the judge's bench. As a boy, William had watched with rapt attention as his father argued cases here. In more recent years, he had been at the defense table in support of one of the firm's senior partners. It was high time William Bartlett had his own day in the sun, he told himself, and what better place for it than this familiar, intimate space. But as the spectators, lawyers, and other interested parties found their seats, and the room grew noisy and crowded, William fought hard to keep his nerves under control.

He had, in fact, not told the full truth to Kent when they were discussing the reverend's female supporters waiting in the lobby. The reality was that William would be eternally grateful to Judge Baker for barring women from the proceedings. Had he not, Sarah would have insisted on being in attendance, which would have been nothing short of disastrous for William. Though he had rehearsed with Kent in private, though he had practiced in front of his employers, in front of his clerk, and in front of his dog, the thought of speaking of these obscenities in public for hours on end horrified and disgusted him. How much worse would it have been had his wife been present? He imagined himself being struck speechless by her presence, which would not have done him or Kent much good at all.

"Mr. Bartlett!" a loud Australian voice intoned.

William turned abruptly to see the large, bulky frame of John Rathom, editor in chief of the *Providence Daily Journal*, standing a few feet away. Alarmed, William gave Kent's arm a gentle squeeze, encouraging him toward a seat at the defense table. "Please sit down, Reverend. I'll join you in a moment." Kent glanced at the big man curiously, then followed the instructions of his attorney.

Rathom moved closer. William would have taken a step back, but a gallery bench blocked his retreat.

"You never returned any of my phone calls," the Australian complained. "What happened to that undying appreciation you spoke of?"

"What are you doing here?" William replied, stone-faced.

"Don't get your panties in a bunch, Mr. Bartlett. I told you I have no professional interest in the story, and I stand by that statement." Rathom paused. "As a private citizen, however, I find this whole thing ever more fascinating."

"Is that why you were calling me?" William snapped.

"I'll have you know I was calling to offer information," Rathom replied cryptically. "Not to gather it."

William looked at the man skeptically. "What information could you possibly have that would interest me?"

Rathom chuckled. "Smug bastard, aren't you? Well, try this on for size: Were you aware that seventeen sailors were arrested the same day as the reverend on similar charges? They're being held on a prison ship in Newport Harbor, awaiting court-martial."

William looked at Rathom, trying to make sense of the news. Seventeen sailors? Such a sudden outbreak of wickedness strained credulity. But was it good news or bad? Certainly, the last thing William wanted was to have Kent somehow associated with still more naval impropriety. "What does any of that have to do with my client?"

Rathom raised an eyebrow. "That's what I'd like to know."

A stout bailiff entered the courtroom. "All rise!"

The newspaperman gave William a final nod, then strolled to his reserved spot at the front of the gallery. William turned to make his way to the defense table. A thousand questions fought for attention in William's mind, none of which he could hope to answer in the near term. The idea of requesting a delay now, in the first moments of the trial, was inconceivable, and certainly unjustified until he could determine the reason behind Rathom's revelation. Was the man truly trying to help, or was he simply attempting to grow the story into something truly newsworthy?

The reverend was already on his feet. Could the poor man have been aware of the level of depravity going on right under his nose?

"In the matter of the *People of Rhode Island versus Samuel Neal Kent*," the bailiff announced, "Judge Hugh Baker presiding, this court is now in session."

William concluded that there was nothing for him to do but forge ahead as he had planned until more was revealed. He had built a solid defense, and if a delay for further discovery seemed called for, he would make that request at the appropriate time. For now, however, Rathom's claims were hearsay at best.

From a door behind the witness stand, a balding gray-haired man entered the courtroom and took his place on high. William was acquainted with Judge Baker, having attended elementary school with one of his sons, and he knew him by reputation to be a stern but fair jurist. William was also certain that Baker, though a congregant of the more traditional Trinity Episcopal rather than Emmanuel Church, was at least acquainted with Reverend Kent and his many good works. On the other hand, the judge had strong family ties to the naval establishment. In a town like Newport, where conflicting loyalties often went back generations, the pursuit of "blind" justice for a well-known figure like Reverend Kent was no small undertaking. Jury selection had posed a similar challenge, as each man's bias was weighed for or against. But the state prosecutor, Randolph Bishop, a tired-looking man in his late forties, had faced the same frustrations, and William was confident that he had given no more advantages than he had received.

"Good afternoon, gentlemen, please be seated," the judge pronounced as he looked over the restless assembly. "I see we have a packed house. I want to thank you for your attendance. Trial by jury is surely the most sacred of the fundamental rights guaranteed to us by our Constitution, and your support of the process is appreciated. However, I also want to remind you that this is a court of law. As you are no doubt aware, much of the testimony you are about to hear will be disturbing, to say the least. Anyone whose behavior is in any way disrespectful of these proceedings will be ejected from the courtroom immediately. That being said, will the defendant please rise."

William and Kent rose again and faced the judge.

"Samuel Neal Kent, you stand accused of three counts of sodomy and crimes against nature. How do you plead?"

William spoke for his client. "Reverend Kent pleads not guilty, Your Honor."

"Thank you, Mr. Bartlett. You may be seated, Reverend."

William and Kent took their seats.

"The esteemed Mr. Bishop is representing the state in these proceedings," said the judge. "Mr. Bishop, do you have any opening remarks?"

Bishop stood. "I do, Your Honor." Bishop strode to the center of the well, paused to look gravely at Reverend Kent, then continued on until he stood before the jury box.

Bishop had gone up against Abbot Phillips three years before in an incident involving one of Newport's wealthier residents. William had assisted Phillips on that case, so he was somewhat acquainted with Bishop's style and tactics. The man had a solid reputation, to be sure, but William found him dull and uninspired. He expected no surprises from Bishop, thankfully.

"Gentlemen of the jury," Bishop began. "We come together today to deliberate in a serious matter. A man many of us have admired, a man whose life mission it is to do only good, stands before us accused of a crime so heinous, we shudder to speak its name. A paradox, isn't it? That someone who appears so upstanding might be guilty of so horrid a betrayal, of his vows, of our trust, of the very young men whose souls he was supposed to protect . . ."

Bishop, William decided, was in love with the sound of his own voice. It was self-consciously resonant, which made him difficult to follow for long periods. For now, at least, he had novelty on his side. The jury had never heard anyone speak of these things above a whisper, so they hung on his every word.

Someone in the front row of the gallery erupted into a coughing jag, so loud it stopped Bishop in midsentence. William turned to see Rathom searching his pockets for a handkerchief. With his huge bulk squeezed onto the crowded gallery bench, every move was a negotiation. In his office, behind his massive desk, Rathom had seemed appropriately larger than life. But here, in Newport, the man looked terribly out of place, like he'd wandered into the wrong party.

What could Rathom's extraordinary revelation mean? Not long ago, just before the war, the Catholic Decency League had blown through town, closing the saloons and chasing most of the prostitutes from the streets. As much as he disapproved of Catholics in general, William had supported the campaign, hoping it would curb some of the city's worst abuses. Had the Navy now followed suit, and had Kent somehow gotten swept up in its zeal? Such a notion, of the Navy embarking on a moral crusade, was on the face of it completely ludicrous. God knew, the Army and Navy YMCA, where the reverend still served part time, had indeed been a hotbed of sin, but naval personnel were the cause of most of the bad behavior in Newport, not the cure. And if the Navy brass had determined to reform their wild recruits, why not announce the policy publicly, enlisting the assistance and goodwill of a relieved citizenry?

". . . a wolf in sheep's clothing, gentlemen," Randolph Bishop's middle-aged voice droned on. William looked up, suddenly aware that he had missed much of his opponent's opening remarks.

"Now, counsel for the defense," Bishop continued, looking at William accusingly, "will ask you to blame the sheep, these boys, who looked to the defendant for guidance and instead found . . . degeneracy. They deserved better, these fine servicemen who until a short time ago were prepared to sacrifice their young lives for your freedom. I ask you, gentlemen, not to be swayed by appearances, by the collar worn by Mr. Kent, but rather to listen to the evidence, and when you do, I have no doubt you will find for these boys, and for justice."

William glanced at the jury as Bishop returned to his seat. At least three of the twelve men were looking at the reverend with an increased measure of suspicion.

"Thank you, Mr. Bishop," the judge said. He turned to William. The moment had come. "Mr. Bartlett, have you any opening remarks?"

William stood, somewhat shakily. "Yes, Your Honor."

He recalled Sarah's coaching to take his time before beginning his speech. There was no need to rush to the defense of an innocent man, she had said. But as he crossed the abyss between the defense table and the jury box, William had to fight the urge to say something, anything to fill the silence. He held his peace as he paced in front of the twelve men, looking each in the eye as if taking his measure.

"The word of three men against the word of one," William began simply. "It will be your responsibility, gentlemen, to decide who you believe. If a thief comes to you, no, if three thieves come to you, claiming that your wealthy neighbor has been stealing from your rubbish pile, do you believe them?"

William stopped his pacing and shifted his gaze to Reverend Kent. The jurors' eyes followed him. "Reverend Kent is that wealthy neighbor, gentlemen, wealthy not in the things of this world, but in the treasures of the heart." He turned back to face the jury. "What use has he for rubbish?"

William fell silent. That was it, the full extent of his opening statement.

Short, but effective, Sarah had assured him.

The courtroom fell into an even deeper silence. They had expected more. But as he walked back toward his place beside the reverend, he could feel the gathered assembly silently asking the essential question William had posed. Coming abreast of John Rathom, seated front and center in the gallery, William spied the journalist giving him a wink of approval. Though William remained deeply suspicious of the man, he was grateful for the support.

"Prosecution will call its first witness," the judge announced.

Bishop again stood. "Your Honor, the prosecution calls Seaman First Class Henry F. Dostalick to the stand."

The doors at the back of the room opened and William watched as Dostalick made his way down the aisle and climbed the three steps up to the witness stand. The court clerk stepped forward and held out a Bible.

"Please raise your right hand and place your left on the Bible." Dostalick did so. On the stand in his gleaming dress whites, the pale sailor seemed almost translucent, somewhere between an angel and a cipher.

"Do you solemnly swear that the testimony you are about to give in the matter before this court will be the truth, the whole truth, and nothing but the truth, so help you God?"

"I do." His voice was young, a colorless Midwestern tenor.

"You may be seated."

The clerk withdrew and Bishop approached. "Please state your name for the court."

"Henry F. Dostalick, Seaman First Class, U.S. Navy."

"Sailor, are you acquainted with the accused, Samuel Neal Kent?"

"Yes, sir, I am," Dostalick answered stalwartly.

"Is he in this courtroom?"

"Yes, sir."

"Could you point him out to me, please?" Bishop asked dramatically.

Dostalick raised his right arm straight as a bayonet and pointed at Kent with a long skinny index finger.

"Let the record show that Mr. Dostalick has identified the defendant, Samuel Neal Kent. Mr. Dostalick, can you tell us how you came to be acquainted with Reverend Kent?"

"Oh, everybody knew Mr. Kent, sir. You'd almost always find him at the Y, where all the men would show up most days at some point. He was real friendly with all of us sailors, especially the new recruits. And the soldiers, too, from Fort Adams, he was real chummy with them as well."

"I see. And when did you first have occasion to spend time with him, just the two of you?"

"One day, well, we'd been talking and he offered to take me to one of them Navy shows, where the women's parts are played by men."

"And did you accept his invitation?"

"I did, sir."

"Did you find that odd in any way, that he would invite you to a show of this nature?"

"Well, to be honest, sir, no, I didn't. They're sort of a tradition in the Navy, you know?" Dostalick laughed. "Fact is, sir, the men who dress up don't much look like women most of the time, but the boys in the audience always hoot and holler as if they did. It's all in good fun."

"I see. And did anything unusual occur during your evening with him?"

"Not at first, sir, no. But then, after a while, we were sitting there, laughing and enjoying all the high jinks, when all of a sudden I feel Reverend Kent press his leg up against mine, like I would with a girl I was trying to get friendly with."

William jumped up. "Objection, Your Honor. Speculation. The witness is trying to assign his own motives to Reverend Kent."

"Sustained," the judge intoned. "And Mr. Bartlett, the objection is sufficient. Please refrain from any speculation of your own."

"Yes, Your Honor," William said, feeling like an amateur.

Bishop picked up where he'd left off. "And after the show, son?"

"He asked if I'd like to spend the night with him in the parish house. Lots of the sailors did, he said, when they got homesick. There was a cot in the living room, he said, for just that purpose. I told him I wasn't homesick, and that I had early duty in the morning."

Kent had indeed taken Dostalick to the show, William knew that much was fact, and he also knew that it was not uncommon for sailors to spend the night on Kent's living room cot. But there was something about the sailor's insinuations, besides being untrue, that seemed suspect, as if expressed in words not entirely his own, his voice devoid of affect.

"What happened then?" Bishop asked gently.

"He asked would I like to take a ride with him in his Buick roadster on Sunday along Bellevue Avenue."

"Can you tell us what happened during that ride?"

"Well, sir," Dostalick began, "Mr. Kent picks me up around noon Sunday and we ride out Bellevue past the big houses toward Fort Adams. After a while, Mr. Kent put his hand on my leg, then moved it onto my privates and started rubbing."

William glanced over at the jurors, who to a man listened with rapt attention, very unlikely to have heard such things spoken of in public or private.

"Did you say anything?" Bishop inquired with an appropriate amount of shock.

"I asked him what he was doing. He said he wanted to make me feel good. I told him I wasn't that kind of fellow, but he wouldn't listen. Then he took it out and played with it till I had an emission."

*Emission?* William pondered as murmurs filled the titillated courtroom. Though the word corresponded to his deposition, it now sounded odd coming out of the young sailor's mouth.

"Thank you, son," Bishop wrapped up. "No further questions, Your Honor."

The judge turned to William. "Your witness, Mr. Bartlett."

William stood. "Thank you, Your Honor." He approached Dostalick, looking at him thoughtfully.

"Mr. Dostalick," he began in a measured tone, "how did you first come to meet Reverend Kent?"

"Well, like I said, sir, at the Y."

"Did he approach you?"

"No, sir, he had stamps to sell at the counter there. I needed stamps."

William continued amiably. "I see. And how did you happen to attend the show with him? I mean, how did it come up in conversation?"

Dostalick thought a moment. "I told him how hard it was for a young man to entertain himself in a wholesome way in Newport, so he offered to take me to the show."

William scrutinized him. "A wholesome way," he echoed. "Of course. Now, Sunday, April 27th. Noon, you said?"

"Yes, sir, about noon."

"The reverend picked you up in his car and you went for a drive."

"Along Bellevue Avenue, yes, sir." Dostalick seemed pleased with himself as he reiterated that detail.

"Inclement weather, was it?" William asked casually.

"Oh, no, sir," Dostalick protested. "It was a beautiful day. We had the top down."

"Did any other motorcars happen to pass along the way?"

Dostalick paused a moment, thinking carefully. "A few," he offered.

"A few?" William offered back, surprised. "On a perfect April Sunday?"

"Well," he said, backtracking, "quite a few, I suppose."

"So, with quite a few motorcars going by, Reverend Kent, in an open car, proceeded to place his right hand on your private parts?"

"That's right."

"Driving with his left, I suppose. And the gearshift?"

"Sir?"

"In this time he was supposedly fondling you, with other cars on the road, didn't he ever need to shift the motor's gears?"

Dostalick looked confused. "I suppose so, sir."

"Mr. Dostalick, you identified Reverend Kent earlier. Do you still see him?"

"Yes, sir. He's right there, sir."

"How many hands does he have?"

A little ripple of laughter moved through the courtroom.

"How many hands does the reverend have, sailor?"

Dostalick smiled, thinking the laughter had been aimed at the lawyer's foolish question. "Well, sir," he answered, "unless he's been in a recent accident, he's got two, sir."

And there it was, William noted, the smirk he had hoped would appear. William smiled back.

"And you, sailor? How many do you have?"

Dostalick held up his hands, enjoying the fanciful exchange. "Two, sir."

"And during the time Reverend Kent was allegedly fondling you, where were they?"

"Sir?"

"Your hands, Mr. Dostalick. Where were they? Had they been tied behind your back?"

Dostalick gave out a pathetic laugh as his face flushed. "No, sir." It must have just dawned on the young man that he had lost control of the situation.

"So," William said, trying not to sound too triumphant, "in other words, Reverend Kent's hands were miraculously performing three tasks at once, while yours apparently lay idle, doing nothing to prevent this unwanted attention."

Bishop shot up. "Objection, Your Honor. The witness is not on trial here!"

William looked at Bishop, struck by this last remark. He glanced over at Rathom, who stared back at him with a Cheshire cat grin. Perhaps the man was indeed on to something.

"Overruled, Mr. Bishop," declared the judge. He looked at William. "Do you have any more questions for this witness, Mr. Bartlett?" But William's attention had clearly wandered. "Mr. Bartlett?"

William continued looking at Rathom a moment longer, considering, then turned toward the judge. "Yes, Your Honor, I do, but . . . may we approach the bench?"

"Counsels will approach."

William moved quickly toward the judge, followed by Bishop. "It's nearly lunchtime, Your Honor, and this is a good place for me to stop. If it pleases the court . . ."

The judge turned to Bishop. "Any objections, Mr. Bishop?"

"None, Your Honor."

The judge banged his gavel and boomed aloud, "This court stands in recess until two o'clock."

William made his way to the defense table and gathered his things. Kent looked at him, concerned.

"William, is anything wrong?"

"No, Reverend, not at all, but I need to attend to something. I'll have one of the clerks escort you to lunch."

"Don't worry about me," Kent replied. "I'll be fine."

William gave Kent an appreciative pat on the back and turned in time to see Rathom exiting the courtroom. He quickly closed his briefcase and hurried after the fat man.

— • — • —

"Do you really believe that?" William asked, incredulous.

At the White Horse Tavern, an ancient inn a few blocks from the courthouse, Rathom dove into an enormous steak smothered in onions. William looked on, his own plate of fish untouched.

"How else do you explain it?" Rathom managed between bites. "The timing of the other arrests? Kent's accusers stepping forward all at once? Coincidence? I doubt it. No, for whatever reason, someone was out to get these men."

William sat back in his chair, dumbfounded. "Who could be behind something like this? And why Reverend Kent? And what of the others? What's to become of them?"

"They're in custody, aboard a prison ship out in the harbor. They've been arraigned and will no doubt be tried eventually. For now, at least, the Navy is focusing all of its energy on the big bad reverend."

William sighed. "So, now the question is, what am I to do with this information?"

"What?" Now, it was Rathom's turn to be stunned. He stopped eating at last. "This was a conspiracy. It's entrapment, Bartlett, plain and simple. Case dismissed."

"Perhaps," William said, troubled. "But it doesn't prove these boys are lying. It doesn't actually prove Reverend Kent's innocence."

"Not technically, no. But at least he'll be off the hook."

"No," William insisted. "No, he won't. His position, you see." But of course, Rathom would never see. What did a newspaperman care about reputation? "This will follow him."

"Not half so much as a prison term. Believe me, Kent wouldn't survive a week at Howard."

William looked at Rathom, contemplating the idea of Reverend Kent as an inmate at Howard Prison, the state penitentiary, a horrible, sprawling Gothic structure of granite block that housed the worst assortment of criminals and mental patients.

"He's actually much tougher than you think," William objected. "But obviously, we don't want him to go to prison."

"I can't believe what I'm hearing." Rathom shook his head. "Decide what you like, but you must at least pursue this line of questioning. You owe Kent that much."

"And if I do as you say," William asked, "do you expect Dostalick to simply fold, just come out and admit it?"

"Mr. Bartlett, the boy is following a script, clearly written by others." Rathom turned back to his steak. "If you can't find a way to trip him up, then I suggest you stick to contract law."

⬦ · ⬦ · ⬦

"Remember, young man," said Judge Baker. "You're still under oath."

Dostalick nodded. The sailor seemed to have been refreshed and renewed by the lunch break.

William approached the witness, thinking back to something he had noted on his own, even before Rathom's revelation. "Tell me, Mr. Dostalick, who taught you that word, 'emission'?"

"Objection, Your Honor." Bishop rose.

"It's a simple question, Prosecutor," William responded.

Bishop ignored William, addressing the judge. "Defense counsel's implication is obvious, Your Honor."

"Objection sustained."

"I'll rephrase," said William. "When you're with your shipmates, discussing things of this nature, would that be the word you'd use?"

"No, sir," said Dostalick. Another smirk.

"Can you offer the court an alternative?" William queried.

"Objection, Your Honor!" Bishop shot up. "Do we really need to get into this?"

Judge Baker looked down at William. "Mr. Bartlett, what is your point?"

William looked at Dostalick, scrutinizing him. The young man looked away and shifted his weight.

"Mr. Bartlett?" the judge repeated.

"I'll withdraw the question for the moment, Your Honor. Now, Henry." William smiled pleasantly. "May I call you Henry?"

"Yes, sir," Dostalick replied.

"I'm going to read something back to you, Henry, something you said earlier. Tell me if it's accurate." William began to read, "'I told him how hard it was for a young man to entertain himself in a wholesome way in Newport, so he offered to take me to the show.' Is that what you said?"

"Yes, sir, that's it."

William drew closer to Dostalick, almost leaning on the witness stand. He smiled, as if speaking man-to-man. "Tell me, Henry, you've been in the Navy for a while. What are some of the more unwholesome ways a sailor might entertain himself?"

"Objection, Your Honor," Bishop shouted, sounding exasperated. "These good people don't need to hear—"

"Overruled, Mr. Bishop." The judge looked at William, intrigued. "I'll allow you some room, Mr. Bartlett, but this better be leading somewhere."

"Yes, Your Honor, I believe it is, sir, thank you." He turned to the somewhat bemused witness. "So, Henry? What does a sailor do on a Saturday night?"

"In port? Well, uh . . . drinking."

William feigned surprise. "What about the prohibition?"

Dostalick offered a sly smile. "You know how it is, sir. We manage."

William smiled back. "I see. What else?"

Dostalick shrugged. "Women."

"By that you mean loose women?"

"Well, sure, yes, sir."

"Awful lot of sailors in Newport at the moment. Doesn't seem like there'd be enough women of that sort to go around."

Dostalick nodded. "Not hardly, sir."

"So," William mused, "what does a healthy young man do, if he's not one of the lucky few, or if, say, he's out at sea for long periods?"

Dostalick looked at William a moment. The lawyer could feel the ponderous deliberations going on in the sailor's mind, as if trying to determine if William meant what Dostalick thought he meant. "Sir?"

"Oh, come now, Henry, we're men of the world. I'm referring to other . . . alternatives to the tender company of a willing female. Similar to what you've mentioned here. Young men can get pretty desperate. We don't like to think about it, but these things do go on, don't they?"

A sweat moustache began to appear on the sailor's upper lip. "On shipboard, you mean, sir?" Dostalick seemed distracted, as if trying to find someone in the gallery.

"Why, is there a distinction?" replied William. "Who are you looking for, Henry?"

"No one, sir." But the sailor's eyes kept darting, an anxious child searching for his mother.

"Then look at me, sailor."

Dostalick abruptly brought his attention back to William.

"Is there a distinction," William repeated, "between what goes on aboard a ship, and what goes on in port?"

Dostalick blushed and fought a smile.

"Something strike you as funny, Henry?"

"Oh, no, sir, it's just that there's an expression some of the boys use . . ."

"Objection, Your Honor!" Bishop nearly shrieked. "Leading the witness."

Judge Baker looked at the prosecutor. "It seems to me that it's your witness who's doing the leading. Overruled."

William resumed. "You were saying, Henry?"

Dostalick suddenly clammed up, realizing he had strayed into dangerous waters.

"Henry? What expression were you referring to?"

Dostalick shook his head. "It's not right, sir. I shouldn't."

"Why? There are no ladies present here. We can be frank."

Dostalick looked to the judge. "Do I have to, Your Honor?"

"At this point," Baker said, "I'm afraid so."

Dostalick turned back to William but didn't meet his eyes. "Well, some of the boys, well, they like to kid, they say, 'It ain't queer unless you're tied to the pier.'"

Scattered laughter erupted in the gallery.

"I see," William resumed. "So, these activities, between men, they do go on, then, on shipboard, at least, do they not?"

"So I'm told, sir."

"So you're *told*?" William looked at him, letting Dostalick know that he didn't believe a word. "What's the Navy's opinion of this sort of behavior?"

"They frown on it, sir," Dostalick insisted.

"I have no doubt. And you, sailor, what's your opinion?"

Dostalick looked William in the eye and said with conviction, "I frown on it as well, sir."

William turned away. "Of course you do. Now, when Reverend Kent invited you to spend the night with him in his quarters, you begged off because of early morning duties. Is that correct?"

Dostalick seemed relieved to be getting back onto familiar turf. "Yes, sir, that's right."

William turned back toward him. "What are your duties, Mr. Dostalick?"

But Dostalick did not respond. Instead, he started searching the gallery again with his eyes.

"Mr. Dostalick?"

Dostalick looked at William and steadied himself. "I'm not at liberty to say, sir."

"Excuse me, sailor," William retorted, indignant. "You're in a court of law. Answer the question."

Dostalick remained resolute. "I'm sorry, sir. Naval Intelligence."

"Yes," said William, dismissive. "So you said in your deposition. But surely you can tell us something without endangering the security of the nation." William repeated, adamant, "What are your duties, Mr. Dostalick?"

Dostalick looked confused. "I . . . I've taken an oath not to divulge the nature of our operations."

William turned to the judge, feigning surprise. "Your Honor . . ."

Baker looked down at Dostalick. "Young man, you have accused a respected citizen of a serious crime. Now I can clear the courtroom if I must, or we can retire to chambers, but you will answer Mr. Bartlett's question. And remember your oath."

Dostalick looked up at the judge, his face now registering full-blown panic. "But Judge, I can't—"

Baker ignored him. "Repeat the question, Mr. Bartlett."

"What are your duties, Henry?"

"I'm . . . I'm assigned to a special unit . . . investigating immoral conditions."

Good God, Rathom had been right. William's heart began to race. "Immoral conditions. So, the early duties you were referring to were, what? A date with a prostitute?"

"Objection!"

"Sustained."

"What are your morning duties, son?"

Dostalick chose his words carefully, struggling to forestall the inevitable. "To report to my superiors whatever . . . whatever happened the night before."

William turned away and faced the jury. "The night before was spent with Reverend Kent, so am I safe in assuming that you were reporting on him, a man you had approached and to whom you had appealed for salvation from various unsavory pursuits?"

"Objection!" shouted Bishop.

"Sustained," said the judge.

William did not relent. "Were you reporting on Reverend Kent, Mr. Dostalick?"

Whatever blood still remained in Dostalick's pale face now drained completely. "Yes, sir," he replied flatly.

William turned back to Dostalick and faced him from a distance. "And after reporting on your evening together, did you receive further instructions?"

"Yes, sir."

"What were they?"

William could feel the hush that had fallen over the courtroom. Dostalick must have felt it, too, as he gave up all resistance, like a gored bull surrendering to the matador's last blows.

"To keep the date with the reverend on Sunday and see where it went," said the sailor.

The surrounding hush now turned into a rising murmur of outrage.

"I see," said William. "This unit you're assigned to, do part of your duties include allowing yourself to be fondled?"

Humiliated, Dostalick looked at William, then up to the judge in a final appeal for salvation.

"Answer the question," the judge barked, giving no quarter.

Dostalick hung his head. "If necessary."

The room full of men erupted. Baker pounded his gavel. "This court will come to order or I will have it cleared immediately!"

Enough calm was restored for William to resume. "If necessary? Necessary for what?"

"Necessary to gather sufficient evidence of perversion."

"I see," said William. "So, you're to use your own judgment, in other words."

"Yes, sir."

"An expert in perversion, are you?"

"Objection!" Bishop shouted as a few titters rose from the gallery.

"Withdrawn," said William. "Young man, did you volunteer for this duty?"

"Yes, sir."

"Knowing what it might entail?"

"More or less, sir."

"Once it became fully clear, did you ever try to get out of it?"

"No, sir."

William paused a moment and asked simply, "Why not?"

Dostalick raised his head, a last hurrah before the deathblow. "Because I think it's right what we're doing. We gotta get rid of these degenerates!"

In the judge's chambers, William stood before Baker's desk trying not to gloat, while beside him the state's prosecutor attempted to shrink into the carpet.

William spoke. "This case has been so undermined that we believe the people will no longer be able to prove these charges. We move to dismiss, your honor."

Baker looked at both men and sighed. "I'm inclined to agree, counselor. Mr. Bishop?"

The prosecutor nodded glumly.

"Very well," said Baker. "Case dismissed!"

· — · — ·

On the following Sunday, at his home on Harrison Avenue, Sarah arranged a small reception to celebrate her husband's victory. He had not had the heart to discourage her, since her attendance in the courtroom had been forbidden, and the least William could do was allow his wife to interact with the various players in the discreet privacy of their home. He only wished that he could feel as proud as she appeared to be. Instead, William stood alone to one side, watching the interested parties mingle in his parlor, sipping champagne and nibbling on canapés.

Loudest among the group of guests were Rathbone Gardner and Abbot Phillips, William's employers, who stood near the piano laughing and chatting with John Rathom. Though William could not hear the substance of their banter, it made him burn just the same. They all seemed so chummy, as if none of this had ever really concerned them at all. Of the three, William had to admit that his clear favorite was now Rathom. At least the man wasn't a hypocrite.

Displaying her customary passion, Sarah was engaged in a conversation with Bishop Perry, undoubtedly trying to enlist his support in one or another of her causes. A dozen other respectable men and women to whom he'd been introduced but whose names he had instantly forgotten made small talk while keeping an eye out for Fanny and her floating tray of hors d'oeuvres.

In a corner, framed in the light of a window, Reverend Kent stood deep in conversation with Sarah's youngest sister, Alice. The man looked immensely relieved. Rathom had been right, of course; the risks for Kent had been too great not to grab at the chance for a summary dismissal. Still, William was troubled. As it was, the sailors' outrageous testimony stood; it had not been disproved but simply ruled inadmissible. Good had not triumphed. William had seen it in the jurors' faces when the judge came out to tell them they could go home. They looked confused, and suspicious, as if they'd been cheated of the truth. In the end, William himself had done precious little, other than humiliate a young dimwit and experience a distinct thrill in the doing of it.

"My hero." Sarah suddenly appeared at his side, kissing his cheek as she offered him a glass of champagne. William managed a weak smile and they clinked a toast. "You were right," she offered with sincere humility.

"About?"

"Those boys."

"Ah. Disappointed?" he mused with a hint of bitterness.

She looked at him askance. "That's an odd thing to say. Of course I'm not. I'm proud of you."

He sighed. "I know. And I appreciate it. But I'd hoped for a cleaner victory."

She took his face in her hands. "William. The reverend is free."

He looked in her eyes and nodded, grateful for her good sense.

"Congratulations, my boy!" Rathbone Gardner approached, smiling broadly.

"Quite a young trial lawyer you've got there, Mrs. Bartlett," Abbot Phillips chimed in.

Sarah looked at them. "You sound surprised."

Gardner laughed, slapping William on the back. "Your biggest booster, eh? Just as it should be, just as it should be. Abbot?"

Phillips cleared his throat. "Well, William, we've been discussing this for some time . . ."

"Wouldn't want you to think it was based solely on your recent performance," added Gardner. "But we've decided to act quickly before some firm in Providence or Boston lured you away."

"William," Phillips intoned. "It's my privilege to offer you a junior partnership at Gardner, Phillips."

Sarah beamed at her husband while William stared at the men. He had expected to lose his position, no matter the outcome of the trial, but it seemed as though his victory had trumped any past infractions. "I . . . I don't know what to say."

Phillips smirked. "'Yes' would do nicely."

Kent joined the group before William had a chance to respond. "Am I interrupting?"

Gardner turned to him. "Not at all, Reverend. Come, Abbot, it's getting late. We old men need our rest." Then, to William, "Bad form to discuss the details at a social event. Tomorrow then?" He turned to address Sarah, taking her hand. "Thank you for a lovely evening, Mrs. Bartlett."

Sarah smiled graciously. "Not at all. Come, I'll see you both out." She led them off, leaving William alone with Reverend Kent.

"More good news?" Kent asked with a smile.

"Yes," replied William grimly. "And I don't deserve it."

"You're too hard on yourself, son," said Kent with concern.

William shrugged. "Someone's got to be."

"Well, there's one thing I'm certain you do deserve," Kent said, "and that's my undying gratitude."

William smiled. "Thank you, Reverend. I'm only sorry I wasn't able to expose all three of them for the liars they are."

"No, William," Kent protested, laying a hand on his shoulder. "We should feel nothing but sympathy for those boys, being used like that by men they were trained to trust."

William looked at Kent, humbled once again by the man's unfailing compassion and selflessness.

"You're right, Reverend," William agreed. "It's horrible."

"Indeed. And it's over," added Kent. "For us *and* them. Now, let's get on with our lives."

William raised his glass. "Amen."

"Amen," Kent echoed with a smile, and the two men clinked.

# TWELVE

Like most New Yorkers, Charlie McKinney had lived his life in the shadow of great wealth. He'd grown up on the Lower East Side, amidst the smell of garlic and pickles and the sweat of the world's surplus population. But as in no other city on earth, the distance between the heaving life of the tenements and that of a far gentler world was measured in blocks. It was a testament to the hope that America still sparked in the hearts of her huddled masses, that these worlds could live side by side, separated at times, Charlie had noted on hungry nights, by no more than the plate glass of a restaurant window. Someday, the outsider believed, he too would be dressed in finery, eating steak off china plates, looking out at the poor kid on the street. It had happened before, and it would happen again.

Often, in good weather, Charlie would jump the turnstile of the Third Avenue El at Houston Street and venture farther to the north, hopping off at Fifty-Ninth or Sixty-Seventh Street, then hoofing it the four blocks over to Central Park. There, in an impossible paradise of flowers and breathing green, he would stroll with the swells, for whom every day seemed to be Sunday, and to whom life in a Fifth Avenue mansion must have seemed the most normal thing in the world.

Life might have turned out differently for Charlie had he been a different sort. Exactly what sort that might have been remained a mystery to him. He only knew that once, when he was fourteen, against all odds, he had found his way into one of the great houses, not as a thief or grifter but as an invited guest, who might just have stayed forever.

Charles Aaron McKinney had been born to shiftless people. His father was a harsh Scotsman fond of the strap, his mother an Irishwoman who liked her drink, and they had little use for children over the age of ten who could not earn a decent wage. One day, when his father tried to hang Charlie from a tree because he wanted to attend school rather than sell apples in the street, Charlie, then twelve, realized he was better off on his own. The eldest of six, he doubted his parents would long weep over his departure, or even much notice that he was gone.

His first few nights, two of them rain soaked, were spent under the Williamsburg Bridge. Alone and undeniably scared, he nevertheless recognized that he was on the brink of a great adventure. It was as if a veil had been torn away and he saw the city anew as a wonder of possibilities. There were plenty of other boys in his situation, and once they saw he could handle himself, they were happy to teach the quick-witted Charlie the skills he'd need for survival. From petty thievery—pinching a hard roll or picking pockets on Orchard Street—he graduated to shining shoes, then found a job in a local saloon, running booze to the poker room in back and keeping an eye out for cops not on the take.

Once the biblically old proprietress determined he could be trusted, the boy was led to a torn and stained mattress in the cellar where the old woman said he could sleep each night after he'd finished cleaning up. God knew where she'd found the mattress, but it must have been infested with lice, because before long Charlie found countless numbers of the varmints crawling through his thick wavy black hair and across his scalp.

The old lady threw the mattress in the garbage and set it ablaze, then proceeded to shave Charlie's head and strip him naked, examining every inch of him as she scrubbed his skin raw. He had scant hair anywhere else on his slender body in which the little creatures might hide except for a patch above his already impressive manhood. She shaved him there as well, but showed no interest in his rising tumescence other than a wry comment that the boy was destined never to lack for company.

The next day, a well-dressed patron in his forties, who Charlie had seen playing poker in the back room several times before, called out for a drink. The fellow had already made a strong impression on the youngster. For besides the fine suits he wore, never the same one twice, the man bore a certain resemblance to Charlie, blue eyes and dark wavy hair, or so the boy liked to think. But even more remarkable to Charlie was how the fellow moved and spoke and laughed with the confidence of someone accustomed to being treated with respect. On this particular night, the man, already deep in his cups, sat engrossed in the card game with a huge pile of cash in front of him. When he called for a drink, Charlie rushed over with a bottle of good English gin. The swell, who had never seemed to notice Charlie before, turned and looked at the lanky boy a moment, puzzled.

"You the kid works here all the time?"

Charlie could hear the drink in the man's otherwise refined speech. He nodded.

"What happened to your hair?" the man asked with a lopsided smirk.

Charlie blushed, suddenly embarrassed. "What's it to you?" he retorted.

The man laughed. "Nothing, young fella, nothing at all. But I've got a lot riding on this hand, so would you mind if I rubbed that bald head of yours for luck?"

Charlie thought a moment, then shrugged in agreement.

The man rubbed Charlie's head roughly, then pushed most of his money to the center of the table. "I'll see your fifty, boys," he said, "and raise you two hundred."

Charlie watched intently. All but one of the other four players judged the fellow a bluffer and saw his raise. The man smiled broadly and laid down his cards, revealing a full house, kings over jacks. The pot, well over a thousand dollars, was his. Elated, he turned to Charlie, laughing, and planted a big kiss on the boy's head.

"You're my lucky charm, kid!" The man handed Charlie a twenty, more money than the boy had ever held in his life. "That's for you."

The other men at the table were grumbling that money always comes to money, and that a swell like him had no business coming downtown to take advantage of a bunch of poor workingmen.

Then the man did the most extraordinary thing Charlie had ever seen. He took the cash he'd just won and tossed it back into the middle of the table. "You're right, boys," he said. "It's all yours. Just make sure you don't fight over it!"

Charlie's eyes went wide. "Jeez, mister, you sure you want to do that?"

The man smiled. "What, you think 'cause I'm a little drunk I don't know what I'm doing? Believe me, kid, I don't come here for the money."

Charlie was puzzled. "For what then, the gin?"

The man's laughter erupted again, straight from his belly. "No, son. I come for the education!" The man shook his head, looking at Charlie with pleasure. "You're something else, you know that? Tell me about yourself. Who are your people?"

Charlie had no interest in his past, so he held his head up proudly and said, "I have no people. I'm an orphan."

The man took another long look at Charlie, his face serious. "Is that so?" he demanded, but it didn't sound like a question, so Charlie did not respond. The man then pushed himself away from the table and marched up to the old lady. Charlie watched as hushed words were exchanged and a big wad of cash appeared from the man's pocket. The fellow kept peeling off bill after bill to hand to the woman. Finally, she leaned in to whisper something in the man's ear. He looked hard at the old hag, as if he were about to lose his temper, then suddenly he laughed again, harder by far than he had up to that point, and he handed her the rest of the money with a shrug.

The old woman came up to Charlie and told him that he was no longer welcome at the saloon, and that his only choice now was to go live with the man, who had been kind enough to offer to take the boy in. Charlie thought a moment as he glanced over at his new benefactor, who was now talking to a girl at the bar. There was no reason to protest, really. He hated the basement and the old lady and the way she smelled. Besides, he was curious about this man and how it was that he could possibly be so careless with money.

Charlie expected to leave immediately. Instead, the man disappeared with the woman, and Charlie fell asleep in a corner of the bar. He had a further dim recollection of a long, drowsy car ride north. He awoke in a large comfortable bed in a darkened room, his head resting on a feather pillow. Through leaded glass windows to his left, he could see that it was still night.

Suddenly, he realized that he was not alone. Just beside the bed sat the man, wide awake, staring at him. Charlie must have recoiled instinctually, because the man reached out to touch Charlie's arm lightly.

"I'm sorry if I startled you," the man said soothingly. "I . . ." He laughed, apparently still somewhat drunk. "I was just watching you sleep." The man gazed at him with a faraway look. "It amazes me that anyone could sleep so soundly."

Charlie looked around, suddenly panicked. What was this place? There were heavy drapes on the windows. The ceiling was high and dark, with all kinds of grotesque animals carved in wood. The stained glass windows beside the bed were narrow, too small for easy escape, and the covers under which he lay suddenly felt heavy. He threw them back to find himself still fully clothed and jumped out of bed. The man reached for him again, clutching his arm.

"No, no," the man insisted, "you mustn't be afraid. Please, you don't understand."

"Oh, I understand plenty," Charlie declared, pulling his arm away. Charlie knew about fairies, knew what they liked to do, and that they'd pay good money if you'd let them do it. Was this fellow one of them? He didn't seem to be, but Charlie wasn't going to let anyone stare at him like that, like an animal in a zoo. His eyes searched frantically for the door.

"No, I'll . . . I'll let you be." The man grabbed at him again, clumsily. "Don't go. I want you to sleep. I want . . . really, I was just—"

And fourteen-year-old Charlie slugged the grown man in the jaw. It must have been a lucky punch coupled with the effect of the drink, because the man went down like a felled tree. Charlie bent close to make sure he was still breathing, then rifled his pockets to take what he could, around sixty dollars.

Charlie jumped to his feet, found the door, and made his exit. From the relatively small bedroom, he entered into a huge interior space and he paused a moment, awestruck. The long carved mahogany balustrade, the paintings and statues, the vaulted ceilings, and the wide set of stone stairs leading down to the front door all made him think of a church. Charlie now understood why the man had given back the money, for he must have had all the money in the world. Gathering himself, the boy raced down the stairs and out the wide front door, running across Fifth Avenue and into Central Park.

Charlie never saw his would-be benefactor again. He never went back to the bar, nor did he return to Central Park for a very long time, fearful of what might happen if he chanced to bump into the man. But as the years passed, and the memory and the fear both faded, Charlie would from time to time find himself uptown. As he walked along Fifth Avenue, he wondered in which of the many mansions he had almost spent a night, and what his life might have been like had he stayed put.

# THIRTEEN

Shortly after his inauguration as twenty-eighth president of the United States in January 1914, a grateful Woodrow Wilson appointed Franklin Roosevelt, then only thirty-one years old, to the post of assistant secretary of the Navy. Fifth cousin to former president Teddy Roosevelt and married to Teddy's niece, Franklin had given support at the Democratic National Convention the year before that had helped to secure Wilson's nomination. And though Franklin was known far and wide as a callow playboy, the handsome aristocrat proved himself well suited to his new role. He had great energy, and his surprising administrative abilities proved invaluable during the trying times of the World War.

Like his cousin Teddy, who he admired immensely and in whose footsteps he longed to follow, Franklin fancied himself a reformer, so he seemed a good match for his direct boss, Secretary of the Navy Josephus Daniels. Daniels was a strong advocate of prohibition and had banned alcohol from all Navy ships in 1914, replacing it with grape juice. The secretary also supported the Catholic Decency

League in its crusade against prostitution, and so convinced Congress to pass a law making it a federal offense to foster any "immoral condition" within five miles of a military base.

Roosevelt was not himself such a prig. As long as there had been warriors, any man of the world had to acknowledge, so had there been camp followers, but the assistant secretary convinced himself that a reduction of their numbers and the outbreaks of pernicious disease did not seem unreasonable.

There was of course the more problematic issue of sodomy, which had bedeviled navies from time immemorial. The choice had always been either turning a blind eye or calling attention to the issue by attempting to weed out the worst offenders. Since no one wanted to discuss the subject even in the best of times, discretion seemed to Roosevelt to be the better part of valor, especially during full-scale mobilization. More importantly, there were certain things of which the general public best not be made aware. Though the Sedition Act had put the press firmly under government control, scandal had a way of metastasizing through various means of its own.

But Newport was a special case. Twenty-five thousand sailors at a facility meant to house four thousand, mingling cheek-by-jowl with the world-renowned summer colony, members of his own class, the wealthiest of whom often made a virtue out of excess and all forms of vice—ingredients that had conspired to bring the issue front and center. Exposure and scandal was a risk, it seemed, even if he did nothing, so why not at least give the investigation a chance? If properly handled, it might have put just enough of the fear of God into everyone to tamp the fires of wickedness back down to an acceptable level. Little did Roosevelt anticipate, however, that arrests would be made amongst the civilian population, and of a popular priest no less. An Episcopalian to boot, and tried in a civilian court!

It must have been a long night on the train from Providence

down to the nation's capital, for the two men presently standing before Roosevelt looked anxious and sweat soaked. They were peculiar and far too serious, and Roosevelt judged them to be, at best, mediocrities. How the running of this undercover operation had fallen to them, he hadn't a clue, but unless it ended here, there was a chance that it could tarnish his newly respectable résumé. Careers were destroyed by things like this, and Roosevelt's had only just begun. Their unexpected appearance was alarming, but it had provided the perfect opportunity for him to put them in their places.

"You assured me, gentlemen," Roosevelt intoned indignantly, "that you had solid evidence. Otherwise, I would never have allowed this to go forward!"

"We did, sir!" Chief Arnold, the taller, distinctly unpleasant-looking one, protested in a gruff voice. "We do! The other two men didn't even get to testify!"

Roosevelt placed a cigarette in a long enameled holder and lit up. "The charges against the reverend have been dismissed," Roosevelt reminded them. "And frankly, as a coreligionist, I'm relieved."

The more bookish-looking of the pair, Lieutenant Hudson, a naval doctor, leaned forward to speak. "Acquitted on *state* charges, sir. There's a *federal* statute, passed during the war, that makes it a federal offense to foster any kind of immoral condition within ten miles of a military base—"

"It's five miles, Lieutenant Hudson. I'm well aware of the statute," Roosevelt said, putting the man in his place.

"Of course, sir, pardon me. My point is, sir, that Kent could be tried again in a federal district court in Providence by a competent judge before a truly impartial jury."

"The charges were never disproved, Mr. Secretary!" Arnold insisted. "He was acquitted on a technicality."

"Entrapment," Roosevelt said pointedly, "is hardly a technicality. Is it true, then, that your men were ordered to do . . . what, what the defense attorney implied? As a doctor, Lieutenant Hudson, you of all people . . ."

Hudson squirmed.

"It's an absolute lie!" Arnold interjected, protesting. "My boys are no angels—what sailors are?—but versus that collar of his, we didn't stand a chance. All his do-gooding, who in that town would have believed this of him? He could have killed his own mother and gotten away with it!"

Roosevelt scrutinized both of them in silence. Hudson seemed nervous and eager to leave the room, but Arnold was adamant.

"Very well," Roosevelt said finally. "I'll assume good intentions and we'll consider the entire affair at an end. Thank you for coming all the way down to Washington. Have a good trip back." And he dismissed them with a nod.

But Arnold did not move. He appeared to be frozen in place. Hudson grabbed at the bigger man's arm and tried to fill the uncomfortable silence with farewells. "Thank you for your time, Mr. Secretary, thank you," Hudson muttered, but Arnold would not budge.

"Mr. Secretary, sir," Arnold queried, "why'd we win the war, do you think?"

Roosevelt looked at him, perplexed. "Because we had better tanks."

"No, sir, we won because we've got something in our gut that tells us right from wrong. The Europeans are finished; they're all rotted out morally. Are we gonna let that same sickness infect us? These fairies, it's just the beginning."

What was he talking about? Roosevelt wondered. "I'm not sure a military historian would agree with you, Mr. Arnold, but I have to admit, you speak with great fervor. You should consider a career in politics. Now, if you gentlemen would—"

Arnold leaned in abruptly, his big hands firmly planted on Roosevelt's desk. "Hear me out, sir, please!"

Roosevelt did not flinch. "Get off my desk," he said icily, "before I call for my adjutant."

Arnold straightened up, giving Roosevelt some breathing room, but the fire in his eyes did not dim.

"Very well," Roosevelt said. "Speak your piece."

"I had an older brother, sir. Navy. Finest man you'd ever want to meet. Had a few bad breaks with women, fell in with the wrong crowd." Arnold fought back emotion as he related his tale. "Once those fellows got through with him, he was never the same. Took to drink, then disappeared altogether. Broke my poor mother's heart."

Roosevelt had to acknowledge the genuine pain that Arnold seemed to feel over his lost brother, lost as surely as if he'd gone missing in war.

"I've made it my mission in life to hunt these fellows down, and I *know* this priest is queer, sir!" Arnold said with wrenching conviction. He wiped at his eyes. "We can't stand by and allow his type to pollute any more fine, young Americans!"

The assistant secretary sighed and observed the horrid creature before him. The man was uncouth and took up far more space in the room than he deserved, but how could Roosevelt dismiss his heartfelt story? He too had seen good men fall to decadence. If there was indeed evidence that this man Kent was abusing his position for unsavory ends, then it was a terrible crime deserving of punishment. The attorney general's office for the First District Court was not likely to prosecute without just cause. Roosevelt would leave it up to them.

"I will speak with the prosecutor's office. If I can be convinced that there are sufficient grounds for these new charges, you may proceed with the support of the Navy Department."

Roosevelt watched the unseemly smile spread across Arnold's face.

"But if not," Roosevelt continued as a warning, "you will drop this, utterly and completely. Are we agreed?"

Arnold nodded. "Agreed, sir. And my men?"

"As before, your work falls under the auspices of the Office of Naval Intelligence. I will therefore continue to guarantee their immunity from prosecution." Roosevelt looked away. "May God forgive me."

———

The train pulled into Providence's Union Station just as the summer sun was beginning to set. Amidst billows of steam and the last of the workaday crowd, Arnold hopped off the train toward the three men who had been awaiting his arrival. Hudson had remained in New York, where he and Arnold had stopped for a day and a night in the hopes of launching a similar operation amongst the society of fairies in that modern-day Babylon. New York was the source, they had determined, the open door that allowed easy entry to the worst the world had to offer. Kent had come to Newport from the city, where moral values were a cause for ridicule, where so-called decent women drank and smoked and bared their bodies, and where desperate men learned to debase themselves with the queers who hung around the honky-tonks on the Bowery.

And New York had plenty of sailors, with enough good men amongst them, he was sure, to recruit a disciplined cadre of undercover operators. It had been a blessing, Arnold realized, losing the first trial, for now they were able to prosecute Kent on federal charges, thereby establishing a precedent for the nationwide operation that Arnold and Hudson had always envisioned. It was within his grasp, he felt certain. He simply needed to bring Kent's trial to a successful conclusion, and the tide of public opinion, once awakened to the extent of the depravity right in their midst, would surge in his direction.

Rudy stood on the platform beside Dostalick, snapping to attention and raising a salute as Arnold approached.

"At ease, sailor." Arnold eyed the civilian beside Rudy, a mid-forties man in an expensive coat and tie who looked suspiciously like a lawyer.

"Welcome back, Chief," Rudy said with a grin.

"Who's he?" Arnold grumbled, though he could as easily have asked the man himself.

The chief could see the man was annoyed by his slight, but the stranger covered it with a stiff smile and extended hand. "Joseph Cawley, U.S. Attorney for the First District."

Arnold shook Cawley's much smaller hand without enthusiasm.

Cawley continued. "Lieutenant Hudson phoned me from New York with the good news."

"I'd say I was glad to meet you, Mr. Cawley," Arnold growled, "but my opinion of lawyers has sunk to an all-time low."

"Well, then," Cawley announced, upbeat, "it's up to me to change all that, isn't it?"

"We'll see," Arnold said. "You think you got what it takes to put this pervert behind bars?"

"I've reviewed the transcripts and depositions. The prosecutor in Newport was clearly out of his depth. The defense attorney seems bright, but he has no experience in federal court. I doubt he's up to the challenge. Moreover, the federal statute has a much broader reach than the state sodomy charge. As long as we all work as a team"—he regarded the two sailors with the slightest hint of skepticism—"I have every confidence that your faith in lawyers will be restored."

Arnold turned to his men. "Are we a team, boys?"

"Yes, sir!" he replied, as if reciting from a catechism.

Arnold glanced down at the lawyer. "Well, Mr. Cawley?"

"I'll speak with Secretary Roosevelt's office tomorrow morning," Cawley replied officiously, "and have an arrest warrant issued by the afternoon."

"That's fine." Arnold gave a broad smile. "And while you're at it, I want you to deputize me and my men here. This time, I intend to make the arrest myself."

—•—•—

"Least we each got our own cell," Hospital Apprentice Second Class Harry Trubshaw said, offering a weak smile as he tried to look on the bright side. "Guess they figure we'd do something evil if they put us in together."

Reverend Kent, a free man, stood on the other side of the bars. Only the gentle motion of Narragansett Bay beneath them gave Kent any sense that he was aboard a ship. In all other ways, the USS *Boxer* was indeed a prison, with its two rows of small cells facing one another across a narrow aisle. One deck below the waterline, the place was dank and without portholes. Caged bulbs hung every three feet along the low ceiling of the center aisle, casting zebra-striped shadows through the prison bars. It had been two months now since Harry, along with sixteen other sailors, had been arrested, charged, and imprisoned here to await court-martial. According to the Uniform Code of Military Justice, the crime of sodomy with which Harry and the others had been charged carried a likely sentence of thirty years' hard labor at the military prison at Fort Leavenworth, Kansas. And as yet, neither Harry nor any of his cohorts had spoken to or been assigned a lawyer.

Kent wondered how he might help these men. He knew that the military was its own world, with its own system of justice. Perhaps he would speak to William about it, though he was loath to further burden this man who had already done so much for him.

"You shouldn't be here, Reverend," Harry insisted. "People might get the wrong idea."

"Nonsense, Harry. It's my job to assure those who've lost hope that they're not forgotten. Besides, *my* ordeal is over. It's you and the other men we have to think about now."

Harry sighed. "Wasn't for you, Reverend, wouldn't be nobody coming to see us. Sometimes I wonder if anyone even knows we're here, my family, anybody. Or maybe it's just that they don't *want* to know." Harry fell silent for a moment. "It's not like I killed anybody or stole something. I try to be a good person. I've helped a lot of people, I think."

"Yes, you have, Harry, many people."

"So, then, why do folks hate me so much, Reverend, me and the others? Can you tell me? 'Cause I don't understand."

Simply put, thought Kent, a simple question that defied simple answers, a question for the ages. One might as well ask why men go to war. Instinct would instruct us to hate those who practice hatred, but if we truly wish to understand the actions of others, we must stand in their shoes. How does one practice compassion toward the wickedly unjust and still fight injustice? Like many men of conscience, Kent had wrestled with this dilemma. Now, he had been asked to resolve it, at least to the extent that he might bring some comfort to this boy. He began slowly.

"People grow accustomed to certain things, Harry: that day will follow night, that the ground will be solid beneath their feet, that those around them will behave in predictable ways. Then something happens, the earth moves, the sky turns dark at midday, someone different appears in their midst, and they're suddenly reminded of how little in this vast universe they understand or control. It's a fear that we all harbor, I think, secretly, that life is arbitrary, that what we believe and build amounts to nothing, and that ultimately it's death that awaits us around every corner. And until people can banish or explain away or assign blame for the inconsistency of life, it makes them very uncomfortable." Kent paused, breathing a deep sigh. "I think it must be God's way of leading us to Him, giving us a glimpse of how much we've yet to learn. It's not meant to frighten us, but rather to encourage us to be more."

Harry nodded vaguely, as if this answer made some sense to him. "So, then, God," the young man asked, just as simply, "well, does He hate us, too, do you think?"

"*Never* believe that, Harry!" Kent said with genuine and immediate conviction. "People use the name of God to justify many horrible things. But *my* God, the God who died on the cross, who told us to love our neighbors as ourselves? No, Harry, He could never hate you, not for simply being who you are."

# FOURTEEN

Small "private saloons" such as this had begun popping up that summer, hidden down dark narrow alleyways, in the backs of warehouses, in the stockrooms of grocery stores, even in the basements of people's homes. By January 1919, two-thirds of the states had ratified the Eighteenth Amendment, the number required to establish prohibition as the law of the land. By the end of February, only Rhode Island, New Jersey, and Connecticut held out against the great social experiment and the paradise its supporters predicted.

The Puritans too had envisioned the establishment of a moral utopia in New England. But even they, in their voyage toward Plymouth Rock, had provisioned the *Mayflower*'s cargo hold with forty-two tons of beer and only *fourteen* tons of water. Virtue, it appeared, had always had its limits.

And so it was a raucous summer in Newport. The country had been given a year to prepare, but everyone knew that come next January, as 1920 ushered in a new decade, Rhode Island too would be forced to fall in line and criminalize the consumption of alcohol.

No one really believed that anybody who liked to drink would actually stop, on that day or any other. They simply looked to the future with a mischievous sort of excitement, embracing the newly forbidden nature of an old vice as little more than an added source of intoxication.

"I got you all set up," Charlie crowed. "She's right over there."

Barker peered through the crowd of drunken servicemen to catch a glimpse of Dottie standing near the bar.

Charlie pulled off his sweaty T-shirt. "It's like the fucking Philippines in here."

"She . . . she doesn't look happy," Barker complained.

Charlie laughed. "Kid, if you hang your hopes on the happiness of women, you're in for a miserable life." He took Barker by the arm and pulled him through the crowd toward Dottie.

"But . . . but she's your . . . she's your girl, Charlie," Barker resisted feebly. "Why . . . why would you . . . ?"

Charlie had asked himself the same question a dozen times: Why was he handing over the best piece of ass he'd ever had, a woman he actually cared for, to another fellow? Because it was Barker, that was why, and after all Charlie had put him through, he wanted to do right by the kid. Dottie was the only one Charlie could trust to take care of the job properly.

"'Cause it's your first time. And I want it to be special for you."

"Was . . . was your first time . . . ?" Barker asked. "What was . . . ?"

"She was fat and fifty and smelled like old cheese and I still loved every minute of it."

"So . . . ?"

"So, you ain't me," Charlie snorted.

"I . . . I don't know, Charlie," Barker pleaded.

Charlie stopped and looked his young friend square in the eyes. "Listen to me. All that pent-up energy you feel, all that power you sometimes dream you have, that crazy hardness in your dick night and day, as if it had a life and a mind all its own, I promise you, all that will suddenly make sense once you're inside a woman. And for a little while, you'll feel like one thing instead of a dozen different voices in your head."

Charlie paused a moment to let the message sink into Barker's brain. It seemed like the boy had stopped breathing.

"So," Charlie resumed, "you wanna be a man, or not?"

Barker looked mesmerized. After a moment, he nodded.

"All right, then."

They approached Dottie. Her arms were crossed, her mouth was set, and she was fuming. But as soon as she caught sight of Barker, Charlie could see her starting to soften.

"Preston Barker is his name," Charlie offered, then, to Barker, "This is Dottie."

"He's just a baby," she said in dismay.

"He's seventeen," Charlie protested. "I was only fourteen first time I got laid."

"Yeah, well," Dottie sneered. "Oughta be a law against the likes of you hanging around with the likes of him."

She leaned in and smiled at Barker. "What do you have on him, kid? Must be something big, 'cause I never known this man to do a thing for anybody but himself, so there must be an angle in it somewhere." She looked at Charlie, raising an eyebrow. "Or could it be that you're growing a heart, Charlie McKinney? *That* would be simply too much to bear!"

Charlie smirked. "You wish," he said flatly. "You and every other broad," he added, and as soon as it left his mouth, he knew that he'd said the wrong thing.

"What do you gotta say things like that for, Charlie?" she complained, a hurt look in her eyes. "'Specially when I'm about to do you a favor."

Dottie *did* care for him then, which made Charlie feel good, which in turn made him feel bad. They *all* fell for him. Why should it matter that this particular woman had as well?

It did matter, though, which made it that much more important that he not be in her debt. "A favor, is it?" Charlie asked. "Don't worry, I'll leave a little extra for you on the nightstand," he added, offhand.

"Bastard," she hissed. "Like a knife in my heart." She put on her game face. "All right, I'll do it. Why not? But on one condition."

"Yeah?" Butterflies had suddenly invaded his stomach.

"I want you there," she said, a clear challenge.

He looked at her, curious.

"I want you to see me fuck this boy all night, again and again," she continued. "I want you to hear me moan. I want you to see that what I do with you, I've done with a hundred men before, and will do with a hundred men after you're gone."

He waited for the phrase that he knew was coming, three little words that summed up the unique bond between them.

"You're nothing special," she declared.

Even this far away, he could feel her heart racing.

Charlie did not want to think about the day when he'd be gone, about the night when Dottie would no longer be in his bed. He suspected that these were the best days of his life. But he knew, like she did, that one day they would be over. His eyes offered a weary smile of recognition. "D'you think maybe you and I were separated at birth?"

"I wouldn't be a bit surprised," she whispered, and she headed off to do what she had done with so many men before. Only this time, for the boy's sake, she would try to recall a time when she hadn't hated them all quite so much.

---

Little Dottie McCann realized early on how meager the prospects were in Belfast for a poor Catholic girl like herself. When Dottie was just seven years old her mother died of consumption, a disease as common as the cold in those years in Dublin, Dottie's birthplace. This left the pretty young girl and her four siblings, three older brothers and a younger sister, in the care of their father, a great lover of Guinness, who promptly disappeared for points unknown, presumably north since he himself had Protestant roots and, it was said, a family of some means. Her twelve-year-old brother, Brendan, being the eldest of the crew, decided they should go off in search of the man and force him to live up to his responsibilities. And so Brendan scraped together what pennies he could from local friends and relations, all of whom were more than pleased to see the five young ones leave town. Brendan was well aware of this and knew how to play it to his advantage. He also knew that these people, in all fairness, had to save their own children from famine and disease, and so he did not resent the encouragement they offered in favor of the children's foggy quest.

Clutching their meager funds and the few clues they held to their father's origins—an ancient railway ticket from the north to Dublin dated a year before Brendan's birth, and their parents' marriage certificate, stating their father's birthplace as Sandy Row, Belfast—the children headed north.

Surprisingly, Brendan did find their father, two weeks after their arrival when they were at the very end of their resources, in a pub in that same neighborhood of Sandy Row. It was a tearful reunion, the father begging forgiveness for abandoning them, claiming his extreme grief at the loss of his darling bride as an excuse, and promising to come collect them the following day, saying he could not face the younger ones in his current state of drunkenness. Or this was at least how the excited Brendan described the meeting to his siblings later that night as they rejoiced at the prospect of being a family once more.

Their father was of course never heard from again. Not a trace could be found of him, nor of any wealthy relations, close or distant, and it was not long before the children were evicted from the tiny room they had been occupying. Trying to keep them alive (youngest sister Megan had already developed a bad hacking cough) until he could come up with a plan to return them to the familiarity of Dublin, Brendan resorted to petty theft, for which he proved to have scant ability. He was quickly caught and brought before the magistrate, and when he explained the pitiable reasons for his actions, the other children were promptly rounded up and they all were deposited in two local Protestant orphanages, the boys in one, Dottie and Megan in another. Megan's cough worsened, and she was diagnosed with consumption, isolated from Dottie, and shortly followed her mother to the grave. It was more than a year after Megan's death that Dottie was informed that Brendan too had died of the family illness. She never heard from or of her other two brothers again.

The orphanage was a Dickensian place, Dottie would later realize when she began to read Dickens, and the fact that she'd been baptized a Catholic, or that she was developing into a lovely, shapely, and naturally vivacious young woman, did not make her life any easier. She was regularly informed that if she did not do exactly as the mistresses said, she was likely to become a whore, and she was often beaten with a strap for the simple fact that she was growing full breasts, or because severe menstrual cramps prevented her from doing her assigned chores.

So, just shy of her eighteenth birthday, Dottie was pleased to accept the offer of a position as a domestic in the home of a wealthy Boston family. Dottie was a good reader (an above-average education being the sole benefit of the Protestant orphanage system), devouring in her youth not only the works of Dickens but also of her countryman Bernard Shaw, of Shakespeare, Milton, and, under cover of secrecy, Marx. She arrived in the New World a "Fabian" socialist, and made sure she was awake when her ship slipped into New York Harbor at dawn.

As they sailed past Lady Liberty, she recited the words of Emma Lazarus quietly to herself, "Give me your tired, your poor, your huddled masses . . ." and she looked forward to a bold new start in this mythical land, or as the Great Emancipator, Abraham Lincoln, had named it, "the last best hope of earth."

It wasn't long, however, before Dottie found herself put-upon by the upstanding father of the home in which she was employed. It started as mild flirtation on his part, which she had failed to discourage, and had in fact enjoyed, since she had never known what it was like to be flattered or paid attention to by a man. But the father, a handsome businessman of forty who had married above his station, mistook her smiles and blushes as encouragement. As his advances grew more aggressive and frequent, Dottie realized that she was in over her head. It never got so far as rape, though it might have on one occasion in the basement of the large Back Bay mansion, had Dottie been less quick on her feet. But she was sure that things were headed in that direction.

Panicked, Dottie turned to the only ally she thought she might have, the lady of the house, a kind woman of obviously high birth who seemed devoted to her four children. Flustered and inarticulate, Dottie tried to tell the aristocratic lady what had almost happened and was met with a calm, concerned response and a promise to look into the matter.

That night as she lay in bed, Dottie gave thanks for the marked improvement in her life. At the orphanage, had she dared to raise even a peep of protest about any sort of mistreatment, she would have been summarily beaten and stripped of privileges. Now, although the circumstances she found herself in were uncomfortable and confusing and likely to result in her having to find another position, she had not been punished for speaking her mind. She had in fact been treated with consideration by a clearly compassionate and enlightened woman.

At that moment, the door to Dottie's room burst open and in stormed the cook, a fat hag of fifty or more who had barely spoken two words to Dottie since her arrival a month before. The cook began shouting at Dottie, calling her a worthless liar and telling her that she'd better have her things together and be out of the house in thirty minutes or there'd be hell to pay. Dottie was nothing if not honest and the implication infuriated her. She began shouting in response and threatening to go to the authorities with her story. The thickset cook, English and of the London lower classes from the sound of it, called Dottie a "rotten mick" and warned her that if she dared to attempt any such thing, the mister and missus would see to it that Dottie was instantly deported, sent back to the filthy "whorehouse" from which she'd come.

Finding herself on the street on a cold Boston night, Dottie supposed that it had indeed been the *men* of earth, not the women, to whom Lincoln had been offering his promise of hope.

In the months that followed, Dottie tried factory work, but the slave wages and hellish working conditions, not to mention the mind-numbing exhaustion, made her feel like little more than a footnote in one of the many socialist tracts she'd read. She met a young man at the factory who had charmed her with his promises of a future together "out west," but once she had fully given over to his advances in a moment of lackluster passion, he discarded her, and in her humiliation and rage she left the factory, never to return.

Hungry, and with her innocence already compromised in more ways than one, Dottie unceremoniously decided upon the street as her best option among the very few that remained open to her. It afforded her some freedom at least, she reckoned, and a modicum of power in her dealings with men. The experience with the young cad at the factory, though hardly memorable, had not been unpleasant, and she was certain she could endure it again as required.

It was not long, however, before the downside of her choice revealed itself amidst the brutal competition in Boston's tough West End. Girls just a few years older than Dottie had already been worn thin, so when one of them bragged of her plans to travel the hundred or so miles to picturesque Newport, where thousands of sailors and soldiers filled the local military outposts and a girl could ply her trade free of the pimps, Dottie packed her few things and moved south in time for Christmas 1916. It was indeed a lovely town, historic and friendly and oddly tolerant, with the sea on all sides, and the fantastic palaces of the wealthy to stroll by and dream upon.

By the time America entered the Great War in April of the following year, and the town was literally overrun with men in Navy blues, Dottie was well established, living in a cheery little rooming house off Thames Street with a reliable clientele that came to her largely through referrals. She preferred the sailors, because most of them were trainees at the war college and so were young, inexperienced, and more than willing to let her run the show.

With the war had come the Catholic Decency League, determined to close the saloons and clear the hookers from the streets of Newport. "Good luck on them," Dottie opined. With thirty thousand men on the hunt, the League was courting open mutiny against their crusade, and riots in the streets. In the end, that particular scourge merely served to thin the competition of the more obvious and less quick-witted of her sisters, allowing Dottie to raise her rates.

The next hurricane to hit was the Spanish flu, which halted business altogether for a brief few weeks as people cowered in their homes or bunks or hammocks, terrified to take a breath in public. But the face of Death, however gruesome, always brings forth its opposite, and Nature, in the guise of eighteen-year-old boys, *will* have Her say, no matter the risk.

Through it all Dottie had endured, by luck, by her superior wits, and by her unshakable belief in the Marxist theory of dialectical materialism. One fine autumn day, Dottie awoke to find that she had achieved a genuine victory of sorts, that she had come to like herself and the principles she seemed to stand for—brutal honesty, kindness to the weak, and a firm belief in her right to care for herself by whatever means necessary.

# FIFTEEN

I t was no use.

Charlie sat across the room in his skivvies, hard as a rock from the moment Dottie had started to unbutton. But for Barker, it had all been a hopeless muddle. No matter what Dottie did, with her hand, her mouth, her whispers in his ear, she couldn't coax an erection out of the kid.

In his heated state, Charlie's first response was relief that a potential rival had been neutralized. Then he remembered who it was, and joy was swiftly replaced by pain and embarrassment for his friend.

*What was I thinking?* Charlie asked himself. How could a shy kid like Barker rise to the occasion with another man watching from the corner like a seething referee? Charlie had told Dottie that Barker was nothing like either of them. They should have just let the kid be, let him find his own way to some farm girl back in Iowa or Ohio or wherever the fuck he was from.

The fan creaked loudly once a revolution. Barker still lay atop Dottie, as if he'd died there. No one seemed able to move.

"It's so bloody hot," Dottie exclaimed. "No wonder you . . ."

Barker chose that moment to crawl off the woman and onto his side, facing away from his companions and toward the door as if longing for escape.

Dottie looked at Charlie and shook her head at him bitterly. Then she reached out and gently stroked Barker's damp hair.

"No matter, boy-o," she cooed. "Lots of fellas have trouble their first time." She laughed gently. "And not just their first time neither."

But Barker did not acknowledge her words or tender touch in any way. He was inconsolable.

Dottie looked at Charlie, desperate for help. Charlie sighed, rose from his chair, and crossed to sit on the edge of the bed nearest Barker. He looked down at the boy's face.

"She's right, kid. Forget it," Charlie said, dismissing the whole incident. "It's no big deal."

Barker looked up at his friend tentatively.

"Truth is"—Charlie braced himself for the lie to come—"it's even happened to me."

Finally, a light of hope seemed to dawn in Barker's eyes.

"A woman's body is real different," Charlie purred. "Especially"— Charlie smiled and winked at the younger man—"when all you're used to is jerking off."

Barker managed a weak smile in response.

"It's like a whole different world," Charlie resumed. "Want a tour?"

Barker looked at him, confused.

"Turn around," Charlie urged. "Towards Dottie."

After a moment's hesitation, Barker did as he was told, turning his body and pressing himself up against Dottie's left side. Charlie went around to lie on her right, then reached over and gently took hold of his friend's left hand.

"There's lots to get used to about a woman," Charlie continued as he moved Barker's hand to Dottie's left breast. "Lots to explore. Gotta learn to make love to every part."

Dottie looked at their joined mitts. "Charlie, what—"

"Shhh!" he cooed in her ear as he gently encouraged Barker to manipulate Dottie's full, firm tit. "Her bosom," Charlie instructed as he began to nuzzle her right breast, laving and biting. Once he'd seen to it that both nipples were hard, Charlie guided Barker's hand down to the little mound around Dottie's navel. "Her belly," Charlie whispered as he moved their hands in a slow circle, just barely touching her hair down there. Finally, Charlie pulled the boy's hand to the space between her legs, already noticeably wetter than the rest of her. "Her thighs," he purred as their fingers entered her.

Dottie let out a little gasp.

"Pretty soon there'll be nothing in the world more natural for you." Charlie knew that he now had Barker's full attention, that he'd gotten the boy's mind off his recent humiliation.

"Uh-oh," said Dottie. "*Some*one's hard."

"No shit," said Charlie, ready to burst.

"I didn't mean *you*, big shot," quipped Dottie.

Charlie looked at Barker, surprised. "Attaboy," Charlie said with a smile, any sense of rivalry long since vanished. Instead, he felt relieved for the kid. "What are you waiting for? Hop on up there."

Barker hesitated, looking at Dottie.

"Okay with you, Dot?" Charlie asked.

She nodded, and Barker awkwardly did as his mentor had instructed. Charlie tried to disengage their hands but this time it was Barker whose strength would not allow it as the young man slipped between Dottie's legs. After no more than ten or twelve thrusts, longer than Charlie had lasted his first time, the boy shuddered and moaned and spent himself inside Dottie, nearly breaking Charlie's clasped fingers in the process.

As Barker basked in the afterglow, Charlie was suddenly filled with an overwhelming sense of pride at the good deed he'd done. In the end, it had all worked out according to plan.

"Good, right?" he asked Barker. The boy nodded, his eyes glazed.

"Now, what do you say, buddy?" Charlie asked. "How about letting your old friend have a go?"

Barker looked at him, still a little bewildered. He released Charlie's hand, as if surprised to find it still attached to his own.

As Charlie maneuvered his way atop this body that he knew so well, fitting with it as if hollows had been carved out of his own, Dottie pulled his head close to hers and whispered, "I don't care what you say. I will love you forever for what you did for this boy tonight."

"Me?" he whispered back. "What about you?"

"Like you said," she cooed. "Separated at birth."

Forgetting Barker now as if he had never existed, they fell to devouring one another. They groaned and howled out their pleasure, until at last Charlie came so hard he thought he'd died. Totally spent, he fell asleep where he was, still wrapped inside her.

———•—•—•———

Barker rolled off, smelling everywhere of Dottie, his cock soft but still wet. As Charlie took his place, mounting and covering the woman with his broad torso, Barker was astounded by the force of his friend's lust, how the man's whole body seemed possessed by it, how the woman wrapped her arms and legs around him, the two merging into a rhythm of thrusts and moans, a dance so violent, so desperate at times it looked as though they meant to kill one another. Barker lost track of time, but he figured it must have been forty minutes or an hour before the pair, drenched in sweat, finally shuddered and cursed, their bodies wracked by simultaneous eruptions that dwarfed what Barker had felt. Shattered, the two lovers fell asleep where they lay. Sometime later Charlie rolled off, staking out a resting place between his lover and his friend.

More hours had passed since. Barker lay there, eyes wide, unable to sleep, turned away from Charlie. He had experienced an awaken-ing this night, as profound as any he had witnessed at his parents' Pentecostal church when he was a boy. On numerous occasions, a younger Barker had watched folks writhe on the floor, possessed by the Holy Spirit, then rise up again reborn as something entirely different. He'd never understood it before. Now, it suddenly made sense to him, for he too had begun this night as one thing and ended it as another.

Barker's transformation had occurred the moment Charlie had reached over and taken hold of his hand. As the man took him on a tour of breasts and belly and thighs, Barker had felt only the heat of Charlie's touch above, his friend's large, sure palm pressing against the back of Barker's own hand. It had been that touch which had gotten him hard, those fingers entwined with his own that had guided him to orgasm. Barker had awakened to a truth about him-self. It was Charlie that he desired, Charlie with whom he wanted to merge, to whom he wanted to cling for dear life. He was in love with his friend and always would be, and this simple truth, as Charlie had suggested earlier in a different context, had at last fastened up all the ragged ends of Barker's stumbling existence.

For an instant, his heart leaped at the sudden uncovering of its one, true desire. Then his mind took over, flashing back to the scene months ago, when the sailor at the Y had whispered strange offerings in his ear. Barker had understood enough to blush, and Charlie and the other men in their group had explained the rest in the months since. These descriptions had always been accompanied by laughter or disgust or wonder at how a fellow would want to degrade himself with another man. In the course of his duty, Barker had allowed several such men, fairies he now knew them to be, to drop to their knees to perform these degrading acts—degrading only to them, as he understood it—upon him. He did not especially enjoy it, often could not get hard, and in his own mind he had also wondered why they would want to do these things if they knew, as they must have known, that the consequence would be their permanent expulsion from the brotherhood of men.

Now, as a crushing need filled him to do all those things and more with Charlie, to taste and touch him in every way imaginable, he understood it fully. He didn't feel himself to be other than who he had been the day before, Preston Barker, the boy from Nebraska, the sailor who couldn't swim, the friend of Charlie and Claude. But he knew that he *was* different, knew that Charlie would label him a fairy, worthy of no more respect than any of the others. And so Barker resolved that Charlie must never know, vowing to take his secret to the grave rather than risk the loss of this man's friendship.

Then Charlie moved his left foot, bringing the tips of his three smallest toes into direct contact with Barker's right shin. Charlie was asleep and it meant nothing, Barker knew, but he figured it would be all right to enjoy it at least, enjoy that hot square inch of skin into which every drop of Barker now poured. He allowed himself to imagine what it would be like to touch the man elsewhere, to explore his friend's body the way they had explored Dottie's. Charlie had been so generous with Barker always, had even shared his woman with him. Was it possible that he would also be willing to share himself, to allow Barker, for whom he cared so much, to do to him what he had allowed strangers to do? No, he determined, it must never happen. Never even be thought of.

The man's scent filled Barker's nostrils and penetrated his skin, making it difficult to think. Just to gaze at Charlie; surely, he could allow himself that much. Slowly, Barker turned toward his friend, who lay on his back, his lovely chest rising and falling in the unhurried rhythm of slumber. A sheen of sweat glistened on his skin, calling out to be touched. Barker had seen Charlie sleep through reveille in a barracks full of shouting men. A gentle hand resting on his chest would not awaken him. Barker burned to reach out, felt he would die if he didn't, but with so much at stake, all that mattered to him in the world, how could he run the risk?

But what if this were his last chance? He knew he could never again allow himself to be naked with Charlie without giving himself away. If this then was indeed the one occasion he would ever have to touch his beloved, could he live with the knowledge that he had passed up that chance forever? A simple touch, that was all he wanted. And if he was caught, if Charlie awoke and threw his hand off and called him a fairy, then Barker would leave, and he would run as far away as he could so that they would never have to see one another again.

The boy reached out, his hand hovering just above the broad muscular chest. He could feel the heat radiating off his friend's body. He almost pulled away, but instead found the courage to rest it tentatively on Charlie's beating heart. When the man did not awaken, his breath still steady and even, Barker allowed his hand to settle, and a whole universe seemed to unfold across his palm and fingertips. If at that moment someone had suggested that the cost of this bliss would be his life, Barker would have judged it a good bargain.

—•—•—

Charlie had been dreaming of a steak dinner. He was seated in a fancy restaurant, dressed in finery, surrounded by swells, and he realized he'd better eat up, that once they knew his pockets were empty, he'd be out on his ass, or worse, sent to the kitchen to wash dishes. Suddenly he felt something; a rich woman had crawled under his table, had pulled out his dick and had begun to suck on it. At that moment, the headwaiter showed up with the bill. Charlie broke into a grin at the thought of his next move. He would stand, exposing himself and the woman.

Instead, he began to awaken, glad to find at least that the mouth was real and that he was approaching what promised to be a major climax. His fingers reached for Dottie's long blond hair, so that he could hold her there as he always did, her mouth against his pelvic bone as he shot. But instead his fingers found a sailor's bristly crew cut. A trick in an alley was one thing, but he never let a fairy share his bed. He looked down and between his legs he made out the unmistakable head of a boy. It didn't take him more than a moment of confusion to realize exactly who the boy was.

"Barker," he mumbled, hoping this was still a dream. "What the fuck . . . ?" Barker glanced up. Charlie's impulse was to kick him away, to put as much distance as he could between them, to prevent this from reaching its fast-approaching and irreversible conclusion. Maybe he could still turn over and fall back to sleep and in the morning, they'd fuck Dottie again and pretend this never happened. But as nature took hold, Charlie's limbs refused to obey and he ground his head back against the pillow, eyes squeezed shut, as Barker finished the job.

———•—•—•———

Sometime after dawn, a persistent pounding at the door yanked Charlie from sleep a second time. The bonds that had strung his dreams together dissolved, while the naked female at his side and the fan above reclaimed their place in his memory.

But as the dream world faded, another image, the craziest of all, stood fast. He struggled to shake it, but it was no use. The shock and revulsion, the bitter disappointment, the orgasm that had been wrested from him hit Charlie like a massive wave. He recalled Barker's expression afterward, a pathetic wordless appeal, his fumbling exit from the room as Charlie rolled on his side, pressing his spent dick against Dottie's comforting behind, and fell back into a heavy sleep.

Betrayal was a concept Charlie rarely entertained. Now, it cut across him like a long, sharp knife. But even more than betrayed, he felt stupid, incredibly, unbelievably stupid that he hadn't seen it coming, that he'd fallen for the kid's innocent act. How many other fellows had Barker done this with? Coming from the rough-and-tumble neighborhood that Charlie did, he had long understood fairies almost as well as he did women. He knew this was like an addiction to them, that they'd do it anytime, anywhere. What a fool he must have seemed defending the kid, covering for him with Arnold and Claude and the other guys, letting Barker tag along day and night wherever he went, like a lost dog. Barker was good. He'd fooled Charlie, not an easy thing to do, enough so that he'd been willing to share his woman with the kid, to help him become a man.

"McKinney!" a familiar male voice shouted over another fierce pounding on the door. "Wake the fuck up!"

It was Rudy, Charlie recognized. What the hell did he want? Charlie glanced over at the clock on the nightstand. Just shy of 7:00 a.m. Dottie stirred beside him.

"What is it, Charlie?" she asked dreamily.

"Nothing," he grumbled. "Go back to sleep."

"McKinney!" came another shout and a pound.

"All right, already, I'm coming! Cut it out, will ya!" Charlie stood and made his way to the door. He secured the chain and turned the knob to peer out at Bart Rudy, in full uniform, with Dostalick, the ventriloquist's dummy, hovering just behind him.

"Do you know what time it is?" Charlie demanded. "What the hell do you want? I'm busy."

"I bet," Rudy sneered. "Well, busy or not, you better throw a uniform over that sorry ass of yours and come with me. We got business."

"What kind of business?" Charlie demanded.

"We're arresting Kent," Dostalick piped up with some enthusiasm.

"What?" Charlie asked, confused.

Rudy glanced at his sidekick, annoyed. "Dostalick, will you shut up?" He snapped back to Charlie. "Look, McKinney, all you need to know is that the chief wants the whole crew down at Emmanuel Church by seven thirty. And that's an order." Rudy then lowered his voice to just above a whisper. "We don't want the pervert getting tipped off, so don't go blabbing any of this to anybody, like your whore in there." Rudy tried to peer into the room.

"Watch your fucking mouth, Rudy." Charlie slammed the door in the man's face.

"All right, McKinney," Rudy yelled through the closed door. "Have it your way. You got your orders. Seven thirty. Twenty-five minutes from now. You don't show up, it's *your* ass, not mine."

Confounded, Charlie stood facing the door a moment as the footsteps of the two men faded down the hall.

"What is it, Charlie?" asked Dottie, sitting up in bed. "What's wrong?" She looked around. "Where's your friend?"

"Who?" He turned to her, distracted. "Oh, you mean Barker? Left." Charlie collected his Navy blues from off the floor and proceeded to dress.

Dottie sat up, wrapping herself in the sheet. "Who was that at the door?"

"Guys from my unit," he said as he buttoned up his fly. It felt to him as if his worlds were suddenly starting to collide, and that would make them much harder to manage.

"What did they want?" she demanded.

"Not much," he tossed off, avoiding her gaze. He found his shirt and pulled it on as he slipped into his shoes. "It's just that something I thought was over don't seem to be over after all." How could they be arresting Kent again? What had the poor old guy done now? "I'll see you later," Charlie muttered as he headed out the door.

179

# SIXTEEN

Emmanuel Free Church stood at the corner of South Baptist and Spring Streets, toward the lower end of Thames, not far from Blakey's Soda Shop, which served the best strawberry malts in town. But though the glorious East window over the altar faced Spring, and the length of the church ran along South Baptist, it was only from Dearborn Street that one could enter, across a wide courtyard, which made Chief Arnold's early morning mission that much easier. The six men he'd stationed at the arched entry could maintain an easy watch over every inch of the courtyard, so that no one could go in or out of the sanctuary, the rectory, or the wood-framed parish house undetected.

Meanwhile, Arnold himself, along with Barker and another young sailor, one Seaman Haynes, prowled the interior of the sanctuary. Instructed by the chief to leave no stone unturned, the two younger men peered under pews, in closets, and up and down adjacent stairwells, while Arnold opened doors until he found the sacristy.

The small room did not look to Chief Arnold like the den of a viper. And yet he knew it was. How subtly, he thought, does the evil within and amongst us entwine itself with the good? Without constant vigilance and a warrior's discipline, humanity was truly lost, helpless against this onslaught. Nature, Arnold knew, was relentless in its war against man's better angels. Like weeds, which time after time sprout anew even in the most prized, ancient, and cultivated of gardens, so Nature finds its way up through the tiniest chink in the armor of civilization. Insignificant at first, the crack widens until eventually, if not rooted out, all structure is lost, and things revert to Chaos, Nature's preferred state, the enemy of divine order.

Arnold approached the bookcase under the window and glanced at the titles. Thomas Aquinas, Saint Augustine, Marcus Aurelius. Shakespeare? He then opened the creaking door of the adjacent armoire and found it largely empty, except for several sets of vestments suspended limply on hangers. He pulled a set off its rack and spat on it, then tossed it back onto the floor of the armoire.

Striding back into the sanctuary, the chief found Haynes seated in a pew near the altar, glancing indifferently through a hymnal, while Barker sat on the floor in the center aisle halfway back, head in his hands.

"What the hell's the matter with you two? On your feet!" Startled, Haynes dropped the hymnal and fumbled to retrieve it as he hurried to attention, banging his head on the pew in front of him in the process.

But Barker did not attempt to rise. If anything, the boy seemed to bury his head even deeper, as if attempting to drive his hands straight through his forehead.

"Barker!" Arnold bellowed. The young man suddenly glanced up, a panicked look on his face. "Get up! Now!"

Barker struggled to his feet. Furious, the chief grabbed the boy by the arm and pulled him up roughly. "What the hell's the matter with you, boy? Have you been drinking?" Arnold leaned closer to sniff the youngster's breath.

Barker instinctively drew back. "No, no, sir, not . . . I don't drink, sir," he stammered.

Arnold looked askance at Barker a moment longer, then released the boy's arm. "Well maybe you should start. Come along, both of you!"

—•—•—

Charlie found himself on the floor of Reverend Kent's bedroom, on his hands and knees, searching under the bed. Claude's face peered at him from the other side.

"Thought you said this was over, Charlie," remarked Claude.

"What the fuck you want from me?" Charlie grumbled as he got to his feet. The last thing he needed was for this rube to start in on him. "Did you look in the closet?"

Claude jumped up and stared at his friend. "What, you getting as crazy as Arnold, now? Kent ain't here, Charlie."

Charlie shrugged, avoiding Claude's gaze. "What do I care? I'm sick of fairies. I just do what I'm told."

Claude laughed cynically. "Since when?"

Ignoring the remark, Charlie walked past his friend. "I'm going to look in the kitchen."

Charlie and Claude found the other men huddled around the closed doors of a garage, trying unsuccessfully to remove the padlock. "Stand aside!" Arnold barked. The men did so and Arnold wedged an iron bar behind the hardware that held the lock and with one tug popped it free. Sunlight poured into the garage, illuminating the shiny blue paint of Kent's late-model Buick convertible.

"All right," Arnold announced, finally satisfied. "Kent must still be in town. Crawford, take a couple men and watch the train station. Cheney, Haynes, check the bus terminal. McKinney, you and your two sidekicks, stay here. The rest of you, fan out. We'll find the little bitch."

The men dispersed, leaving only Charlie, Claude, and Barker behind. Barker stared at the ground in obvious discomfort. The kid was too pathetic to hate, and Charlie was on the verge of forgiving the punk, when Barker made the mistake of opening his mouth.

"Charlie, I . . ." said Barker, more a gasp for air than an attempt at communication.

"Shut up, Barker," snapped Charlie. "Just shut the fuck up." Then Charlie turned and walked away.

Claude yelled after Charlie, "What the fuck is wrong with you today, McKinney?"

Charlie stopped and looked at Claude, then nodded at Barker. "Ask *him*."

"What?" Claude looked at the young sailor, but before he could say a word Barker hurried away.

— • • —

Samuel Kent had awakened at five forty-five that morning, half an hour earlier than usual. Feeling uncommonly cheerful, he dressed quickly and set out for a brisk walk through the yellow dawn. Striding along Thames Street, he paused at Long Wharf to gaze at the sunrise over Narragansett Bay, then continued out Fairview all the way to the old cemetery, which lay chilly and bleak under the teal sky. He stopped for a moment to say a prayer for all those boys who had not made it home from the war, or had been cut down by the flu and lay buried here, far from loving hands. Then he started back, his mind working at the sermon he was to deliver at morning service.

A few blocks shy of Dearborn Street, the reverend stopped at Blakey's Soda Shop to indulge in one of their famous strawberry malts. The sweet scent and taste of fresh strawberries was almost too good, and he considered having another. He had certainly earned it after such a lengthy constitutional, but in the end, Kent decided against it, not wanting to spoil the singular pleasure with overindulgence. Instead, he savored the last few drops of berry and milk and malt, paid his check, and turned his attention to the business of his day.

Moments after emerging from the shop, Kent recognized the two young sailors walking in his direction. They were nice young men, one rarely seen without the other, who had always been eager to engage the reverend in conversation on their frequent visits to the Y. Kent smiled as he caught their eye and was about to wave when their somber faces alerted him that something was amiss. He turned only to see two more grim-faced young sailors heading his way from the other direction. The fear that now clawed at Kent's insides had no name or apparent cause until, searching for an escape route, his glance fell upon Rudy and Dostalick bearing down on him from across the street. A larger, coarse-looking man in his middle forties strode beside them. The reverend froze.

"Samuel Kent," the coarse-looking man proclaimed as he pulled something shiny from his pocket. Kent felt the blood drain from his face, as the something that the horrible man now extended turned out to be handcuffs. "You are under arrest!"

• • •

William sat in his office, unable to focus on the stack of documents piled on his desk. He was once again awash in the tedium of small-town life, a dull parade of aggrieved parties and sorrowful victims, lightened by a wealthy man's occasional death and the transfer of riches to his heirs. Was this to be his future? Those few weeks leading up to Kent's trial, as distant now as a dream, had been his first real taste of what a life of purpose might resemble. Had the trial continued as planned, William was confident he would have proven himself a more than adequate criminal defense attorney, and who knew what path his life might have taken then? Though he tried to content himself with the dismissal, there was no doubt that William was once again bored.

A respectful knock on his office door brought him back to his duties. "Yes?" William called out as he rearranged the papers on his desk, trying to make it look as though progress had been made.

The door opened slightly and Thomas, the youngest of the new clerks, poked his head in, a troubled expression on his face. "Sorry to bother you, Mr. Bartlett, sir, but Mr. Gardner says it's urgent you come speak with him immediately."

William sprang up, grateful for the temporary reprieve and hopeful that a minor adventure might be lying in wait. He followed Thomas through the outer office, oddly empty for this time of day, and started toward the old man's lair.

"Uh, Mr. Bartlett," Thomas spoke up, stopping William. "Not in there, sir." And the younger man pointed outside.

Intrigued, William followed Thomas into the cloudless morning only to find his employers, Messrs. Gardner and Phillips, standing with the rest of the firm's half-dozen male employees in a rough semicircle facing the door, a silly grin plastered on every face. At the moment of William's appearance, the group erupted in applause. The ancient Gardner pulled William by the arm and directed his attention to the newly mounted sign above the door that read, "Gardner, Phillips & Bartlett, Attorneys-at-Law." The men gathered round to shake William's hand as a bemused smile spread across his face.

"All right, gentlemen," Gardner announced good-naturedly. "Let's get back to work! It's hardly meant to be a holiday." The group chuckled and grumbled and started back inside.

William found himself at the rear of the retreating pack beside Abbot Phillips. He continued to dislike the man and had no doubt that had Kent's trial gone in another direction, he would have been out on his ear. Still, he was willing to acknowledge the importance of this step for him, and for his family, and that called for some level of gratitude. He turned to Phillips to offer thanks, but before he could, William noticed some sort of commotion in progress a block or two farther down Thames Street.

Following William's gaze, Phillips turned to train his weaker eyes on the scene. "What is it, William?"

"I don't know," William muttered. "Probably nothing."

The two gazed a moment longer, then, not recognizing anything of relevance, followed the others into the law office.

## SEVENTEEN

One phone call was all it took to alter William's situation completely.

"Your man's back in jail," the Australian said. "In Providence, this time."

"Excuse me?" William asked, confused.

"Kent. He was picked up today in Newport. They're booking him now. I'm sure you'll be getting a call any minute."

William heard several telephones ringing in the outer office.

"You must be mistaken," he insisted.

"William, trust me. We have a reporter at the police station twenty-four hours a day. I'm speaking the truth. It appears the Navy's not done with the reverend yet."

"But . . . this is outrageous!" William exclaimed, wondering how such a thing could be possible. "By what right—"

"Federal morals statute passed during the war," Rathom explained. "What's really outrageous is that the arrest was carried out by a gang of sailors this time. Deputized by the federal district prosecutor."

Two doors slammed in succession. Then his own swung open and Thomas once again stood before him.

"I'm sorry to barge in, Mr. Bartlett, but Mr. Gardner wants you in his office immediately."

"Of course," William said. "Tell him I'll be right there."

Thomas nodded and vanished.

"John," William said into the phone, "I have to go. I'll call you again when I can, but I need to know what you plan to do—professionally, I mean—with this news."

A disturbing silence filled the line.

"You know I like Kent," the journalist said. "But I'm afraid this is bigger than him now. The military is arresting civilians, William. I'll do what I can, but I can't completely ignore the story. Now, hurry up and make bail for the poor soul. The jail in Providence is not a very nice place."

William sat with his two new law partners. Gardner was at his desk, his head nearly in his hands. Phillips paced, emitting an occasional "humph" under his breath.

Gardner raised his large, gray, aristocratic head and managed to speak. "The bishop has called the judge assigned to the case. They will allow Kent to go free on bail."

"Well, of course they will!" stated William, indignant.

Phillips stopped pacing and glared at William. "The prosecution was claiming that he was a flight risk. They were demanding that his motorcar be impounded."

"You're joking!" William exclaimed.

"They mean to get him this time, William," Gardner said. "The decision to take such drastic action had to have been made very far up the naval chain of command. Their intention from the start will be to paint Kent in the worst possible light."

"Cawley is no fool, and he rarely loses," Phillips informed

William. "He must feel he has a very strong case this time around. And he's a big one for last-minute surprises."

"What about the judge?" William asked. "Who is he?"

"Name's Brown," said Phillips. "He's tough. Not easily swayed by sentiment. And he will certainly have no personal reason to like Kent, as did the judge and jury here."

"Federal law or state law," William complained. "What difference does it make if I've proven entrapment!"

"You haven't proven it," said Phillips. "Not really. The first time out, the prosecution simply rolled over at the mere mention of the word. Cawley will have no such scruples, and he clearly believes he can withstand your accusations."

"And Judge Brown?" William asked. "Can I at least get a hearing with him? If I fully explain the situation, perhaps he'll see reason and dismiss the charges."

"That's a good one," Phillips chortled.

Gardner sighed. "I suppose it couldn't do any harm."

Phillips shrugged and turned away. "Very well. It'll be good for you to see what you're up against. I'll arrange it."

●—●—●

It was long after dark by the time William's black sedan pulled into the driveway of the Bartlett family home. Kent had said little during the forty-minute drive from Providence, and William had not tried to draw him out, fearful that his own anxiety would betray him. But neither man had any illusions about the challenges that lay ahead. They had defeated a very small dragon, it now seemed, only to find an army of much bigger ones waiting just over the next hill.

There was a chill in the air that evening, which hinted at an early fall, so the fire Sarah had lit in the parlor was a welcome sight. With her lightest touch, she guided the reverend to a velvet wing chair near the hearth, as if welcoming an old friend. Gratitude rushed in, overtaking William in a way he had never known before. A beautiful, loving spouse, three healthy children, a fine home, clean linen folded in drawers, carpets and heirlooms and wealth and position, *history*, all that this moment possessed down to the soft orange glow of the fire and the smell of fresh lemon cake coming from the kitchen. Nothing, it seemed, short of war or revolution or another outbreak of plague, could undo the enduring edifice of William's life.

Yet here, in its midst, the desperate circumstances of one he held in such high regard, a man with nothing and no one, who had done so much for so many, disturbed him profoundly. If they were to lose the upcoming trial and Kent was sent to prison, something would break inside of William, he was sure of it. He was not a child; he knew there was injustice in the world. But such an egregious example would upend his belief in the world as a fundamentally logical place. Never again would William be free to view his own life of patrician ease as something he somehow deserved. After a lifetime of doing only what was required of him, his privilege would seem to be nothing more than a careless trick of fate.

Fanny chose that moment to appear from the kitchen with a tray of jasmine tea and the lemon cake, newly sliced.

"Thank you, Fanny," Sarah said. "Milk, no sugar, I believe you said, Reverend?" She smiled as she poured tea for Kent.

"You're very kind, Mrs. Bartlett," Kent replied weakly. "No cake for me, thank you."

Fanny stopped in her tracks and looked at him. "Beg your pardon, Reverend," the woman announced, "but I won't be hearing that. This is my mother's recipe and you need your strength."

"It's useless to resist, Reverend," William offered. "I suggest you eat the cake."

Kent smiled. "Very well, perhaps a small piece."

Satisfied, Fanny retreated to her kitchen. Sarah served the cake, then settled beside her husband on the sofa with a cup of tea for each of them.

Kent stared at the flames, lost in thought. "I came to the ministry quite late in life, did you know that, William? I was nearly thirty-five before I took my vows. Perhaps this is God's way of telling me I made a mistake."

"Never!" William insisted. "You must never think that!"

Kent sighed. "I don't know what to think anymore."

William set his tea aside and leaned forward. "Listen to me, Reverend." Kent turned his gaze from the fire and looked at William. "They could try you a *hundred* times and a hundred times you'd be acquitted. But if you lose heart, then whatever the verdict, the other side wins."

A flicker of hope seemed to appear in Kent's eyes. Or perhaps it was only William's imagination and the play of firelight. He felt Sarah's hand on his arm and a gentle squeeze of encouragement. His wife had not been fooled by his bravado.

Still, if William believed in anything in this moment, beyond his wife, beyond this house, he believed in Reverend Kent. He would not roll over, as Abbot Phillips had put it, no matter how determined and powerful the forces arrayed against them might be. He simply would not allow either of them to be broken.

—◆—◆—◆—

From where he stood, just beyond the door of the tiny room, Samuel Kent could see a world in miniature. White wallpaper with a thin red stripe, a Gainsborough landscape above the bed, a small window draped in burgundy and below it a window seat with a red and gold striped satin cushion. A well-worn teddy bear lay facedown on the cushion and next to it, a red rubber ball. Near the bed, a wooden floor lamp cast the softest glow.

Sarah Bartlett placed two fluffy white towels and a washcloth on the neatly made single bed. Having turned down the bed, she stepped toward Kent into the light of the hallway. Her face was revealed to him once again, serene and patient and so filled with compassion that he felt the need to either flee or drop to his knees. He did neither.

"The bathroom is right across the hall. If there's anything at all you need—"

"No, Mrs. Bartlett, really," Kent insisted, blushing. "I feel terrible troubling you this way."

She laid a hand on his wrist. "Don't be silly, Reverend. It's an honor to have you grace our home."

He took a deep breath, accepting the fact that this moment of peace at least was real. "Thank you."

She gave him a smile and turned to go.

"Mrs. Bartlett?" He stopped her.

Sarah turned back to him, her eyes alert.

Kent looked down, embarrassed by the emotion he felt stirring in him. "Your husband continues to stand by me against all reason. I am . . . I am greatly in his debt. And yours."

Sarah closed the gap between them. "William adores you, Reverend. If I can tell you how affected he was, the night he came home from meeting you. He's been a different man since then, a better man. You've given William something to believe in. You mean a great deal to him. To both of us."

Kent knotted his eyebrows, fighting tears. "Sorry. I'm an old fool. The fact is, I don't . . . I don't feel I deserve such devotion, and, well— pardon me, there's no other way to put it—so much love, really."

Sarah took Kent's hand and held it gently between her own. "Love is something we all deserve, Reverend. Every one of us."

Kent yielded to her gaze. He could not have described in that moment what passed between them, but he felt as though a heaviness that had been about him for years had lifted all at once.

"Sleep well, Samuel." She released his hand, touched him lightly on the shoulder, and turned down the hall to the room she shared with William.

When we stand before our maker, Kent had long ago decided, it's the little things that we have done to and for one another—the healing touch, the kind remark, the forgiven slight—that are tallied into our final account. By this measure, Sarah Bartlett was indeed a woman destined for heaven. Of this, Samuel Kent had no doubt.

# EIGHTEEN

The tightly rolled copy of the *Providence Journal* slammed onto the porch of the Bartlett home at 7:32 a.m., somewhere near the middle of the paperboy's delivery route. By that time, he had already visited the town hall, the opera house, and most of the businesses along the upper half of Thames Street. The papers lay on doorsteps and sidewalks, in puddles or on the tops of hedges, awaiting the start of the day and the havoc soon to be wrought upon so many lives.

For the last fifteen minutes, the patrons at Blakey's Soda Shop had been quietly passing copies amongst themselves over breakfast. Finding no acceptable words with which to share their dismay, they simply blinked in shock, and only the bravest amongst them managed a brief shake of the head.

The soldiers at Fort Adams, awakened by a 6:00 a.m. reveille, were not so squeamish, and were in fact less shocked than amused, counting this as simply the latest bit of evidence that, as they'd always known, Navy men were *all* a bunch of fairies.

On the Island, where sailors were understandably abuzz, the mood was entirely different. Scuttlebutt had been rampant even before the trial in Newport, but the furor had died down just moments after the charges against Kent were dropped. Most men who knew him held a generally favorable opinion of the reverend, and the average sailor, with more than enough troubles of his own, simply chalked the incident up to the never-to-be-underestimated stupidity of the military brass.

But this time, with their collective shame committed to paper for every eye to read, they hung their heads and searched for villains. However much they may have detested the last two years of war and idleness on land and sea, they were still men, and the Navy was their tribe, and the tribe must be defended. Few were sure exactly where to focus their bitterness, at the queers, the brass, or the so-called operators, but most agreed that there was plenty of blame to go around.

The common sailor wasn't the only Navy man boiling over with impotent rage. Captain William Campbell, commanding officer of the training station, the man most directly responsible for the training and well-being of the twenty-five thousand young men currently in his charge, had been staring at the headline "NAVY SCANDAL EXPOSED" on and off for over an hour. A youthful fifty and highly decorated, Campbell had done an outstanding job meeting unprecedented wartime demands, and he was fully aware of the impact this event was likely to have on his promising career.

He remembered the day Assistant Secretary of the Navy Franklin Roosevelt had visited the Island, how full of pomp and circumstance it had been, the dress parade, the tours of ships and barracks and training facilities, dinner for a hundred at the fabulous Breakers, grandest of Newport summer "cottages," hosted by Roosevelt's boyhood sailing chum, Cornelia Vanderbilt.

Squeezed at the last minute into this insanely busy program had been a brief untoward meeting with a decidedly unpleasant man. The tall, homely chief petty officer, with a prominent nose and a face scarred by acne, had written Roosevelt in advance of his visit, complaining to him of the horrendously immoral conditions in Newport and claiming he had a plan to address them once and for all. Roosevelt had insisted that time be made for this monstrosity, who spent the fifteen minutes allotted to him ranting about fairies and prostitutes and cocaine joints. Together with his bland-faced colleague, a Navy doctor holding the rank of lieutenant, the chief had requested a modest sum to embark on a crusade to clean up the city and thereby save the "finest of American youth." To the extent that Roosevelt actually listened between interruptions for cablegrams and telephone calls, the assistant secretary appeared swept up in the drama of the thing, and with a wave of his irritating, ever-present cigarette holder he gave his official blessing to the endeavor. Campbell had thought little more of it beyond the fact that it had given twenty-five idle sailors something to do. The war was fast approaching an abrupt conclusion and since no one had floated any sort of a plan for demobilization, the captain's greatest concern at that moment had been in keeping occupied the twenty-five thousand bored young men he had struggled so long and hard to train.

Now the same horrid chief petty officer, whose name he knew so well but which he refused to utter, stood before him, stone-faced, as Campbell vented the rage he felt for this nobody, for Secretary Roosevelt, and for his own stupidity. He had not taken the deranged chief seriously enough to contemplate where his missionary zeal might lead them. Campbell fought to remain behind his desk, certain that if he were to get up, he would strike the idiot, or worse, challenge him to a duel.

"Why didn't you simply arrest Kent on Sunday morning in the middle of worship service?" Campbell demanded, his sarcasm appearing to have no effect on Arnold.

"We were concerned that the suspect might attempt to flee, sir," Arnold responded flatly.

Baffled, Campbell stared at the man.

"Are you a fan of detective stories, Mr. Arnold?"

"Excuse me, sir?" Arnold asked, not following.

"Is that where you've picked up all this hokum?" Campbell elucidated.

"I was a private investigator in Bridgeport before enlisting, sir," the big man explained.

"I see," said Campbell. "Well, judging from these *headlines*, the *'private'* aspect of your duties seems to have escaped you!"

"Captain, sir." A bead of sweat appeared on Arnold's brow. "Please believe me, I never meant to cause the Navy any embarrassment. But, you see, I've seen what these types can do to good, clean boys!"

Campbell could hear genuine passion rising in the man's voice. "And what *you're* doing to them?" the captain shot back, incredulous. "Does that appear *insignificant* to you? Clearly, the *Journal* thinks otherwise." He picked up the paper. "Have you seen what they're calling the affair? The Newport Navy Vice Scandal!" Campbell read from the text. "'The details of the operation are unprintable'! Well, at least *someone* still has a sense of decency!"

"These are difficult allegations to prove, sir," Arnold protested. "We needed hard evidence!"

"*Hard* evidence?" Campbell could not help but emit a bitter laugh. A moment later, the intercom on his desk buzzed loudly. "Hard evidence, indeed!" the captain added as he pressed a button and barked, "What?"

A young adjutant's voice replied, "I have Secretary Roosevelt on the line for you, Captain, sir."

"Roosevelt?" Campbell began to panic. "Already?" He wasn't prepared for this. "No," he reconsidered, "he couldn't possibly have seen this yet. Very well," he said into the device, "put him through."

A moment later, the phone rang. The captain took a deep breath, regaining some measure of composure, and announced, "Good morning, Mr. Secretary—"

A sudden tirade from the other end of the line quickly shut him up. Even Arnold reacted to Roosevelt's onslaught, audible from six feet away. Campbell felt as if the floor had dropped out from beneath him.

"But, Mr. Secretary, how did you—? Oh, yes, of course. The *wire* services . . . The *New York Times* . . . ? *National* news? No, sir, *believe* me, I had *no* idea . . . ! Of *course* you didn't, sir . . . I agree . . . Yes, sir." Campbell glared at Arnold. "He's in my office as we speak, Mr. Secretary." If the captain had had a cauldron of hot oil handy, he'd gladly have boiled the man alive in it. "I will be *sure* to tell him that."

But the next thing out of Roosevelt's mouth sent Campbell even deeper into despair. "But Mr. Secretary, do you think that's *wise*, sir . . . ? Yes, sir, by all accounts Kent does appear to be guilty of . . ." Campbell looked for confirmation from the detested Arnold, who was even now nodding his enthusiastic support. "Yes, sir," Campbell replied into the phone. "I understand . . . Yes, sir, I'll keep you informed . . . Yes, sir, *before* you read it in the *Washington Post* . . . Good-bye, Mr. Secre—"

And the line went blessedly dead.

The captain remained frozen for a moment, then gently returned the receiver to its cradle as if Roosevelt were somehow still a part of it. The man resolved to bury his fear of the secretary in the fury he felt toward the scoundrel before him. For the first time, Arnold looked genuinely worried.

"Captain," Arnold began desperately, "Mr. Roosevelt *approved* this entire—"

"Do you think," Campbell interrupted, in a cold and clipped tone that had withered better men than Arnold, "that the secretary, that *any* of us, imagined what you had in mind?"

Arnold opened his mouth but nothing came out.

"Now, you listen to me," Campbell continued. "You and your 'operators' will cease all 'undercover activities' at once, do you understand?"

"But Captain, we're—" Arnold protested feebly.

"Do you understand me?" Campbell repeated in a roar.

"Yes, sir," Arnold managed, but Campbell could see the man was fuming.

The captain took a deep breath as he swallowed the disturbing orders he'd just received from Roosevelt. "As the Navy is not in the habit of apologizing to sodomites," he resumed, "Kent's trial will go forward."

Campbell could feel Arnold stifling a satisfied smile. He wanted to slap the man, or beat him with a sword, but instead the captain stood and slowly approached the much taller Arnold. "However," he continued quietly, now inches away from Arnold's scarred face, "if it is proven that the reverend has been falsely accused, the world will not be a big enough place in which to hide from my wrath or the wrath of this administration. Is that clear?"

Arnold waited, whether out of respect or defiance Campbell could not tell, before he uttered, "Yes, sir."

The captain turned away, seething. "Now, get out of my sight." Behind him, Campbell could hear Arnold salute, turn, and exit the room.

Once the door had closed, Campbell picked up the paper, glanced at the headline one last time, then threw it into the wastebasket along with his thirty years of fine service.

—•—•—

"What's this, Charlie?" Dottie asked.

He was at the washbasin, in his undershorts, halfway through a leisurely shave. In the mirror, he could see the woman behind him seated at the room's one small table, reading the morning paper. She wore the silk slip he'd bought her a week before and she had her feet up, shapely calves and narrow ankles resting perilously close to the black coffeepot, which bubbled on a single-burner hot plate. He could smell the rich brew and he imagined that he could smell her as well, as if the scent of this woman were with him always now.

This had become their routine. After morning sex, always his favorite, they would wash up and partially dress. He would put the coffee on and shave while she scoured the paper for heaven knew what obscure bits of knowledge, and she would read aloud certain choice items that she thought might interest him. He would nod or shake his head or utter some other wordless acknowledgment, but the truth was, Charlie had no interest in the papers, on this or any other day. He'd had enough of grand and petty events, of the world outside of this room.

What interested him was this ritual, the closest he'd ever come to a home life. Over the last few days, Charlie had paid special attention to each smell and sound and taste, every random touch or glance. The casual mattered most to him, for it spoke of a belief the woman had in the future of their affair, an assumption that this was one of a thousand mornings to come, each more or less the same as the last.

But Charlie had the inside dope. He knew the hayride was over, and with it the extra money that had made his life with Dottie possible for all these months. They didn't have much, but he couldn't imagine her settling for less, especially without a reasonable explanation. Charlie could dodge with the best of them, but the closer he got to this woman, the more difficult it became to lie about important things. In the end it was nothing more than useless chatter anyway, for he would soon be transferred, far away perhaps, far enough at least that he and Dottie would be over, as thoroughly as if they'd never happened.

"What now?" he asked, stroking away the last bit of whiskers. "Did we declare war on Canada?" When she did not answer, he wiped his face with a hand towel and walked over to her. The expression on Dottie's face was one he'd never seen before; the woman was shocked, and thoroughly engrossed in what she was reading.

"Son of a bitch," she whispered.

He knelt close to her, trying to discern the source of her dismay. "What is it, Dot?" he asked, his own curiosity growing.

She gazed into the distance, lost in her thoughts, and said, "You got your name in the papers." Then she rose, allowing the *Journal* to fall to the floor, and quickly began to dress.

Charlie watched her odd behavior. "What are you talking about?"

"Don't play innocent with me, Charlie. It's the worst kind of insult." She shimmied into her dress.

"What the fuck is wrong with you?" Charlie said simply. "I thought we were having a nice morning."

She looked at him again, shook her head, then marched over, picked up the paper, and handed it to him. "You're a celebrity."

Charlie took the paper from Dottie's outstretched hand. He had not saved any drowning children recently, nor had he been elected to public office, so there was only one story that could possibly involve him. He hoped the newsprint would dissolve in his hands before he could read it, but the paper failed to cooperate.

And there it was. The writer, a Mr. John Rathom according to the byline, didn't go into the sexual specifics of the operation, but anyone with half a brain could read between the lines. Kent's name was there, listed as the accused in a new federal indictment. Also described by the author were his extraordinary contributions to the Episcopal community both before and during the war. Charlie, Rudy, and Dostalick were mentioned as the aggrieved parties, with little else to their credit other than their military ranks. But most extraordinary were the names and ranks of every "operator," each listed as having been assigned to a unit investigating "immoral conditions in and around Newport." The implication was clear.

"And to think I felt *close* to you!" Dottie exclaimed.

He looked again at the paper, at his name, "Charles A. McKinney, Seaman First Class," printed in black type like in the obituaries of dead sailors he'd known in the past. Somehow, a part of him was somewhere else now, outside of his control, a lost twin trapped in this story. He considered defending himself, but the natural instinct to do so faded in the face of the most common kind of sense. Dottie knew he was capable of the things implied here, and of a whole lot worse. Judging by these headlines and the trial that was sure to follow, he figured he may as well start getting used to this sort of humiliation. Folding the paper and tossing it on the bed, he grumbled, "I was just following orders," as he searched for a cigarette.

"And they had to twist your arm, I'm sure!" she exclaimed, laughing bitterly. "Oh, I knew all along you had something funny going on! But this? My one question, Charlie, how'd you convince the Navy? They couldn't have been dumb enough to come up with this on their own. It *must* have been your idea."

"You got it all wrong," he squawked. "I was recruited, see? Even said no at first, but they told me it was either this or . . . or something a whole lot worse."

She stopped and stared at him, hands on her hips. "And what would *that* have been, I wonder?"

He avoided her glance. "Something plenty bad, don't you worry."

"No, Charlie," Dottie insisted, "I want to know. What would that worse thing have been, huh? Turning in women, maybe? *Me*, for instance?"

"Never!" he protested, hoping that it was true.

"*What*, then?" she demanded.

Charlie looked at her, weighing his options. The woman would not back down, and lying was now out of the question. He could walk from the room, or remain and stonewall, but in either case, were he to display such cowardice, he would lose her for good. Despite his knowledge that the days left to them were few, he could not bear the thought of losing her now, not today, not in this moment. His only choice, it seemed, was to come clean and run the risk that the shame and rage he'd been bottling up for the last eight months would boil over, and he would be reduced to a pathetic sap, whimpering on the floor. In which case, of course, he would again lose her for good. But she had left him no alternative.

He sat on the bed. "All those hot little evenings we had, back before you moved in, when you made me pay every time." He paused and looked at her. "You knew where I got the money."

He could see the recognition in her face. She tried to hold his gaze but had to glance away.

"Not all the time," he admitted. "Sometimes I got lucky at cards, but often enough it was the other."

Dottie looked away silently.

"Yeah," Charlie said bitterly, "you didn't say anything then, either, long as you got your money. Business is business. We buy and we sell. But when they brought me in for my 'recruitment' interview, turns out you weren't the only one aware of my little business. They told me I had to choose, one side of the operation or the other. If I didn't help them, they'd nab me as a fairy. *Me!*" he yelled in indignation. "Oh, and they knew all about you, too. Said if I didn't play ball, they'd send you back to Ireland!"

Dottie smiled. "My savior! So, it was all my fault, was it? Sweet, innocent little Charlie, pure as the driven snow till the evil Dottie made him take to the streets. I've known plenty of sailors, boy-o, and they don't all sell their bodies to be with me. And what about that little farce you made me go through? Was that my doing, too? I knew the kid was a fairy the minute I met him. Just some bizarre fantasy of yours, I figured, so why not?"

"You shut your filthy mouth," Charlie warned her. He already had enough feelings to deal with. If she added Barker to the mix, he would surely blow his top.

"Did you find it amusing, Charlie, humiliating the boy like that? Made you feel like more of a man by comparison?"

He leaped up and grabbed her by the arms. "Did you hear me? I told you to shut the fuck up about Barker!"

"That's right," she taunted him. "Go ahead and hit me! I knew you would one of these days! Your kind always does!"

Charlie howled in frustration as he squeezed her arms one last time, so hard he knew it would leave a bruise, and then he let her go and backed away. "What difference does any of it make? You made your point." He finally found a cigarette and lit up. "We're both whores. Separated at birth, right?"

"No." She shook her head. "There's still one big difference between us."

Charlie smirked. "And that would be?"

She came right up to him and looked in his face. "I don't bite the hand that feeds me. I don't rat out my johns."

She grabbed her hat and handbag and headed for the exit. "Good-bye, Charlie." Opening the door, she stopped and looked at him one last time. "Mr. Top Secret, fighting our nation's enemies! Bunch of poor, silly fairies. And to think *you* were the one gonna make an honest woman out of *me*."

With that she left, slamming the door behind her.

And Charlie knew that he had indeed lost her for good.

# NINETEEN

William did not know this judge, a large balding man in his sixties by the name of Arthur Brown. There were no family connections between them and they shared no common history of which William was aware. Nor did there appear to be any prejudices, one way or another, that the jurist might be harboring behind his deeply lined, impassive face. Brown's chambers on the third floor of the U.S. District Court building in Providence testified to a distinguished career on the bench, so William pinned his hopes on the assumption of a level playing field, at least at the outset.

"Your Honor," William stated, "my client has already been cleared of these charges."

"No, Mr. Bartlett," the prosecutor rebutted with something approaching a smirk. "Not *these* charges, he hasn't."

William already disliked Joseph Cawley, the federal prosecutor and his opponent in this case. Cawley was undoubtedly smart and a far more experienced trial lawyer, but William had known these things before this meeting, and however unwelcome, he would have agreed that they were qualities worthy of admiration. Only a coward, thought William, dislikes a man for simply being a better man. Rather, it was Cawley's arrogance that had aroused William's disapproval, for it seemed to be a pose designed to intimidate and undermine his opponents. Simply put, the man was a bully.

"Move to dismiss, Your Honor," William maintained, trying to keep his focus on the judge.

Cawley turned to William, a perplexed look on his face. "On what *grounds*, counselor?"

Unfortunately, Cawley's strategy was having its desired effect. William was already feeling agitated. "Are you saying these men were *not* under orders to engage in sexual relations with certain persons?"

"Are *you* admitting that Reverend Kent had sexual relations with my clients?"

"I most certainly am not!"

"Well, you can't have it both ways, Mr. Bartlett. You see, an innocent man cannot be entrapped by anyone." Cawley looked at the judge as if they were the only two professionals in the room.

As infuriating as Cawley was, William couldn't help but contemplate the dozens of times the man must have argued cases in these very chambers.

"Your Honor," William resumed, fighting his insecurity, "I am calling into question the basis of this investigation and the character of the men making the accusations."

"Men? These are boys, Your Honor, investigating immoral conditions in and around the Naval Training Station. Hazardous duty as it turns out, exposing them to a practiced seducer like Kent."

"Save it for the jury, Mr. Cawley," William fired back. "And you will kindly address my client as the *Reverend* Kent, a title he has earned. Your Honor, these 'boys,' as he calls them, have accused a respected citizen of a crime of which, by their own admission, they themselves are guilty."

That comment seemed to land with the judge, and William watched with anticipation as Brown fixed his gaze on the prosecutor, raising an eyebrow. "Mr. Cawley?"

"Men do all sorts of horrible things in wartime, Your Honor." Cawley had clearly thought this through, offering William a taste of what he was likely to face in court. "They are even encouraged to kill, a behavior that would certainly lead to prosecution in civilian life. These sailors, and their superiors, saw this as a kind of war, so they took actions, however misguided, that they deemed necessary under the circumstances. Reverend Kent's behavior, on the other hand—"

"*Alleged* behavior," William interjected.

Cawley sighed and repeated, mocking William's emphasis, "*Alleged* behavior, if *proven*, demonstrates a 'persistent inclination,' which, because of the position of influence he holds over so many young men, created an immoral condition within five miles of a military base, a federal offense as you know, Your Honor."

Now it was Judge Brown's turn to sigh. "I'm sorry, Mr. Bartlett, but the prosecutor is right. As sordid as this whole business is, the charges stand. We'll let the jury decide as to their merits under the circumstances."

"But, Your Honor—" William protested.

Brown looked at him sharply. "I've made my ruling, Mr. Bartlett." William offered a brief nod of surrender. "That will be all, gentlemen."

—•—•—

Outside the judge's chambers, Cawley approached William. The man towered at least three inches over William.

"Bravo, Mr. Bartlett! That was a spirited defense you made in there. I can see I'm in for it. Bet you were a real star on the debating team. Princeton, was it?"

William met Cawley's half smile with a grim face of his own. "Yale."

"Really?" Cawley looked him up and down dismissively. "Would have taken you for a Princeton man."

Cawley started to walk away, then stopped and turned. Each of the man's gestures appeared timed for maximum effect.

"If I might offer you a bit of advice," Cawley said intimately. "Judge Brown? I've argued at least a dozen cases in front of him. I'd watch my p's and q's, if I were you. He doesn't like to be crossed." Cawley paused and smiled. "See you in court." Then he turned and strode away.

William knew that the moment called for a witty response, a sharp line to toss back, but he could think of none that would not further weaken his already damaged position.

The loss of round one had always been a foregone conclusion, so William resolved to take it in stride. He was learning to appreciate little victories, however, among them the prize that Cawley had handed him today. For William hated bullies, and if he'd had any doubts going into this hearing today, he was now more determined than ever to win this case.

◆—◆—◆

By late afternoon, most of the men had gathered at the basement headquarters, drawn there for mutual support and protection. A quick glance at the article or glimpse of the headline had been enough to bewilder all but the most stalwart amongst them, as if what they had done had not really been done until they'd seen it in print. It was like waking from a dream to find that you had not been dreaming at all but had in fact been living a life that you could not now recognize as your own.

They huddled in small groups near the corners of the large room, some passing tattered copies of the *Journal* from man to man, speaking, if at all, in hushed tones.

Charlie searched the room and was pleased to find that Claude had not joined any of these cliques but rather sat alone, his chair leaning against a wall, the paper folded on his lap.

"Hey," said Charlie as he approached, grateful for the easy intimacy they shared. But the man kept staring straight ahead, his gaze so fixed that Charlie glanced in the direction of Claude's focus. "You all right?" Charlie asked, concerned.

"Thirty years in Leavenworth," the big Texan stated flatly. "That's what Kent stands to get, and Harry and the others. And that's *if* the poor bastards ever get to trial."

Claude looked up and Charlie couldn't tell if it was disgust or astonishment that had so profoundly altered his friend's face.

"'Just like it never happened.' Ain't that what you said after the Newport trial?" Claude shook his head. "What a dope I was, listenin' to you!"

"Come on, Claude," Charlie protested, offering a faint smile. "Gimme a break. I didn't know—"

"Really? And here I thought you always had the answers, Charlie," Claude growled, an unambiguous look of contempt painted across his freckled face.

Yes, Charlie recalled, that had indeed been his boast more times than he could count, but he could think of nothing now to say in response.

"Speechless?" Claude asked, and snorted, "Well, *that's* worth something anyhow."

The man rose abruptly, ready to walk. Charlie grabbed his arm and leaned in, his voice low and urgent. "Claude, I'm no lawyer. How the hell was I supposed to—"

Claude yanked his arm away. "Just stay the fuck away from me," he warned, and walked across the room to join a group of men.

"Charlie, I . . ." a familiar voice pleaded.

Barker was standing right behind him, too close by half. The smell of panic on the boy brought out the devilish worst in Charlie, who fought the impulse to lift the kid by the throat. *Go away*, Charlie thought, *just go away.*

"They said it was secret, Charlie!" Barker blurted. "Who's gonna know about this, huh? My folks, they can't know! They—"

"What the hell you expect *me* to do about it?" Charlie snapped.

"You . . . you—"

"What?" Charlie demanded in a furious whisper. "You telling me this is *my* fault now? You *wanted* in, Barker, remember that, so try acting like a fuckin' man for once, instead of a goddamned little fairy!"

Charlie knew before the words landed that they should never have left his mouth. But they had, and he watched with concern as the face in front of him turned a shade paler. Barker appeared to have stopped breathing, and it was only the blinking of his eyes that assured Charlie the young man was still alive. He offered no resistance, absorbing Charlie's spite as he would anything else the man had to give, and Charlie realized for the first time how completely one individual could control another. Barker would have thrown himself under a moving train if Charlie had asked him to, and the thought made Charlie oddly nauseous. He turned away momentarily and took a deep breath, hoping to start fresh, but when he turned back, he saw a boy as shattered as any he'd seen evacuated from the blood-soaked fields of France.

"Look, kid, I'm sorry," Charlie said sincerely as he laid a hand on the boy's shoulder. Barker looked at it, and it was clear that this touch held a different meaning for each of them. Awkwardly, Charlie withdrew his hand. It was no good, he thought, once and for all. He had nothing to offer Barker.

"Your folks," Charlie asked simply, "can they read?"

Barker nodded slowly. Charlie looked at the boy a moment longer, then shrugged and walked away, hoping as he did so that Barker would remember once again to breathe.

— • — • —

An hour later, Arnold and Hudson entered the basement room followed by prosecutor Joseph Cawley, who stopped just inside the door, surveying the clusters of men skulking in the corners. "Jesus!" Cawley muttered. He had expected to meet quietly with the three men directly involved in the proceedings, but there must have been thirty sailors in the basement room. Had they all been involved in Arnold's scheme? "What is this?" asked Cawley.

"Don't worry, counselor," Arnold replied. "They're all sworn to secrecy."

Cawley shook his head. "What were you people thinking?"

Arnold glared at the lawyer. "I'll round up the plaintiffs." He walked off, leaving the prosecutor standing beside an awkwardly silent Dr. Hudson.

"Did you really believe this . . . operation would go unnoticed and unreported, Lieutenant?" Cawley asked. But the doctor merely shrugged his shoulders, clearly at a loss. "I've been told you're an expert in the science of fingerprinting," Cawley continued, hoping to draw the doctor out.

Hudson brightened. "Yes, Mr. Cawley, that's correct. I made a study of it before joining the Navy."

"And were you anticipating that this skill of yours might prove useful in your current endeavor?"

Hudson puffed up his chest proudly. "Yes, Mr. Cawley. Most certainly, it has."

"I'd keep that fact to myself, if I were you," Cawley replied, his quip drawing a confused look from Hudson. The man was clearly an idiot, thought Cawley. Worse than that, he had no sense of irony, a very bad sign.

The lawyer shook his head, trying to clear it. How odd it was, he pondered, that in a society founded on due process, Americans would so often revert to their native religion, the dime novel, reducing the world to a battle between cowboys and Indians in which a posse of righteous citizens was deemed the most effective instrument of justice in a lawless frontier society. But the frontier was long gone, if indeed it had ever existed the way people imagined it to have been. America now was a "civilized" society and, as such, some things were best left unexamined. Foremost among those were the sexual peccadilloes of others. Everyone had something to hide, Cawley had long ago determined, and nothing upset people more than being forced to confront peculiarities vastly different from their own. Perversity, once brought to light, invited public scrutiny, reputations inevitably suffered, and little satisfaction was to be gained for any of the parties concerned. Even successful prosecution of such "crimes" was rarely worth the political capital, which would, in Cawley's mind, be put to far better use advancing the careers of one's friends and undermining those of one's enemies.

Once undertaken, however, nothing was more harmful to one's future than a high-profile failure, especially a scandalous one. Cawley knew what had to be done. These lost souls must be brought into line, their stories, true or false, must be made to match, and the obviously queer priest—fifty, single, and obsessed with sailors—must be convicted and put behind bars.

Franklin Roosevelt, immensely wealthy and heir apparent to an American dynasty, clearly had political ambitions of his own. The man's potential was far greater than his current title of Assistant Secretary of the Navy implied, and it might someday prove extremely useful to have delivered this victory to him today.

Arnold waved Cawley over to a corner of the room where three young sailors sat in a glum semicircle. Cawley had read their depositions as well as the testimony of the one sailor, Dostalick, who had managed to testify to such ill effect at the first trial in Newport before the charges were dropped. Each of the accounts of sexual misconduct carried its own unique measure of implausibility. But if the stories were utter fabrications, made up out of whole cloth, then at least one person in this room, Arnold, was horrendously depraved. No, Cawley decided, there *had* to be a kernel of truth here, enough at least upon which to build a successful case. None of these three men were the picture of innocence. But no matter. Once properly prepared and in dress whites, their youth would stand in stark contrast to the crusty middle age of the unmarried clergyman.

In the end, it would come down to experience, and his fifteen years as a trial lawyer on the district court level made the contest a laughable mismatch.

There was one thing, however, that Cawley found unsettling about the young defense attorney, and that was his almost religious belief in his client's innocence. Either he was incredibly naïve or a very good actor. In either case, it was a quality that could sway a jury, and of which Cawley would need to remain acutely aware.

"Gentlemen." Cawley nodded at the sailors.

"Have a seat, Mr. Cawley," Arnold snapped as he planted himself in one of two empty chairs.

The lawyer scrutinized the men as he slowly sat. In the middle, spine pressed ramrod straight against the back of his chair, Cawley recognized Bart Rudy as the handsome young fellow he'd met at the train station. A prominent jaw advertised the pride Rudy felt at being a superior specimen of a man, a leader amongst his peers. But an individual so committed to his place in the natural pecking order could be easily led, so Cawley thought it safe to count Rudy as an asset.

The fellow on Rudy's right was the youngest of the three, no more than twenty, with a shock of golden blond curls and a boyish, slightly demented face, as if he'd spent a good part of his childhood drowning kittens. This had to be Dostalick, Cawley determined. It would not be easy squaring his testimony at the Newport trial with what was to come, but Cawley had navigated more treacherous waters before and come through unscathed. If he could just keep the boy from humiliating himself again, Cawley could then rely on the testimony of the other two sailors to seal the reverend's fate.

The third sailor, however, the one on Rudy's left, was difficult to read. His jet-black hair and startling good looks would command a jury's attention under any circumstances. But there was something more about this twenty-three-year-old, a sadness in his gas-blue eyes, that hinted to Cawley of secrets within, the depth of which would likely have withered a lesser soul. Yet the young man seemed defiantly unburdened. This was McKinney, the lawyer decided, and if experience was any judge, it was likely upon this prodigy that Cawley's case against Kent would succeed or fail. Next to him, Rudy was a mere cipher.

"Mr. Cawley," announced Arnold, "meet your star witnesses, Seamen First Class Dostalick, Rudy, and McKinney."

"A pleasure to meet you, gentlemen," Cawley intoned.

"Tell the man what he wants to hear, boys," Arnold commanded.

The three sailors looked at one another uncomfortably.

Seizing the opportunity to win their trust, Cawley took the boys' side against the schoolyard bully. "And what would that be, Mr. Arnold?" he asked with a smile.

"Never mind," he insisted. "They know. Tell him."

Finally Rudy spoke up, reciting mechanically. "Kent forced himself on us, sir. If we'd resisted, we might've compromised the operation."

The lawyer's work had clearly been cut out for him. He looked at the other two. Dostalick's face showed only a hapless need to be pointed in the right direction. But McKinney was regarding Rudy with unvarnished contempt. Cawley decided that now was as good a time as any to assess the magnitude of the problem this one sailor might pose.

"Well, Mr. McKinney?" he asked. "What do you say to that?"

Charlie looked askance at Cawley, as if the answer were obvious to both of them. "Excuse me, sir?"

"The defense attorney is no fool, I assure you. Mr. Bartlett will undoubtedly try to prove entrapment a second time." Cawley drilled McKinney with a look that had intimidated the most hard-boiled of witnesses. "You were *not* ordered to commit these acts, is that correct, young man?"

McKinney hesitated under the prosecutor's practiced glare, and that was all Cawley needed to see. The sailor glanced toward the glowering Arnold and Rudy, then looked down, caving in bitterly. "That's correct, sir."

Cawley released an inner sigh. Perhaps this boy was not as unpredictable as he had feared.

"Very well," Cawley said gravely. "But I suggest you go over your stories and stick to them closely. You each filed an affidavit in Newport. Those affidavits serve as the basis for this federal indictment. Perjury is a serious crime, gentlemen, punishable by up to five years in prison. And against *that*, you have no immunity."

Cawley was pleased to see the men, McKinney included, acknowledge their shared predicament with an exchange of worried glances. Yes, the lawyer thought to himself with satisfaction, there was without a doubt enough here on which to build a winning case.

— • —

It was after nine when the men finally dispersed. They wandered off together into the night, reluctant to face the world alone. Only Charlie emerged solo. Standing in the cold, he briefly scanned the clusters of men for his two former comrades—a force of habit, since he had already seen Claude slipping off with a band of brothers who until then he had barely acknowledged. Barker, for his part, had been oddly invisible all evening. Shortly after the jamboree had begun, Arnold had called the roll and locked the door, so it would have been impossible for Barker to steal away during the meeting.

This was the natural state of things, Charlie affirmed, being alone, relying once again on no one but himself. It was a cold but familiar suit of clothes, and he assumed it without effort. But as he lit a cigarette and turned to head back to his room, a room he knew he would find empty, Charlie spotted Barker just outside the basement door. The boy's head was down and he'd failed to notice his beloved friend standing not more than thirty feet away.

Charlie hesitated, then started toward Barker, still feeling guilty over the way he had treated the sorry soul earlier in the evening. But by the time Charlie took his second step, another figure had emerged from the basement and Charlie halted. The man, still in the shadows, turned back to slam and lock the door behind him, and even before the figure moved into the crescent moonlight, Charlie knew it was Arnold. He watched as Barker looked up at the much bigger chief, who laid a proprietary arm across Barker's shoulders and resumed what appeared to be an authoritative lecture on the facts of life according to himself. Barker, now an empty vessel, hung on Arnold's every word as they turned toward an alternate path.

Charlie felt an urge to follow after them, to somehow defend his former protégé from the distorted mind of such a monster. But again Charlie hesitated, and after a moment, he shrugged off the instinct, recalling how little he knew of other men's demons. He had already tried taking charge of Barker's education, and look where it had gotten them. Unless he was willing to unravel the strange obscurities of the boy's desires, and he was not, it was hardly his business where Barker went, or with whom.

# TWENTY

The first thing William noticed when he emerged from his motorcar was the man selling popcorn and hot dogs at the base of the courthouse steps. No one was buying, but he clearly expected a crowd. Two red helium balloons flew high above his oversized parasol, and the front page of the *Providence Journal*, headlines screaming, had been plastered to his cart.

It had not been a good morning. To start off, his wife had chosen that day to have the painters come. She'd claimed it was a mistake, that in fact they had been scheduled for the following week, but when they arrived at seven and began draping the dining room with drop cloths and filling the house with the toxic smell of oil paint, William couldn't help but suspect revenge. Three days previous, he had informed his wife that she would not be allowed at the trial. Not because of the judge's ruling this time, but because William couldn't bear the thought of it.

"Sarah," he'd implored her, "*I* can hardly endure these proceedings. What kind of woman wants to listen to such filth?"

"The kind," she'd replied, furious, "that would like to think her husband wants her support on the most important day of his career!"

The only reason he had agreed to her painting project at all was because he knew that this day was coming. Sarah had been at him for months to paint white the oak wainscoting and crown molding on the first floor of their home, claiming that the house was dark and dreary and needed modernizing. He had firmly resisted until the day he'd made his decision to keep her from the trial. He agreed to let her try it in one room, in the hopes that it might take her attention off the trial, all the while imagining his father turning in his grave.

"I do want your support, you know I do! But if you were there, I . . . I would be struck dumb. For God's sake, Sarah, you're my wife! I'm supposed to protect you from things like this!"

With a sigh she'd relented, allowing William to embrace her. "Thank you," he said, relieved. "Pray for me, darling. Please. Pray for all of us. If I lose this case, the reverend could go to prison for thirty years. And I will likely lose my job, and my reputation."

"You won't lose," she assured him confidently, a trace of sadness still in her voice. "I'm certain of it."

William tried to hold on to that certainty as he endured the anticipation of his debut in federal court. But when he saw the reverend's face on the morning of the trial's commencement, his fears resurfaced. The man looked as if he hadn't slept a wink in days.

"Are you all right, Reverend?"

Kent smiled. "Don't exactly look my best, do I? Nightmares." He shrugged. Then he laughed, laying a hand on William's shoulder. "Don't worry, son. I'll be fine. Because *you'll* be brilliant."

＊ ＊ ＊

Flashbulbs exploded as they entered the courthouse. Once his eyes adjusted, William picked out amongst the crowd various faces conspicuously absent at the first trial in Newport. Bishop Perry was there with a claque of black-clad clergymen. William Campbell, CO of the Naval Training Station, led a procession of heavily medaled Navy brass with the three plaintiffs in tow, dazzling in their dress whites. Near the courtroom doors, Prosecutor Cawley held court with a group of reporters while just behind him, a pair of unknown Navy men stood, one exceptionally tall and homely, the other middle-aged and bland. William made a mental note to find out more about them as a surge in the crowd carried him and Kent toward the chamber. Faceless reporters from a half-dozen national newspapers swarmed around them, firing questions and trying to elicit comments. Kent obediently followed William's instructions and kept his head down until they were safely within the sanctity of the courtroom itself.

"Mr. Bartlett!" a familiar male voice called out.

It was John Rathom, approaching rapidly. William was astonished to find himself so happy to see the man.

"Mr. Bartlett." Rathom extended his hand and the men shook.

"Call me William, please. And thank you, sir."

"That would be John," Rathom replied. "And why on earth are you thanking me?"

"You were true to your word," William said. "We're very grateful for your portrayal of the reverend in all your coverage, the references to his history of good works."

Rathom shrugged it off. "Simply stating the truth, Mr. Bartlett."

"William, please," he insisted.

"As you wish. Well, William, if you're happy with our coverage so far, tomorrow's paper should make you jump for joy."

"How so?" William inquired.

"In tomorrow's morning edition, the *Journal* is publishing an open letter to the president," Rathom announced, "protesting the persecution of Reverend Kent, and signed by twenty of the most prominent clergymen in New England."

William looked at Rathom, confused. "The president?" he asked. "The president of what?"

Rathom laughed. "Of the United States of America."

William was speechless.

"I'll explain over dinner tonight. On me, of course, since this is my hometown. You're invited as well, Reverend."

William turned to see Kent watching the two men expectantly.

Rathom continued. "I'll take your silence as a 'yes.' Good luck today, gentlemen." He gave them a polite nod and maneuvered his bulk to a seat in the front of the gallery.

William remained frozen in place, stunned by how high the stakes had suddenly become.

"William," Kent muttered, stirring the lawyer from his reverie. "Shouldn't we . . . ?"

"What? Oh, yes." The two men headed toward the defense table.

A second jury of twelve white men was settling in as William and Kent found their seats. Within moments, the gallery was full and the bailiff appeared, announcing the arrival on the bench of Judge Brown.

"All rise!" Everyone shuffled to standing. "In the matter of the *People of the United States versus Samuel Neal Kent*, the Honorable Arthur Brown presiding, this court is now in session!"

"You may be seated," the judge announced as he took his place. "Mr. Bartlett, how does your client plead?"

"Not guilty, Your Honor," declared William.

"Opening statement, Mr. Cawley?" Brown asked, all business.

Cawley rose and moved slowly to the jury box, looking each man in the eye.

"Not guilty," the lawyer repeated. "What exactly does that mean, gentlemen? A child of five years may commit an act outside of our established moral code, but we do not blame him, nor does he experience guilt, until we teach him to do so. But as we grow, in age and in wisdom, as we rise through hard work to a position deserving of respect and, indeed, 'reverence,' surely, the bar, the standard by which we are judged innocent or guilty, rises as well. The defendant in this case, 'Reverend' Kent, by virtue of his position, knows the difference between right and wrong. Indeed, he is among those we rely on to help the lost sheep among us return to a righteous path. Now, counsel for the defense will remind you that Kent has already had similar charges against him dismissed. This is true. But he has never been found 'not guilty,' gentlemen. That"—he paused solemnly—"will be for you to decide."

——•——

Cawley was perfect, William acknowledged to his dismay.

But judging by Dostalick's direct testimony, this man at least was the same flawed witness that William had taken apart in Newport.

"And were you ever," Cawley asked, "at *any* time, instructed to allow Reverend Kent to perform these acts upon you?"

"No, sir," Dostalick replied with conviction. "Never, sir. It was forced upon me, sir. If I was to preserve the integrity of the operation, I had no choice. I had to submit."

"Thank you, Mr. Dostalick," Cawley said with a supportive nod. "I have no further questions, Your Honor."

Judge Brown turned to face William. "Your witness, Mr. Bartlett."

"Thank you, Your Honor." William stood and walked toward the witness stand. Dostalick was the least of his worries, and he expected to make short work of him.

The sailor tried to remain cool, staring straight ahead as William approached.

William rested a hand on the front railing. The sailor glanced down at it nervously. William smiled.

"Hello, Henry."

"Hello, sir," said Dostalick.

"You remember me, don't you, Henry?" William asked pleasantly.

"Yes, sir."

"Good. Now, Henry, you've just testified that, prior to your alleged encounter with Reverend Kent, you had never experienced anything of this sort, is that right?"

"That's correct, sir."

"And since?"

Finally, Dostalick looked William in the eye, puzzled by the question. "Sir?"

"Since the alleged encounter," William elaborated, "have you had experiences of this nature with other men?"

Dostalick hesitated.

"Yes, sir."

"So you found that you liked it?" William suggested. "Wanted to continue on with it?"

Cawley rose. "Objection!"

"Sustained," Judge Brown agreed.

But William had not imagined that his question would pass muster. He simply wanted to plant a seed in the minds of the jury that Dostalick and his two cohorts were natural degenerates. Jury selection had proceeded smoothly with little contention, for both lawyers had chosen these twelve for much the same reason—a strong and immediate aversion to such behavior. Ultimate victory would come down to who they considered most likely to commit or even consider these acts. If William could successfully impugn the plaintiffs, the character witnesses that William would bring forth in support of the reverend should tip the balance. The jury would come to believe as William himself did, that it was not possible for such nobility and corruption to coexist in the same individual.

"Isn't it true, Henry," he continued, "that you were specifically instructed to engage in sexual relations with 'suspected deviants'?"

Dostalick held firm, his confidence growing. "I was instructed to get evidence, sir."

"And didn't that include allowing things of this kind?"

"No, sir. Those were never my instructions, sir."

"I see," said William, taking a breath. "Henry," he continued as he walked over to the defense table and reached for a transcript. "Henry, you testified in the court in Newport to the following: 'This unit you're assigned to, do part of your duties include allowing yourself to be fondled?' Your response was, 'If necessary.' Do you remember saying that?"

"No, sir," Dostalick replied, stonewalling. "I don't remember."

"You don't remember?" William asked in disbelief. "You then went on to say, if 'necessary to gather sufficient evidence of perversion.' Do you remember that?"

"No, sir, I don't recall."

"Don't you recall *anything* you said down in Newport?"

"It's been quite a while, sir," Dostalick replied with a straight face.

"Yes," William quipped. "Three whole months! I suppose I should be flattered that you remember *me!*"

Scattered laughter erupted across the courtroom, confusing Dostalick.

"It's been even longer since your alleged encounters with the reverend. Why should we trust your memory there?"

Dostalick hesitated a moment and William filled the silence before he could answer.

"But of course, you have the transcripts and your depositions to refer to in that case, don't you?"

"Yes," said Dostalick, sounding wary. "Yes, sir."

"Very well," William continued. "So, allowing for your sudden lapse of memory, are you able to tell me now? Were you under orders or were you not under orders?"

"I was not under orders to do it. No, sir," Dostalick said definitively.

"So then what you said in Newport was a lie. You perjured yourself in a court of law, is that it? You committed perjury? You do realize that's what you're saying, don't you?"

"Objection, Your Honor," Cawley announced. "Badgering the witness."

"I'll sustain it. Let the witness answer, Mr. Bartlett," the judge said.

William focused his gaze on Dostalick, who had clearly been rattled by the back and forth. "Mr. Dostalick?"

Dostalick looked at him. "Yes?"

"Yes, you committed perjury?"

"No," Dostalick insisted. "No, sir. I . . ."

"What? You heard the judge, Mr. Dostalick. Answer the question. Did someone order you to have sex with other men?"

"No! Never!"

"Then you lied."

"No, well, I . . . only if . . . if it . . ."

"If it *what*?" demanded William.

Dostalick's body went visibly limp as he conceded defeat a second time.

"If it came to that," the sailor mumbled.

"Speak up, please, Henry," William ordered. "I couldn't hear you."

Obediently, Dostalick did as he was told, under the sway of a new master. "If it *came* to that, sir, it was understood that we would do what was best for the cause."

Cawley rose to his feet with somewhat more energy than before. "Objection, Your Honor. I move that this last statement be struck from the record. It has nothing whatsoever to do with the charges under consideration."

"I'm merely following the prosecutor's own line of questioning, Your Honor," William fired back. "Besides, it goes to credibility."

"Objection overruled, Mr. Cawley. You may proceed, Mr. Bartlett."

"Thank you, Your Honor." William looked at Cawley with satisfaction. "No more questions, Your Honor."

— • — • —

They were halfway through Bart Rudy's direct testimony, and so far, the prosecutor had failed to impress. Nothing in Cawley's style gave William any indication of surprises to come. His manner of questioning was strictly by the numbers, and he seemed to be leading this witness, like Dostalick before him, straight down the garden path that William had hoped for. If anything, Rudy's arrogance and his fluency in the language of perversion made him an even easier target than Dostalick.

"He wanted me to make him come," the handsome Rudy declared. "I refused. Did up my trousers, went on my way."

"Thank you, Mr. Rudy," Cawley said with a respectful nod. "No further questions, Your Honor."

"Your witness, Mr. Bartlett," the judge grumbled.

"Thank you, Your Honor." William stood and made his way toward Rudy, who met William's gaze defiantly, his mouth edging into a smirk.

"You find this amusing, sailor?" William asked.

"Sir?" Rudy questioned, confused.

"This sort of talk, behavior," William clarified. "You find it amusing?"

With an indignant snigger Rudy replied, "I most certainly do not, sir."

"Then why are you smiling?"

Rudy's eyes darkened as he wiped the smile off his face.

"Thank you. Now, Mr. Rudy, you testified that on the evening in question, you approached the reverend for advice on your future, that you might be interested in a career as a clergyman. Is that correct?"

"That's correct, sir."

"Correct, yes. But is it true?" William probed.

"Sir?"

"*Are* you considering a career in the ministry?"

Rudy fought hard to suppress a smile. "No, sir."

"I see," replied William with obvious disdain. "So, then, under these false pretenses, you were invited to the Reverend Kent's quarters that same Friday evening."

"That's right," said Rudy.

William turned away from the witness, strolling the length of the jury box as he continued. "And there you were, Mr. Rudy, discussing your future as a clergyman, when suddenly he threw his arms about you, and . . . all the rest of it."

"That's right, sir."

William turned and faced Rudy from a distance.

"Was this a surprise to you, young man?"

Rudy raised his eyebrows as if the answer was obvious. "Yes, it was, sir. Certainly."

William included the jury in his next questions, a faint smile on his face. "So, what did you do? Knock him down?"

The sailor glanced at the jury, then back at William. "No, I didn't knock him down."

"Well, were you accustomed to having fellows do these things to you?"

"No," Rudy assured the jury.

"Nothing like this ever happened to you before?" William asked, dubious.

"No," Rudy declared.

"Never?" William pushed. "Remember, sailor, you're under oath."

Rudy hesitated. "Well, only . . . in the line of duty."

"Ah," said William. "So in the line of duty, over the last six months, not including your alleged encounter with the reverend, how many so-called degenerates did you discover?"

"Objection, Your Honor."

"Overruled, Mr. Cawley," said the judge.

William repeated the question. "How many, sailor?"

"Five," replied Rudy, assuming his stony face.

"Hard at work for six months," said William, taken aback, "and you only found five such persons! Well, perhaps Newport's not as depraved a place as you all feared."

Laughter erupted in the courtroom. Judge Brown pounded his gavel. "The gallery will come to order or I will have it cleared." And the laughter slowly subsided.

"It took some time to work on them," Rudy asserted, growing defensive. "So's they wouldn't suspect."

"I see," said William. "Any of them women?"

"No, sir."

"Interesting. Now once you'd 'worked on them,' as you say, gaining their trust, how many sexual encounters would you typically have with each?"

Cawley shot up from his seat. "I most strenuously object, Your Honor!"

The judge said nothing but instead glowered at William. "Mr. Bartlett?"

"Your Honor, the reverend has been accused of crimes of immorality, for which the prosecution can produce no witnesses. The personal history and character of those making the accusations must be examined in order for the jury to render a just decision as to whom they believe."

The judge looked at Rudy, then back to William. "I agree, Mr. Bartlett. Objection overruled."

Cawley took his seat in obvious frustration.

William locked eyes with Rudy. "How many, sailor?"

Rudy glared at William, beginning to burn. "I can't recall."

"You can't recall?" William asked, feigning astonishment. He faced the jury. "Seems to me a wholesome fellow like yourself would recall quite well having a sexual encounter with another man."

"It varied," offered Rudy in an authoritative manner. "Depending on how much evidence I thought was needed to bring them up on charges."

William continued to direct his gaze toward the jury. "I would've thought once would be quite enough. Perhaps I'm naïve." He turned to Rudy. "Twice? On average."

Rudy squirmed under the pressure, reluctant to respond, as William bore down on him.

"Three times?" William posited. "Four? Forty-four?"

Rudy's anger was growing visible as William pressed his advantage.

"Mr. Rudy," William asked, patronizing, "do you understand the term 'persistent inclination'?"

"Objection, Your Honor!" Cawley shouted desperately.

Finally catching on to William's inference, Rudy looked at the lawyer in genuine disbelief. "You callin' me a fairy?"

William turned to the judge, ignoring Rudy. "Withdrawn, Your Honor. No further questions."

"You may step down, Mr. Rudy," said the judge as William walked away.

"IS HE CALLING ME A FAIRY?" Rudy turned to the judge, his rage now boiling over.

"You will step down, Mr. Rudy," repeated the judge.

Rudy stood, trying to contain himself, but instead of stepping down, he turned a fierce glare on William. "Fucking queer-loving lawyer!"

"Bailiff!" the judge called out, pounding his gavel. "Please have the witness removed from the courtroom!"

"You're probably a cocksucker, just like him!" Rudy pointed at Kent as two court officers approached the witness stand, each grabbing one of Rudy's arms. "Let go of me!" he protested. They struggled to escort him down the aisle. "I'm no fairy!" exclaimed Rudy. "Don't you know that? What the hell is wrong with you people?"

*Yes*, thought William, *just like Newport, only better*. This time, against men like these, William was certain he'd have the chance to clear the reverend's name, once and for all.

— • —

Charlie sat in the lobby, watching the crowd mill out of the courtroom. First had been Rudy, shouting, restrained by court officers. The young photographers cooling their heels nearby had simply started snapping from where they sat, recording the sailor's disgrace as his protests echoed down the marble halls.

Then the doors had been shut again, and Charlie waited. He had expected some sort of harassment by the photographers and reporters, and had prepared a repertoire of sarcastic remarks to fend them off, but the onslaught never came. Earlier in the day, they had snapped a few photos of him, but other than that, and the occasional awkward glance in his direction, it was as if he were not there.

Then the doors opened again and the boisterous crowd made their way out of the stuffy courtroom, bound for home and dinner. At the head of the pack was Cawley, who rushed to Charlie and began babbling, clearly upset by the wretched performance of his first two witnesses. Charlie only half heard the lawyer's exhortations, watching the crowd instead. And there, amongst the faceless gawkers and gossips, Charlie saw Kent, with the smug lawyer at his side.

Just as Charlie had expected, the priest appeared unruffled, distant, radiating the same innocence and compassion that he always did. It was impressive, Charlie had to admit, that any man accused of these things, a priest no less, could undergo such proceedings with so much apparent composure.

"Mr. McKinney," the lawyer at his side pleaded. "Are you listening to me?"

Charlie turned halfheartedly to the prosecutor. "Yes, sir."

"I don't want you to be rattled by what happened today to Mr. Rudy."

Charlie looked at Cawley as if the lawyer were speaking another language. "Are you kiddin'?" Charlie smirked. "Like I care what happens to Rudy."

Cawley looked at him oddly. "Excuse me?"

"I don't rattle easily, counselor," Charlie replied.

"I'll confess to you, Mr. McKinney, I've always seen you as our strongest witness. At the same time, I've also questioned your commitment to these proceedings. Chief Arnold expressed a concern that you might harbor some sympathy for the reverend. I hope I don't need to remind you of the serious consequences—"

"Look," Charlie interrupted, his patience at an end, "I don't want to tell you your business, but do you really think anybody on that jury's stupid enough to believe that Kent forced himself on me or Rudy or even that retard Dostalick?"

Charlie enjoyed the stunned look on Cawley's face.

"I . . ." the man stammered, "I need to know what you intend—"

Again Charlie felt no need to let the lawyer finish his sentence. "Far as I can see," Charlie announced, "Kent never did nothing bad to nobody. Tough luck for him. Don't worry. You'll get what you want. I ain't going to prison, that's for damn sure. But let's not pretend we don't both know who the *real* scumbag is here."

And as if by command, Ervin Arnold appeared at the other side of the lobby. A full head above the crowd, Arnold stood like a rock diverting the river of people to his right and left. The two men locked eyes and Charlie felt the hair on his neck bristle. Somehow, in his gut, he knew that something had changed. The self-satisfied smile on Arnold's face told him that the prick had some new strategy. And so, Charlie asked himself, what was wrong with that? As much as he hated the man, they were still on the same team. A victory for Arnold equaled absolution for Charlie. Then why was he certain that the chief's new ploy, though it might save all their skins, would not be to his liking? And why was he sure that Arnold knew this as well, and took enormous pleasure in the fact?

Charlie could feel Cawley at his side, watching Arnold with anticipation as a clerk approached the chief, handed him an envelope, and whispered in his ear. Arnold's face broke into a big grin, and he held up the envelope for Cawley's benefit. Charlie looked at the lawyer, who smiled, visibly relieved.

Charlie fought his misgivings. It would all be over soon, he reminded himself, for him at least if not for Kent. He simply needed to keep his powder dry a little while longer and he would be home free.

But Charlie well knew his own temperament and the limits of his tolerance, and as he sat there, chafing under the thumb of these men, the sailor suspected that playing along with this new game might prove a difficult task.

# TWENTY-ONE

The waiter pulled the cork on the bottle of Bordeaux and poured the deep red liquid into the goblet. John Rathom raised the glass to the light, swooshed it about, and brought it to his nostrils. This was one of his favorite moments of any day, when all six feet three inches, two hundred sixty pounds of him was focused at the tip of his nose, inhaling fruit, wood, and tannin. Incredible, he pondered, how much drama an area the size of the human tongue could withstand. Nothing challenged those discerning taste buds like a fine vintage red. And like water rushing over rapids, the flavor would twist and turn from subtly sweet to tart to savory, sometimes separately, sometimes all at once, leaving one both refreshed and dry as dust, parched for more. It was the taste of history, Rathom opined, the pageant of human evolution summed up in a sip.

There was something fundamentally wrong with a government that wanted to rip this pleasure from him.

"I still don't understand," said the reverend, perplexed, as the waiter filled his glass with the 1909 Châteaux Margaux.

"The current law forbids selling alcohol, Reverend," William offered with forbearance, "not drinking it."

"It'll come to that soon enough," Rathom complained.

William held his hand over his own glass, turning the waiter away.

"Oh, come now, William," Rathom sighed. "How can you refuse one of the great vintages of the last twenty years?" Rathom turned to Kent. "The wine is served at no extra charge, Reverend. Of course"—he smirked—"meal prices have more than doubled."

"Very clever," Kent chuckled. "How inexorable is the human spirit!"

"Observing the letter rather than the spirit of the law, Reverend," William pronounced with obvious disapproval.

"Oh, it's all right, William," Kent assured the younger man. "The Lord himself served wine at Cana. We're not hurting anyone."

"I'm an officer of the court, Reverend. Whether I agree with the legislation or not, someone must set an example."

"I'll drink to that," Rathom exclaimed. "Just so long as it's not me!" He raised his glass toward Kent and the two men clinked collegially.

"Delicious," said Kent. "There was one question I had, though, which perhaps you gentlemen could answer. Once the stricter laws are enforced, will I still be permitted to use wine at mass or will I have to make do with grape juice?"

Rathom shrugged. "You referred to Cana. Christ turned water into wine. Don't suppose he'd object to your turning grape juice into, you'll pardon the expression, his blood."

Kent smiled as he cut into his beef filet. "I take it you're not a believer, Mr. Rathom."

"Oh, I have my beliefs, Reverend," barked the Australian. "But none of them have to do with God or any sort of salvation. Mostly I believe in maintaining a healthy sense of humor."

"There are worse religions," said Kent graciously.

What an interesting man, thought Rathom. He had rarely taken the time to get to know any clergymen beyond the superficial, but this one seemed worth the effort. "Thank you, Reverend, I'll take that as a compliment. And you, William?"

Startled, William looked up from his meal. "Excuse me?"

"What is it you believe in?" Rathom pressed.

The lawyer shrugged, nonplussed. "Well, I . . . what all good people believe in, of course. God. Justice. The rule of law."

Kent stopped eating and looked at the younger man. "And do you never find those to be in conflict?" the reverend asked.

Rathom regarded Kent, impressed. The question appeared to be genuine.

William tried to keep up a good front, but he was clearly unsettled. "Not really, no," he asserted. "Certainly, there's injustice in the world. What's being done to you is an obvious example, but then we all know which side we're on, don't we?"

"And what about silly laws?" Rathom queried. "Like prohibition, which doesn't have a prayer's chance of succeeding? Do you find that to be a reasonable piece of legislation? If people are caught drinking in their own homes, do you suppose the authorities will haul them off to prison?"

"Now who's being unreasonable?" William scoffed. "Look, John, personally, I agree with you. If people want to destroy themselves with liquor, that's their right, isn't it? But it *is* now the law. It's our job to follow it and trust in time to bring about the appropriate corrections."

"Trust in *time*, did you say?" Rathom asked, incredulous. "Is that the same time that allowed the death of millions in a four-year catastrophe known as the Great War?"

William was momentarily speechless.

"Mr. Bartlett?" A slender maître d' stood half bent at William's right. "I beg your pardon, sir, but there's a telephone call for you."

William glanced up brightly. He seemed relieved. "Oh?" He looked at his dinner companions. "Excuse me, gentlemen." William rose from the table and followed the maître d'.

The journalist and the reverend spent an awkward moment in silence until Kent raised his glass to offer a second toast. "Thank you for the invitation, Mr. Rathom. I can't remember when I've dined in so fine a restaurant."

"My pleasure, Reverend. Thought we deserved a little celebration. I'm sure William told you about the letter we're printing in the *Journal*, the top clergymen in New England petitioning the White House on your behalf. The *New York Times* has agreed to run it as well."

"Really!" Kent said, impressed. "Is that . . . is that good?"

"For you?" Rathom offered with a smile. "Most definitely. The jury is forbidden to read the papers, of course, but they can't help being affected by the atmosphere, and you're about to become the latest *cause célèbre*. Anyway, the important thing is, you picked the right lawyer."

"Yes," Kent agreed. "I'm very grateful." Kent looked in the direction William had gone and murmured, "Strange, I sometimes find it hard to believe that such a man still exists."

Rathom regarded Kent. "Rather an odd sentiment, coming from someone in your line of work."

"I only mean . . ." Kent hedged.

The lighting in the room was subdued, but Rathom would have sworn that he'd seen the man blush.

"I mean," Kent continued, "his ability to view life in such stark black and white. Can I even remember a time when things were that simple for me?" Kent looked at Rathom, both men over fifty, and smiled sadly. "A luxury of youth, I suppose."

Yes, Rathom thought, this was indeed an interesting man, worthy of a real conversation once he was no longer newsworthy. "Not even the *youth* of today are afforded that luxury, Reverend. Not with what they've seen. No, William is unique, I'm afraid, like an ancient specimen caught in amber, a species whose time has long since passed. Good riddance, some would say. On the other hand, I'm willing to bet his kind will be missed."

It was Rathom who first saw William reapproach the table, with an expression so pale and troubled that both men rose to meet him. "Good heavens, William," said Kent. "What is it? What's wrong?" William looked back and forth between them, not seeing either, then dropped his gaze to the tabletop. "Another sailor has stepped forward, Reverend, accusing you." William's eyes finally found their way to Kent's. "He's seventeen."

After their brief conversation, Rathom would not have been shocked to learn that Kent had robbed a bank or was a secret Bolshevik sympathizer, but molesting a seventeen-year-old boy seemed highly unlikely. He had been wrong many times before and no doubt would be again, so he scrutinized the reverend, awaiting a second blush or too quick a denial, but the journalist saw only the blank-faced stare of an innocent man.

- • - • -

Cawley and Arnold had both quickly disappeared, but it didn't take Charlie long to discover what was up. The news was all over the base, that the degenerate reverend had loved up a seventeen-year-old kid. Anyone who'd been on the fence regarding Kent's guilt or innocence had come down on the hard side now. The other operators were no angels, a fact widely known, so whatever mess they'd gotten themselves into was well deserved. But Barker was another story altogether. Over the months since the war had ended, the quiet, stammering kid from Nebraska had become something of a mascot for the sailors of Newport, an object of harmless ridicule. When men gathered, bored to tears, desperate for scarce women and drink, any lull in the conversation would inevitably be filled with the question "Now, what would Barker say about this?" Then someone would respond, not getting more than three words out in as many minutes, and the other men would laugh to the point of pissing themselves.

The teenager himself knew nothing of his own celebrity, since any man who dared mock the boy to his face would have had his head handed to him by any given bunch of sailors. Most of the men had never even met Barker. The ritual had become a kind of paean to Barker's innocence, a hallelujah to its continued survival in their sordid, brawling midst. It was an assault on this sacred thing that Kent had apparently perpetrated, and for that, there could be no forgiveness.

Charlie was certain that Kent had done nothing to or with the kid. As for Barker's innocence, it had been violated long before this accusation, it seemed to Charlie, and if anyone other than Barker was to blame for that loss, it was Charlie himself.

---

Long after taps, Charlie finally gave up his search for the boy. Exhausted, he hustled through the sleeping training station toward the main gate, hoping to hitch a ride back to the boardinghouse before the roads emptied for the night.

He'd spent most of the last several hours thinking about Barker. McKinney had hoped to be a mentor to the boy, to allow the younger man to benefit from the lessons Charlie had learned in the school of hard knocks. Like everyone else, Charlie had been drawn in by Barker's vulnerability, by an instinct to protect the boy from the harsh realities of the world. And it had made him feel surprisingly good, doing something for someone else for a change, with nothing in it for himself.

How, he'd asked himself, had Barker made it even seventeen years with such childlike innocence still intact? Maybe if Charlie could wise him up to the hustle, to women, Barker might retain some of that goodness that he and the others saw in him, an eyes-wide openness that Charlie had long since abandoned in the pursuit of self-interest.

And then the night with Dottie happened, and the moments after. It had been a crushing disappointment to discover that Barker had been nothing more than a fairy all along. Charlie felt like he'd been played somehow, and it frightened him that he'd missed the signs that must have been there from the start. Charlie had made it as far as he had in life because of his ability to read people, usually before they could read him. He had concluded that his instincts had failed him with Barker, and he felt like a chump, so he'd kicked the kid to the curb like a dog.

*But was that the case?* Charlie asked himself now. Had his instincts failed him? He had grown closer to Barker in the last eight months than he had to almost any other person in his life. He didn't think he would ever comprehend men who didn't desire women, who longed for something as dreary as other males. But should that one thing, that one profound difference between them overrule everything else his gut told him about the boy? Charlie's expectations of other people were universally low, so why should he expect this one person who had proved so much better than most to be everything Charlie imagined him to be?

What happened that night had been a shock, but thinking back, he was convinced it had likely been a first for the boy. Perhaps Barker had not even known himself until that moment. Queer or not, he now decided, Barker was as innocent and guileless, and as good, as he had appeared all along. It was either that, or Charlie would have to throw out all he knew of human nature.

"Where you rushing to, McKinney?" the despised voice cooed from somewhere in the darkness. "You should be home in bed by now, resting up for your big day in court."

If he couldn't find Barker, Arnold was the next best thing.

"What did you say to him?" Charlie demanded.

"I don't know what you're talking about," Arnold replied, emerging from the darkness, puffing on a foul, fat cigar.

"It's all over the base that Barker's testifying against Kent tomorrow," Charlie growled. "I saw you the other night, talking his ear off. What did you say to him?"

"I told him to do his duty," Arnold proclaimed. "Kid's got quite a story to tell. Didn't think he had it in him."

Charlie had never killed anyone, not in war, not in his hardscrabble youth, but for the first time, he felt the urgent need to end another man's life. "You rotten son of a bitch!"

"Watch your mouth, punk!" Arnold warned sharply.

"Fuck you! Barker was never anywhere *near* Kent and you know it!" Charlie insisted. "Kid never did anything on his own! Practically had to hold his hand every time we went out!"

"We've all got secrets, McKinney," Arnold said. "Maybe there are some things about the little man that you don't know. Then again," Arnold spat through his teeth, "maybe you do."

Charlie stared at Arnold, incredulous. "Why does all this matter so much to you?" he asked.

"If you have to ask," Arnold replied, contemptuous, "you wouldn't understand."

"You've got me and the others," Charlie offered. "Why can't you just leave Barker alone?"

"Aw!" the other man said mockingly. "Isn't that sweet? Defending your little darling. Out of character for you, McKinney." Arnold flicked his cigar into the darkness. "But I think I understand. After all, the kid is one helluva cocksucker."

Before either man knew it, Charlie had opened up with a hard right and a left, knocking the giant back on his heels. He readied a haymaker but Arnold blocked it and pushed him back. Charlie steadied himself quickly and assumed a defensive posture, preparing for Arnold's counterattack as he tried to calm his raging heart.

Arnold licked the blood from his lip and dropped his arms. "You're not worth fighting," he sneered. "As if I'd let that little fairy touch me. See, that's the difference between us, McKinney. I'm a man, not an animal."

"I'm warning you," Charlie seethed, breathless, "you put Barker on the stand tomorrow and I swear I'll—"

Arnold laughed. "You'll what?"

All these months, Charlie had always come up short in his dealings with Arnold, as if the chief were a hand wielding a pin and Charlie a slow, flightless bug. Suddenly, the power Charlie possessed became apparent to him and he fought the urge to grin. "I'll change my testimony, that's what. I'll tell them Kent never touched me. Then I'll tell them how you ordered us to lie."

But rather than blink as Charlie had expected, Arnold stood taller. "Go ahead"—the man shrugged—"admit to perjury. Only five years in prison. I'm sure you'll do just fine."

Charlie stopped dead. He'd forgotten about prison. He would not do just fine and Arnold knew it—controlled every moment, told when to shit, when to eat, where to sleep and with whom. Worse than the Navy even. Five years was an eternity in a life like Charlie's and he would be the worse for it, he was sure of that.

"Something on your mind?" Arnold continued sarcastically. "Funny thing is, Barker's the one they're likely to believe, so why waste your time? Once that rosy-cheeked boy wins the jury's heart, they'll see Kent for the pervert he is; then the rest of us can go home knowing we did *some* good, at least."

"You . . ." Charlie muttered. He'd been outmaneuvered again.

Arnold shook his head. "Pathetic. I always knew I could count on you, McKinney. Know why? 'Cause you're trash, and trash'll always find a way to get over." Arnold gave him one last look. "Sweet dreams," he said as he turned and walked off.

Charlie felt the pin slide in, felt his heart and guts wriggling on the end of it. He'd endured a thousand wounds like this in his life, from Arnold and others like him. He knew from experience that it would not kill him. The difference was that this time, he wished that it would.

# TWENTY-TWO

It was impossible for the court to bring a fourth count against Kent and include it in the same proceeding, so they settled on introducing the boy's testimony as corroborative evidence. William still tried to have it declared inadmissible, claiming that the defense had not been given adequate time for discovery, but Judge Brown would not hear of it. "I'll give you one day," the aging jurist declared.

William spent that day mostly by himself. He had not read the boy's statement the night before when it had been hand-delivered to him, telling himself it would be better digested after a good night's sleep. He did not read it first thing in the morning as he had intended, preferring instead to share a pleasant breakfast with his wife and children before stepping back into the underworld he had inhabited for much of the last six months.

The worn leather briefcase containing the affidavit still sat on the hall stand by the front door where he had dropped it the previous evening. And though it was the first thing he spied when he passed from the staircase to the breakfast room for his morning meal, it was the very last thing he picked up when he left the house for the day.

At his small office in Newport, William busied himself with the trivialities he'd always detested and which now miraculously seemed so urgent. As first the morning passed, then lunch, then the afternoon, the leather satchel, carried with him wherever he went, grew heavier and more insistent. Finally he found himself back at home, the leaden briefcase in hand, still unopened. He had tried to drop it again on the hall stand but it refused to release his fingers, and so he carried it to his study, closed the door, and sat in his leather chair with the hated thing balanced on his knees as the room filled with sunset.

Surely, he reasoned, the resistance that had gripped him since yesterday was not simple revulsion. He would have welcomed revulsion at this point, like a long-lost friend, a sign that the wanton things now commonplace to him still remained at some level unimaginable. No, it was something deeper that had filled him with dread, a fear that he remembered feeling in this very room not that many years ago. He choked on it like something caught in his throat, something rotten that made him nauseous. And as he did, the thing clarified itself, took form, and offered up its name.

Doubt, he recognized at last, was the thing that had been gnawing at him, the sickening ambiguity he'd always felt in the presence of his father's ancient resolve. He'd banished it in the years since the old man's death with a string of mundane victories: college, law school, marriage, children, a measure of professional success. But from the moment William received the phone call telling him of this new accusation, a cold breath had been whispering at his heart. *Are you sure?* it asked, and he recognized his father's voice, that clarion of conviction no more diminished by death than it had been by the daily vicissitudes of life on earth.

He undid the two heavy brass buckles that fastened the briefcase and slid out the slim, typed affidavit. It did not take long to read and contained no spectacular new revelations, simply more of the same. If anything, the story seemed even less plausible, more crudely fabricated than those of the other men. Immediately William saw, point by point, how he would refute each claim. There was of course the boy's age to contend with and, depending on the fellow's demeanor, any natural sympathy he might evoke in the jury. But by the time William had finished reading, he felt reasonably confident that this new testimony posed no undue threat, and that the string of impressive character witnesses he had assembled to testify on Kent's behalf would more than outweigh any potential damage the Barker boy might inflict.

And still the doubt persisted. He knew the reverend as he knew few other men, and nothing in this latest twist had prompted William to reconsider his assumption that these three, now four, were abject liars. Kent had denied any acquaintance whatsoever with this fellow, and William believed him. What then was the source of his discomfort, which sat perched on his left shoulder, licking at his ear like a whore?

It could derive of only one question, he concluded, a puzzle that had plagued him from the first and for which he had never found a satisfactory solution. *Why* had the reverend been targeted? Even after their bumbling defeat in the first trial, why had these scoundrels persisted in their zeal to the point of corrupting a seventeen-year-old boy, inducing him to lie under oath? William could continue to rattle off the old arguments about Kent's goodness and the sailors' need to bring everyone down to their level, bromides that had served him well enough up to now. But the determination his adversaries continued to demonstrate strained these simple answers and hinted to William of something fundamental in the human spirit, something at which he could hardly even guess.

Once identified, the riddle refused to release him, and he found himself still preoccupied by it the next day as he sat at the defense table beside his client and friend. The courtroom was filled to capacity, and from the stand the picture of dewy innocence spoke of his alleged abuse at the hands of Reverend Kent. The boy had some sort of speech impediment, which seemed more emotional than physical. Not a stutter exactly, more of a stammering insecurity that made even William's heart break for the lad.

"But when . . . when I came out . . . out of the bathroom," Barker continued, "he wanted . . . he asked me if I'd get . . . if I'd get into . . . into bed with him."

Cawley nodded like a wise and solicitous uncle, encouraging his new star witness. "Did you accept his invitation, son?"

"Yes, I . . . yes, I . . . yes, I did, sir."

"Why?" Cawley asked gently.

Barker looked down. "Because . . . well . . . out of . . . out of respect."

"I see," said Cawley. "Then what happened?"

"Then he started . . . he . . . he kissed me and he . . . he tried . . . tried to . . ." Barker trailed off.

The young man was blushing. This sounded far worse to William's ears than a string of lifeless words on paper. The boy's speech problem could easily be interpreted as a struggle with difficult memories, rather than the hesitations of a perjured witness. A glance at the faces of the jurors confirmed to William that his fears were well justified.

"I know this is difficult, son." Cawley knew exactly how to maximize his advantage, playing directly into the jury's sensibilities. "But we need you to tell us. Then he . . . ?"

Barker continued with genuine difficulty. "He tried to push . . . push me down, make me . . . but I wouldn't. Then *he* did . . . I was . . . I couldn't move. Then . . ." He trailed off again and the court was left to imagine the most horrible of infamies.

"Yes?" Cawley coaxed, struggling to hide his glee.

"Then . . ." The boy looked down, ashamed and visibly deflated, referencing either an unwanted sexual climax, or relief at a lie well told. "Then I left," Barker finished.

Cawley gave a last, long sympathetic gaze at Barker, then addressed the judge. "No more questions, Your Honor."

Judge Brown turned to William. "Your witness, Mr. Bartlett."

"Thank you, Your Honor."

Kent grabbed his sleeve and pulled him close, whispering frantically, "William, I've told you, I don't even know this boy! You must believe me!"

William simply looked at Kent, disturbed by the man's behavior. Perhaps he too had been upset by the boy's testimony and concerned about its possible effect upon the jury. Still, it seemed an uncharacteristic moment of panic for the reverend, who up to now had been a rock, and William hoped it did not presage a general collapse. A centerpiece of William's defense strategy involved putting Kent himself on the stand, and now was not the time for him to come unhinged.

William placed a calming hand on Kent's shoulder, then stood and walked toward Barker, weighing his options. The boy was far more delicate than he had anticipated, and though he could not let the testimony go unchallenged, he knew he would have to tread very lightly with Barker or risk alienating an already sensitized jury. He began gently.

"Mr. Barker?"

Barker looked at him cautiously. "Yes . . . yes, sir?"

"You never did anything like this before joining the Navy, did you, son?" William adopted Cawley's affectionate tag, though he was clearly not old enough to be the boy's father.

"No, sir. Never. Nothing . . . nothing like . . . like this."

"So how is it," William asked earnestly, "that a good, clean boy like yourself wound up doing this sort of work?"

"I . . . I was . . . I was asked to go into it. They, well, they picked . . . picked out certain . . . certain men. There was a . . . a list. I . . . I was on the list."

"So they asked," William repeated simply, "and you said yes. Knowing what it would entail?"

Barker shook his head emphatically. "No. No . . . no, sir."

*Could this be true?* William asked himself. "They never told you your duties?"

"No, sir. Not . . . not until . . . well, until we were, uh, in the organization. It was . . . it was secret . . . until we took the . . . the oath."

"Well," William continued, hitting on the right tone, as if he and Barker were the only two people in the room, "how did they know you'd be able to stomach such awful things?"

"They kinda . . . well, they tried . . . tried us out."

"I see. So you had to go out and do the work, show that you were able to do it, before the Navy would swear you in as an operator?"

"No. I . . . I helped . . . helped a couple of fellows, went . . . went around with them, but I never . . . I didn't do any work."

"But you learned enough that you thought you might enjoy it."

For the first time, Barker failed to provide a prompt response.

"Objection, Your Honor," Cawley intervened.

"Sustained," agreed the judge.

William resumed his gentle tone. "Why did you join up, son?"

Barker looked at William with a different sort of confusion. "Because I . . . it seemed . . . important. I didn't . . . I never got to fight. The war, well, you see . . . it ended. I thought . . . I wanted to do some good."

A plausible and monstrous explanation, William thought to himself. How tragically simple it was to convince young men to do wrong by telling them it was right. Millions of recent war dead could testify to that. "Once you realized exactly what your duties were, son, did you ever speak to anyone, parents, friends, anyone, to try to get out of this work?"

A look of panic came into the boy's eyes. "No . . . no, sir. Never, sir. My . . . my parents? I could . . . please, I could never . . ."

There were indeed aspects of the human heart that William did not understand, he thought to himself. Here Barker sat, testifying in the most public of trials, yet still he believed that somehow his parents would never know what he'd done. William could not help but feel sympathy for this boy.

"Mr. Barker," William continued, "were you ordered to get evidence against Reverend Kent?

"Yes . . . yes, sir." Barker still seemed rattled.

"Against him, specifically?"

"Against . . . against any lewd men. We were . . . They said he was a lewd man."

William hated to do it, but it was time to move in for the kill. "And yet," he continued with a tone of disappointment in his voice, "a good, clean boy like yourself agreed to get into bed with this supposedly lewd man?"

"I . . . yes, sir."

"Mr. Barker, how many other men did you work on prior to the reverend?"

The panic returned to Barker's eyes. He looked down. "I . . . I don't remember."

"Oh?" William replied, taken aback. "Were there that many?"

"No, I don't . . . I mean I couldn't remember . . . I never got . . . I never got their names."

William looked at him, genuinely puzzled. "You never . . . ? But wasn't that the whole point? To collect names?"

Barker was now visibly sweating. "Yes, but I . . . Charlie said that—"

"Charlie?" William queried, his interest piqued. "You mean Mr. McKinney? *What* did he say?"

Barker shook his head, suddenly protective. "Nothing! Nothing! He . . . he was . . . he was my friend. It wasn't . . . I never . . ."

It was clear the boy was beginning to fall apart. William had to risk pressing his advantage now while he had the chance.

"Mr. Barker," he said in a somewhat more strident tone, "isn't it true that you were instructed to 'get' Reverend Kent at all costs?"

"No," Barker insisted, "I . . . not—"

"You dutifully gave your body over to the most abhorrent acts, abhorrent to yourself, your parents, to all good men and women. Isn't it reasonable to assume that you would just as willingly obey an order to lie?"

"Objection, Your Honor!" Cawley jumped up.

"Overruled," declared the judge.

Barker looked from one to the other, confused. Clearly, something in William's last barrage had struck home. "My parents, they . . . they . . ." he stammered, "they can't . . . they . . ." He turned to the judge, desperate. "Please, Judge, it'd just about kill them if they . . . if they found out. They can't . . . they can't know about this. They just . . . Please, I'll . . ." The boy trailed off in seeming shock as a deadly silence filled the room. William knew that he dared not push the young man any further.

"Answer Mr. Bartlett's question, son," the judge insisted as compassionately as he could.

William shook his head. "Withdrawn, Your Honor. No more questions. This boy's been through enough."

"Very well," said the judge. He turned to Barker and spoke gently, "You can step down now, son."

Barker looked up at the old man helplessly; then, in a daze, the young fellow did as he had been told and walked out of the courtroom.

— • — • —

It had been excruciating for Charlie, sitting outside the courtroom as Barker testified within. He couldn't hear much. It had still been dark when he'd dressed that morning after a night of fitful sleep. Shortly before six, he'd stepped into the new whites that Arnold had delivered to him, Cawley having decided that his only other set looked somewhat stained and worn. That'll happen, Charlie had remarked, when you go to war. From six to seven, he simply sat on his bed, waiting for the honk of the shuttle that would transport him and Barker and Arnold and Hudson to the courthouse in Providence. They would have an hour at least to ride together, and though their conversation would be restricted, Charlie figured he could at least offer the kid some words of encouragement before his march into the lions' den.

But when the military bus arrived, there was no one in it but the driver and an Army MP whose express duty was to make sure Charlie made it to court on time.

"Where's everybody else?" Charlie asked.

"Gone in another car," said the MP.

Arnold's hold on Barker must be pretty tenuous, Charlie thought, if he felt the need to keep the boy so far out of his reach. Perhaps Arnold was not as cocksure as he had played the night before.

He beat the others to the courthouse, arriving just after it opened for business. He took his old seat near the oak doors, waiting for any chance of a word with Barker. Whether by accident or design, his coconspirators arrived just before nine, amidst the last crush of humanity anxious to find a seat in the gallery. Charlie stood when he saw Barker being escorted through the crowd, Cawley's hand firmly attached to the boy's right bicep. As the two approached the courtroom, Charlie seized what would be perhaps his only chance, took a step forward, and called out, "Barker!"

Cawley tried to draw the boy back out of Charlie's eyeline, but the moment Barker saw Charlie, his pace slowed to a crawl. "Back off, Mr. McKinney!" barked Cawley.

"Listen to me, Barker," Charlie urged. "I don't know what Arnold told you, but whatever it was, it ain't true!"

Barker looked at Charlie, nervous and confused.

"What did he *say* to you, kid?" Charlie demanded.

Cawley tried to pull Barker along, but the boy was now frozen in place. "I'm warning you, McKinney," Cawley snarled.

"He . . . he promised if I testified," Barker said, "he'd . . . my name would stay out of the papers. I could . . . I could just go home like it never even happened." Barker looked down, embarrassed.

"He's lying to you," Charlie insisted.

"No, no," Barker maintained, adamant. "No, he said . . . he said it. And he said if I . . . if I didn't testify, it would . . . you would have to go . . . to go to jail, and I'd never . . . you'd just be . . . gone." And Barker looked up at him then with more pain than Charlie had ever seen in a man not dying.

Charlie stood speechless. An instant later Barker was swept into the courtroom and the doors were closed behind him. A court officer blocked the way.

And so Charlie waited, an hour or more, until the doors again swung open and Barker walked out, his gaze focused a hundred yards off in the distance. "Barker!" Charlie called. The boy looked at him a moment, unseeing, then continued on.

From the courtroom, Charlie heard Cawley's voice announce, "The prosecution calls Charles A. McKinney to the stand!" The court officer took his arm to escort him into the courtroom, but Charlie shook him off and took a step after his lost friend.

"The judge'll find you in contempt!" the court officer warned as the MP grabbed Charlie's other arm. Torn, Charlie glanced for a moment toward the courtroom, then back at Barker, but the boy had already disappeared through the courthouse doors and out into the world beyond.

# TWENTY-THREE

The flu ward of the naval hospital was dark at 3:00 a.m. on that November night. A world away, the Great War had ended, Charlie remembered, but here, men who only days before had been in the bloom of their youth were still dying for no good reason. Charlie laid in bed, flanked by a pair of purplish-blue hulks, while Kent occupied the chair beside Charlie's bed as he had done with so many other victims of the dreaded disease, if reports were to be credited. In Charlie's case, however, the reverend could hardly have believed that this particular sailor had ever been sick a day in his life, and Charlie made no attempt to mimic the symptoms of the illness. In fact, he felt ridiculous lying there, healthy as a horse amongst all this horror. It would have served him right, Charlie thought at the time, if he really *did* come down with it. And he'd have had just one person to thank for the favor—Ervin Arnold.

But in spite of the deceit that hung between them like so much smoke in the air, the reverend never challenged the charade. Kent must have wondered, Charlie thought, what desperate circumstances had driven this strapping fellow to feign a deadly illness. He must have puzzled over how the man had managed to convince the doctors to assign him a scarce bed in the overcrowded ward. For his part, Charlie wondered what motivated the priest to come here night after night to stare death in the face. The stench alone was almost more than Charlie could bear. And yet, here Kent was, placid as a mountain lake, ready to give whatever comfort was needed.

The temperature in the ward had been turned way up in a futile attempt to calm the shivers of the feverish men, most of whom were either delirious or comatose. But Charlie felt the heat and peeled off his sweaty T-shirt. And as the priest gazed at his young body, then forcibly looked away, Charlie watched the ripples appear in Kent's tranquil demeanor.

"Go ahead," said Charlie without judgment. "No harm in looking."

Charlie could see the surprise in Kent's face as the man looked up and their eyes met. The sailor shrugged. How foolish people were, Charlie had thought in the moment, to believe their secrets so safely hidden.

He watched Kent struggle, debating whether to deny what was now obvious to them both, or to give in to this moment of darkness, surrounded by death, and do what he longed to do. It was an unfair fight from the start and Kent surrendered, growing visibly younger as he allowed himself to gaze with deep appreciation at the perfection of the young man's body.

Charlie was accustomed to being looked at. He held no opinion on the subject, other than being glad that he hadn't been born ugly or misshapen. To him, his body was just one more asset to be used as required. But no one, he had remarked to himself at the time, had ever looked at him in quite this way before. Had he been asked to describe how this gaze was unique, Charlie would have come up short. He only knew that there was nothing bad about it. It was as if Kent had never seen a human before, and now judged man to be the jewel of God's creation.

"May I . . . may I touch you?" Kent asked in a near whisper, torn between terror and anticipation.

Charlie simply looked at him.

"You . . . you seem like a young man who might understand," Kent continued. "I've seen so much death. It would be proof of God to me." Kent laughed. "That sounds ridiculous, doesn't it?"

Charlie shook his head. "I don't believe much in God." Then he added, "Sure."

Kent slowly reached out and took hold of Charlie's hand.

"My hand?" Charlie asked skeptically. "You wanted to touch my *hand*?"

The two men exchanged another glance and Kent smiled sadly, shaking his head.

By now, Charlie had forgotten why he was there, what his orders had been, and he watched, fascinated, as Kent's hand released his own and moved to rest atop his sternum, feeling Charlie's heart as though it were beating for them both. With the greatest reverence, Kent ran his hand gently over the bare torso. He looked as though he might weep. Kent looked up at the young man helplessly, and it seemed to Charlie that he was awaiting some silent permission.

———•—•—•———

"And then?" Cawley asked as the packed courtroom sat in rapt silence. William had to remind himself to breathe.

"He took hold of me," said the sailor.

"Where?" asked Cawley.

McKinney flashed the prosecutor an unmistakable look of contempt. "Where do you think?"

"Tell the court," Cawley insisted, determined to milk every moment.

McKinney stared at Cawley, challenging him.

"My privates," McKinney said.

"What did you do then?" Cawley asked.

The sailor was silent for a moment, then dropped his head. "Nothing. I felt sorry for him. And I felt guilty about what I was there for. Pretending to be sick."

The entire courtroom hung on McKinney's every word. Not a soul appeared to be breathing. Finally, McKinney looked across at Kent with what appeared to be genuine sorrow in his eyes.

"I'm sorry about this, Reverend. I am. It's nothing personal," the sailor said.

The whore of doubt that had been whispering in William's ear now stood atop the defense table, laughing, her legs spread toward him in defiance. He dared not look at Kent, afraid of finding what his gut already knew, that this sailor with his oddly simple story had just made a joke of William's great crusade.

A shared intimacy now connected McKinney to the man at William's left, sucking up all the air in the room and pulling several hundred sets of eyes Kent's way. Unable to resist the tug any longer, William turned to face his client. Kent's pained expression confirmed the lawyer's worst fears, that he had spent the last four months defending a guilty man.

"Christ," shouted the sailor, reclaiming his pivotal role in the drama. "It's just sex! What do you all gotta make such a big deal out of it for?"

—•—•—•—

William sat at the wheel, peering through the torrential rain that pummeled the motorcar's roof and turned the windshield wipers into a useless annoyance. Pedestrians dashed, their heads covered with newspapers or purses or jackets pulled up high, since all but the sturdiest of umbrellas had been inverted by the wind.

Samuel Kent sat beside him. The two men had not spoken since they'd shoved their way through the crush of people in the courthouse, avoiding the newspapermen eager for a statement. John Rathom had slipped out a few moments earlier and was lying in wait just outside the courthouse doors. But instead of badgering them with questions, he had helped the two men to William's car, running interference along the way.

And now they crawled along through the nasty weather. At this rate, it would take them two hours to get back to Newport, hours lengthened by the weight of the sudden truth that hung between them. Clearly, something needed to be said, but William had not a clue how to begin the conversation. It was as if he had never met the other man in his car. He no longer even looked the same to William, but seemed older and smaller and awkward in a way William had never noticed before. And Kent had not made the situation any easier. Far from showing any discomfort, the man seemed content to sit silently by, locked in his thoughts, almost as if William were simply his chauffeur. That change in relationship would have suited William just fine had he been able to convince Kent to sit in back, out of sight, or find himself another lawyer.

Then again, William reflected, trying to calm his racing mind, perhaps he was jumping to undue conclusions. He hadn't been himself the past two days, and Barker's testimony, true or false, had upset everyone in the courtroom. Why should he, or Kent for that matter, be any different? Abbot had warned William to expect surprises from Cawley, and the one-two punch of Barker and McKinney had been a brilliant maneuver. But the trial was far from over. After all, he still had his own ace in the hole, the reverend himself, whose testimony was certain to outweigh the claims of these depraved men.

William released a sigh, ready to break the unbearable silence. "This was not our best day, I'm afraid, Reverend," William offered, his voice hollow against the pounding of the rain. "The Barker boy won the jury's heart, I think, and McKinney . . ." He stumbled a moment as he uttered the sailor's name. "We must put you on the stand."

But Kent seemed not to be listening. Instead, he peered out his window. "Stop the car," the reverend abruptly ordered.

Concerned that the older man might be ill, William immediately pulled over and stopped the motor, whereupon Kent opened his door and jumped out into the driving rain. William leaned over and called out, "Reverend!"

But Kent did not turn or respond. William watched, dismayed, as the man mounted the steps of Saint Joseph's Cathedral and entered through the heavy bronze doors.

His panic returning, William remained in the car until he realized, reluctantly, that he must follow his client. He parked the motorcar and made a mad dash for the sanctuary.

It was not unlike other papist churches he'd seen in Boston or New York or Europe. Massive pillars of somber concrete soared to a vaulted ceiling above. In the nave a hundred yards ahead, a huge freestanding structure of polished bronze housed an altar and a wooden pulpit, now empty. Above the altar a rose window one hundred feet across displayed deep reds, blues, and golds that on a sunny day, William surmised, might contribute a modicum of charm to the space. Today, however, it could only be described as dark and damp and excessive. Intermittently, rising through the floorboards, the voices of a children's choir could be heard rehearsing. It was sweet, but distant and faceless, and made him ache desperately for the comfort of his home and the nearness of his children.

Kent sat alone in a pew halfway up the center aisle. William half hoped the reverend *was* ill, if only to justify his bizarre behavior.

"It's so beautiful," Kent said, gazing up at the stained glass window.

"What are you doing, Reverend?" William blurted out, exasperated. "Isn't this a *Catholic* church?"

Kent sighed, ignoring the remark. "Sit down, William. Please."

"Reverend, we really—" William protested.

Kent looked up at him. "Please," he repeated simply.

William felt he had no choice but to agree, so he squeezed past Kent and took a seat a respectful distance from him.

"William," the reverend began, "were you aware that a thousand years ago, had you and I been unfortunate enough to be born left-handed as we are today, we might have been burned as witches?"

How long had it been since he'd found Kent's every word an inspiration? "Is that so?" was all he managed in response.

"Even today," Kent continued, "in our own country, parents will often tie a child's left hand behind his back, forcing him to use his right."

"Reverend," said William, out of patience, "I really don't see what—"

"The great question, William, that any thinking man, any man with a sense of history must ask himself, is this: How much of what we call virtue is an accident of birth? The right century? The right culture? The right parents?"

William clammed up, fearful of where this road might lead.

"I won't get on the stand," Kent said simply. "I won't bear false witness. I—"

"Stop right there, Reverend," William interrupted, alarmed. "Whatever you're about to say, I really don't need to know. In fact, as your lawyer—"

"Is that all you are, William?" asked Kent. "I thought you were my friend."

William knew there was no escape for him now. The river had been crossed, the bridge demolished behind them. He looked down. "What is it you expect me to say?"

"I'm truly sorry, William." Kent laid a hand on William's shoulder. "I know I've hurt you."

William shook off the hand and stared ahead in stony silence.

"But I didn't think you'd understand," Kent sighed, looking away.

"My career, my family's future," William fumed, half to himself. "All of it put at risk because I believed in you!"

"And have I changed so much in the last few hours?" Kent demanded.

"You're a liar!" William shot back.

A sad look came over the older man's face. "Granted," he replied. "But would you have me spend the rest of my life in prison, for one moment of weakness?" Kent asked reasonably. "Does that make sense to you?"

None of it made sense to William at that moment, not Kent, not the law, not his own muddled place in it all. "That's not for me . . . for us to decide! Society condemns—"

"But who is society, William, if not you and me?"

William shook his head. He would not go down that slippery slope with Kent. "It's wrong! Plain and simple! What you did! What I did to that boy today! And the others!"

"They lied!" the reverend insisted.

William turned to Kent, infuriated. "Then *tell* me! *What* is the truth? *Did* you or did you *not*?"

"Barker, and the other two, I never touched!" Kent swore. "Only McKinney spoke honestly of what happened between us. I think I had convinced myself that it wasn't real, that I had imagined it." He smiled sadly. "I was reminded today how very real it was. And it made me ashamed."

Four months as his lawyer and nearly a year of knowing the man. How many words had he uttered on Kent's behalf? How many decisions had he built upon his absolute knowledge of Kent's innocence? All swept away. "I should think it would," William declared.

"You're so sure, aren't you?" Kent snapped back. "The lines are so clear for you. Then explain to me, please, the precise point at which love stops being love. When exactly does it become a thing so obscene that it can't be mentioned?"

William looked at him, speechless.

"What I am ashamed of," Kent clarified, "is that I lied to myself, and to you. I'm not ashamed of what I did. I would not take it back for anything on earth, or in heaven for that matter. It was as pure and authentic a moment as I have ever had in my life."

"Stop it!" William insisted, his eyes darting about for the closest exit.

"Do you have any idea," Kent continued, with a smoldering rage, "how many young men I have prayed over in the last two years, boys, torn apart by that stupid, senseless war, or cut down by disease? Yet, somehow, someone somewhere decided that shooting a man in the head or stabbing him with a bayonet is more acceptable than touching him with love. In fifteen years, never have I broken my vows, until now. I must answer for it. But it's God I must answer to, not the whimsical laws of men."

And just like that, it was over. William remained silent a long moment, struggling to find a path back to a world he recognized. "Under the circumstances, Reverend, I'm . . . I'm not certain I can continue to represent you."

Kent closed his eyes. "You must do as your heart tells you, William." The reverend sighed. "But before you decide, would you accompany me on an errand of mercy? It's not far out of your way. And I promise I won't lecture you anymore."

William looked at Kent, suspicious. But courtesy would allow him only one response. "Very well, Reverend."

Kent gave a small nod of appreciation and stood, faced the altar and made the sign of the cross, and left. William pulled himself to his feet and followed him.

# TWENTY-FOUR

The rain had stopped along Cliff Walk. Despite the weather, despite the public scandal of Kent's trial and the heightened fear of discovery and arrest, Nature still demanded that those so inclined answer her call.

So on this night, ignoring the clouds that threatened a second downpour, two teenaged servicemen made love in the dark as best they could. It had been sweet and awkward and passionate, as the two offered up to one another their beauty and inexperience. Rather than a one-sided affair, as many of these encounters often were, the attraction and desire to please had been mutual and had left them both wanting more of the other's company. The bigger of the two, a strapping Irish-looking soldier of nineteen with black hair and blue eyes, turned to his shy, somewhat younger sailor companion as they both buttoned up. "So, d'you think you'd like to get together again?" The soldier laughed, embarrassed. "I don't mean here. Maybe we could go to the pictures or something, then get a room?" he suggested. The sailor simply shrugged, looking away. Concerned, the Irish lad approached his new lover and laid a gentle hand on his shoulder. "You all right?"

The other boy said nothing.

"Hey," the big one said as he took his new friend's face gently in his hands. "I know how it is," he said. "Don't worry," he whispered and he kissed the other boy.

As their lips parted, the young sailor looked up at his dark-haired companion. "You . . . you're so . . . you're so beautiful," he said. "I can't . . . I wish that . . ." Then he broke off and kissed the soldier passionately, wrapping his arms around the bigger, stronger fellow, grasping on as if to a lifeline.

"Take it easy," the more confident boy laughed nervously, coming up for air. "I can't breathe."

The shy one gazed up at the young soldier. "I . . . I mean, I . . . I'm not . . . you . . ." And with that, the sailor turned abruptly and ran like the devil, as fast and as far as he could.

— • — • —

Having grown up in Newport, William was an able sailor and a strong swimmer, so he rarely found himself uncomfortable on the open water. That night, however, on the small, motorized tender that carried him and Reverend Kent across the harbor to the USS *Boxer*, William experienced an uncommon anxiety. It had been building for several days, of course, but that was little comfort as he found himself clutching the sides of the bouncing boat. All control seemed to have vanished from his life, and he saw no reason why the sea should not be the next to betray him.

A silent young Navy man ferried them to the floating under-world that loomed black and ominous ahead. As they drew closer, it became clear that the ship itself was a reject, with a rusty and pitted hull that looked only marginally seaworthy. They disembarked and were escorted by a gnarled hellhound named Kowalski down several narrow flights of stairs to a damp, dark chamber below the waterline, in fulfillment of William's deepest fears.

"A few minutes is all I can give you, Reverend," the aging salt cautioned. "I shouldn't really be letting you in here at all."

The old sailor inserted a large key into a gray steel door, turned the thing with difficulty, and swung the door open, scraping metal against rusty metal. A long corridor stretched into the shadows ahead of them, with random streams of light escaping through the bars that lined each side.

*So this is a prison ship,* William noted.

"Come," said Kent. At this point, William had no choice but to follow the reverend through the portal and into the corridor. The door banged shut behind them. He glanced side to side and saw a man asleep in each of the first two cells.

"Yoo-hoo, Reverend," a voice called from farther on. "How 'bout a root beer?" William looked in the next cell and saw a slender, effeminate young man lounging in his skivvies.

"Sorry," said Kent with a smile. "Not tonight, Jimmy."

"Hello, Reverend," from the other side, a homely and heavyset man in his fifties called out.

"Sergeant," Kent said, nodding a hello.

"Why have you brought me here?" William asked.

Kent turned and looked at him. "I wanted you to see the newest part of my ministry, my fellow sex offenders, William, detained for nearly five months now. No legal counsel, no date set for court-martial. Over there . . ." Kent pointed to a young man sleeping soundly in another cell on their right. "Decorated twice for bravery. Pulled three men from a burning ship."

William regarded the slumbering young hero, wondering how on earth he could have become involved in such sordid doings.

"You'll hurt your eyes, Harry," the reverend admonished. William turned to find Kent gazing into yet another cell on the opposite side of the corridor. Within, a young man of no more than twenty sat on his bunk, attempting to read in very poor light. The sailor looked up and smiled broadly at Kent.

"Hi, Reverend," he said, jumping to his feet.

"Harry, I'd like you to meet William Bartlett. William, this is Harry Trubshaw."

Trubshaw reached his hand through the bars to shake with William, who reluctantly obliged. "Nice to meet you, Mr. Bartlett, sir."

"Yes," William managed awkwardly.

"William has been defending me in my court case, Harry," Kent explained. "Very successfully, I might add, up to now."

"Good for him, then," Harry said with enthusiasm. Then, to William, "It's not right what they've been doing to the reverend, Mr. Bartlett. He's a real saint, if you ask me."

Kent laughed grimly. "I'm afraid not everyone would agree with you, Harry." He explained to William, "Harry is a hospital's apprentice. He showed particular dedication all throughout the flu epidemic. Quite courageous, really."

"That's only 'cause I hate boats, Mr. Bartlett," said Trubshaw, brushing off the compliment. "I'd do anything to stay off one. And now look where I wound up! So, Reverend, what'd you bring me tonight?"

Kent pulled a book from his coat pocket and handed it through the bars.

"Thanks, Reverend," said Trubshaw. He turned to William as he examined the gift. "I want to be a nurse if I ever get out of here. The rev keeps bringing me the books I need for my exam. Isn't that swell of him?"

"Um, yes. Very," William replied.

"Darn right," agreed Trubshaw.

"The least I can do, Harry," Kent scoffed. "It has to be a short visit tonight, I'm afraid. Mr. Bartlett needs to get home to his family."

"No problem, Reverend," Trubshaw replied amiably. "Thanks for this. Pleasure to meet you, Mr. Bartlett, sir."

"You, too, uh . . ." William hesitated.

"Harry, sir," Trubshaw said helpfully.

"Of course. Harry. Good to . . . good luck to you."

"Thank you, sir. Keep doing your best for the reverend, Mr. Bartlett. We all appreciate it. Best friend I've ever had."

William nodded.

Kent looked at the lawyer. "A very effective use of personnel on both sides of this operation. Don't you agree?"

Back in the tender, the two men rode in silence. William experienced a twinge of nausea, something he had not felt in a boat since he was five years old.

"Are you all right, William?" Kent inquired.

"Not really," he replied. "You brought me here, showed me these men. What is it you want from me, Reverend?"

"Nothing," Kent replied simply. "I believe that your feelings of revulsion are genuine. I can't explain the differences between people. I only know that there's a reason for all of it. God is either God or He's not, and unless He's horribly cruel, He would never have made so many mistakes."

William could not be sure if it was his seasickness or the conversation that had him sweating. He only knew that if he didn't get on solid ground soon, he would likely be sick.

———•—•—•———

War makes men brothers and until a few hours ago, Charlie would have done pretty much anything to resolve the differences between him and Claude. But having recently fought his way back to a tolerable indifference toward the world, Charlie viewed the approach of his former comrade with apprehension. His life here was over. That much was clear. Best leave things as they were.

"Mind if I join you?" Claude asked in the familiar drawl.

Charlie shrugged, dragging on his cigarette.

Ignoring the slight, Claude took up residence on the porch steps beside his brooding friend. They sat in silence.

"You gonna offer me a cigarette, at least?" Claude asked.

Charlie jerked his pack of Camels toward Claude. The man took one, then made use of the burning end of Charlie's cigarette to light his own. Claude took a few drags and found his voice.

"Look, Charlie." The Texan's voice was laced with regret. "Last time we spoke, well . . . I'm real sorry 'bout what I said. Wasn't your fault I got involved with all this bull crap. Got a mind of my own, after all." He grunted. "Someday I should try usin' it."

"No," Charlie said without emotion. "You were right. People should just stay the fuck away from me." *So scram,* Charlie wanted to add, but didn't.

Claude looked at his friend and shook his head, frustrated. "Why do y'always gotta go to extremes, Charlie? It's all or nothing with you. So, what is it now, huh? All you did today was tell the truth. Can't hardly blame yourself for *that.*"

"Right." Charlie blew out a long plume of smoke. "I been sitting here asking myself what I would have done if the truth hadn't been in my best interests. What do *you* think, huh?"

Claude looked down, his silence the answer Charlie had been expecting.

"Exactly," said Charlie with a smile, at peace once again.

"Just be glad you didn't have to make that choice this time, that's all," said Claude, looking on the bright side.

"Yeah," Charlie replied with a laugh. "I've always been a lucky guy. Didn't you know that?"

And the two men fell silent.

— • — • —

Someone had turned out the porch light. "Must have been Fanny," William grumbled over a whiskey burp as he fiddled with his key in the chilly darkness. The meddlesome housekeeper had likely sat up with his wife, the two of them worrying till all hours, then decided to make her disapproval known to the master of the house in her none-too-subtle manner. His father would never have tolerated such defiance. The monstrous old woman would have been on the next boat back to Dublin or Cork or whatever god-awful place she was from. "Changes are going to be made in this house," he insisted as the keys slipped from his hand. He bent for them, and a sudden attack of wooziness forced him to the welcome mat.

"No more rebellion," he muttered as he sat to regain his balance. No more painting perfectly fine wood on a whim for fashion. No more lights switched off, risking the lives of innocent passersby. No, he insisted silently, time to return to the tried and true, to values that had stood the test of time.

He heard the grandfather clock in the hall strike two. "Can't be right," he protested pulling out his pocket watch. Just as he'd thought, it was seven minutes *before* the hour. The hall clock, in his family for generations, had never kept decent time. "Or is it my watch that's always wrong?" he wondered aloud. Like the clock, the watch had been his father's before it was his and his grandfather's before that. In any event, both machines were far older than he was and required constant maintenance, and even then it was difficult to know which to trust.

It had been just after ten (according to the tower bells) when he'd dropped Reverend Kent at the parish house. Barely a word had passed between them since they'd left the harbor, though William was fairly bursting with rage, all the more so since Kent, apart from his brief outburst in the church, had remained cursedly tranquil throughout. Every fiber of William's being was screaming in protest, though he could put no words to his complaints. He simply knew that the place he'd just come from had been dreadfully, fundamentally wrong, and that Kent had somehow tilted William's horizon, conflating things William knew and held in esteem with others whose existence he could barely contemplate.

He left Kent feeling dirty and sick and in desperate need of a drink. So he walked the short distance over to Thames Street, then wandered the half mile or so to Long Wharf, where the ever-present trail of sailors and soldiers would no doubt lead him in the right direction.

Sure enough, before long, he found himself in a damp cellar, drinking alcohol shoulder to shoulder with all sorts of desperate, unknown people. *Was this even Newport?* he wondered. A colored ensemble played lazy jazz. Patrons dropped change into a green vase, clapping intermittently, as smoke billowed in great plumes and people shared conversation and salacious smiles.

But no one approached him. No woman draped herself across his shoulder, and no inebriated fellow offered temporary brotherhood. He seemed to be invisible to all but the bartender, whose job it was after all to dip into the private hells of all sorts of drunkards.

"Prohibition is doomed," he said to himself, as he always knew it would be. Why did people, most of them ignorant and uninformed, feel the need to go on tinkering with the world? There were loose ends, to be sure, but on the whole, the ascent of man, led by the Anglo-Saxon race, had been fairly relentless and running as near to perfection as it was ever likely to be. Even the war seemed to fit in with this credo at the start. A rough slap on the wrist, and the upstart Germans would quickly see how much they had to lose by upsetting the status quo.

But then the war had dragged on year after bloody year, as the fair-minded British failed to vanquish the tyrannical Huns. Reports of unimaginable barbarism filled the newspapers each day, with no end in sight. The Bolsheviks captured Russia and left the field of battle, only to unleash the ancient furies of envy and retribution upon the propertied classes with their obscure philosophy. America, the world's last great neutral power, had been compelled to join the war effort and brought upon herself the scourge of the Spanish flu, killing hundreds of thousands of her citizens. Watching his world torn apart, filled with frustration and feelings of impotence, William had longed for a battle to fight, a rampart to climb.

"Seek and ye shall find," the Bible declared with unfailing irony, William noted. It now seemed laughable how ignorant he'd been of the world, of the depth of its corruption, how close to the bone it grew, how impossible to separate the veins of it from the good meat. How urgent the need for worldwide redemption, as his wife had always claimed, and how much more unlikely it would no doubt prove to be. William longed to crawl back inside his old ignorance, to lock the doors and pull up the covers, drawing a line at the wrought-iron fence that surrounded his home. Time would stop there and the world would forever end at his property line.

But first, he would have to fire Fanny.

His career was over, that much was sure. And he would likely need to find a new place to live once all the chickens had come home to roost.

As drink followed drink and his problems receded to where they might almost belong to someone else, William was resolved on one point and one point only—that he would steadfastly refrain from sharing any of the awful truth of the past twelve hours with Sarah.

As the hall clock struck two thirty, William hoisted himself from the mat to his feet to make another assault on his ancestral home. This time, he managed to slide the key into the lock and turn it successfully, opening the heavy door in a single push. He crept into the foyer, closed the door gently behind him, and started toward the stairs, anticipating their riotous creak. But first he turned toward the big clock, opened the dial glass, and moved the minute hand back seven, no, eight minutes, to match the time on his watch.

"Where on earth have you been?"

William started, surprised to hear his wife's voice coming from behind him rather than from the darkness above. He turned and there she stood in the doorway of the unlit parlor.

"Nowhere on earth," he replied, then turned again and started heavily up the stairs, swaying slightly.

"You're drunk," said Sarah, shocked.

"Does it show?" he joked bitterly, mounting the next tread. He felt her hand grip the banister. There would be no escape.

"William," she said urgently. "It's two thirty in the morning. Do you have any idea how worried I've been?"

"Yes, dear," he replied. "I have no doubt, and I'm genuinely sorry for that. But I'm tired now and, as you observed, very drunk indeed, and I desperately need to sleep."

"No, William." She stood her ground. "Something has happened, and I insist that you tell me what it is."

William stopped again, turned, and glared at her. "You insist?" he barked.

She refused the bait and replied simply, "Yes, William. Or I'm afraid neither of us will get a very good night's sleep."

William looked at her. It was no use. She'd known his father, and his pale imitation of the man was ludicrous, like wearing a pair of pantaloons. He gave a brief nod and spoke without emotion. "Samuel Kent is a sodomite."

He walked down the stairs, past his stunned wife and into the parlor, making a beeline for the large walnut credenza that occupied the far corner of the room. Dropping to his knees, he began opening and closing the cabinet doors.

"Where is it? I know it wasn't thrown away, in spite of your instructions. She *is* Irish, after all. No doubt she still enjoys a nip now and then. Or three, bless her heart. Ah!" William rose to his feet, a half-full bottle of Napoleon brandy in his right hand. "Care to bend the law with me? No? I didn't think so. Well, if it's all the same to you . . ." He pulled a dusty snifter off a shelf, blew into it, then poured himself a brandy and downed it in a quick gulp as Sarah approached, stopping just behind him, still silent.

"Nothing to say? Truthfully, dear," he remarked with a smile, "I can't remember the last time I left you speechless. It's really quite a powerful feeling."

"How did you . . . ?" Sarah struggled. "I mean—"

"Someone told the truth in court today," William announced, "difficult as that may be to believe, a sailor, actually. This prompted a sudden attack of conscience in the reverend. He made a good confession, to me alone of course, in a Catholic church of all places. Are you sure you won't have one?" he asked as he poured himself another. "It's really quite a nice brandy."

"I don't think so," she sighed. "William . . ." said Sarah, her voice full of compassion.

"No, don't you dare," he declared. "I will gladly suffer your reproach, but *not* your sympathy." He dropped back onto the sofa. "That would be cruel, if not so unusual."

She said nothing. He looked up at her and smiled again.

"You had plenty of sympathy for the good reverend, didn't you," he added sharply.

"Of course, I—"

"You knew all along what he was!" He chuckled.

"I—" she protested softly.

"Yes, you did," he repeated, then ticked off the list on his fingers. "You. My partners. The bishop. John Rathom! In fact, I'll wager

I'm the only person from Maine to Florida who believed he was innocent!"

"Darling, please . . ." Sarah murmured.

"No, it's funny." A fit of laughter rose and began to overtake him. "Really, it is." He could not remember laughing with such intensity in a very long time. It made breathing difficult and William soon found himself wondering with indifference if he might suffocate.

"William!" Sarah urged. There was anxiety in her voice, but he found it impossible to care. "I can imagine what you're feeling," she continued, "but try to get hold of yourself!"

He looked up at her, wide-eyed. "Get *hold* of myself? Oh, that's *really* funny! Now you want me to get hold of myself? All right, dear," he said, struggling to his feet. "I'll do my best." He looked at her and the laughter died as quickly as it had come. "Just tell me, please," he asked sincerely, "what part of myself should I get hold of, do you think?" William could see fear in his wife's eyes, that he was coming unglued.

"I only meant—" She struggled.

"Never mind." He shrugged. "This isn't your fault." He bent over suddenly and put his head in his hands. "What an idiot I've been!" he cried desperately. "How do I make my way back?" It felt to him as though a trapdoor had opened beneath his feet.

A moment later, a pair of arms wrapped him in a comforting embrace, pulling him from the brink of destruction. His eyes snapped open. "Don't!" he warned, and he pushed her away, surprising both of them. It took a great deal to get Sarah angry, but as he watched her color change, even in the dark parlor, he knew he'd succeeded.

"Very well," she shot back. "Yes, I knew, or *thought* I knew! Enough at least to recognize he wasn't all you'd imagined. My God, who *could* be? And, yes, I tried to tell you, but you refused to consider any opinion but your own! So now you know, and what *difference* does it make? *Nothing* has changed! You're still fighting against a horrible injustice!"

"Am I?" He looked at his wife blankly. "Let's assume for the moment that what you say is true, that I'm fighting against some ill-defined 'injustice.' But what am I fighting *for*, Sarah? What am I *defending*?"

"A man, William," she offered gently, taking his hands in hers. "A kind, gentle man who by any sane measure does not deserve thirty years in prison."

"Yes, well"—William smiled—"saving him after today would require a miracle. And I'm afraid he's not a likely candidate."

"That's not your concern," she said sharply. "You must simply do your best."

William dropped back onto the sofa and Sarah sat beside him. After a moment, he sighed and took her hand. "And am I allowed nothing, then?" he asked, feeling again like a child in school. "Nothing at all that I can hold on to? No guiding principle on which I might base a life?"

She gazed at him a long moment. "Love fiercely."

It was the answer he'd expected of her.

"And doubt often," she added.

William looked at her curiously.

"Doubt is an affliction," William protested.

"Only if you're afraid of it," she replied.

# TWENTY-FIVE

Charlie wasn't sure if they were his own hands or someone else's working the piece of heavy rope, tying a knot at one end. The boarding-house room looked like the one he'd inhabited for the last eight months, except that one end of it opened out onto a big common shower area, like the ones they had over at the barracks on the Island. He hadn't noticed at first, but there seemed to be one guy showering all alone. He thought it was Barker, but when Charlie waved at him, the guy didn't wave back. Upon second glance, Charlie wondered how he could ever have guessed it to be Barker, since the guy was so old. He was taller too, and balding.

Charlie climbed onto the wooden chair in his bare feet and wound the knotted end of the rope around a metal lighting fixture that hung from the ceiling, similar to the ones in the shower room. Deftly, as only a sailor could, he fashioned a slipknot, pulling it tight. He did not remember removing the old ceiling fan. Dottie must have done it, he reasoned, while he was sleeping one off, which was just as well since it never worked right anyway. The hands that seemed to be his then took hold of the other end of the rope and tied it into a noose.

Claude stood there laughing at him. "No way that's going to fit around your head, Charlie," he joked. "You sure you're not tying that for someone else?"

Charlie looked down at himself standing next to Claude and shook his head. The two of them shared a laugh, both on the floor, and looked up at Barker standing on the chair as the kid slipped the noose around his neck.

"All right, Preston." Charlie realized he'd never used Barker's first name before. "A joke's a joke. Now, get down off there. You're gonna hurt yourself." But Barker paid no attention. It was as if Charlie weren't even there. "Talk some sense to this kid, will you please, Reverend." Charlie laughed nervously. "He's just trying to get me up there with him and you know as well as I do that ain't gonna happen." Charlie turned to Kent, but he saw that the reverend was all the way across the street, talking with Claude in hushed tones in the shadow of a big willow tree. Charlie wished he'd remembered to put his boots on before venturing outdoors since there was still some snow on the ground. He watched through the window now as Barker, still on the wooden chair, rose onto his tiptoes. Charlie shook his head. "Dumb kid's gonna wind up getting a splinter. And it'll serve him right." He banged on the window hard enough to break it, but the glass was sturdy as steel. Charlie felt his heart drop as a copy of himself pulled the chair out from under Barker. Charlie kept banging on the glass as the boy dangled, laughing with an abandon that Charlie had never seen in Barker before.

"Come on, open up!" Charlie heard over another round of banging. "It's me, Claude!"

He woke to find his feet sticking out from under the blanket. Relieved, Charlie caught his breath and made his way to the door. He was grateful to see his friend and was about to share his crazy dream when he took note of the horrified expression on Claude's face.

"What's wrong, Claude?"

"It's Barker. He's . . . He . . ."

# TWENTY-SIX

Dottie sat with Charlie on the edge of her bed as dawn stole past the tattered shades. He had wept on and off for the better part of an hour, some of it in her arms, some of it pacing frantically as he choked on the story of what his friend had done to himself. Now, drained of everything but breath, he sat motionless, eyes fixed on a point somewhere in his near or distant past, she would have guessed. Dottie had never seen him like this and it worried her.

"Come on, baby, come to bed," she coaxed, taking a seat beside him.

But he didn't move or even look at her. "That's not gonna help, Dottie. Not this time."

When a man like Charlie crumbled, Dottie reckoned, he was not easily mended.

"You didn't make the boy what he was," she insisted.

"True," he acknowledged. "But I promised I'd look out for him. And he believed me. Poor stupid son of a bitch."

They sat in silence a long moment.

"Well," she said at last. "It was his decision to do what he did and it can't be undone, not by all the tears in the world. Question is now, what are *you* gonna do?"

Charlie looked up and let out a laugh that frightened her even more than his silence had. She didn't know if what she felt for this man was love, but right then the need to protect him from himself overwhelmed all other feelings.

"They haven't left me with a lot of options," he mused.

Slowly, Charlie pulled himself to his feet and walked the few steps to a side table, where he poured a tumbler of whiskey.

"This is gonna make things even worse for Kent," he said. "What do you want to bet the jury blames him for all of it?"

"I don't care much about Kent, to be honest," Dottie objected, going to him. "What I care about is you." An idea that had been knocking around in the back of her mind suddenly sprang forward. "Look, things being what they are, a girl can't hardly make a living in this town anymore, so . . . I'm leaving, for New York, maybe farther. I have quite a bit of money saved. A lot of it used to be yours. Come with me. Now. Today."

He downed his drink and poured himself another.

"We're two of a kind, Charlie," she insisted.

He turned and gazed at her. Taking her face in his hands, he drew her in for a long kiss and Dottie remembered why she had been so crazy about this fellow. In those few moments, she imagined a bright new future, a fresh start for both of them together.

Then the kiss ended and she thought again. Who was she kidding? Though they might indeed run off to New York or Philadelphia or San Francisco for that matter, their future together was unlikely to be bright, or fresh, or enduring. But she would take what she could get. As for Charlie, she just prayed he'd have sense enough to grab hold of this lifeline rather than any of the darker alternatives she imagined were swimming through his grief-addled brain.

————•————

Samuel Kent sat alone at the defense table in the nearly empty courtroom, wondering if a new attorney had been chosen for him, and if so, by whom. Rising early, he had driven himself to the courthouse in his beloved blue Buick convertible, top buttoned up against the early autumn wind off the bay. Kent had paused more than once during the ninety-minute drive, his car idling at some major crossroads as he pondered a more or less permanent detour from his life. It would be so easy to simply turn the wheel, north, south, or west. California was a world away, but Canada or Florida seemed plausible enough, exotic destinations for a man from Massachusetts who had never ventured farther than the Lehigh Valley. From Florida, he could sell the car and make his way to the Caribbean, or even farther, to the Amazon basin, where he would work amongst the natives. Or, if he chose north, he might go to Montreal, a taste of France, he'd been told, at his very doorstep. Simple as that, he'd be in another country, beyond the reach of those who sought to hurt him. Why not a total break, board a ship and escape to Paris? More than once he'd heard dying boys whisper of the French capital in their last moments, their fevered delusions delivering them to an earthly paradise of beauty and grace.

But in the end, unable to break right or left, he had surrendered to the fate that lay directly ahead. And as a great weight rolls inevitably downhill, so had he been delivered here, to the courthouse of the First U.S. District, fulfilling a destiny that in hindsight he knew had always been his. To flee would have been an admission of guilt, and Samuel Kent did not feel guilty, not for offenses of a criminal nature, at least.

He had, of course, sinned against his church, in not one, but two ways. First was the despised sin of sodomy, a heavy name it seemed to him for a transgression as light as the one he'd committed. Next was the sin of having sexual relations of any sort outside the bounds of marriage. A Catholic priest must forswear *all* sexual activity, but an Episcopal clergyman may marry and thereby enjoy physical love sanctioned by God. It suddenly struck Kent as terribly unfair that his kind alone should be forced to live a solitary life, or suffer damnation.

But it was a transgression of an entirely different sort that weighed most heavily upon him, a personal betrayal that he would not have judged kindly in another and that might indeed cause great harm to a good and blameless man. William had come to him again and again, to help, yes, but more often to wrestle with his better angels. Somehow, out of all of them, this earnest young man had found wisdom in Kent's tired old sermons. He could not fault William for turning his back on him now. But as he would have with any sinner, Kent tried to chart his own road to this point, to understand how he, who did not fear death, would so run from the truth within himself that he would deceive a man he had come to care for like a son.

As a young actor, Sam had been encouraged to experiment, and since he had been drawn to women as well, he had assigned no great importance to the feelings he'd begun having toward men. The few experiences with other fellows that he'd allowed his younger self had been furtive and unloving, so following his spiritual awakening he'd made what seemed a sensible choice, to deny his body entirely and choose a holy life. Compared with the divine union he had recently tasted, sex of any sort seemed a pale substitute. A life of devotion, however, in which he could openly demonstrate his love for his fellow man, appeared to be the logical road back to that time-less, blessed place.

For nearly two decades, Kent dutifully ministered to young and old, male and female alike, but not once did he ever approach that ecstatic moment of his youth. Then God, in His infinite wisdom, carved out a purpose for him, leading the pastor toward what he loved most and did best—the spiritual guidance of young men. Time and again, as Kent gazed into the eyes of a troubled youth, he would feel his soul burst open, radiating outward until he knew himself not as a man, but as the heart of a much larger being, without personal needs, desires, or self. Gazing with the sort of love that God must surely feel, how could he have anticipated what was to come?

But summoned to Newport to act the pastor's ultimate role of Death's apologist, Kent was shocked to find his body stirring once again. He had been trained to stand fast against the illusion that life had an end, but instead, Kent found himself enraged by the river of youth that emptied each day before his eyes. As scores of young men were ripped from their blameless lives, the value of each individual took on supreme importance to him. Eternity was a long time and would no doubt be filled with an endless amount of whatever it turned out to be. But this flaming instant of life, its carnal exceptionality, the rage of need and desire and brilliant promise dying all around him, provoked Kent's aging flesh to rebel against its own inevitable demise. As McKinney lay before him, so beautiful in his blooming health, the only one to vanquish Death amidst weeks and weeks of carnage, Kent was struck by the most obvious of epiphanies, that God had made us body *and* soul and that to deny either was not just a lie but an affront to creation itself. As the flame of life passed between them, as McKinney offered himself up to the other man as graciously as he might extend a hand to one who had stumbled, Kent knew that there was no power in heaven or earth that could have dissuaded him from this act of love, of lust.

Now he sat in an empty courtroom, facing an uncertain future that likely included ruination and prison, the central player in a conundrum as old as civilization itself, but one which served, he had to believe, some yet-to-be-illuminated divine purpose.

•—•—•

As the courtroom began to fill, as people maneuvered to their seats, bits of dialogue found their way to the reverend, reflections on the previous day's dramatic events and speculation about what the new day might bring. Mutual pleasantries were exchanged, lunch and squash dates confirmed, off-color stories shared. They were male voices mostly, going about their day's business. Many he recognized from his two years in Newport, while many more had become familiar to him during his brief tenure in this court. They were old and young, sympathetic or cynical, and their chorus was punctuated by brief bursts of rueful, rumbling laughter. To most, he would be hard-pressed to attach a face. Yet Kent felt certain that the great majority of these souls had already made up their minds about him. This had long been true, Kent realized, and it had been William's faith that had shielded the pastor from the glare of reality thus far. The sudden loss of this left Kent feeling bereft and utterly disconnected from his fellow man.

"Well, that's a relief, anyway," William announced, taking his place beside his client. "I thought perhaps you'd bolted."

Kent looked at the lawyer, scarcely believing his eyes.

"I . . . I didn't think I'd see you again," Kent muttered as he gazed at William, in a rare moment of genuine surprise. Besides his own personal relief, Kent felt an overwhelming sense of pride for William.

"Yes, well," said William with a sigh. "Here I am." He looked at Kent. "I am certain of nothing, Reverend, including whether or not I will be here, or anywhere, tomorrow, or how exactly I feel about you. But as I could discover no compelling reason *not* to be your lawyer, I'm willing to take it one day at a time, if that's all right with you."

And Kent's heart burst open once again, his faith restored. "Thank you, William."

# TWENTY-SEVEN

M r. Bartlett?" Judge Brown began the day's session.

"Your Honor," William replied, rising to address the court, "the defense calls Seaman First Class Charles A. McKinney to the stand." William stepped from behind the defense table, preparing to do battle with the most formidable opponent of his career. Not only was the sailor smart and engaging, he was also telling the truth. William would need to forget that fact and proceed as planned, using the sum totals of these two unique lives, Kent's and McKinney's, to cast suspicion upon the sailor's testimony and sow doubt in the minds of the jurors, making the twelve rethink in retrospect what their every instinct had recognized as genuine in the moment. Time and natural prejudice were on his side, as well as, he was willing to entertain, justice.

The truth, however, was not. He turned to steal a quick glance at his wife, seated amidst the throng of male faces in the packed gallery. Sarah smiled at him, while John Rathom, seated beside her, added his own nod of support. William was not too proud to admit that he would need all the support he could get.

The doors to the lobby swung open as the court clerk sang out McKinney's name. William turned in anticipation of that first moment when the sailor would appear and their eyes would meet, each man taking that all-important first measure of the other. Would the fellow's natural self-confidence hold up under hostile cross-examination? Would William find his opening to drive a wedge between witness and jury? They would not need to wait much longer to find out.

But no one entered. As a wave of murmurs rippled through the gallery, a court officer appeared in the doorway and shrugged at the clerk, shaking his head. The clerk relayed the message in similar gestures to the judge, who glared down at the prosecuting attorney.

"Mr. Cawley," asked the judge, "do you have any idea where your witness might be?"

Cawley stood to address the judge, but a young clerk from the prosecutor's office ran in to whisper in the lawyer's ear. William had never seen a man's jaw literally drop open until that moment. Cawley's face went white.

"Mr. Cawley!" Judge Brown insisted.

"Judge, I, uh . . ." Cawley stammered, looking over at William. "May I . . . The prosecution requests a sidebar, Your Honor."

"Very well," Judge Brown acceded, clearly displeased. "Counsels will approach the bench."

Cawley moved slowly, as if in shock, meeting William at the bench, where the two faced the judge.

"All right," said Brown. "What is it, Mr. Cawley?"

"I . . ." Cawley began. "A dreadful thing . . ." He took a deep breath. "Preston Barker, well . . . it appears." He shuddered. "I've just been informed that he's taken his own life."

William felt his own mouth drop open.

"Good God," Judge Brown said, visibly distressed. "As if enough young men haven't died already." He looked at Cawley. "Is this the reason for McKinney's absence?"

"I . . . I suspect so, Your Honor," Cawley replied. "Although I can't be sure."

Brown sighed heavily. "Very well. Mr. Bartlett, are you ready to proceed?"

William's heart sank as he remembered his own assault on the fragile young man. "Yes, Your Honor."

Judge Brown looked between the two of them. "Neither of you are to say anything about this. I will order that the jury be sequestered for the remainder of the trial. As deeply tragic as this is, it should have no bearing on these proceedings. Is that understood?"

"Yes, Your Honor," said both William and Cawley, almost in unison.

As the two men made their way back to their respective seats, William could hear Cawley whispering urgently in his young clerk's ear, "Find McKinney!" whereupon the clerk fled.

Kent leaned toward William as he sat. "What is it, William? Has something happened to Seaman McKinney?" Kent asked with genuine concern.

William looked at him. "No, Reverend. Nothing has happened to McKinney. As far as I know." But if the sailor didn't show up, however tragic the reason, William could all but guarantee Kent's case was as good as won.

"Do you have any other witnesses to call, Mr. Cawley?" Brown demanded.

Cawley rose again clumsily. "The people rest, Your Honor."

"Mr. Bartlett." The judge turned his attention back to William. "The floor is yours."

"Defense will proceed, Your Honor," William replied, "provided we can cross-examine Mr. McKinney if and when he arrives."

"Very well, Mr. Bartlett," Brown allowed. "Call your first witness."

"Your Honor," said William, "the defense calls Herbert I. Fair to the stand."

The court clerk called out in turn, "Will Herbert I. Fair please take the stand?"

A moment later, a young man entered the courtroom, tall, blond, and fit, twenty-five perhaps, a paragon of American manhood in a well-tailored suit, who strode gracefully toward the witness stand. He sat facing the court with one of the most sober and handsome faces William had ever seen.

"Please raise your right hand and place your left hand on the Bible," said the clerk.

Fair did so.

"Do you solemnly swear," the clerk intoned, "to tell the truth, the whole truth, and nothing but the truth, so help you God?"

"I do," said Fair simply, in a deeply resonant voice, as if he truly meant it.

This witness was almost too good to be true. In spite of everything, William thought to himself as he approached the young man, perhaps God really *was* on Kent's side, or, if not God, then maybe the other fellow.

"Will you state your name for the court, please?" William asked.

"Herbert Isaiah Fair, sir," the young man replied, looking William squarely in the eye.

"Mr. Fair," William continued, "you recently served your country in the World War, did you not?"

"Yes, sir, I did."

"The Army, was it?"

"Yes, sir," said Fair. "I served as a lieutenant in the Yankee Division from the time they left home for France until they returned in '18, at which time I went to England and studied with some other American officers and men. A program they made available to us."

"While in France, did you see combat, Mr. Fair?"

"I did, sir."

"And when did you return to this country?" William inquired.

"I only just returned, sir. One week ago. On the *Olympic*."

"And may I ask *why* you chose this time to return?"

Fair looked over at Kent. "I was informed that the Reverend Kent was in some sort of trouble, sir, and that some fellows were needed to speak in favor of his character."

"And you wished to speak on his behalf?"

"Without a doubt, sir."

"Mr. Fair, how long have you known the Reverend Kent?"

"Since 1915, February of that year."

"And how did you become acquainted with him?"

"Midway through my junior year, Mr. Kent took over as warden of Leonard Hall, one of the dormitories of Lehigh University, where I was a student."

"I see. And what were his responsibilities at Leonard Hall, as warden? Goodness, sounds rather like a prison."

Fair laughed genially. "Hardly, sir. The warden functions more or less like a parent. Most of the boys, well, it's their first time away from home. A lot of them wind up frightened or lonely or lost in one way or another, and the warden is there for them to talk to if need be, to help them in their studies. And of course, like any good parent, to discipline them if they get seriously out of line."

"Hmm. Maybe not a prison, then, but not so different from the military, would that be fair to say?"

Again, Fair laughed. "Without the live ammo, but yes, sir, I suppose it would."

"And you were at that same time a proctor at Leonard Hall?"

"The following year, my senior year, yes, sir."

"And did you live with Reverend Kent?"

"Just down the hall from him, sir."

"And when did you graduate from Lehigh, Mr. Fair?"

"June 1916."

"So you lived just down the hall from the reverend for about sixteen months? Is that correct?"

"Give or take, yes, sir."

"And what were your duties as proctor?"

"Well," Fair said, "if the warden is the parent, then the proctor is sort of the older brother. He's the line of first defense, you could say, to spot a boy in trouble right at the first and try to nip things in the bud, to speak to him in his own language. Then to talk with the warden about those things as necessary."

"So, then you would be in a good position to hear from the boys if they'd ever had a problem of any sort with Reverend Kent, a disagreement, or if they disliked him for any reason, wouldn't you?"

"Oh, yes, sir. If the warden is disliked or not respected for any reason at all, the students are sure to talk about it amongst themselves and complain to the proctor."

"And nothing like that ever came up with the reverend?"

"Absolutely not, sir, never. He was universally well liked by all the students."

"About how many students room there?"

"About fifteen when I was there," said Fair.

"And during that time, Mr. Fair, those sixteen months that you lived down the hall from him, especially during the time that you were proctor and he warden, would you say you had a close relationship with the reverend?"

"Very close, sir. We were constantly talking about the boys just by the nature of things, but I'm honored to say that I believe the reverend and I became friends as well. And I daresay I had the better of the deal, and gained a tremendous amount from his wisdom, which he was always generous to share."

"Now, Mr. Fair, were you familiar with the estimation in which

Reverend Kent was held by the officers and other students of Lehigh University?"

"Most emphatically so."

"And what was his reputation with them?"

Again, Fair looked over at Kent. "Words could not portray the high esteem in which the reverend was held at Lehigh."

"And that applied to every feature of his character?"

"Absolutely."

William directed his attention to the jury as he asked his last question of the witness. "And have you ever, Mr. Fair, on any other occasion, found it necessary to speak in defense of the reverend's character in this or any other way?"

"Never once, sir, though on my own, I admit I have never missed an occasion to speak most highly of the good work he has done wherever he has gone. Everyone who knows him from those days, whenever his name comes up, only praise is spoken for the great good he did for the men of Lehigh and elsewhere."

William turned back to look at Herbert Fair, a perfect name for a perfect young man. Had this scene taken place twenty-four hours earlier, William might even have looked upon Fair as a carbon copy of himself. The high esteem in which Fair held Kent, and the place the reverend occupied in the fellow's private pantheon, were reminiscent of the feelings William had, until yesterday, so jealously guarded. And judging by the faces of the twelve jurors, it had done the trick. The momentum had indeed swung back in Kent's direction.

So, why then did William find himself resenting the young man? Why did he feel that he now had more in common with McKinney than with Herbert I. Fair? Placed side by side, unvarnished by dress or title, by personal history or lawyers' fancy arguments, William had no doubt that McKinney's truth would ring with far greater resonance than Fair's, that it could still sink Kent like a stone, if not in the eyes of the jury, then at least in William's own heart.

William looked at the judge. "No more questions, Your Honor."

◆—◆—◆

And so it went for much of the day. Others with whom Kent had worked over the last twenty years testified enthusiastically on his behalf. The Right Reverend Dr. Alfred Mottet, rector of the Church of the Holy Communion in New York City, where Kent had been posted just prior to his Lehigh assignment, praised his unique abilities.

"We have many young men among our parishioners," said Mottet, an older man with a round belly and a narrow fringe of hair. "Reverend Kent seemed particularly fitted in temperament and general knowledge of how to influence young men for good."

Under Cawley's withering cross-examination, riddled with innuendo, Dr. Mottet took umbrage, stating adamantly, "I will say this, if you will allow me, everyone in my parish who got to know Reverend Kent and who remembers him today, remembers him with the most profound respect and gratitude, because he is a perfectly splendid and manly man among boys and men."

Even James DeWolf Perry, bishop of Rhode Island, made an appearance before the court and cameras. He could hardly have stayed away, what with the *Journal*'s open letter to President Wilson, signed by a dozen prominent clergymen from across New England. But never once did Perry testify to any personal knowledge of Kent, despite the fact that the reverend had worked for him for almost two years, but spoke only of reports he had received from third parties.

"During the flu epidemic, at great personal risk, or so I have been told," the bishop offered, "Mr. Kent spent many a night visiting the sick boys in hospital, writing letters to their loved ones, staying with them when they were dying."

"So you have been *told*?" William queried.

"The principal source of information that I have of his standing and character," Perry stated for the record, "is the report made to me by Colonel Straub of Fort Adams, in Newport."

"Reverend Kent was held in high esteem, you said, by Army and Navy officials," William pressed him.

"By the Army officials there," Perry repeated.

"By the Navy as well?"

"By the Navy," Perry added, "so far as the officers reported to me, and so far as I could gather in Washington."

But Perry's faint praise had not been enough to undermine the portrait of devotion that William had carefully painted for the jury; it was, after all, what they *wanted* to believe, what William had wanted to believe until yesterday, so it was a far easier climb than the prosecution faced throughout the day without their star witness.

During the many tributes, William often allowed his gaze to drift to Kent, who watched the proceedings with what appeared to be genuine gratitude and humility, like a kind, old man at his retirement dinner or on his deathbed, tallying up accounts as his life flashed before his eyes. Even William had to admit that for so many to have stepped forward, swearing before God and the court on the priest's behalf, Kent had to have done many fine things, touched many lives in his decades as a pastor. And the men who owed him the highest praise, for whom he had done the greatest service, were not present at these proceedings. They were dead, or languishing on that prison ship. Yes, William acknowledged, whatever Kent's sins, the man had a noble heart. How the two aspects could coexist in one individual, William could not fathom, but he supposed, as his wife had said, that that part was none of his concern.

•　•　•

The witness stand was empty.

"Mr. Bartlett?" Judge Brown inquired. "Have you any further witnesses to call?"

William rose to address the judge, barely able to contain his pride at a job well done, already tasting victory.

"But for the sailor McKinney's absence," William announced, "the defense rests. And may I say at this time, Your Honor, the contempt that this prosecution witness has demonstrated for these proceedings is but another testament to the frivolous nature of these charges—"

"Yes, yes, Mr. Bartlett," the judge cut William off. "We know. Save it for your closing state—"

At that moment the doors at the back swung open, drawing the attention of Judge Brown and most everyone else in the courtroom, including William. A court officer entered, hurrying up the aisle to the bench. Judge Brown lowered his head as the other man stood on tiptoes, trying unsuccessfully to speak into the judge's ear. The court officer finished his address and looked at the judge for instructions.

Brown nodded brusquely. "Very well."

The officer turned and quickly retraced his steps through the rising chorus of murmurs. The judge rapped his gavel, bringing the court to order, and looked over at William. "As I was saying, Mr. Bartlett, don't count your chickens."

"Your Honor?" William questioned.

"It appears that Seaman McKinney has arrived at long last," the judge explained. "Does counsel for the defense still wish to cross-examine?"

William wondered if he'd heard correctly. "I, uh . . ."

The judge shrugged. "It's your choice, Mr. Bartlett."

As often happens to people involved in a terrible accident, time slowed to a crawl. William looked at the jury. They were on his side now, fully, he was certain, and had McKinney not shown up, William had no doubt that the twelve men would have quickly

291

returned a verdict of "not guilty." He was not required to cross-examine the sailor, it was true. Simply leaving well enough alone was probably the wisest course at this juncture.

Yet as William gazed at the jurors, he thought he could detect in at least half of them a sudden sense of anticipation. This was the inevitable moment toward which all great drama builds, individual combat, the climactic battle between good and evil that he himself had longed for, and which he had been promising to his audience all along. To cheat these spectators now, when it was within their grasp, would invite resentment and suspicion, pointing the finger of doubt once again in Kent's direction. The twelve had watched William make short work of each of the prosecution's other witnesses. Why shy away from McKinney, unless William were frightened, unless *this* one had spoken the truth?

"We're waiting, Mr. Bartlett," Judge Brown announced, shaking the attorney back into real time.

"I beg your pardon, Your Honor—"

"Do you wish to cross-examine the witness?" the judge asked with exaggerated patience.

"Yes, Your Honor," said William, suddenly resolved. "Yes, without a doubt. Defense calls Charles Aaron McKinney to the stand."

# TWENTY-EIGHT

Charlie stood in the corridor, the hubbub caused by his sudden arrival floating to him through the open doors. He'd put on his Navy blues this morning instead of the dress whites, mostly because he hadn't known till an hour ago whether or not he'd show, and so he hadn't had time to get the whites pressed and ready. But the blues seemed more right in any case, considering the disgust he felt for himself and for these proceedings.

Dottie had spent most of the day trying to convince him to move to New York or Panama City or anywhere with her. Her vision of a new life together, complete with roses and a little house for two, had been tempting but ultimately laughable. Both knew they needed someone better than they were themselves if they were ever to amount to anything.

Even their lovemaking had gone south that day, which made good-byes easier. After Charlie finally announced the decision he'd known all along he would make, he promptly got up and dressed. Dottie watched from the bed, both of them aware that this would likely be the last time they'd see one another. Charlie walked to the door, stopped, and waved good-bye halfheartedly. The woman did not glance at him, but simply returned the meager wave through a haze of cigarette smoke, as determined to let go of this man, it seemed, as he was with her, along with some unidentified part of himself.

As he made his way to the CO's office with his urgent request for a ride to Providence, Charlie noted that he had for a time known someone better than himself, had indeed loved his friend for that, wanted like hell to keep Barker that way. But the boy had been the wrong sex, and in any case he was dead now.

Once Charlie had been identified and a few calls made it up the chain of command, a Navy bus appeared as if by magic to hurry him to Providence. During the trip from Newport, Charlie tried to fathom the choice he'd made, but could arrive at only this clumsy fact: that there are no heroes and that each of us simply does what he needs to do in each moment.

—  •  —  •  —

William watched as McKinney settled onto the witness stand, the sailor's face somber.

"Young man," Judge Brown addressed the sailor sternly, "I won't waste any more of the court's time by demanding an explanation, but be aware that I may still fine you for contempt."

"Yes, sir," McKinney addressed the judge with a respectful nod.

"Your witness, Mr. Bartlett," said the judge.

William approached McKinney, their gaze meeting for the first time. The sailor's deep blue eyes were opaque to William. A hint of sadness perhaps, but the lawyer could discern nothing of the strategy with which the young warrior had entered the field of battle. Of course, William noted, it was possible that McKinney had no strategy. He didn't need one, after all, since he was telling the truth.

"Mr. McKinney," William began, his mind a jumble of competing voices. "Yesterday you stated before this court—"

"I lied," said McKinney abruptly.

William looked at the man, wondering if he'd imagined that last response. And the scattered whispers behind William told him that everyone else in the courtroom was asking the same question.

"I beg your pardon?" asked William.

McKinney looked past the lawyer, connecting squarely with the jury. "What I said yesterday," McKinney continued, "it was a lie. Well, not all of it. Kent did hold my hand, just like he held the hand of a lot of other scared, sick boys in that hospital. But the rest I made up." The sailor threw a hard-edged look at William. "That clear enough for you, counselor?"

William stood speechless. Around him, William noted, was silence.

Judge Brown looked down and addressed Charlie curiously. "Young man, do you realize that you are admitting to perjury, a very serious crime?"

McKinney seemed to swallow whatever anger he had expressed, and nodded again to the judge. In even tones, he said, "I'm aware of that, Your Honor."

The fellow must have felt William's quizzical gaze. He turned back, their eyes met again, and the realization of exactly what William knew seemed to dawn on McKinney. A veil dropped from the fellow's blue eyes and William wondered if the sailor felt as young and vulnerable as he suddenly looked. Of the two hundred people in the courtroom, besides Kent himself, only William and McKinney knew the truth of what had happened in the hospital ward on the night in question. Never before, William noted, had he experienced such a profound moment of intimacy with another man.

"Why, Mr. McKinney?" William asked sincerely. "Why would you lie?" *And why are you lying now?*

Charlie leveled his gaze and William felt the man was speaking only to him. "Because I was instructed to."

At that, the gallery behind them erupted at last. But their agitation was no more than a bothersome distraction to William, who from the first had wanted nothing more than to prove McKinney and his cohorts guilty of precisely what he'd just admitted. Now, however, as a genuine revelation hovered on the horizon, William wanted a deeper answer. One thing was damnably clear: this young man, with little other than youth, looks, and native wit to his credit, had marched in here with a kind of plaintive grace, carrying within him the power to unravel these proceedings, and the will to do it. How and why such a man would risk what little future he had, and to what degree William would allow him to do so, had suddenly become a matter of intense importance to both of them.

"Order!" the judge shouted from above as he pounded his gavel.

William could read the suspicion in McKinney's gaze, as if the man feared the lawyer might rob him of this moment.

"By whom were you instructed?" William demanded, giving the sailor an almost imperceptible nod.

"By Chief Arnold and Dr. Hudson," McKinney said.

McKinney looked into the gallery, raised his arm triumphantly, and pointed to where the two responsible parties sat side by side.

"Arnold said he didn't need no evidence to convince him Kent was guilty. Said if we couldn't get him to do the lewd, we should lie about it." McKinney locked eyes with Arnold, whose face was red with rage. "Made us sign an oath, warning us that if we told anybody, we'd go to jail."

William stared at McKinney, searching for the trap that he was certain must lay buried within this stroke of incredible good fortune. *No doubt what you say about Arnold and the doctor is true, sailor,* William thought. *But as for the rest of it, I know what you know. I know that you are lying now.*

"Why are you doing this?" William asked, in a tone so low they might have been the only two people in the room. "Putting yourself in jeopardy this way?" *Needlessly. The proof of entrapment alone would be evidence enough to get Kent acquitted.*

McKinney took a moment before he responded. "I realized too late," he said at last, in a voice oddly filled with emotion, "that some things just ain't right. What we did to Mr. Kent. And the others." The sailor looked away and remained silent for several palpable seconds. "Too many people have been hurt," he determined. "Some of us should've known better."

McKinney's audience, and that was all they were at this point, was rapt. It was an extraordinary performance, even better than his first. And of all the absurd conclusions William Bartlett had ever drawn in his thirty-odd years of life, this had to beat all; the fact was he actually believed that McKinney was once again telling the truth. McKinney, a man who had proven to be little better than a common prostitute, and who, in his young, brutish life, had no doubt committed countless other dishonorable acts of one sort or another. But in that moment, it seemed to William that he had never heard truer words than those just spoken by this young miscreant.

All well and good, William thought, but he still found himself on the horns of a dangerous dilemma. Keeping Kent's ill-timed confession to himself had been one thing. Unpleasant though it had been, that particular encounter was thoroughly protected by attorney-client privilege. William could not have divulged what Kent had revealed to him even if he'd wanted to. But if he allowed McKinney's false testimony to stand, William would in effect become an accessory to perjury. He was bound legally to disclose some of what he knew to the judge in chambers, at least enough to provoke a mistrial. Under the circumstances, it was highly unlikely that the state would elect to retry the case, so it would be as good as an acquittal to Kent, and William could remain true to his duty as an officer of the court. As for McKinney, the sorry soul, any effect on him would be negligible, since either way he was guilty of perjury and was likely bound for prison.

"Any more questions, Mr. Bartlett?" Brown asked.

William did not answer. He stared at McKinney, who stared back, each trying to fathom the motives and intentions of the other.

"Mr. Bartlett?" the judge repeated with growing impatience.

Finally, William broke away and looked up at the judge. He had to do what he knew was right. "I have something to say, Your Honor."

"Proceed, Mr. Bartlett."

William again looked at McKinney, the sailor's eyes defiant in anticipation of what William might say.

"I . . ." William hesitated. "I wish to state, for the record . . ."

"This is a court of law, counselor," barked the judge. "Whatever you say *will* be for the record, I can assure you."

William looked at Brown. "Yes, well," he continued with sudden conviction. "I wish to state that . . . that the courage this young man has displayed in the name of justice argues strongly against perjury charges. No more questions."

As he glanced back at McKinney, William detected the beginnings of a wry smile at the edge of the sailor's eyes.

"So noted," said the judge. "You may step down, Mr. McKinney."

McKinney looked at the lawyer once again. He glanced over at Kent, gave him a nod, then stood and walked out of the courtroom.

"Your Honor," William announced, "the defense rests."

## TWENTY-NINE

The jury adjourned for deliberation.

Outside the courtroom, cameras flashed as William and Kent emerged into a crowd of well-wishers, the majority of whom, William was certain, would have been equally ecstatic if the tide had suddenly turned against his client. It was all the same to them.

Sarah made her way to her husband and wrapped her arm around his waist.

"I'm glad you were here," William said to her.

She smiled knowingly. "You're a liar, but thank you for saying so."

"I love you," he said.

She nodded with a different kind of smile. "Yes, you do."

He looked to find Kent standing by awkwardly. William reached out and placed a hand on Kent's shoulder. "Everything's going to be fine, Reverend."

"Yes," Kent said in disbelief, still absorbing the day's events. "Such an extraordinary . . . McKinney, I . . ."

William brought a finger to Kent's lips to gently silence him. "Inexplicable, yes. Someday, perhaps soon, I'd love to discuss it with you. But today is not the day." He looked between Kent and his wife. "If you two would excuse me for a moment? Look after one another, would you?"

"I'll take care of that," John Rathom said from behind.

William turned to face him.

"Don't go far," the big Australian advised him. "This won't take long."

— • —

William cupped his hands under the faucet, then leaned down and splashed his face. He stood up and looked at his reflection in the mirror, his eyes wide, his face and the front of his hair shiny and covered in droplets. Reflected in the far left side of the mirror, William could spy one-half of the stand of urinals, unoccupied at the moment, and was struck all at once by how absurdly large they were. Massive blocks of porcelain as high and twice as wide as a man's shoulders, as if they had been built long ago for a race of giants now extinct, powerful men who'd known what they were about, who had taken action decisively when the need arose. But men had never stood that tall, William realized, except perhaps in their own minds. The war had proved that much, if little else. A sword of any kind was as likely to cut down the innocent as the guilty, no matter how many monuments man might build to the grandeur of his own self-importance.

But perhaps, William conjectured, in this one instance at least, in this building, the designer had meant to have a laugh on posterity, to remind men, at their most vulnerable, of how small in fact they were, how insignificant in the face of justice. William would like to think that was true, to believe that some of those who made such

decisions had a sense of humor, an awareness of the proper importance of things, and were simply waiting patiently for the rest of us
to catch on. Perhaps, he speculated, the urinals had been designed
by a woman.

Then there was a flush and William realized that he was not
alone. Not eager to be caught staring at himself, he buried his wet
face in the stiff white towel that hung from the contraption on the
wall to his left. The man's footsteps came closer until he arrived at
a sink not far from where William stood. The water was turned on
with a squeak, and William could hear the sound of hands being lath-
ered and rinsed. William looked up from his towel and saw that the
young man standing abreast of him wore a dark blue sailor's uniform.

William and Charlie took note of one another's reflection in the
same instant and the men shared an awkward silence.

At last, William acknowledged Charlie with a nod.

Charlie shook his head. "It fits, you know? Guy like me, I finally
figure out what's right, and I have to lie to do it."

"As an officer of the court," William offered, "it is my duty to
reveal any act of perjury."

"Yeah?" Charlie asked, curious. "So, why didn't you?"

William simply shrugged.

Charlie nodded. "Well, then. Guess we're even."

"I guess so," William replied, and he knew that he meant it.
After a moment, William extended his hand and the men shook.
Charlie looked once again at William, then dropped his eyes and
walked out of the men's room.

◆——◆——◆

The jury foreman, a small red-haired man in a brown tweed suit,
stood to read the verdict.

"We, the jury, find the defendant, Samuel Kent, not guilty."

The courtroom erupted in thunderous applause. William turned to the individual beside him, Samuel Neal Kent. There was much more to this human being than he could ever have imagined. Most of it he liked, and much of it he didn't. But William felt content that justice had been served. Kent looked at him tentatively for a moment until finally William smiled and shook hands with the grateful man. William actually felt moved to hug his client, but settled instead for a supportive hand to the shoulder.

Outside the courtroom, a mob of reporters crowded around them both and William momentarily lost sight of Kent.

Breaking free at last, he found the man standing at the top of the marble stairs just outside the courthouse. Following Kent's gaze, William found Charlie McKinney, standing alone at the bottom of the stairs, looking up. The priest and the sailor shared a moment's eye contact, then McKinney waved a final farewell, turned, and walked away.

## EPILOGUE

The day was cold, the sky cobalt blue and clear as a pane of new glass, making the edges of everything hard and brittle. Charlie and Claude, each with a full duffel slung over one shoulder, made their way in awkward silence through the doors of the Newport train station. There were so many travelers, civilian and military, urgent and all bundled up in dark fur and peacoats, that if not for the brightly wrapped Christmas bundles sprouting from bags or in outstretched arms, it might have been an evacuation in progress rather than another holiday season. Charlie remembered seeing the grainy pictures in the papers, before America joined the war in '17, of the carnage under way in Belgium and northern France. It wasn't until he was there himself, however, that he realized that even the worst horror happens in color, that lovely spring days visit war-ravaged cities, that flowers bloom and birds sing and the sun shines and flesh is pink or gray and blood red or dried black, and what a small thing it was that separated joy from sorrow, life from death.

Claude checked his ticket against the numbers on the side of the cars and found his carriage. He looked at the numbers for far longer than he needed to and then turned to Charlie.

"Guess this is it," Claude said at last.

"Good," Charlie uttered with a nod. "Wouldn't want you to get on the wrong train."

Claude shook his head. "That'd be just like me, right? Have to change in Chicago. If I find my way all right, I should be home by Christmas."

"Oughta make your momma real happy," Charlie said with a smile.

"How 'bout you, Charlie?" Claude asked. "What time's your train?"

Charlie shrugged. "Little while," he offered.

And the silence fell between them again. Claude dropped his duffel and gripped Charlie's shoulder hard with his right hand. "Come on, Charlie, come with me to Texas. We sure could use your help. It's a wide-open country, you know? Anything's possible. Might just be the start of a whole new life for you."

Charlie shook his head and laughed. "Can't you just see me on a farm? Tryin' to scam the chickens into laying a few more eggs?"

Claude smiled. "Yeah." He shrugged. "Silly idea, I guess."

"I'm a big-city boy, and I always will be," Charlie affirmed. "Thanks, though, Claude, for the offer," he added with sincerity. "Means a lot."

"Guess you're just glad you ain't in prison, huh?" Claude offered. "Sure was nice of that judge not to push those perjury charges."

Charlie smiled. "I'm a lucky guy, remember? I'll bet the Navy Department calls me down to Washington to testify. Just you watch. I'll be in the papers again."

"The Navy investigating the Navy." Claude smirked. "Like asking the wolf to guard the henhouse."

The train conductor let out a long whoop. "All aboard!"

"Well, I better, uh . . ." Claude indicated the train with a jerk of his head. "You come see me at least, you hear?"

"You bet!" Charlie responded as they shook hands, but both men knew this was good-bye.

Claude again shouldered his duffel. "No bullshit, Charlie," Claude said, his face filled with concern. "You gonna be okay?"

Charlie took a moment to consider before he answered. "No bullshit, Claude. I don't know. But for the first time in my life, I'm just fine with that."

Claude looked at Charlie and offered a brief nod, acknowledging his friend's honesty. The train began to move. Claude hopped aboard but remained on the steps to wave good-bye to his buddy. As the train picked up speed, the big Texan shouted back, "None of it was your fault, Charlie!"

Charlie lifted his arm in response, grateful for any kind of absolution.

———•—•—•———

William stood beside Samuel Kent's blue Buick convertible, guarding the contents of the open trunk—a single leather suitcase and a box of books. There was something to be said for a life like Kent's; he traveled light and when he made his exit from this world, there would be little to distribute, just the memories he had left with those who had known him.

The day was cold, but William had always loved this time of year—the clean, bracing air, the scent of fallen leaves and fires burning, the holidays just ahead. Now, especially, it felt like a time of renewal for him, amidst all the dying, as if nature was sloughing off the good and bad of the previous months in equal measure, leaving an empty canvas for the year to come.

As he looked up toward the sun, his gaze lingered on the enormous copper beech that rose beside the parish house. Bereft of leaves, it was still beautiful, exposed and more vulnerable certainly, without the confidence that the fullness of summer would bring, but honest and determined, its dark and gnarled branches reaching for the light and whatever else the winter sky might hold. Perhaps William would visit this tree after Kent's departure, or just as likely, he would fill each of his remaining days and years with other things and never again make the short trip from his life to this spot. Yet he knew that he would see the tree in his mind's eye at each turn of the season. And he knew that it would endure, long after he was gone.

Kent emerged from the residence, looking subdued, relaxed in civilian clothes, an additional suitcase in his left hand. He approached William and the car, deposited his burden in the trunk, and slammed it shut.

"That's the last of it," said Kent. He was trying to be cheerful, but William could sense the sadness in the man.

"Thank you, William," he said, extending his hand. "For all your help. And for your forgiveness."

William shrugged, accepted Kent's hand, and the two men shook. "We should both thank my wife." He smiled wryly. "Are you sure this is the right decision, sir? At this point, there's really no need—"

"I discussed it with the bishop," Kent declared with a weak smile. "I'm quite sure I sensed relief."

Kent turned back to gaze up at the church. William could see the pain in his face.

"No," Kent declared. "If a man takes vows, he should be prepared to keep them." He sighed, then faced William with a hearty optimism. "There are other ways to serve God." He walked to the driver's side, opened the door, and got in. William closed the door firmly and remained standing at the window as Kent started the car.

"Reverend, I—"

"Call me Sam," Kent said warmly. "Please."

William nodded, feeling foolish. "Very well. Sam, then." He took a deep breath. "I'm sorry for . . . for any . . . for my lack of . . ."

Kent smiled. "Do you know that old parable about the three blind men and the elephant?" he asked.

"I'm afraid I don't, sir," William replied, at a loss.

Kent continued. "Well, the first blind fellow grabs the tail, claims it's a rope. The second wraps his arms around a leg, certain it's a tree, while the third touches the trunk and jumps back, convinced it's a snake. We're each of us entrusted with only a portion of the truth, William. That's why we all need one another so desperately."

Kent smiled and William nodded his understanding.

"Good-bye, my friend," said Kent. "Take good care."

William watched as Kent drove off for the last time. He was acutely aware of the emotion welling in his chest, and savored it, along with a certain regret. He wished he'd hugged the man.

＊　＊　＊

On a lonely, undeveloped stretch of two-lane asphalt bordered by wild grass, Charlie McKinney stood with his duffel, peacoat collar turned up against the cold, his thumb out, hitching for a ride. One car passed, then another.

Finally, a black Model T Ford slowed, then stopped. Charlie walked up to the car and opened the door. He leaned in.

The elderly man at the wheel asked, "Where you headed?"

"Well, I . . ." Charlie began.

Just then another car passed by. Through the windshield Charlie caught sight of the familiar-looking blue Buick convertible as it sped off to points unknown. He watched as it vanished over a rise in the highway.

"You all right, son?" asked the old man.

Charlie looked at the driver, a kindly looking gentleman in his seventies with blue eyes not unlike Charlie's own. The young sailor nodded appreciatively. "Yes, sir. Thanks for asking."

The driver looked at him, expectant. "Well? Do you have a destination, young fella?"

Charlie shrugged. "I'm sure I do, sir. Just not sure what it is yet."

The man chuckled. "Well, I'm going as far as New York if that's any help."

Charlie smiled broadly. "That'll do for a start."

Charlie hopped in and the car pulled off. And though he could only see as much of the road ahead as the horizon would allow, Charlie considered his own unlikely past and the varied futures that lay in wait along that endless ribbon of time.

—•—•—•—

*The Navy and the U.S. Senate conducted separate investigations of the Newport incident. In six months of hearings, few operators and none of the accused were asked to testify. In the end, no one was punished. Those men still being held aboard the prison ship* Boxer *were finally released and cleared of all charges.*

*On August 10, 1921, Franklin Delano Roosevelt was stricken with the first symptoms of polio. In 1932, he was elected president, led the nation through the Great Depression and the Second World War, and was elected to an unprecedented four terms. He is universally remembered as one of our most beloved and compassionate presidents.*

*There is no record of what became of Samuel Kent, Charlie McKinney, or any of the other operators or victims of what came to be known as the Newport Navy Vice Scandal.*

*The man this author has chosen to call William Bartlett continued practicing law in and around Newport, Rhode Island. He is listed in the 1920* Who's Who in America, *no doubt because of the prominence of Kent's trial, and in that same year, he and his wife, Sarah, had another child, a daughter, whom they called Hope.*

## Author's Note

Long ago, on a chilly autumn evening, I was walking down lower Broadway in New York when a sudden rainstorm sent me ducking for cover into Shakespeare & Co., a rare gem of a bookstore. It was there, in an essay by historian George Chauncey, that I first encountered the facts and personalities of the Newport Navy Vice Scandal of 1919. So began a relationship that would consume me off and on for the next two decades of my life, first in crafting fact into fiction as a screenplay, then as this novel. Though these characters are based on historical persons—much of the trial testimony is lifted verbatim from naval transcripts—they and the events herein are, of course, informed by my own life and by people I have known whose experience in some ways, it seemed, echoed through these events. A few surnames have been changed, where I took the most creative license, while others remain as given in the historical record. I hope that I have done some justice to all the lives that have contributed to this tale. I know that the telling of their stories has deepened my own life immeasurably.

## Acknowledgments

First, I want to thank Terry Goodman at Amazon Publishing for taking a chance on a first-time novelist. Thanks to Charlotte Herscher and Jon Ford, my Amazon editors, for their patience and insight, and Dennelle Catlett for getting the word out about this book; Nicole Op Den Bosch at Audible, an early and passionate advocate for this book; and Jen Bassuck at A-Pub, who got my manuscript to Terry in the first place. Countless thanks to all my friends and colleagues at Audible.com and ACX.com, especially Mike Charzuck, who encouraged this novel from the first; Audible CEO and founder Don Katz, a wonderful, generous man without whom none of this would have been possible; and Keith Reynolds, Hannah Wall, Christina Harcar, and Jason Ojalvo for their awesome support along the way. I would also like to thank my beloved friends Linda Rattner Celle, David Thompson, Francis Lyons, Christer Hokanson, Chic Eglee, Tom Fontana, and John Carlino for their unfailing belief in me and their willingness to read this story again and again over the years in all its incarnations. I'd like to thank my first editor, Kat Bailey, whose insightful notes helped me to cut *Certainty* down to size, and Ron Baker, whose wisdom guided me past doubts of all shapes and sizes. Finally, I would like to thank my family, especially my mother and my sister, Sue, both of whom have always supported me in my creative endeavors in every way a person can support another.

# About the Author

*Photo by Bill Strong, 2012*

For over thirty years, Victor Bevine has worked as an actor, screenwriter, audio book narrator, director, and more. His acting credits include many prestigious roles onstage as well as roles in the film version of *A Separate Peace* and countless television shows. He has read over one hundred and eighty titles as an audiobook narrator; in 2010, he received an Audiophone Award for his narration of the Pulitzer Prize–winning book *The Beak of the Finch*. He has written several screenplays, including *Certainty*, which was chosen for two prestigious writers' conferences and which served as the basis for his first novel. His thirty-minute short film *Desert Cross*, which he wrote and directed, won accolades at the Athens International Film Festival. Currently, he serves as CEO of the World Freerunning Parkour Federation (WFPF), of which he is cofounder. Victor is a graduate of Yale University. He resides in New York City.